Hunter's Moon

Dear Readers,

Welcome to a new reality! Shapeshifters live among us, hidden in plain sight. The Sazi are wolves, bears, snakes, cats, and raptors. But they're also fathers and mothers, business owners and public servants, living and working beside regular humans. Tony Giodone is an attack victim, turned Sazi against his will. Since recovering from his injuries he's been forced to try to understand his new nature and to fight to fit it into his life.

People ask authors: where you come up with these ideas? The truth is that we haven't a clue! Usually we start with a question: What if? What would happen if werewolves existed? Would modern humans be tolerant of them? Would shapeshifters have to hide what they are in order to survive in society?

Absolutely. Rules would have to be strict. The secret would have to be clouded in smoke, hidden in shadow and wrapped in an enigma. Punishment of those who tell tales would be necessarily harsh, because discovery would bring the very real risk of slaughter. Sad, but true.

It's taken a lot of sweat and tears to bring Hunter's Moon to this final form, to create and apply rules for an entire society, and we're very proud of this wonderful new reality. We hope you enjoy visiting the world of the Sazi. We certainly enjoyed writing it!

Hunter's Moon

CATHY L. CLAMP

AND C. T. ADAMS

tor paranormal romance

A TOM DOHERTY ASSOCIATES BOOK
NEW YORK

This is a work of fiction. All the characters and events portrayed in this book are either products of the author's imagination or are used fictitiously.

HUNTER'S MOON

Copyright © 2004 by Cathy L. Clamp and C. T. Adams

Edited by Anna Genoese

A Tor Book
Published by Tom Doherty Associates, LLC
175 Fifth Avenue
New York, NY 10010

www.tor.com

Tor® is a registered trademark of Tom Doherty Associates, LLC.

ISBN-13: 978-0-765-35735-9
ISBN-10: 0-765-35735-6

First Edition: December 2004
Second Edition: November 2006

Printed in the United States of America

0 9 8 7 6 5 4 3 2

DEDICATION and ACKNOWLEDGMENTS

This book is dedicated first to Don Clamp and James Adams, who have offered patience and unswerving moral support through the years. Then to our parents, families and friends for their love and willingness to read through version after version (really, *really* thanks for that!).

We would also like to thank those people who helped us make it this far: To Thia, Bonnee, Dara, Gina, and Trace for being wonderful and helpful. Special thanks go to our agent, Merrilee and the wonderful Ginger, and our terrific editor at Tor, Anna.

Lastly, but most importantly, our most sincere thanks to Laurell K. Hamilton and Darla for their steadfast encouragement and help, and just being all 'round terrific people.

Without all of you, this wouldn't have been possible. We know that words aren't enough, but they're what we do best.

Chapter one

Nick's Tavern is in the worst part of town. The front door opens onto a back alley and the back door dead-ends inside another building. The Fire Code wasn't in effect when the building was built. Nick's has been there that long. My Dad remembers going there after work for a schooner of beer—twenty-four full ounces—and a plate of cheese. A buck bought both in the 40s. It was big enough for lunch for two or dinner for one. They don't do cheese plates anymore. Pity.

One time I went around the back of the building just to see what was on the other side. It's an upholstery shop. Big frigging deal.

Most of the buildings that surround Nick's are vacant now. Multi-colored graffiti scars plywood-covered windows. God only knows the last time someone cleaned the trash from the sidewalks.

I'm known as Bob to my clientele. That's not my real name. I'm the kind of person you would expect to find at Nick's. Call me a businessman who works the wrong side of the street. All sorts of people have need of my services: high class, low class, quiet suburban mothers, good church-going men. At one time or another all of them give into their primal instincts and call me. I meet them here at Nick's to talk details.

I'm not a hooker or a drug dealer. Too many risks, not enough money. There are no drug deals at Nick's. You'd get bounced on your ear if you even thought about it.

I'm an assassin. A killer-for-hire. If you have the money, I'll do the job. I like puppies, kids and Christmas, but I don't give a shit about your story—or your problems. I'm the person you call when you want the job done right the first time with no sullying of your name. Yes, I am that good. I apprenticed in the Family.

Oh, there's one other thing I should mention. I'm also a werewolf.

Yeah, I know. Big joke. Ha. Ha. I never believed in "creatures of the night" like vampires, werewolves, or mummies. They're the stuff of schlock movies and Stephen King novels. I'm not.

The door to the bar opened and the figure silhouetted in the doorway almost made me laugh out loud. I stifled the laugh with a snort of air. Then I let my face go blank again. Talk about stereotyping. The woman wore an expensive black pantsuit, odd enough in a low-class part of town. But the part I liked was that she wore a dark wig-and-scarf get-up like something you'd see in the 60s, and huge round black sunglasses. Oh yeah, she'll blend right in with the steel workers and biker babes. Sheesh.

My client had arrived—and she was early. No big deal. We'd only set the appointment a few hours ago. I hadn't even unpacked from my last job. The quicker we finished, the better I'd like it.

The woman in the doorway was forced to take off the sunglasses to look around the darkened bar. I got a look at her face. Nothing special. Deep, green eyes looked out from a relatively plain face. She stood about 5'5". I felt like I recognized her, but she was like me—a blender. She could probably get dolled up and look pretty but she would never be stunning. She was a woman that a man would fall in love with for her mind or personality. Or maybe her body, which was on the good side of average. She was probably a size ten—Maybe a twelve. She carried it well and comfortably. The suit spoke of money. Good. She could probably afford me. The rest of the get-up spoke of nerves.

She scanned the bar, looking for someone she had never met. You can't mistake the look. The person just stands there, hoping that someone will wave or pick them out. I let her feel uncomfortable for a moment, just long enough to size her up. She wasn't a plant or a cop. Nobody can fake that level of nervousness. She wasn't wringing her hands, but close.

I was sitting in the back booth—my usual table. I looked around the bar while I counted slowly to ten. It's a comfortable, familiar place. A Family hang-out. See, it hasn't been too long since the Mob ran this town. Nick's was one of the neutral taverns. Not upper-class. Nick didn't run "no hoitsy-toitsy gentlemen's club." His words, not mine. Nick's son Jocko runs the place now. Yeah, really. Nick actually named him Jocko. Poor guy.

The bar looks old. Not elegant old, just old. Dark wood covers the floors and walls and surrounds a real marble-topped bar. Remnants of old sweat and stale cigarette smoke cling to every surface. You can't see through the nicotine haze on the windows. Jocko doesn't do windows.

I finished counting, raised my hand, and caught her eye. She walked toward me, both hands clutching her purse like someone was going to lift it. A pleasant jingling reached my ears. Jewelry of some sort. When she reached the booth she looked at me, surprised. Apparently I wasn't what she expected.

I don't wear an eyepatch or have a swarthy mustache. I even have all of my teeth. I look absolutely ordinary. Collar-length black hair, blue-grey eyes the color of gun metal, and a build that shows I work out but not to excess. I was dressed in a blue cotton long-sleeved business shirt with the sleeves rolled up, grey slacks and black sneakers that look like dress shoes as long as I keep them polished. The jacket that matched the slacks was folded on the bench next to me. I look like I could be a lawyer, a writer, or a mechanic. I don't look like someone that would as soon shoot you as look at you. That's the idea. I gave her my best mercenary look; cold, uncaring. I wouldn't want her to think that I was just some guy hitting on her. She looked away, rattled.

Her scent blew me away. I notice smells more since the change. Nice term—"change". Her scent was stronger than it should be, but not perfume. This was just her. The woman smelled sweet and musky, with overtones of something tangy. I learned from Babs that means she's afraid. Fear reminds me, although Babs said I'm nuts, of hot and sour soup. Every emotion has its own particular scent. And lies! When someone lies, it smells like black pepper. I don't mind; it helps me interview clients.

Most scents are soft and not particularly noticeable. They rise off a person's skin like ghostly presences, only to disappear into unseen breezes. I have to concentrate to catch a person's real scent.

My client slid into the opposite side of the booth. I didn't stand. She didn't expect me to. Good thing. She sat with her back to the room. Another good indication that she wasn't a cop. Cops, like crooks, have a thing about having a wall at their back. Nobody can hit you from behind or pull your own gun on you.

"Um," she began when I just stared at her without saying anything. "Are you Bob?"

I nodded but still made no sound. It unnerved her and amused me. She was having a hard time looking at my face, whereas I looked straight into her eyes.

"I'm hoping you might be able to help me," she tried again. It required no comment, so I didn't make one.

My nose tingled. The client smelled like blood; like prey. But that's true of most people. Especially near the full moon. I never used to think much about the moon phases. Now I plan my life by them.

People didn't used to smell like food. Some days it pisses me off. But I didn't get a choice in the matter. A hit went bad. The woman I was stalking stalked me back. I wasn't prepared for a being with superhuman speed and strength. She ripped my throat out of my body and left me for dead. I should have died. She said so later. Guess I was too damn stubborn to die.

The wash of emotions from the client overpowered my nose. I could handle the fear and the blood. I was used to them. I don't meet with clients until after I've had a large rare steak for lunch. But this lady smelled of heat and sex. Heat, not sun—heat and something that I couldn't place that reminded me of a forest. Warm, dewy, sweet, salty. It was a safe, comforting smell unlike anything I've ever been in contact with. It was a smell that I wanted to soak into my pores. Breathe in, roll in. I had to blink and sneeze to clear my senses. Then I returned to staring quietly at her.

She couldn't meet my eyes but kept scanning the room. Her fingers tapped restlessly on the table, then on her lap, then on the table again while she bit at her lips as if looking for something to say or do. The hot and sour smell of fear, the burnt metal of frustration overwhelmed me as if they were my own. That was new. My muscles tensed against my will. Suddenly she stopped fidgeting, took a deep breath and looked right at me.

"Would you please say something?" she asked in frustration. "I'm drowning here."

That won her a quick smile. "Would you like something to drink? It's not much cooler in here than outside. That dark suit has to be hot."

She looked at her outfit and had the good grace to blush. "It's a little trite, isn't it? I didn't even think about the heat. I was trying to be inconspicuous." She smiled a bit as if she felt my amusement the way I was feeling her emotions, but she smelled embarrassed. A dry smell, like heat rising off desert sand, mixed with other things I didn't recognize yet. I don't know a lot of the emotions yet. Babs told me that I'd get the hang of identifying them. I'm in no hurry.

I didn't believe it at first. Didn't want to. But Babs followed me around for three days, and taped me with a camcorder. I avoided her like I avoid everyone, but she filmed enough to prove that she was telling the truth. Babs was a sadistic bitch about it, too. She made sure she immortalized all of the most embarrassing moments of a dog in living color. Pissed me off. I stopped returning her calls after that.

"I don't exactly blend in, do I?" The words brought me out of my musing.

Lying to save her feelings would be diplomatic, but I try to save lies for important things. "Not really."

I raised my hand to signal Jocko. He moved out from behind

the bar, wiping his meaty hands on a snow white bar rag. Jocko's a big 6'8". He looks beefy but it's mostly muscle—he was a pro wrestler for a few years. Jocko wears his waist-length black hair in a ponytail because of state health regs. A scar cuts his left eyebrow in half. He's second-generation Italian but he looks Native-American because of the hair.

Jocko smells like bad habits. Whiskey and cigarettes and sweat. He walked slowly toward the table—almost lethargically. Jocko moves slow because he threw his back out in the ring years ago and since there isn't any worker's comp insurance in wrestling he came home to run the family business. But he's hardly a cripple. Jocko can still throw a man through the front window if he puts his mind to it. Everybody knows it. Like me, he doesn't talk much. He just stood at the table waiting for our order.

"Draft for me." I turned to the client with a questioning look.

"Um—rum and Coke, I guess." Jocko started to walk away. She raised her voice a little bit to add, "Captain Morgan, please." He nodded without turning or stopping. "And Diet?" a little louder still. Anyone that didn't know Jocko would presume he hadn't heard her. I knew he heard her and that he was chuckling softly under his breath. The mild orange smell of amusement drifted to me. A rum and Coke is not the same thing at all as a Morgan and Diet. Not to a bartender.

She glanced at me. "Do you think he heard me?"

"He heard. Now, what can I do for you?"

"I want you to kill someone," she said calmly. "I can afford to pay whatever the cost."

Well, that was direct! I shut my mouth again, closed my eyes and reached my hand up to rub the bridge of my nose. It eased the tension behind my eyes.

"Is something wrong?"

There's a certain code in my profession. The client doesn't actually ask and I don't actually admit what I do for a living. It's just sort of understood. Money is discussed but only because both parties know what transaction is being, well, transacted.

I lowered my voice. "I would appreciate it if you could be a little more *discreet* about our business here."

That stopped her cold. She suddenly realized what she had said, and that she had said it in a normal tone, in a place of business. Her face flushed and her jaw worked noiselessly. The blend from the combination of emotions made me giddy.

"That was stupid, wasn't it?"

"Well, that sort of depends whether you *want* to spend the next twenty or so years in prison. It's called 'accessory before the fact'."

She shrugged. "Actually, for the job I'm proposing, I'd never see the inside of a prison."

"That might be a little overconfident," I replied, "There's always the chance of getting a very good investigator. I always make it clear to clients that there is risk involved. I'm good. I'm very good. But there is always a risk."

She shook her head. "You couldn't know since I haven't explained. But it's not an issue."

I believed her and I didn't know why. No black pepper smell of deceit, maybe. I shrugged my shoulders. "Fine. You've been warned." I drew a breath and began my list of conditions. "I'll need the name of the mark, a photograph, and home and work addresses. I work alone. I will choose the time and place of the job. Not you. If you want it public, I'll pick the time. You can pick the method if you want. If you don't specify, it could be by a variety of methods. I vary them to fit the situation and the mark. I don't do extras like rape or torture for the same money. There will be an additional charge for that kind of thing."

She listened intently and without comment. When I mentioned rape and torture, she grimaced slightly. I could feel her disapproval beat at me like heat from a furnace. I shook off the feeling and proceeded on.

"If the mark meets his end without my assistance, there are no refunds. I require payment in advance. Cash only, small bills. If the money is marked or traceable you will forfeit your life at a future time of my choosing. Don't presume that I can't find you. I can."

She nodded, as if she had heard my speech a million times. She leaned forward, eyes intent on my face—focused. Good. I like it when people listen.

Jocko arrived with the drinks so I stopped speaking. He put them on the table, then looked at me. "That'll be four-fifty."

I motioned for him to ask the lady. He turned his attention to her and she opened her little purse quickly. She extracted a ten dollar bill and held it out to him. "Keep it."

Jocko pursed his lips in approval and moved off silently.

"Go on," she said.

I tried to remember where I left off. I hate to get interrupted mid-stream. "If the police somehow get wind of me through you, I will make sure that you never live to testify. If there are family members involved and they get in the way, I will remove them. I don't charge for removal of witnesses. That's for my benefit, not yours. However, if there are potential witnesses that you do not wish removed, make sure they are kept out of the line of fire until after the job is complete. I won't be held responsible for mistaken identity, so if the photograph is not absolutely clear, or up-to-date, there could be a mistake."

The client sipped her drink as I spoke. It's a long spiel. Now's the only time I ask questions like whether she needed proof that the job had been accomplished. She smiled. "No, I think I'll know." That meant that it was someone close to her; possibly a husband or boyfriend. Her amusement smelled sweeter, more like tangerines than oranges.

When I finished, my beer was almost gone. "Do you have any questions?" I asked.

She had a mouthful of complimentary peanuts and she didn't respond immediately. Jocko puts out peanuts to increase drink sales. It works, so I don't indulge.

"No," she said when she'd swallowed, "That about covers it. When do I have to get the cash to you? And how much?"

"How much depends on who. Public figure or private? Who is the mark?"

She spread her hands out, showing her chest to perfection. It was a nice view but, "I don't understand."

"*I'm* the target. The mark. Whatever."

I raised my eyebrows. "Excuse me?"

"I'm hiring you to kill me. The time and place don't matter. But soon. How much will it cost?"

Alarms started ringing in my head. "There are a lot less expensive ways to do yourself in,"

She nodded her head once. "Probably. But this is the method I choose. Is there a problem?"

There was something wrong with this situation. I couldn't think of what specifically was bugging me. I really don't want to know a person's story but I was missing something. Something important. I needed to dig.

I leaned back in my seat. "Who are you and why do you need to die?"

Her eyes shifted. Yeah, there was something there all right. "Does it matter?"

"Normally, no," I admitted, "But this is a first for me and it's making me nervous. So, give. Why do you need to die in such a way that it *doesn't* look like a suicide?"

Intense emotions washed through my nose, blending and then splitting. I couldn't identify them all. I'm still new at this shit. I suppose a little part of me is annoyed that I haven't picked them up faster. It's been almost a year. But I'm not curious enough to contact Babs.

"I don't need to die. I want to. But you'd need to hear my story and you told me on the phone that you didn't want to hear it. I'm a nobody. No one special. Just take the money and do the job." Her eyes were bright, too bright, and her voice too intense. I didn't like it.

"What's your name?" In any event, I'd need it if she turned out to be the mark.

"Wh—" she began and then corrected herself. "Oh, that's right you need the name. Quentin. Sue Quentin."

Sue Quentin. That name rang a bell. I leaned forward and put my arms on the table. "Take off the wig," I ordered.

She looked around her nervously. Yeah, it probably wouldn't do to have her reveal herself in full view of everyone. That sort of thing is remembered.

"Fine," I crooked a finger and slid out of the booth. "Follow me." She stood and followed me down a hallway to the bathrooms. It was dark but my eyes are exceptionally good—funny thing. I knocked on both doors and waited. No response. I turned around to face her. "Take it off."

She slid the black wig with attached scarf from her head. Underneath were medium-brown permed ringlets that reached her shoulders. The hair changed the shape of her face. Even in the dim light of the hallway I instantly recognized her. The disguise was better than I'd credited. With the wig, I hadn't had more than a vague recognition. Fortunately, no one else in the bar would probably make her, either. I knew her but couldn't imagine why she would want to die.

I shook my head. "Huh-uh. No way. You're a *very* visible lady. I'd have to wait until the heat surrounding you dies down."

She stood very still, eyes closed. The hot blanket of sorrow pressed on me and tightened my throat. A single tear traced silver down her left cheek. "How long?" Her voice was barely a whisper.

I turned and walked back into the room, not able to answer right away. I had to get away from that distress. She got under my skin way too easily. That alone made me nervous. Some instinct told me if I didn't run from her, she was going to change my whole life. I didn't want this job.

I slid back into the booth. She followed me a couple minutes later, in control again. The wig was back in place and she had wiped the tear from her face. She looked relatively calm but her hands trembled a little. She folded them in front of her and held herself stiffly, as if hanging onto her control by her fingertips.

I'm not moved by tears. I've turned down jobs before. But she'd asked a question and I could at least give her an answer. "I don't know," I replied. "With all the publicity—a year, maybe more."

Her gaze was steady on me but the unshed tears made her eyes shine. "So I can count on that? A year from now you'll do the job?"

I held up my hands in front of me. "Whoa, lady. I didn't say that. I said, 'a year, *maybe more*'. I can't judge that. You could be in the papers again next week and it would start all over. I don't predict the future. No. I can't take the job."

"If you only understood," she began.

"Stop." She did. "You were right the first time, Ms. Quentin. I don't want to know. I don't *care* to know your story. I'm not a psychologist. I'm not a social worker." Except this time, I *did* want to know and I couldn't explain why.

Her eyes went cold for a moment, almost as though she could sense my thoughts. "Fine. How much?"

I felt my brow wrinkle. "For what?"

"To listen." She leaned forward a bit. "You're absolutely right. You're not a psychologist or a social worker. You're a mercenary. How much will it cost me for you to listen to my story?" Her anger bit at my nose. It smelled like coffee burning.

"It won't change anything," I said. "I don't want the job."

"So don't take it. There are other people out there with less *scruples*. I just want an ear. I just want you to shut up and listen to my story." Her voice tightened as she spoke — colder, harsher, more brittle. She was blinking back tears again. "You don't have to care. Just make the right noises in the right places. How much for a couple of hours?"

"It's not scruples that would stop me from taking the job, lady. It's self-preservation. Too many people know your name. Investigators would work a lot harder because you're newsworthy. And I'm not for rent on an hourly basis."

That was supposed to be it. The end. I don't know why I said the next. "But, fine. If you want to buy my ear for the night, it's for sale. A thousand up front and I'll let you know how much more when the story's over." I half-stood and half-slid out of the booth. "Let's go."

She looked startled. "Just like that?"

There I go again — being impulsive. I should walk out. My gut told me I should run. I've learned to trust my wolf instincts even when I don't understand them. And yet, I shrugged and smiled tightly at her. I had nothing better to do right now. I had no reason to fear this person. No logical reason, anyway. Money's money. It's just another job.

"Just like that. You're driving. But I have to make a call first. So finish your drink, go to the john or whatever. I'll meet you out front in a couple of minutes. What are you driving?"

Her eyes got wider. I could smell the hot tang of fear, the soured milk smell of disbelief and rising under both, the lighter smell of hope. She had been expecting me to walk out. Probably thought I was playing a cruel joke. Not a chance. For once I'd be able to indulge my curiosity. In my position, the less I know about a client or a mark the better. Except this time I wanted to know more. Maybe I'd find out how many people had walked out on her in the past. Or why she wanted to die. Maybe I'd walk out too. We'd see.

Chapter 2

I left her in the booth looking dazed. I went down the back hallway again. A payphone hangs on the wall in the corner near the door to the men's room. It's an old phone but it works.

I dialed a number and a man answered. "Plaza Hotel, how may I direct your call?"

I used my harried-but-professional businessman voice. "This is Anthony Giodone. May I speak to Max, please?"

"Good evening, Mr. Giodone. This is Max speaking. How may I assist you?"

I glanced at my watch and noticed a crack across the crystal. Damn it! I'd have to get it repaired. I like this watch. But still, not quite three o'clock on the 11th. Three more days until I checked in.

"Max, I know it's unusual but I was hoping my suite might be available."

"We always try to assist our loyal customers, sir," came the appropriate reply. "When did you want to book your suite?"

"For right now." Before he could continue I added, "I know it's unusual and short notice but I'm meeting someone on urgent business."

There was a hesitation. "No, it's not short notice, sir. When did you want to arrive?"

"Thirty minutes?"

"Oh!" his voice sounded relieved. "I understand now. Of course, we'll make the suite available immediately. We'll look forward to seeing you in a few minutes, Mr. Giodone."

I hung up the phone. The call had solved the *where*. Now to go outside and meet the *who*.

A bright yellow Mustang of this year's vintage sat purring

quietly by the curb. Well, I guess if I had won the state's largest lottery jackpot ever I'd probably splurge a little bit too. Two hundred sixty eight million dollars. Wow! I took in a little over a million a year, but even after she paid taxes, I'd have to live a hundred eighty years to accumulate what she had fallen into with a one dollar ticket. I guess that proves that money doesn't buy happiness. Susan Quentin was the least happy person I had met in some time.

She still had on the wig and scarf, which I was going to suggest anyway. I opened the door and slid onto the soft white leather seats. All the perks. A CD player played a soft rock ballad that I recognized from the radio. The wind blew her scent right at me. For a second I forgot to breathe. I could feel my nostrils flare as they willingly saturated with her fragrance. She watched me get in the car. It wasn't a casual look. Whatever was happening between us, she could feel it too. Her eyes were wide. I could smell her excitement—desire and fear. Heat, for lack of a better word.

When I was seated and closed the door, I looked at her. "Yes?"

She looked forward again and flushed. "Nothing. Sorry."

She blushed easily. This could be fun.

"Drive," I commanded. She put the car in gear.

"Where are we going?" she asked after we had traveled for a block or two.

I had already worked up a cover. "Head to the Plaza. Drop me off about a block from the hotel. Park the car. Wait ten minutes. No more, no less. You'll be Jessica Thornton, a broker."

The CD was still playing. I reached over to turn it off so it wouldn't be a distraction. She reached over at the same time. Our hands touched. She jerked back suddenly, as though burned. I felt it too. Electric, like when you scuff your feet and touch metal. But it was deeper inside, not just a surface shock. It felt good enough that parts of my body reacted forcibly.

I grabbed her hand, fast but gentle, and got the same reaction as before. Thrills of electricity up my arm that raised all the hair on my skin. It wasn't painful. The sensation was wild. It was scary but intoxicating. Almost addicting. The hand wore a small opal ring in a nice setting. Expensive and elegant but not gaudy. Probably new. The office-length nails were cared for, though not professionally.

I got glimpses of her mind as we touched. Since the change I can sometimes sense what other people are thinking. Only when I touch them, though. My hearing went berserk too. Some days if I stand real still, I can hear the neighbors talking two or three doors down. During the full moon, the humming of the refrigerator hurts my ears. I bought a stock of foam earplugs. Why is he doing this? Is he going to hurt me? Stop. Don't stop. I'm not supposed to like this. What's happening to me?

She glanced at me. It wasn't fear—not exactly. I turned her hand over and looked at the palm. I forced my voice to remain cold and rational. "I won't specify stock or real estate. It's none of the hotel's business. I'll ask at the desk whether you've arrived. Then I'll head to my suite and ask that you be directed to the room when you get there."

She drove silently, listening intently while I traced the lines and the callousing on her palm with my thumb. Her mind couldn't come up with a complete thought. Even in the heat I saw her shiver.

I wanted to raise her hand to my mouth. Kiss the skin, roll the taste of her in my mouth. Shit. This is too weird. I released the hand and she pulled it away slow, like she had just started to enjoy it. I shook my head once to clear it and turned off the music. "When you go into the hotel, ask the desk clerk for Anthony Giodone. That's not my real name so don't bother to remember it. He'll either direct or escort you to Room 935. It's on the top floor. I'll have dinner delivered from room service. How do you like your steak?"

She didn't respond for a moment and I looked at her, waiting for an answer. "That was impressive," she finally said.

"What was?"

"You said all that in one breath. I'm impressed. And I like my steak well done."

I almost laughed but held back. "I'll let room service know."

It was about twenty miles on the freeway to the Plaza Hotel. It's very nice and comfortably furbished. It's also extremely expensive. When it was first built I met with the owner to discuss renting a suite on a permanent basis. It was about five months after the change occurred that I realized I needed somewhere to go for three days that was absolutely safe. I'd tried to lock myself in my house, but I always managed to get out. I would wake up and find a window broken and bloody feathers or fur littering my bed. Any idea what that stuff feels like coming out the other side? Once I found the refrigerator hanging open and groceries scattered through the house. It was a pain in the ass to clean up.

The client suddenly shifted into fifth gear and I once again heard the delicate jingle of metal. It must be a bracelet. I just couldn't see it under the jacket sleeve.

The hotel was in sight. I needed to go shopping soon. I always bring food with me for my visit. Then I lock the door and stay in the room for three days. They leave me alone; no maid service, no calls, no nothing. When I come back to my senses I clean up the mess, or pay for anything I've damaged. It's worked well so far because I've never told anyone I go there.

Except now I was bringing this client to my hideout. Go figure. Weirder still was that I was glad that the room could be ready.

I heard her swallow and noticed the nervous tapping of her fingers on the wheel. She was shifting back and forth in her seat restlessly.

"So, how did you get my number?"

She relaxed back into her seat. The tension drained from her like air from a balloon. She smelled of gratitude. Warm and slightly musty like air from a dryer's vent. "You would not *believe* how difficult it is to find someone in your profession."

I said nothing. It's not supposed to be easy. That's how we stay out of jail.

"I mean, it's not like you can just look in the phone book." She put her hands on top of the steering wheel, resting her wrists on it and pretended to be flipping pages. "Let's see, here we go, *assassins*. See *hired killers*." Amusement edged her voice.

I chuckled. So much for my fear she'd get maudlin.

"I remembered reading a few years ago in that magazine from Colorado . . . oh, you know the one. I can't remember the name."

"I know it," I responded, "Go on."

"Well, I remember they got into real trouble because they were running ads for mercenaries."

I nodded. "I read about that. The people who put in the advertisements weren't real bright, either."

"Well, I hoped that maybe even though they got busted they might still be doing it."

I raised my eyebrows. "And were they?"

"Sort of," she conceded. "There weren't any actual ads but when I called the magazine and talked to the classified department the clerk had a list of people who *couldn't* put ads in."

A back door approach. I like it. I grinned.

"It must have been a private list. He started to tell me but I guess his boss came in 'cause he hung up. I tried to call back later but he wouldn't take my call."

"So what did you do?"

"I went to the library and looked up some back issues. The ones that *did* have the ads in them."

"Attagirl."

She blushed and smiled. She was bright. It won her a few more points. It almost made up for the '60s spy movie get-up. Smart, with black humor. And hey, she wasn't bad-looking. I looked her up and down. Decent figure, great hair under the wig, nice smile. Not bad at all. Yeah, I could do her. Happily, if that little taste earlier was accurate. She glanced at me and must've seen something of what I was thinking. Her eyes widened and her head snapped forward again. Her knuckles whitened on the steering wheel. I smelled the sharpness of her sudden fear and the musky heat of desire.

"So, anyway," Her voice, now, was just a little shaky, "I

called two of the numbers I found but they were both on 'extended leave of absence'. I presumed that meant they were in jail."

"Or on the run."

"Either or," she agreed. "But one woman gave me a number of someone that she said was good. That her 'man', as she phrased it, respected."

"And that's how you called me?"

She shook her head. "No. I got the number of another person. *That* was the weirdest meeting I've ever had in my life." She shivered. "I got a message to meet him at this little video arcade that has a lunchroom. I sat down at the table that I was told to, and up comes this kid wearing baggy blue jeans and a striped T-shirt. Dark blonde hair cut long on the front so it covered his eyes and shaved in the back. You know, typical teenager."

Ah. Him. I nodded, unable to suppress a smile.

"Anyway, I figured that the kid was going to try to sponge money. So I ignored him, hoping he'd go away. I mean," she looked at me somewhat pathetically, "I was supposed to *meet* someone."

"Not realizing that he was who you were coming to meet?"

She looked at me, shocked. "You mean you know him!?!"

"Go on."

"Well, apparently, he *was* who I was coming to meet." Her brows were buried under the bangs of the wig, as if she was still startled. "He sat down at the table and asked if I was Sue. He was very professional. Very business-like. It was incredibly unnerving."

"Scotty has that effect on people," I agreed.

She looked at me again, newly surprised. "You really *do* know him."

I nodded.

"He's a baby!!"

I laughed out loud. "Lady, Scotty wasn't a baby when he was born!" She smelled sour-sharp with disapproval but at the same time oozed wet, fog-bank sorrow.

"He can't be more than, what, twelve?" She gestured with

her fingers while controlling the wheel with the heels of her palms. She was agitated enough about the kid that she couldn't sit still.

"I mean, he's only a few years older than my nephew who still plays video games and is shy around girls."

I nodded agreement. "He just turned thirteen. He's already had two strikes so he'll have to keep his head down. Next time, they'll charge him as an adult. And he *does* still play video games and *is* shy around girls."

"You mean he's been *caught* before? Killing people? Then why is he still out and . . ."

"Talking to people like you?" I asked with a smirk. "Because he's a minor. He got the maximum five years in juvie hall for the first one. They had to drop the case on the second one. Witnesses kept disappearing."

She glanced at me in horror. "But if he was in juvenile hall for five years, then . . ."

I completed the thought, "He did his first job, sloppily, at the tender age of six."

Her eyes went wide. "The poor baby!"

I shook my head. "Don't feel real sorry for him. He's the way he wants to be. I checked him out. There's no history of abuse. The kid's just a psychopath. He doesn't look like anything other than a normal kid. It's his trademark. Nobody expects him, so he can sneak up on people." I thought I knew but asked anyway. "Why'd he turn you down?"

She shook her head with a small laugh. "He said that it wouldn't be any *fun* to 'do me', because I'd know he was coming. He said he does 'close in' work, whatever that means and he couldn't sneak up on me."

"That's with a knife or other arm's length weapon. A blade, a golf club, whatever. For Scotty, it's a visceral pleasure for him to watch a person die. He actually gets a physical high. Maybe even a sexual high." I shrugged. "To each his own."

"That," she said with a shiver, "is just so . . . bizarre! He really scared me."

I looked at her with a questioning smirk. "And I don't?"

She paused. "Not in the same way," she said thoughtfully. "He gets his kick out of pain. You can see it in his eyes. You look like you'll do it, but it's just business."

Not at the full moon. I nodded in agreement anyway. I stared hard at the side of her face for a minute and abruptly decided she needed a dose of reality. I admire the kid's work. He's talented. I wouldn't want her to go all socially conscious on him and turn him in "for his own good."

"You know, you should be happy that he does this for a living."

"Why in God's name would you say that?" Her eyebrows climbed high on her forehead. She spared a horrified glance before returning her attention to the freeway traffic.

"Because as long as he does it for a living, it satisfies the need and he doesn't do it for *fun*." She glanced at me stunned. "Understand? A lot less dead people. Scotty's damn smart. He won't get caught easy. He'll be a serial killer if he ever stops being an assassin."

A sign whizzed past. The next exit was ours. She flipped on her turn signal and changed lanes. Her eyes blinked in time with the sound. "I guess."

I rested my elbow on the car windowsill. "You still haven't said. How'd you find me?"

Silence for a little while, then she took a deep breath. She shook her head and straightened in her seat. "From him. He wouldn't do the job but he gave me your number. Said you were the best, if I could afford you."

Huh. Didn't know the little bastard even had my number. Maybe I'd return the favor on the next blade job.

As instructed, she stopped the car about a block from the hotel and parked at the curb. All the reasons why this was a bad idea came rushing back to me. I had never invited another soul to the suite. Too late now. I was actually enjoying talking to her—looking at her. That worried me. My voice was harsher than I had intended when I steered the conversation back to business.

"Before we go any further—a thousand up front. Remember?"

"Oh!" It seemed like she had truly forgotten and wasn't just trying to burn me. She opened the clutch purse. My eyes opened wide. Inside the little black bag was a huge wad of cash! That explained her death grip on the purse.

She pulled the roll of currency out of the bag, in full view of whoever was walking by and counted out ten one hundred dollar bills. I shook my head wearily as I accepted the money. I carry around a lot of cash, but get real! She was a robbery waiting to happen.

"I wouldn't flash that wad of money around, if I were you," I warned. "You've already got a target painted on your back from the car. No need to advertise."

She looked mortified and hurriedly stuffed the money back in the bag. "I wasn't sure how much you would charge but I figured you would want cash."

I smiled. "You wouldn't have enough there. Not unless those are thousand dollar bills. My base price is fifty grand and goes up from there."

She cleared her throat. "Fifty. I see. I've only got ten here."

"Like I said, not nearly enough. But it would have been enough to show good faith. I would have accompanied you to the bank for the rest. *If* I had agreed to the job."

She looked at me slyly. "You haven't actually refused, you know."

"Close enough." I pocketed the money and got out of the car.

As I walked to the hotel, I heard the rhythmic beat of soft-soled shoes behind me. Seconds later, a jogger passed me by, headphones drowning out the world. The muscles in my legs instantly tensed to run—to start the chase. I forced myself to keep walking. I could hear the pounding of the man's heart over the music feeding into his ears. The light dew of sweat on his forehead and trickling down his back from the heat was like some intoxicating perfume that turned my blood to fire. I fought down the desire to snarl and take off after the runner; to bring him down. To quench the hunger.

I have this problem a lot. It makes jogging in the park tricky. People seem to resent it when you chase them. Go figure. And I *have* to run. I *have* to chase. It's part of me now. It gets harder and harder to control the closer it gets to the full moon.

When I reached the hotel, the doorman quickly moved to open the door for me. "Afternoon, Mike," I said cordially. He'd worked here since the place opened.

"G'day, Mr. Giodone," he responded with a grin. Mike is Aussie, right off the boat. He always smells like eucalyptus and mint and the citrus smell of happiness, penetrating and bright as his smile. The smell cleared out the musk from the client and the prey-smell of the jogger. I slipped him his usual tip. A crisp twenty keeps his smile genuine.

Max Holcomb met me halfway across the room with a slight bow. He's the Concierge; tall, thin, and always immaculately dressed. In another time, he would probably have been a butler or a gentleman's gentleman. He has the temperament for it. Obedient and dependable, the smell of a well-tended lawn with overtones of cookie spice. It's a comforting smell. Another deep breath calmed me down the rest of the way.

"Good afternoon, Mr. Giodone."

"I've told you before, Max, you can call me by my first name."

"Now, Mr. Giodone," he said somewhat reproachfully, "That would hardly be proper."

I smiled. The same game every time I came in. "No, I suppose not." I looked around the room, as though searching for someone. "I was to meet my broker here. Has she arrived yet? Her name is Jessica Thornton."

He pursed his lips as though concentrating. Yeah, right. He knew each and every person in the building and their location. "No, sir, nobody by that name has come in. Would you like to wait for her in the lounge?"

I gave it a moment's thought. "No, just have her shown to my room." He nodded and handed me the key card. I started to walk to the elevator but then stopped and turned briefly. "Oh, and have a bottle of Captain Morgan and some Diet Coke delivered to the suite for the lady. Is there draft on tap?"

Max raised his eyebrows and the scent of his surprise drifted to me. "Of course, sir. You asked that the room be ready. It is." It made me smile. "Will there be anything else?"

I remembered to order dinner before I took the elevator to the top floor. There was a bellboy already waiting for me at the door with the requested items. I slipped him a five. He accepted the proffered bill and left quickly. That's the way I like staff.

Once he was gone, I opened the door and tossed the key card on the marble-topped table inside the door. The blast of cooled air greeted me like a welcomed friend. Exactly as I remembered it. The stone fireplace with the natural gas logs stood ready if the need arose. The drapes had been opened to reveal the excellent view. Clear blue skies stretched to the horizon and the mountainside looked just ready to begin to turn colors. Next month this time, it'd be stunning.

I kicked off my shoes and padded to the wet bar opposite the fireplace. There were two taps available. Guinness Dark and whatever was on sale. Today it was Bud. That suited me.

I removed one of the mugs from the small freezer below the bar and filled it. A slight layer of frost formed on the outside of the mug and I took a grateful sip. It really was hot outside. I hate heat. I've always been a cold weather person. Give me a forty degree day anytime, no coat, no sleeves, and I'll be happy. Heat is even worse since I became a wolf. It's like I have fur even in human form.

I sat on one of the two recliners across from the couch and put up my feet. Not enough sleep for a couple of days now. It's been a rough week. I glanced at my watch again. My brow furrowed when I saw that it hadn't changed since we left Nick's. I tapped on the crystal. The second hand grudgingly moved a second forward and then stopped again. Damn! I'd not only cracked the crystal, I broke the whole watch! When had that happened?

I closed my eyes and sighed when it hit me. Oh, yeah. I knew *exactly* when I'd done it. It was during that second car theft, when I'd had to roll the hot Mustang into a ditch and high-tail it before the cops arrived. I'd forgotten to grab the

portable police scanner from the front seat after I got out and
the door had slammed into me when it started to roll. Yeah,
this last job in Atlantic City had gone very, *very* badly.

If Carmine had given me the mark's real name instead of
his current alias, I would have refused the job. I'd gambled
with Jeffrey a couple of times. He knew me on sight and
would see me coming. Granted, the guy had to go. He'd
tried to slice a piece out of Carmine's pie. If that wasn't bad
enough, he'd taken out one of our guys in the process. Under
the circumstances, it didn't matter that he was the son of a
cooperating family in Atlantic City. Nobody, but *nobody*
invades Carmine's turf. The minute Jeffrey spotted me, he
knew what was coming and ran home to daddy. I had no
choice but to follow.

Carmine had called ahead. Vito, the daddy, had said
he'd handle the situation. But Daddy wasn't my client.
Carmine was, and he wanted the job done anyway. A
strong message needed to be sent. That's when Jeffrey
decided to go to the police for protection. Not his best
plan and not what Daddy had in mind, either. They went
to stop him and bring him home.

My one and only chance to avoid Daddy's goons and to
get the job done was when the kid was walking up the police
precinct steps. Granted, I would have preferred *any* set-up
over that. Atlantic City's so hot for me now that I may *never*
be able to go back. It's going to take some serious negotiations for Carmine to repair the damage with Vito.

The police threw a dragnet around the city in record time
from sheer embarrassment. My only option was to steal cars
and take forgotten back roads. It took a lot more time than I
planned—how long had it taken me to get back? Shit. I'd
lost track of what day it was.

Speaking of time . . .

I started to glance at my watch and swore again. I walked
to the bedroom and checked the digital readout on the clock
radio. Nearly eighteen minutes had passed since I got out of
the car. She should be here by now. I sat back down in the
recliner and reached to my left to pick up the telephone and

dialed an extension I knew by heart. It and room service were the only two numbers I ever dialed.

"Concierge," came Max's voice. "How may I be of service?"

"Max, this is Tony Giodone. Has Ms. Thornton arrived yet?"

There was a pause that I didn't like. "Could you describe her for me, Mr. Giodone?"

"She's about thirty-five, 5'5", dark hair, black Chanel pantsuit. Seen her?"

"Yes, sir. She's arrived but hasn't checked in at the desk yet. She's in a rather odd conversation with another woman."

The devil, you say. Why hadn't I listened to my instincts?

"Odd, how?" I asked, as I grabbed at my shoes. The phone wouldn't reach and I had to lean back in the chair and stretch to drag them over with my feet.

"It appears that a woman is insisting she knows your guest. Ms. Thornton is trying to ignore her but the other woman keeps stopping her to talk to her. Would you like me to intervene?"

"No," I replied, holding the phone with chin and shoulder as I hurriedly tied a bow in the second shoelace, "I'm on my way down. Don't let either of them leave."

I hung up the phone and raced to the door.

Chapter 3

I realized that I'd forgotten the key card as the door slowly swung closed behind me and snaked my arm between the double doors to grab it before the lock latched. The heavy oak crushed my arm. White flowers erupted in my vision for a second and I bit back a curse.

Key card safely in pocket, I closed the door and headed for the elevator. I got out at the second floor. Old paranoid habits die hard. This could still be a set-up. I'd rather not have the elevator door open in the lobby to a waiting group of police. I turned the corner and entered the stairwell. I took the steps two at a time. When I reached the ground floor, I peered through the small rectangular window in the stairwell door.

Susan was trying, without success, to escape a blonde woman who kept grabbing her arm to stop her. The blonde bore a strong resemblance to the client. She was taller and slimmer; with a sharp angular face. Each time, Susan would back away. She wasn't making a sound. My guess was that she did know the woman but didn't want to be identified, and since she wasn't very good at lying, she didn't speak. That won her a few more points.

My payment for listening to the story included ensuring that she had the opportunity to tell it. I opened the door and entered the lobby.

"I don't know what kind of game you're playing, Suzi Quentin, but you're not going to get away with it," I heard the blonde say as the door quietly latched behind me. "I don't care if you talk or not—you're my sister and I know you. So just give it up. You might as well stop and talk to me. And," her hand shot upward, "take off that ridiculous wig."

I quickened my step and just as the blonde's hand reached Susan's shoulder, I reached out and grabbed her wrist.

"Who the hell are you and why are you bothering my friend?" I asked, with quiet menace that wasn't faked. The smell of this woman made me fight down a growl: rotten meat, like a buzzard. She set off alarm bells. It made no sense. I turned to Susan, still holding the wrist. "Jessica, are you all right?"

Susan didn't have a chance to answer. The blonde tried to pull her arm out of my grasp but I merely tightened the grip. A part of me wanted to hurt her badly. "Let go of my arm!" she exclaimed. "Who do you think you are?"

"I'm a friend of the woman that you're accosting," I explained. Quiet was useless, but I was determined to keep this confrontation as low-key as possible. "You seem to have mistaken her for someone you know." My eyes were steady on the woman. She finally stopped trying to escape my hold. She glared at me.

I turned to Susan again. "Jessica," I stared hard at her, hoping she would take the hint to play along. "Do you know this woman?"

She shook her head, trying to look confused.

"You see? You've simply mistaken her for someone. I would appreciate it if you would just leave us be."

The woman gave me a look that said she didn't buy it for a moment. The conversation had started quietly, but her voice kept raising. "I don't know who you are but this has nothing to do with you. I want to talk to my sister." She started to move closer to Susan, but I snapped her wrist backward, stopping her abruptly.

"This woman is not your sister," I hissed. "Her name is Jessica Thornton and I've known her for years. She doesn't have any sisters." My voice was steel cold. "You've made a mistake." I saw Max out of the corner of my eye, mock-casually walking toward our little group. I was surprised it had taken this long. Security should have arrived some time ago. Then I glanced over his shoulder and saw the matching charcoal suits standing right near the check-in. Max had apparently hoped I could handle the situation without intrusion.

"Please don't force me to become... *insistent*." I tightened my grip until she gasped. Her eyes stared into mine and slowly lightened from defiant to anxious. A part of her clearly understood that I *wanted* to injure her. I smelled it and saw it in her eyes.

We continued to stare at each other until Max reached us. "Mr. Giodone, Ms. Thornton, is there a problem here?"

Susan was still frozen, gazing with something approaching wonder at my confrontation with her sister. I spared him a relieved glance. "Yes, Max, there is. This woman is bothering us. Would you please escort her out?"

The blonde looked at Max in surprise when he addressed Susan as Ms. Thornton. Max follows a lead well, whether or not he believes it.

"Madame," he said, "I would appreciate it if you would please leave this establishment. I'm afraid you're creating a disturbance."

The woman's anger escalated and she yanked her wrist out of my hand. She winced at the effort and rubbed it with the other hand briefly. I raised my brows when she glared. No apologies. That's what you get for being a bitch.

Then she pointed a finger at Susan. "This isn't over, little sister! Don't forget I was with you when you bought that pantsuit. You can't hide under some fake hair and silence. I don't know why or how you buffaloed these two into protecting you, but I *will* get the truth out of you. You have no business leaving her alone. If anything happens to her, I hold you responsible!"

I grabbed Susan's arm and led her toward the elevator. The moment I touched her, a little electric breeze sprang up. The fear of discovery and guilt flowing from her nearly overwhelmed me. "Max," I said pleadingly over my shoulder, "take care of this."

Max raised a finger in the air and the two security guards

appeared on either side of the woman. They each gently took an arm.

She stopped short and looked from one to the other. "I am a customer here!" she exclaimed in outrage. "You can't do this."

"We can carry you out, ma'am," said the man on her right, who was built like a linebacker, "But it might embarrass you. Could you *please* come with us?"

The elevator dinged. Susan and I stepped in through the opening doors. I watched as she suddenly realized that we had escaped and that the entire lobby was looking at her as though she had grown a second head. She tried to regain a little dignity. She squared her shoulders and raised her nose.

"Very well. If you insist, I'll go. But you will never have my business again," said the blonde.

As the elevator doors closed, I heard Max say, "I'll make note of that in my records, madame." A chuckle escaped me.

Chapter 4

I hit the button for the seventh floor. When the doors opened, I gestured for Susan to follow me. I didn't touch her again. The flow of emotions every time I did set me on overload.

Susan looked confused. "I thought you said the top floor. Which room are you in?" I just walked away from her and she eventually followed to the stairwell and up. If the woman watched the elevator, she wouldn't know what floor we were really on.

We arrived at the room with her a little out of breath from climbing stairs in three-inch heels. I used the key card on the door and waved her inside. I took off my jacket and automatically checked the weapon concealed at the small of my back in a specially made holster.

I removed my billfold, counted out five hundred dollar bills and offered them to Susan. When she didn't take them, I reached down, grabbed her hand and stuffed the bills into it.

She looked down at the money, then up at me.

"What is this for?"

"I just bought your pantsuit," I explained. "You don't own it anymore. You sold it to a consignment shop three days ago. You can leave out the date, if you don't lie well. If the issue is ever brought up, you can honestly say that you sold it."

The startled look on her face gave way to a look of relief. "That never would have occurred to me! I can do that. It's not a lie. Not really."

I walked back to the wet bar. I could see in the mirror behind the bar the moment when she noticed my gun. A flicker of fear disappeared in quiet resolve.

I picked up my beer, then turned to face her. "Were you followed, or was that little scene an accident?" Self-preservation and professional pride made me ask. I hadn't noticed a tail and she'd already proven she couldn't lie worth shit.

"I don't think I was followed." Worry edged her voice and thick fog rose from her. "I tried to be careful. I know her car, unless she rented one like I did." She began to pace in small circles. "This was a stupid idea! Stupid, stupid, stupid! I should have known that I couldn't have even a few moments of peace. Are you *sure* that you can't kill me right now?" Her cheeks were flushed with embarrassment, voice thick with frustration.

A burst of bitter laughter escaped me. "Here? After *that* scene? You've got to be kidding."

She looked chagrined, as she should. Low-key was a distant memory. All I could hope for at this point was polite embarrassed silence from the gossip pages. I was just glad that I have a good enough relationship with Max that he didn't call the cops. One particular homicide detective has it in for me. He'd loved to run me in, even on a "disturbing the peace" charge.

Time to change the subject. "I had the bar send up Morgan and Diet. Help yourself. You look like you could use one."

She looked from me to the bar and back again, brightening. "That was *nice* of you." She smelled surprised, a shock of scent but warm. Warmth?

"Don't look so shocked," I said in reproach. "I can be nice."

She flushed again. I seemed to have that effect on her.

"I mean . . ." she stammered. "In your profession . . ." She stopped, biting her lip as if she didn't know how to finish the sentence without insulting me.

I let it go. Not important enough to make an issue. I ended the silence with, "Don't worry about it. Grab a drink and sit down."

She moved a little too quickly to the bar. She mixed a Morgan and Diet in one of the beer steins. It was a pretty large glass for a mixed drink. She sat down on the couch but couldn't get comfortable. She restlessly shifted in her seat, body rigid. She wouldn't look at me.

"Why death?" I asked as I turned and walked farther into the room. I faced her and then sank into the overstuffed leather recliner.

She didn't appear surprised by the quick questioning. "Mind if I get comfortable? This will take a while."

I waved my hand at the empty couch and took a long draw of beer.

She pulled off the wig and flipped her hair several times to get the sweat out. It gleamed softly in the light. She gave her scalp a quick scratching. I hid a sympathetic smile in my beer. I know how wigs itch.

Then she unbuttoned and removed the top part of the pantsuit. Underneath was a white silk shell. The chiming sound was from a small silver charm bracelet with tiny bells and little bunny rabbits. I suppressed a chuckle and let my eyes keep roving. Small circles of sweat were beginning to form under her arms. The cool air hit her bare skin and raised goosebumps. My eyes automatically rose. Yes, she felt the cold there too. She stretched and arched her back, outlining the hardened nipples against the thin silk. Definitely enticing. She ended the stretch abruptly and stared at me in shock as if she'd heard what I was thinking. Her scent was embarrassed but a little turned-on. The musk was a very nice touch.

The air blower stopped just then and I could hear her heart beat in the sudden silence. I didn't turn my gaze. She did.

When she sat down, she slumped slightly as if to hide her figure. She looked as though carved in stone. Drink in one hand, legs tight together and crossed at the ankle. Gaze anywhere but at me. My psych professor in college would have said that she had "closed" body language. I'd say more like "slammed shut."

I shook my head and smiled. "Would you please mellow? I won't bite." I paused, allowing myself another good look. "Unless you want me to, of course."

She glanced at me and saw the hungry look in my eyes. I

heard her heart rate increase and could smell heavier musk with overtones of hot and sour soup brush my nose. She flushed again and looked away. Yep, definitely interested, but timid. Fine with me. If she didn't turn out to be an absolute basket case, we could have fun. But I didn't want to make her a wreck. "You wanted to talk. So talk."

She looked at me then. I leaned back into the sofa and put one arm across the back. See, completely relaxed. Just two friends chatting. Except one was a hired killer and the other a multi-millionairess. I sipped the beer. "Well? Why death, Susan?"

"My name's not Susan."

"You're not Susan Quentin?" My hand tightened on my stein but I kept my voice calm. "That's who the papers called you."

"They got my name wrong," she replied angrily. "It's not Susan. It's *Suzi*."

I took a deep breath, shrugged and allowed myself to relax again. "Same difference."

Burned coffee filled the air, thick and pungent. I was a little surprised at the intensity. "No. It's not the same at all."

She hesitated a moment. "My parents named me Suzi. It was supposed to be cute. Suzi Quentin. Suzi-Q. I've spent most of my life being called SuziQ. Makes me sound like some fluffy-headed cheerleader. I hate it."

Her voice vibrated with that hatred. I could smell it too— jalapeño pepper, strong and hot, had joined the burning coffee. There were some other emotions roiling underneath. Too many smells. I couldn't concentrate. I fought for control.

I took a deep whiff of the beer in my hands before I took a drink. Hops. Barley. Alcohol. The emotions faded in the sharp smells. Good. I swallowed deeply. "So what should I call you?"

"Anything but that." She hesitated. "Actually, nobody's ever asked me before what *I* wanted to be called. I don't know."

"What's your middle name?"

She wrinkled her nose. "Lynette. Why?"

I looked her over head to toe then nodded. "You look like a 'Lynette'. How about that?"

She repeated the name to herself several times. Then she shook her head. "Nah. I've never liked it. Just call me Sue."

I nodded in approval. "Sue it is." I stood and walked to the bar to get another beer. She took a swig of her own drink.

"So, *Sue*, you still haven't answered my question. Why death?"

She hesitated not as though she didn't know but like she wanted to collect her thoughts. Trying to give an honest answer. Finally, she looked at me very intently. "Have you ever been used?"

I smiled at that. "I spend every night being used. I'm in a . . . *service* industry."

She shook her head. "Not like that. You have a job. You get paid for your time. I mean really used. Forced to do something you don't want because of duty or obligation or even guilt. With no payment and no thanks?"

My brows raised. "No, using that definition—never."

Her face hardened and she held her glass tight in both hands. "Well, I have. I've spent my entire life being used."

"Why would you want to do that?" I was honestly curious.

She laughed. It was sharp, like broken glass. "I didn't want to. I was born with no backbone. I can't say no. People ask me to do things and I can't think of a polite way to refuse. Or the person sets it up so that I can't refuse without hurting someone. My family is famous for that."

I shrugged. "Tell them to go to hell."

"You don't understand." She sat deeper into the sofa.

I didn't. I mean, why would a person do something just so they wouldn't hurt someone? "So explain it to me."

She thought for a moment and then nodded. "Okay, an example. Years ago, I worked at a fast food place. Just part-time while I was getting on my feet." She looked up and I nodded. "I started at the bottom. You know, cleaning the floor, making fries, that stuff. The boss found out that I could do books and keep money straight, so he started to ask for little favors: 'Could you help me with next week's

schedule? I can't get it right', or 'Would you mind dropping
off the deposit on your way home? I can trust you.' It made
me feel important at first and I was flattered that I'd be
asked to help with important stuff but then it became part of
my assigned duties. Pretty soon, I was doing all the man-
agerial stuff and he was taking off more and more time. Just
not showing up. So I would have to open the store and count
the cash and make sure everything was closed properly. . ."

I held up a hand to stop her. "W*hy* did you have to?"

She swallowed another large mouthful of her drink and
tried to answer. Another wash of emotions—burnt coffee,
burnt water, anger and bitterness and the heavy fog of sorrow all mixed together. It almost took my breath away. I
took another whiff of beer.

"Because although he was a jerk it wasn't the fault of
other employees whose hours would be screwed up without
a schedule, or the customers who expected the business to
be open even when he didn't show up. I felt an obligation to
them, if not to him."

"But every time you did that, you saved his butt from being
fired. He deserved to be canned if he wasn't doing his job."

She sighed, like my words were old news. "But then I
would feel guilty because it also wasn't his wife's fault. She
was confined to a wheelchair and depended on his salary.
Who else would give the jerk a job?"

I chuckled. "You weren't born without a backbone,
sweetheart. You were born with an overdose of guilt. But
that's nothing to die for. You can fix that."

She jumped at the endearment, then plowed on shakily.
"If that was the only problem it wouldn't be so bad. I even-
tually quit, which was my way of solving the problem with-
out confrontation. I don't like confrontation. It's why I say
I've got no backbone. Which leads me back to my family.
More specifically, my mother." She paused and stared at me,
like I was going to walk out on the conversation. Fat chance.
It was just getting interesting.

I raised my eyebrows, encouraging her to proceed.

"I'm the adult care-giver for my mother."

I've known a few of them. Tough life. Watching your parent become a child again, less and less able to provide for themselves. It explained the comment from her sister about leaving "her" alone. "That's a rough job. Is she terminal?"

Another dose of burned coffee. "Some day she will be," she said matter-of-factly and then her eyes narrowed with fury. Thick coffee boiled on the breeze. "But not now. Right now, I'm the adult care giver for a perfectly healthy manipulator."

My surprise must have showed because she smiled bitterly and continued. "Oh, she's good. She's very good. The rest of the family believes that she needs full time care. You only see the truth when you live with her every day. The problem is, I can't get anyone else to believe it. And I can't get rid of her. She possesses my every waking moment. *Demands* my every waking moment."

She finished her drink in a three-gulp wash and stalked to the bar for another.

"She moved in with me two years ago. Back then I truly believed she was failing fast, just like everyone else. She looked like death. She had lost a lot of weight and was having trouble remembering things. Of course, I'm the youngest with no husband or children so it was *decided* that Mom would come to live with me. My input wasn't sought. It was *DECIDED*." Her voice seethed with bitterness. "Everything has always been decided for me." She paused. "But you probably don't want to hear me whine." She took a long draw on the new drink. She was going to get toasted if she didn't slow down. But maybe that was the point.

I took the opening anyway. "I want to hear anything you want to say. Whine or not." She looked at me with surprise. Like even for money I wouldn't want to hear it. Actually, since I had given back half the retainer, I was operating solely on curiosity.

The drinks were starting to take effect. She sat down on the couch and swung her legs up, kicking off her shoes in the process. She grabbed a pillow from the other end and stuffed it behind her back. She had to turn her head to look at me. I felt like a psychiatrist sitting in the chair while she reclined on the couch.

She was silent for a little while before speaking again. She was thinking. Working out where to start. "When Mom moved in with me, I was like everyone else in the family. I believed that she was going senile. The first thing that happened was that she failed her eye test and lost her driver's license. Everybody felt sorry for her. Sorry for the loss of freedom; of independence. We all took turns driving her around to doctor's appointments and the grocery store and other places."

I nodded. Not having a car is a bitch.

"Then, one by one, the rest of the family started getting too busy. I still felt sorry for her and I really did have more time than anyone else. So I guess it sort of made warped sense when they decided for her to move in with me. She just showed up on my doorstep one day; my sister dropped her off. They sold her house and she had nowhere else to be. See what I mean about setting up situations?" She looked to me for agreement.

"Pretty sneaky trick."

"Oh, twice as sneaky as you think. But not on my sister's part; on my mother's. I found out later that Mom had known full well what was happening. She told them that she'd discussed it with me. But she didn't. I had my own life. I had a nice job and a comfortable apartment. I even had a long-standing relationship." She looked sad for a moment. "But they're all gone now. God, I miss it."

"Miss what?"

"My life! She got me fired, and then had me evicted. She even alienated my boyfriend." I could smell it again—the seared caramel that coffee makes when it scorches, muffled under the rising foggy smell of sorrow. Tears came to her eyes and she took another swill.

Oh God, I hoped I wasn't in for a crying jag.

"I don't make friends easily. Relationships are even harder. I knew when she drove Robert away from me that

she'd never let me have another. She set it up so *slick*." She
glanced at me to see if I was uncomfortable having her talk
about a former lover.

It didn't bother me and I said so: "I'm not bothered by
much. There's not a lot you can surprise or embarrass me
with. Talk away." She blushed and looked away again, then
she shifted uncomfortably on the couch and switched sub-
jects. "When she moved in it started innocently enough. I let
her have my bedroom. It was only a one bedroom so I took
the couch. I figured that she would only be there for a few
weeks until she found a new place. But she had no intention
of leaving. My neighbors hated her. She made so many complaints against everyone that eventually I got evicted."

Wow. That takes effort. I've lived next to some real
annoying people, but could never get them kicked out.

"Once I found my current house she started making
requests. Just little ones, you know, like 'Oh Suzi, could you
help me with my medicines? I can't remember which ones
I've taken today.' I figured if her memory was failing, it
would probably be best for me to take control of her medicine. You know, so she didn't overdose."

I nodded.

"And little by little, she just *infringed* into my space. 'Oh,
no, Suzi, you can't buy *that* soap. I'm terribly allergic to it.'
And, 'Suzi, dear, must you play that rock music? It's so difficult to concentrate.' I tried to make her feel like a guest but
she didn't want guest status. She wanted to run the show.
No, that's not right either," she said, shaking her head. "She
wanted to run the backstage, and have *me* in front of the
camera running the show."

The beer had run through me. I excused myself to the
bathroom. She nodded politely and sat staring into space
running a slow fingertip around the lip of her glass.

I didn't waste any time. I wanted to get right back. I was
enjoying her company, despite my better judgment. I even
liked her. I spent the minute or two trying to figure out what
it was. She had a certain—I don't know, maybe *stamina* that
was refreshing. A "grin and bear it" attitude. But if she

wanted to die then things had taken a turn for the worse. I
wanted to hear chapter two.

I returned to the living room. Her glass was full again. A
glance at the clear bottle of rum on the bar confirmed that it
was another full strength job. Nearly a quarter fifth gone in
three drinks.

I walked over and took the drink out of her hand. She
looked at me, startled. "Slow down a little," I said. "If you
pass out, you can't talk. You're plenty relaxed now." I put
the drink on the bar and poured a second glass of just Diet
Coke. She took the glass, nodded, and sipped the soda. Then
she began talking again as if she hadn't stopped and I had
missed part of the conversation when I left the room.

"Becky was the pretty one. Tall and athletic with blonde
hair to her waist. She could have anyone she wanted. I wasn't
born pretty. I'm not tall or blonde. I got reminded of it every
day. That was Becky downstairs."

"Well," I responded glibly, "At least you have manners."

She smiled at that. Smiled at me. A fog of spiced tangerines drifted to my nose. Happiness stronger than gratitude. "Becky's never had to be polite. She's pretty. People
excuse bad behavior in pretty people." I shrugged. I
couldn't disagree.

"Becky thinks that I'm just being selfish. That I want to
have this wild life or something now that I've got money.
She's just sure I want to throw Mom into the street."

"Do you?"

"Honestly? Sometimes. But I can't. And I probably
wouldn't, given the choice. After I won the money I bought
a big house, way larger than I needed. I figured that Mom
could have space and I would have a room or two where I
could be alone. I've always liked being alone. But Mom
can't be alone. Actually *can't*. It drives her nuts. I sit down
to take a bath and she's knocking on the door, wanting to
come in to talk. It drives me insane!"

"Well, if she really can live alone, why don't you buy her
a place of her own? Move her out and be done with it."

She shook her head so hard that her hair whipped with the

force. The alcohol, I thought—her movements were getting bigger, stronger, as if overcompensating.

"Don't you think I tried? That was the *first* thing I thought of. I have two doctors on my side and they're very well respected. When I got the money, the first thing I did was hire a team of doctors to give her a full exam. I mean a *full* exam." Her arm swept the air and almost knocked the drink out of her other hand.

"X-rays, CTs, blood tests, the works. I got a neurological specialist because she said she was losing feeling in her fingers. She swore she was growing taller so she had an MRI to see if she had a tumor. All negative. Oh, and her eyes are just fine. But if she had a license I wouldn't have to drive her. The doctor confirmed that she is as healthy as a race-horse. Healthy for someone half her age. More healthy than *me*. She called them quacks and demanded we see some Chinese herbalist that a friend told her about. I couldn't imagine what *friend* told her that. She doesn't have any friends. I wish she did!"

She shook her head wearily. "I thought the money would help. But things are even worse. I finally convinced the family to let her try to live alone. I bought her an apartment. I even offered to pay for a full-time nurse." She sputtered angrily. "You know what she did? Huh?"

"I can't imagine."

"She broke her hip!"

I raised my eyebrows. "Not intentionally, I'm sure."

Her eyes were cold but calm. "She *absolutely,* intentionally broke her hip. I was finally going to be free and she just couldn't stand it." She said it as if it was a fact, not merely suspicion.

I began to understand.

Chapter 5

"How do you know she hurt her hip intentionally?" I asked.

"She was taped." She waited for a reaction. I carefully leaned forward and set my stein on the table. Then I leaned back and put up the footrest. The slow movements were meant to cover surprise. This was getting even more interesting.

"You videotaped her?"

She smelled embarrassed. "Not on purpose. When I bought the house, there were six months left on a security contract. You know, a burglar alarm company?"

I nodded knowingly.

"Part of the contract is to replace tapes in the hidden monitors around the house every few weeks. It's a real expensive house, but I have them set on pretty low-resolution and on the longest run time since I don't really have much to steal. I don't even think mom knows they exist. Anyway, I was out making the final arrangements on the apartment. She helped pick the colors and the wallpaper. She seemed excited about having her own place again. Something that didn't remind her of Dad. When I got back, she was nearly unconscious on the floor. I couldn't move her. I called an ambulance."

Sue was quiet for a moment. Her scent shifted again. The burned coffee of anger twined with the sour, bitter smell of guilt.

"I felt horrible," she said at last. "Just horrible. I really did feel selfish. When I was out that morning I had been feeling so smug. I was going to be free of her. Then I found her on the floor with her leg bent wrong. She was whimpering."

"When did you get the tape?"

She ignored the question at first. She was in her own little world. Another dose of emotions. Too many to sort out. Time for another long sniff of beer.

"She looked so helpless. I couldn't help. Not even a little. She's a big woman. I couldn't even move her. I was afraid to. So I waited for help. I sat on the floor next to her and tried to make her comfortable. I felt so guilty. I wondered if I had imagined all of the mind games. Whether I really was the selfish one for wanting my own space when she needed me." Tears came to her eyes and she didn't bother to wipe them away. They ran down her face unchecked.

She snuffled and then coughed. I leaned over to the table next to my chair, rummaged a moment, then tossed her a box of tissues. She missed the box but it landed on the floor within reach. She set her drink on the table, grabbed a tissue, and blew her nose. Unlike most people, she actually cried well. Her face flushed and looked better than normal, even with red-rimmed eyes.

"I got a call from the insurance company months after her fall. I had been acting so apologetic. She just ate it up. I bought the apartment anyway; I had a contract. But I never finished the decorations. I stayed home all the time in case she needed something. She had to have a hip replacement. It took months to heal. I literally put my life on hold for three months."

"What did the insurance company tell you?"

"I guess they routinely investigate accidents like this. They saw the monitor in the hallway when they came to the house and checked with the security company. They said they were denying the claim because it was faked. Not the injury. It was real. But the accident was set up. I didn't believe them. Not at first."

She hesitated and I prodded gently. "But they convinced you, didn't they?"

"They showed me the tape. There was no mistaking it. In clear black and white. She knelt down at the top of the bannister and removed the screws from the handrail. She jiggled it to make sure it was loose. Then she calmly climbed the stairs and started back down. When she got to a certain point right near the top she pushed her whole body weight sideways and went right through the banister. It was so cold and calculated. She said something when she was wiggling the banister. Even though it's not the kind of system that picks up sound, her face was clear on the camera. It showed her lips moving."

She looked up at me, very intent. "I never told her that the monitors worked. It never came up. I haven't told her since. I took the hit on the medical. Luckily, I can afford it now. Then I took a copy of the tape to a deaf school. They read her lips." Her eyes were tearing up again. She smelled of anger and heartbreak. Like she wished it never happened.

"What did she say?"

She pursed her lips angrily but her eyes were pained. "She said, 'Now let's see her kick me out.' Is that cold, or what?" Crystal tears glittered at the edge of her swollen lids.

I tried to absorb that. Tried to fathom a family member doing that. My mind rebelled. Family just didn't do that. I spoke before I thought. "That sort of makes me glad I don't have parents."

"They're dead?" She wiped at her face with a handful of tissues. Her voice was already more steady.

I nodded. "When I was ten. Well, my mom anyway. My father died before I was born."

"Who raised you?"

"My father's people. He was a small-time courier for the Family." I said it to imply the capital F.

She dropped her tissues in the wastebasket and shuddered visibly. "I'm really glad they were run out of town."

That made me glare at her with a surprising amount of venom. "I'm not! I had a home with them!" She winced and looked away again.

I took a deep breath and tried to explain. It was probably better if she didn't know about my past but the odds were good that I'd do the job for her, especially if she knew too much. That's what I told myself. And hey, I felt talkative. "They didn't have to take me in. My father was a two-bit hood, a wanna-be. My mom was a whore." She didn't say anything but I could hear her stiffen on the couch and smelled the sharpness of her shock, underlain with the dusty smell of shame.

I shrugged in response to the scent. "Prostitutes are moms too, you know. The Family didn't have to do anything. I was nothing to them. But my father got killed on a run. They felt responsible. He had told someone high up about this real lady that he was seeing. He was one of her regulars. He told everyone how beautiful she was and how he was going to make 'an honest woman' out of her and that they had already started a family. Patrone took him at his word. Gave me a home when she died of syphilis. Treated me like blood."

Her smell shifted again; wet, foggy, but not sorrow. Not exactly. "You're right. They didn't have to do that. I'm sorry for what I said. Is that why you do what you do?"

I shrugged again. "It's what I know. It's what I was raised with. Like, the boys in the Appalachians who don't know that they're not supposed to sleep with their sisters until they get into the outside world and find out it's considered deviant. It's the same in the Family. It's the way things are."

"But," she said, looking truly confused. "How can you take another person's life?"

I smiled coldly. "It's supply and demand. If there was no demand for killing, there'd be no supply. I don't wish anyone ill, but others do. I only carry out other people's bad intentions."

She shifted position again, tense, disapproving. I didn't have to smell it to sense it and it made me uncomfortable. I shifted the subject away from me. "The Family had standards." She gave me a disbelieving look. "No. really. Before two years ago, did you ever see a drive-by shooting of a little kid? Or graffiti sprayed on street signs?"

She thought briefly and shook her head. "Not really."

"Exactly!" I held a finger in the air to accentuate my words. "We kept our business internal. Our fights stayed within our factions. The general public saw few, if any, signs of our presence. These new gangs have no respect for anything or anybody. Before, if someone was killed, there was a reason. Now it's open season on little kids and the elderly. The gangs are scavengers; they take down the weakest. Anyone they can get. We allowed the weak and the innocent to pass by unharmed. We concentrated on our equals. It was the Family that kept the gangs under control. They feared us; respected us." I leaned forward in my chair again, my gaze intent on her.

"I know that most people wanted them out of town. But right or wrong, they were my people. I'm sorry they went to jail. They're family. You stand by them even when they do wrong. I'll stand by them again when they get out."

She nodded, accepting that without question. "I wish I had family that would stand by me. I want them to like me, to love me. But they just don't."

"Oh, I doubt that. I'm sure they love you."

"No," she disagreed, "they really don't! They have no respect for me. No empathy for me; no desire to know about me or my life. You can't feel love for someone if you're not even interested in them." She said it very matter-of-factly. "They don't care. All my life they've told me I'm worthless. Not smart enough, not talented enough, not pretty enough. I'm apparently just not enough of anything to make them love me. My only purpose in life is what they can use me for."

Tears glittered again in her eyes and she stood and walked to the bar. Even without the wolf senses, I could feel her hurt at saying those words. She made herself another drink, ignoring the one from earlier. I watched her in the mirror as she took a healthy swallow. I didn't feel pity for her. She intrigued me, even broken like this.

Then she abruptly began talking again. "It was hard when Robert left me. Harder still when it was Becky he left me for." *That* made my eyebrows climb.

"He said he was sorry but he just wasn't attracted to me anymore. It was understandable, of course." Her voice trembled. There was a sing-song quality to it as though she'd repeated the justifications over and over, trying to believe. "Given the choice, why would he pick me over her? I'm just absolutely insignificant. She's breezy and funny and gorgeous. But it still hurts that he would believe Mom's lies."

No. I stood and walked up behind her.

"I'll never be anyone that a man lusts after. I know that." She took a deep, quavering breath. "But every time I see him, the few times I can't avoid it, he feels so guilty that he has to remind me. He apologizes and then says he hopes that we can be *friends*."

She picked up her glass again just as I stopped behind her. This close, I could hear the catch in her voice.

She raised the glass to her lips once more. "I always wonder—if I had been prettier, would he be married to me instead? I'm rich now. I could have plastic surgery." She turned and found me standing there nearly touching. There was pain in her face that didn't need to be there.

I met her eyes and said softly, "I think you're just fine." She didn't speak but just looked at me.

I breathed in the tang of fear's hot and sour soup. The smell made my jaw tighten. It rolled over the summer forest of her own smell and the musky hot scent of desire. This time, the wolf inside wanted something that was against my better judgment. I needed to taste her. I took the drink out of her hand and set it on the bar. Then I leaned forward and braced one hand on either side of her on the bar to brush my lips to hers. Her lips were supple and her breath had a hint of vanilla.

Dear God! The sensation that passed through me as our lips met was incredible. Heat flowed between our mouths and thrills of electricity spread along the skin of my face; then across my scalp. I felt her rear back in surprise and apprehension. The power of the first meager brush of lips raised every hair on the back of my neck. A brilliant flash awakened each nerve along my spine until I shivered. Oh, I wanted more of this! I wanted to reach for her and pull her against me until I pulled her inside my skin.

Instead, I leaned into her and opened her mouth with mine. My jaw worked slowly against hers. The kiss was soft and gentle until I pressed my body forward and pushed her against the bar. Tingles slid up and down my body, center-ing in my groin, until I could barely think. My tongue slid into her mouth to tease hers. After a pause she kissed me back. I don't think she could help it any more than I could.

When she gave in, it was complete. She wrapped her arms around me and slid them up my back. I moved one arm around her shoulders and tightened it. The other hand stayed on the bar for balance. I hardly remembered doing it. I felt her heart flutter where our chests touched. I could feel the hard press of her nipples through my shirt. I wanted to lie her down on the floor, tear off her clothes, and run my hands over her; taste every inch of her skin. But I knew better than to push. She accepted this, needed it—but too much and she'd run.

I ended the kiss as gently as it began, and when I moved away, I put the drink back in her hand. Damn! I walked back to the sofa, my knees unsteady. My heart raced like I'd been running. My lungs were heaving almost painfully for air. I checked the thermostat on my way back to allow me to col-lect myself. I'd never felt like that from just a kiss. I let out a slow breath and closed my eyes. I felt hot but it was proba-bly just the heat of attraction. Because I was attracted to her.

Bad plan, Tony. Then again, what was one more risk?

Chapter 6

I fought to get my voice back. I cleared my throat. "Why do you think your mom had anything to do with your man leaving?" My voice was still a little shakier than I liked.

She walked to the window and looked out over the city. I followed her with my eyes and watched her stare at the setting sun. It would be time to turn on the lamp soon.

"Robert knew Becky the whole time we were together. He said he thought she was annoying. I found out things Mom said one time when he was a little tipsy at a Christmas party. It was after he and Becky were married. He wondered why I had never told him I thought he was boring and why I *told* Mom that he'd be better suited to Becky. She apparently told him that I thought they were both superficial and egotistical." She laughed harshly. "I never said any of those things. I never talked about Robert with my mom. But he wouldn't believe it. After all, why would my mother lie? That's when I knew. That's when it became crystal clear." She glanced back at me over her shoulder, then returned to staring out the window.

"The rest of the family is all the same. My other sister, Mitzi, brings her dogs over and just leaves them at my door."

"Mitzi, Becky and Suzi?" I shook my head in amazement. "Well, at least Becky is semi-normal."

"Sure," she replied sarcastically. "If they would have spelled like sane people. But it's B-e-*k-k*-i."

I rolled my eyes. God save me from cutesy parents! Mind you, I've heard worse. I knew a Candy Sweet in school and once worked with Jett Black. She had a brother—Cole. Sad. Truly sad.

"Some days I walk outside and there they are. But at least the dogs are always glad to see me and they keep the geese away."

I smiled. "Geese?"

"I used to like geese. They're so pretty in the air." She wrinkled her nose. "On the ground, they're disgusting. Apparently, the previous owners of my house encouraged a whole flock to live by the swimming pool. Built boxes and stuff for nests. Now I can't get rid of them."

I stifled a smile. "Let me guess. It's not the geese's fault that they were invited in the first place, and you can't just kill them." Again that sense of *noblesse oblige*. This quirk of hers seemed to be the root of all of her problems.

Her smile shone brilliant in the window's reflection. "Exactly. But Mom doesn't like them either, so sometimes I can hide from her outside. She's afraid of them." She paused as she gazed out, shifting restlessly to one side. "The sky is pretty tonight. You can see the full moon while the clouds are still colored."

I looked beyond her and saw the pale, almost full moon rising in a blood red sky. My heart started pounding uncontrollably. I must have screwed up my calendar when the watch broke. Did it really take me three days to get out of Atlantic City? No wonder Max was confused when I asked to have the suite tonight. I already had it!

I had to get her out of here. Already I felt hot, the unnatural heat of the change. It might be too late already. I bit off a curse but my voice was harsh. "You have to leave. Get your things and go! Now!!"

She turned back to me, startled. "What? Why?" Smells, emotions, eddied over me. The thick tang of fear spiked with the even sharper smell of worry. Too much, too much—

I grabbed her jacket and threw it at her. One of my legs gave out and started to spasm. "Go! Get the hell out now, or you'll die *tonight*, instead of a year from now."

My vision started to go. Flashes of black and white flowed back to color with a red haze bleeding into everything. Still she stood there gaping at me, as if unable to understand what was happening. She would understand in a minute. Too well. *I'm sorry,* I thought and staggered toward the bedroom. *Give her . . . a chance—*

I got the door shut before I totally collapsed, nearly screaming with the pain of the transformation. Even through the soundproofing I heard her pounding at the door, asking if I was okay. "Get out!" I screamed but she couldn't hear.

I threw the lock and then the change had me.

Chapter 7

I woke up sprawled across the bed. It hurt to move—but then, it always did after. Human limbs don't willingly bend into the shape of a dog.

I stood and stretched. As always, I was naked. I don't know how I get my clothes off. Don't remember. It was odd that I hadn't destroyed the room. I had on other occasions. That and the fact that I wasn't hungry had me worried. I didn't want to go out into the main room. I suspected there was a chewed up millionairess out there and I wasn't looking forward to cleaning it up. My gut turned taut and hollow. For being a part of my life for such a short time she was already leaving a large dent. Damn it!

I walked to the closet and retrieved underwear, a T-shirt, and a pair of shorts from a secret drawer that only me and the owner knew about. The few items are all that would fit in the space but are enough for me to be decent in public. I put on the underwear but not the rest. I needed to take a shower. Makes me feel human again. I twisted the doorknob but stopped short. I really didn't want to go out there. I've seen what I've done to a human being in the past. Only once but it was enough.

I grabbed my gun from the dresser, took a deep breath, and quickly opened the door. Light shone in from the open drapes, highlighting surfaces and creating shadows on the clean floor. No bloody body. The coil of nerves inside my gut released slightly and I let out a slow breath.

A sound caught my ear suddenly. I wasn't alone.

The tumult of running water came from the direction of the bathroom. I moved quietly toward the door. Warm steam, fragrant with eucalyptus and cloves, curled under the closed door and licked at my bare legs. The aroma overpowered the scent of the person inside even when I concentrated.

I counted silently in my head as I flipped off the safety. When I reached three I raised up my foot and kicked in the door.

The flimsy lock gave way immediately and the broken door bounced against the wall with a bang. A shriek came from inside the room. I moved through the doorway, crouched low, gun leading me.

Sue raised frightened eyes over the lip of the marble tub. My head reeled from the sultry combination of her forest scent, the sudden piquance of her fear, and the bath oil hanging thick and strong. When she sat up I got a clear view of her body to the waist, adding visual stimuli to my already aroused body. I couldn't stop a wolfish smile.

She suddenly realized that she was naked and blushed furiously. She quickly grabbed a royal blue towel to pull around her. The towel sank heavily into the hot water and darkened to nearly black. The cloth enhanced her curves and made her eyes seem a much more vivid green. Nice.

"You're back," she said.

Well, that certainly made me nervous. "Have I been anywhere?"

I'm what Babs calls "A three-day dog". That's the day before a full moon, the full, and the day after. I'm not sure how much time I spend human when night arrives. I don't remember the stuff I do when I'm in wolf form. It's not like I have human thoughts. Since I can't control the change and don't remember it, I lock myself away for the whole three days, even though I'm human for part of it.

She seemed comfortable suddenly. Spiced citrus and baking bread rode the steam to my nose. "Physically? No. But mentally? Let's just say you weren't a real great conversationalist. On the plus side, you listen well that way and that *is* what I was paying you for." She gave me a short grin that showed her amusement.

I didn't know how to respond to her. She was happy?

Comfortable? "What happened?" I asked. I needed to know how she survived.

She looked surprised. "You don't remember? Really?"

That was none of her business. "Just tell me your version."

She leaned back in the tub, keeping the towel in place as she moved. She was absolutely sober now and looked more in control of herself. I shut the door to keep in the warmth and the incredible scent and set the gun on the sink. She'd never reach it before me if it came to that. I moved further into the spacious room and sat down on the edge of the tub, near her knees, facing her. It made her a little nervous but it was either that or sit on the stool. If I sat there she'd have to twist her head the whole time. She tightened the towel a bit in unconscious response.

"Well, you threw my coat at me and told me to get out."

"Which you didn't do," I admonished.

"You looked like you were in pain and you screamed." Her voice was calm, as though it was sufficient reason.

I gave an annoyed shake of my head. "That room is supposed to be soundproof."

She shrugged. "You screamed before the door shut completely. After that, it was. You wouldn't let me in and I didn't know what to do. So I went downstairs."

The sudden panic of discovery knotted my gut.

"You didn't tell anyone? Tell me that you didn't say anything!"

She gave me a withering look, completely unafraid. "Do I look like a complete idiot? I just asked the concierge— Max?—if there was a separate key for the master bedroom because I had accidentally locked up my jacket. He offered to come up but I told him that you were in a foul mood and it wouldn't be a good idea. You apparently have a reputation. His eyes went real wide and he agreed."

Smart man.

"Anyway, he gave me a master key that I have to give back before I go. He said it would open anything in the room. It does, by the way. I got bored and tried all the locks."

That's why everything smelled like her. "And you got up the nerve to open the bedroom door?"

"I had to. I thought maybe you had a seizure or something."

"Or something," I said wryly.

"It was something, all right. I unlocked the door and there you were, in full glory! Black and white and teeth all over." She looked impressed but not frightened.

"This is supposed to bother you, ya know. It's not a real normal thing."

She shrugged again and the towel slipped. She caught it before it showed anything interesting. When she saw me watching she flushed, sending a burst of desert-like scent into the room. You'd think that was impossible in a steam filled room, but that's what embarrassment smells like.

"It probably would if it was the first time. But I've seen it before."

"What?" I exclaimed. "Me, personally?"

"No. Not you. Someone else. I don't even know his name. Probably never will. I had completely forgotten about it. When I opened the door and saw you sitting on your haunches ripping off the rest of your shirt with your teeth, it reminded me."

"Then what?"

"You turned to me and whatever is human inside you wasn't home. The look was all animal. Have you been this way your whole life?"

I shook my head. That was all the information she was getting about me for now.

"What then?" I'd never had a blow-by-blow narration before. Mild burned coffee rose to me. She was getting irritated by my interruptions.

"I didn't know what to do. I backed up and you followed, stalking me. I think you thought I was dinner."

I had a flash of memory just then. I'd never had one before. Visions in black and white, of seeing Sue and having to look up at her. Of being a wolf. I saw her wide eyes, smelled her fear. But she smelled like me. She had my scent on her and I liked the combination of smells. She didn't smell like food, she smelled like . . . a mate. I knew why I had stalked her. I couldn't tell her that I hadn't wanted to eat her, I had wanted to screw her. That's way too weird, even for me!

Sue's voice cut through the memory. It frayed at the edges, then fell away from my mind. "I had no choice but to accept what I was seeing. Then there was a knock on the door. You growled and backed into the bedroom. I shut the bedroom door and answered the knock."

"That was stupid." I was annoyed more at myself than her.

"I asked first! Give me *some* credit. The man said he was room service with dinner. You told me you were going to order."

Oh.

"There was no one at the door, just a cart with covered dishes. So I wheeled it inside. The food smelled great. I heard you snuffling at the door like you could smell the food and I figured that if you weren't hungry, maybe you wouldn't be so...aggressive. So I took the plate with the rare steak and moved it close to the door. You snuffled louder so I opened the door a little, slid the plate inside and backed up."

"Thanks for the dinner."

She shook her head. "You wouldn't eat it. You sniffed it and gave the steak a lick but your eyes went right back to me. I didn't like that look so I closed the door again."

I coughed to hide a smile. Yeah, I am a little single-minded. I probably would have eaten the steak without her there. "Why didn't you leave?"

"I didn't know how long you'd be like that or what would happen next. I couldn't just leave you trapped in the room. You couldn't open the door. You might starve or die of thirst if I just left."

I sighed and shook my head. "That soft heart is going to get you killed."

"That's the plan," she replied smoothly. It made me smile. I like black humor.

"So why didn't you let me make you dinner if that's the plan?"

"Because how would you explain it? It'd be a horrible mess."

She wasn't lying. "So you weren't afraid of me?"

She shrugged her shoulders. "As much as I am of any dog, er—wolf. I like animals."

"You said you've seen it before. When?"

"Oh, God, a long time ago. It's just bits and pieces of memory. I'm not even positive that it was real."

"Tell me," I ordered. I need to know if there are others like me. Other than Babs. She hasn't exactly been a fountain of information and it's not like I can sniff them out or something. At least, I don't think I can. Maybe I should have let Babs give me some instruction like she wanted to.

"I must've been about four years old." She scooted down further into the water, reaching up with a toe to turn on the hot water spigot. She spoke louder although she didn't need to. "My parents took us all to the woods. Mom was really great back when Dad was alive. Sweet and thoughtful and just wonderful." She smiled. "I remember Mom made a special trip to the grocery store to buy me bologna for the trip. My favorite sandwich back then was bologna with ketchup on white bread."

She giggled, really giggled. I'd never heard one that wasn't faked. It was cute and I smiled at her. The smile reached all the way to my eyes. She blushed again and averted her eyes. Musky desire rose from her. Her toe stretched again for the faucet but I beat her to it. My hand brushed her bare foot and electricity raced through us both. She gasped and glanced up at me in shock. Our eyes locked briefly but then she looked away uncomfortably. Her foot dropped back into the water.

Sexual tension crackled in the air.

Not yet, I told myself sternly. Business first.

"So, you were camping?" I prompted, after her sudden fear tickled my nose.

A relieved breath exited from her lips. She nodded. "We had just eaten and I was playing near the edge of the woods with my favorite doll. Her name was Jessica. Strange, huh?"

I raised my brows slightly in agreement. I've always liked the name. It's why I picked the fake name for her to use.

"She was one of those dolls that had adjustable hair, you know?"

I didn't. I shrugged and shook my head. "Sorry, dolls aren't my thing."

"Well, she did," she said firmly. "My sisters decided to tease me. I think it was meant as a tease. I try to remember it that way. They took my doll and threw it into the woods. They told me that Mom would be mad if I lost my doll and I'd better go get her. They were right. They wouldn't get in trouble for throwing the doll; I'd get in trouble for losing her. It was the way it was in our family."

"Kids can be cruel."

"Yeah. But they're supposed to grow out of it. Bekki and Mitzi didn't." The anger that she still felt all these years later surprised me again. There was no mistaking the scent.

"Sorry." It was the only thing I could think of to say.

She shrugged. This time, she didn't catch the towel in time. Yes, I watched. I waited for the blush. She didn't disappoint me.

She quickly tightened the towel around her body. "Anyway, I went into the woods to find Jessica. It was hours later when I did. If my parents called me I never heard them. When I found my doll and turned around to head back, I didn't know where I was. I was absolutely lost and the sun was setting. I wasn't a Girl Scout or even a Brownie. I didn't know directions. I knew I'd get spanked for running off so I started to cry."

Sadness and fear rose from her in a sudden burst, engulfing me in her memory. The emotions shadowed her voice as she spoke. "I still had part of my sandwich in my pocket and my doll for company so I sat down under a tree and waited. But nobody came."

"What happened then?"

"I heard a sound and thought it might be Mom or Dad. I called out but it wasn't them. It was a big dog, white as snow with blue eyes. It was beautiful. I didn't know a wolf from a dog. I did remember that Dad always told me a doggie without a collar doesn't like people so I shouldn't pet it. But it was a pretty dog and I was lonely."

I closed my eyes and sighed. "That wasn't real bright."

"Hey!" she retorted. "I was *four*! What can you expect?"

"Okay, yeah, I know. What did you do then?"

"I thought the doggy might be hungry because I was. I shared my sandwich with it. All dogs like bologna."

I wrinkled my nose. "Don't *ever* feed me bologna. I know what's in that stuff." I was startled that I said it as though it would come up again.

"Said by a man who just ate a raw turkey," she replied snidely.

I didn't understand the apparent dig. "So I guess the 'doggie' didn't eat you."

"The wolf was very sweet." The ground clove smell of pride; self-satisfaction burst into the air. Maybe the cloves weren't in the oil.

"He stayed with me all night. Kept me company. That's what reminded me. When you laid down on the couch and just stayed with me. Warm and just, well, *there*. It's hard to describe." Cinnamon and sugar blended with the cloves in the air.

"So why did you think the dog was a man?"

"I didn't. Not that night. The next morning I finally heard the search party. I found out later that they'd been looking for me all night. When I heard Mom's voice I ran off, forgetting about the dog. I was halfway to the voices when I remembered the nice doggy and went back to say good-bye. But when I got there . . ."

"It was gone?"

"Sort of. I saw a bright flash of light and then saw a man—a naked Hispanic man with long black hair. He dropped to his hands and knees and collapsed on the forest floor. I tried to wake him but he was unconscious.

My brows raised. Maybe she really had seen one of us.

"I knew," she continued, "that I'd get in trouble for being with a strange *man* a lot more than a strange dog. Somehow

I knew that he was the dog. But my folks were calling. I left Jessica with the man so he wouldn't get lonely. I've never told anyone about that night."

I smiled and she stared at the water, looking shy. "That was sweet of you. But I doubt he'll remember you. Not if he's like me."

"What else could I do? I was four."

"So, what did you do with *me* after I started to stalk you?"

Cloves dusted the steam once more. She warmed to the new subject. "I decided that you wanted raw meat, not cooked. Even rare is cooked. So I went downstairs and snuck into the kitchen." She started to grin, "And I found the perfect meal."

"What did I have for dinner? I don't exactly recall."

"I told you! Turkey! There was a nearly raw turkey in the oven. It was bloody and warm, hardly cooked at all. I put it on a silver platter and covered it with one of those domes and snuck back into the elevator. I should have taken a cart. I almost dropped it twice. It weighed, like, twenty pounds and once it started to bleed, it got really slippery on the tray. Nobody saw, thank God."

I nodded admiringly. Impressive.

She smiled. "You were so cute!" That made me frown. I don't like to be thought of as cute.

"I put the platter on the floor next to the bedroom. I opened the door just a bit then backed up. You looked at me first, then the turkey. You were real suspicious. You sniffed it a couple of times and then picked it up in your mouth and came here into the bathroom with it. I followed you to see what you would do. You jumped into the bathtub, lay down, and ate the bird. Bones and all. Hardly left a scrap."

Damn! No wonder I wasn't hungry. Twenty pounds of turkey had better fill me up!

"Thank you." I'd only say it once.

"After I fed you, you were real nice. I took the flowers out of that big bowl on the coffee table and filled it up with water. You drank almost all of it. I sat down and stayed on the couch so you'd have room to move around. But you jumped up on the recliner and just watched me. Like you're doing now. Interested in me. I've never had that. So I kept talking and you listened. I got a lot out of my system. I appreciate it."

She blushed and it reddened not only her face but her neck and chest, as well. "I'm sort of glad you don't remember some of the stuff I said."

"Now I'm sorry I missed it." My smile was genuine.

I looked at her; really looked at her. Her hair was wet and tangled and her face was still blushing. Our eyes locked and the flustered smile on her face slowly slid away, replaced by nervous anticipation. The sultry musk that rose from her was stronger now. The scent of her desire filled me completely.

The soft lighting in the bath turned her eyes an even deeper green. She wasn't stunning, but she was pretty, even without makeup. Her eyes went dark and bottomless while I stared into them. Like earlier, the wolf roared to the surface. Before I could stop myself I leaned over and kissed her. It started slow, like last time, but deepened and grew. I snaked a hand behind her head to pull her closer. The tingles where our lips touched nearly scalded but it didn't hurt. It felt incredibly good. I couldn't breathe past the sensations that engulfed me.

My other hand slipped into the water and I helped the towel float away. I stroked a hand down her naked body and she made little noises in the back of her throat. I tried again to remind myself that she was off limits but my body didn't care. It hungered for something that has no name, something beyond logic right at the edge of sanity.

I pulled back and asked for a third time, whispered it into her mouth because I needed to know. "Why do you want to die, Sue?"

She answered this time. Maybe the time she spent talking to my wolf form allowed her to come up with the answer. "To deny them. To escape everybody that has used me."

She gave a harsh laugh. "I've worked when I was delirious with fever; worked when there was no pay, no thanks.

There's never any appreciation. Never a reward. I keep setting aside my own dreams for someone else's. Even the money isn't a reward. It's a curse." A single tear caught the light in flashes as it rolled slowly down her cheek.

"I've been drained of everything independent and useful by a bitter, hateful family. I've been used and used until I'm all used up. I have nothing left to give and it will only keep hurting to give more. It will only end when I'm gone. Because I can't stop them. I can't escape them. I don't know any other way."

"You're wrong. You *could* escape them," I said strongly. A rotten family is no reason to die. "Set up a trust. Disappear in the night. Go to Argentina, Brazil—even Switzerland. You can buy a new identity and be someone else."

She shook her head again. "They'd find me. They would spend all the money and they would track me until the day I died to get the rest. So I have to die."

The next words were whispered with eyes closed. Her voice trembled. "But I'm not even strong enough to do it myself. I figured if I hired someone and paid them it would just happen. Sometime when I wasn't looking." More tears joined the first. They flowed down her cheeks unchecked. I ran fingers through her hair and wiped the tears away with the back of my hand. She shuddered from the electricity as our skin touched.

"Why don't you pay me to hit her instead? Then you could go on."

She smiled but shook her head. "Because she's family, and no matter how bad they screw up, you stand by them. Remember? I can't kill her but I can eliminate myself. Then she'll be forced to move on. Be forced to grow up. I know she's lonely and scared of being by herself. But I can't give any more of me. There's no more to give. She's made me bitter and cynical and not able to love or be loved. I hate her for that. I hate them all." Peppers, strong enough to burn my eyes, made me believe it.

"And I hate myself for allowing it." She shook her head sadly. I couldn't smell the sorrow over the fog-filled room but I knew it was there. "If all that's left inside of me is hate then I don't want to live. I'd rather die."

"Well, I don't want you to die. Not today." I reached into the water and placed my arm under her bent legs. I lifted her out of the tub, and her arms closed around my neck. A mild burning sensation quickened my breath. She still wore the delicate silver charm bracelet. Each movement brought pain as the silver singed my skin. Did she somehow know that silver prevents the infection? How?

Back when I was still speaking to Babs, she mentioned, with a smile, that sex would be a whole new experience—as long as the woman wore silver. There was no problem with damage to me. I'd heal and not infect her as long as I didn't draw blood from her. Probably a good idea for Sue to keep the bracelet. Wish I would have had one when I took on Babs. I wouldn't be what I've become.

Chapter 8

I looked into Sue's eyes. Water streamed off her body and soaked me. I tightened my arm around her shoulder. I turned to take her to the bedroom. The sudden sour ammonia of her panic and the frantic pounding of her heart struck me full in the chest. It stopped me where I stood. I looked into her eyes, trying to decide whether to end it here. She held my gaze with wide eyes but she made no move to stop.

I brushed my lips against hers. She pulled me into the kiss deeper and accepted my tongue hungrily. Hot musk. Enough to drown in. Then the fear hit me again. Still so afraid. So very afraid. Why?

"We can stop." I said quietly. I set her back onto her legs but continued to gently trace the curves of her waist with my hands.

"It's just that . . ." Too many emotions rose from her to sort out so I gave her time to respond. I moved a hand up and brushed her cheek. She shuddered and moved into my touch but couldn't look me in the eyes.

She stared at my chest. Her fingertips traced electrifying patterns on my skin. She tried again. "I mean, someone like me with someone like . . . *you.*" She dropped off again.

Ah. I understood now.

A one-night stand with an assassin wasn't in her plans. It wasn't allowed. Not in her world. Or maybe it was the whole supernatural thing. She couldn't know that it only worked if I broke skin *and* she wasn't wearing silver.

"You're allowed to want this; to enjoy this. Nobody has the right to tell you otherwise. If you want to stop, I will. But you can't become like me doing this. Just keep your bracelet on.

It'll protect you." I lifted her chin until her eyes met mine. "As for being an assassin, if we go on, no one has to know. That's up to you. I'm pretty good at keeping secrets." My eyes reflected humor. A quick smile played across her face.

"I really shouldn't," she said weakly, without conviction.

I brought my lips closer to hers, drawing her body against me. "But you want to." The words lowered to a whisper that breathed into her mouth, "And so do I." Our lips met just as her body pressed against me. The sudden spasms in my groin from the combined contact almost dropped me to my knees. It was difficult to pick her up and carry her into the next room.

I laid her on the bed and she released my neck. I bent down and removed the water in her navel with a quick pull of my tongue. A sudden gasp made her chest move heavily as she became aroused. I fought back the desire to have her as my body wanted, fast and furious. God! I wanted to wrestle with her until we were both sweat-soaked and exhausted. But no. I decided instead to move slowly.

It's easy to be aroused by a gorgeous woman. But a beautiful woman is accustomed to being admired. It'll be good sex but not memorable. On the other hand, if you spend the time to make a plain woman feel desirable, she'll reward you with enthusiasm. It will become more than sex.

Sue's musky scent was stronger now. It blended with the bath oil to create a smell that ignited every desire I'd ever had in my life, and several that I'd never even imagined.

I started by licking the tiny droplets of water and tangy oil from her skin. Not the obvious parts where most men start, but the less common erotic spots. I turned her over and licked her shoulders, the small of her back, the backs of her legs. Light, delicate flicks to barely move the hairs. She tasted salty, like grass and woods. The smell and the taste and the electric charge that ran between us made me moan and nearly lose control. Her breathing grew heavier as I bathed her with my tongue. As I had wanted to earlier, I rolled the taste of her in my mouth and a new part of me realized that I was marking her as my own. Her mind was awash with uncompleted thoughts, but all of them were urging me on.

Next, I blew lightly along the skin I wetted with my tongue. She shivered and whimpered. I blew cool air down her spine and watched goosebumps form as she squirmed on the bed. I flicked my tongue behind her knees and down her smooth calf. I picked up her foot and gently blew air onto the sole. She clutched the pillow in tight fists.

By the time I turned her over, she was panting and so was I. When she looked at me she gasped and her eyes went wide.

"What?" I asked in a husky voice.

"Your eyes . . . they're glowing."

I'd never made love to a woman before during the full moon, but the wolf part of me knew that this was normal, natural. "Is that okay? Does it scare you?"

She looked at me and I could smell surprise when she answered. "Actually, no. It sort of turns me on."

I smiled and listened to the thoughts running through her mind. *It really does turn me on! I don't know if this is such a good idea or not. I'm scared but, oh, God, I want this.*

I stared into her eyes as I again started at her feet. She watched me lick her legs slowly and deliberately, and her thighs spread almost involuntarily. The rush of musk to my nose was almost too much to stand, but again I ignored the invitation and moved higher to trace slow circles with my tongue on her stomach. She made low sounds in her throat. Her eyes closed and her mouth moved but no sound emerged.

"You have a beautiful body," I said softly.

Her voice was sad. "No, I don't.

I raised up on my arms and stared at her. "Are you calling me a liar?"

"N-n-no. I didn't mean . . ."

"Either that, or you're insulting my taste. I like what I see. Do you have a problem with that?" *Sometimes you have to be aggressive to get it through their head. A lot of women have a hard time taking compliments.*

She smiled then. "No problem." She lay back and closed her eyes. "Thank you."

I slid my body up hers, fast and hard. Her eyes opened to find me staring at her. Her hips writhed where I was pressing against her. "Just checking," I said and lowered my mouth to hers. My tongue filled her mouth forcefully and she shivered and ran her hands along my spine. Strong fingers dug into my back and she wrapped her legs tightly around my hips. I forced my arms under her and locked her against me. The tingling was driving me insane and I craved more of it. Needed to go further, faster.

My mouth moved to her neck and I kissed and nipped the skin gently while I ground myself against her. I needed more. My teeth sunk deeper into her neck. Her breath started to erupt into short shallow pants. What I wanted next wasn't at all like me. I had to, *had to*, master her. Make her submit. I moved my hands up her arms until they rested on her wrists and lowered her arms to the bed. I nipped at her skin harder, then even harder, but stopping just short of drawing blood. That was a no-no.

Her smell was still only of desire and hunger. No fear at all. She liked what I was doing. I read it in her thoughts and in her scent. I stared at her. She stared back into my glowing blue eyes and accepted me. I bit her again softly. She seemed to know what I needed from her. She cried out even though I didn't bite hard.

I knew that whatever I felt she felt too. It scared her; exhilarated her. It was a closeness that she'd never had before. Hearing her submit settled the part of me that needed mastery.

I wasn't ready to go farther. I could hold out for some time yet. She had satisfied my hunger earlier. I wanted to do the same for her.

I rolled until I lay beside her. She started to roll to face me but I stopped her.

"Just relax," I said. I pressed her shoulder down so she remained on her back. I touched her with light fingertips to stimulate the nerves on her skin. Across her collarbone, between her well-formed breasts and down her stomach. Muscles contracted where I touched and her breath was shaky. She fidgeted, nearly frantic for me to touch where she needed to be touched. She hungered to feel that electric caress inside her body. Somehow I knew it was all she could think of.

I moved my fingers slowly up the inside of her thigh while I nibbled her breast with my lips. Her hands moved to my face as though to push me away. Her fingers trembled on my cheeks as I suckled her, pressed teeth into her flesh. I ran my hand across her stomach and toyed with the nerves near her hipbones. As a small cry escaped her, I felt her suddenly tug at my hair, pulling me tight against her. Her legs spread as if by magic. Already I could see wetness on the tips of the hair.

She tried to raise her hips toward my hand. No, not quite yet. I traced lazy designs all around the area without actually touching anything. She was whimpering in earnest now, and mumbling incoherently. I kept just out of reach. I teased her and took her even higher.

Minutes later my fingers brushed her dark curls and found them slick. It was enough to turn my mind to fire. Enough to remind me that I needed release as much as she.

When I finally eased a finger inside her, it was actually three. It was more than she could stand. Her back arched and she cried out. Her hands clutched at anything and everything and strong muscles contracted around my hand, pulled on the current of electricity. I moved with her, pulling when she pushed, and then she actually screamed. Leaving my hand where it was, I kissed her breasts and then her mouth, muting her cries.

She grabbed at me. I winced briefly as her fingernails tore at my back and then her bracelet scorched my skin in long lines through the blood. I didn't think it was intentional. That's okay. I could take a little pain. It didn't interfere with my pleasure at all. I was a little unnerved that I was enjoying it. A lot.

She abruptly broke away from the kiss. She moved her hands away from my back and looked at her fingernails with wide eyes. Small bits of bloody flesh were lodged under them. She moved on the bed in such a way that I realized that she had felt my pain in her own back. I saw it in her mind. Her breathing sped up in a moment of panic.

I smiled lightly. "Go ahead. You can't hurt me and it won't hurt you."

Her eyes widened even more and a shock of surprised scent rose from her. The smile reached my eyes and she let out a little nervous laugh. After a heartbeat's pause she closed her eyes and accepted the connection. Her hands returned to my back and relaxed slowly. I butterfly-kissed her cheek and neck as I prepared to indulge my own enjoyment. I slipped off my briefs as I caressed her body.

"I want you. Now. Please . . . ."

"And you'll have me," I promised softly. "So hold that thought for just a second."

I eased off her and knelt on the bed. She watched as I reached to the night stand and retrieved the pale blue foil pouch from my wallet.

She moved up onto her elbows. "Let me." *I want to touch him* eased into my mind.

A half-smile came to my face. One of my favorite things. I handed the square to her with one hand and stroked one of her calves with the other. "Be my guest."

She sat up, bringing us face to face. She carefully set the condom on the bed and stroked the front of my thighs gently. Tingles went through me and an appreciative "mmm," escaped me.

Her hands traveled across my hipbones and up the taut muscles of my stomach. Spasms wracked my groin. I lost my willpower to be the seducer and agreed to be seduced. "Just relax, lover." she said.

The way she said the word made it more than just seduction for today. I looked at her sharply and she looked back, confidence growing in her gaze. "Say that too often," I replied, surprisingly serious, "And you might not be able to get rid of me."

"That might be nice." She eased toward me. I moved my

mouth to meet hers but she dipped her chin and found my chest. She planted slow lingering kisses in a line across my collarbone. I reached up and ran my hand through her drying hair. I separated the tangled curls with my fingers as her hands caressed my lower back and then gently squeezed my buttocks. Nice.

My chest was starting to heave as the kisses descended lower. She adjusted herself on the bed to travel downward. Her hands reached around my body and moved up and down my thighs as she licked and kissed my nipples. I jumped as I felt the gentle pressure and resulting tingles from her hand between my legs. My breath fell out in a shuddering sigh. I sat back on my heels so I wouldn't fall over. I placed my hands gently on her shoulders, caressed her skin and allowed her to tease me.

When her kisses reached my navel, I tightened my hands on her shoulders and stopped her. I didn't want her to stop. In fact, I couldn't think of anything I wanted more. I couldn't even imagine what it would feel like, considering. But I wanted to take her over again before I reached my peak. Wanted to please her; not just me. I reached for the foil packet again. "You'd better stop now or I won't last long enough to use this." I handed her the packet and she smiled. She ripped the foil and eased the sheath over me, taking her time. It made me groan.

I reached for her waist and laid her down gently. I felt her hot, exhaled breath on my cheek; shallow pants that increased as she opened to me. I entered her slowly and then thrust a second time, hard. The feeling of her body, still slick with oil, as she writhed under me was almost too much. I'm a little better than average in size, but at that moment it felt as though I was too large for her. She was swollen and wet but all that I could think was that her fragile body shouldn't be able to contain the swell of magic that filled me. A blaze of blue light burned behind my eyes and threatened to fill the room. It sparkled and danced in my vision as my hips moved against her, faster and harder.

My mouth closed over hers. Small, hungry sounds

climbed out of her throat to exit in my mouth and I responded in kind. We ate at each other's mouths, tongues tangling desperately. I felt her nails in my back again, digging deeper into the previous wounds. I dug my hands into the bed sheets to keep from digging them into her skin. The hunger that I had been suppressing since I met her consumed my mind. The need was driving me onward. It was hard to concentrate. I didn't want to concentrate. I didn't want anything more than my body plunging inside her. I lapped hot musk and sweat from her skin almost deliriously. I rolled the sharp, sweet scent in my mouth and lifted her legs to wrap around my waist.

I drove into her more frantically, seeking the phantom of the release I knew must exist, but couldn't quite imagine. I wasn't sure I could last long enough to take her back over the edge. But I wanted to make sure she would remember today. I didn't think I was going to be able to forget it. It was too intense. Every movement built the tension, built the magic. The moon itself seemed pressed against my back.

Every woman can be multi-orgasmic if you take the time to get them back there. We had the time. Her face flushed a second time, her back arched and she screamed soundlessly. Her every nerve tingled and sang with effort and I watched. Finally, it was too much.

As I neared the top, she rode the wave of sensation with me. I'm no innocent, but I'd never felt *anything* like this. The intensity was incredible. Bursts of silver light exploded in my vision and passed through me in waves of mind-numbing pleasure so great that I couldn't breathe. I could feel the moon call me, entice me. I poured my magic into her like a great roll of liquid. It welled through her, filled her, until the silver blaze filled her eyes, too. Distantly, I heard screams and realized that they were mine.

My senses were saturated by the light, heat, and the scent of fulfilled desire. The orgasm was like a spiral. When I flew over the edge she went with me. I felt her climax and my own increased, which intensified hers leaving us both exhausted.

I rolled off and out of her and lay beside her. I pulled her to me and expected to doze to sleep as I normally do. My body would have none of it, though. She stroked a hand across my chest with a sigh, nails curving in just enough to lightly scrape the skin. The electricity wasn't gone. The appetite hadn't been quelled. It lay just under my skin like a great hungry beast. Her nails awoke it a second time and it flowed through my skin. Every muscle was suddenly invigorated. I drew in a sharp breath and looked down at her with desire again filling my eyes. She caught my gaze and held it. Her eyes held the same need but surprise was there too. Not so soon, surely.

I started to turn her over to take her again but stopped. I wouldn't without protection. Not on a bet. I'm not that stupid. With reckless hope I reached over and opened the drawer of the night stand, silently willing some previous tenant to have left an extra. When I opened my eyes I laughed. I couldn't help it. A brand new box of condoms lay in the drawer— the only occupant. I could only imagine what Max had thought when I told him I was meeting someone in the room. I'd never brought *anyone* here. I'd have to remember to thank him.

The daylight hours passed by without notice as we sated each other over and over. It was probably the longest lovemaking session I had ever been involved in. It was definitely the most intense.

Chapter 9

I woke in semi-dark with Sue curled around me. I pulled her against me and watched her sleep. Somewhere in the middle it stopped being just sex for me. It became something deeper, something I had no name for. I realized that I hadn't gotten close to a woman since I lost my humanity a year ago. I've been afraid to let anyone get too close in case I accidentally mangled them.

But I hadn't. Given the chance, I hadn't killed her. Hell, I hadn't even bruised her during sex. It was like I *couldn't*. Something inside pulled me up short. It gave me hope. But it also caused problems for me. I'm a loner. I like my space. As much fun as this time had been, I didn't know what tomorrow would bring. I did know one thing. I didn't want her to die. I have never believed in love at first sight. Maybe it's real, maybe not. I didn't even know if I felt love for her but lust? Oh, yeah.

I realized that I wanted to wake up beside her tomorrow and the next day. The problem was, if I didn't kill her, I would be just using her like everyone else. I couldn't change her past. If she wanted to die, I should let her. Help her. Keeping her alive for my own needs would make me as bad as the others.

I rose and went to the bathroom, then walked naked through the living room and poured myself a drink. Something stronger than beer. I sat in the late afternoon sunshine just thinking.

I could feel her sleeping in the other room. In some part of my insides I could feel her. I didn't know if she could sense me in return but I knew when she woke. I felt her

lying in the dark. Conscious; thinking. Somehow I knew
that if I concentrated I could read her thoughts. But I didn't
know if it flowed both ways. I needed a few minutes alone
and it seemed like she did too. I had an overwhelming fear
that if I tried to increase the connection between us, even as
an experiment, I wouldn't be able to reverse it.

Paranoia isn't logical.

So, alone—as the night of the true moon neared—I con-
templated this woman. What was happening between us?
My brain should be flashing lights and blaring warning
sirens at the thought of having a bond like we seemed to
have formed. But it wasn't. Did that mean there was a
future? A future with someone who could accept me—my
profession—*and* what I had become? Could she survive in
my world? Would I want to be part of hers? Then I imagined
the rest of my life without her. None of the options seemed
a good idea in the long run.

An hour or so later she made an appearance but kept her
distance. She lingered just near the doorway. Her body was
clothed only in sunset's crimson, cut with shadows thick as
ink. She tilted her head as she watched me. One eye disappeared into darkness.

"Are you all right?" she asked tentatively.

"Fine." I could feel the moon trembling at the edge of the
horizon. Warmth flared over my skin as I waited for the rush
of energy.

She padded toward me, footsteps silent in the thick carpet. I watched the light and dark play across her skin in sultry patterns as she moved. I lifted my glass to my lips and
she suddenly became two, then three, through the thick crystal as I took a sip. Each movement of her muscles as she
walked, every breeze that stirred her scent toward me tightened my body with desire. I wanted her again. I closed my
eyes until the feeling passed. It was too near to true darkness
to risk it. This was only day two and it would be time soon.

She sat down next to me on the couch and I automatically
put my arm around her and pulled her against me. Scary.

"I've been thinking," she said as she snuggled into the

curve of my arm. She slid a slow hand across the hair of my chest and tucked it around my waist.

"Me too. Will you be here when I wake up tomorrow?" I looked down at her.

She seemed startled. "I don't know. I should probably go home." She didn't sound like she wanted to. "Nobody knows where I am. And Mom's alone . . ."

I didn't comment on that. It was her decision. "I'd like you to stay, if you want to. I won't force you. If you have to go, you have to." I shrugged but I wanted her to stay. "What were you thinking about?"

"What just happened between us? There's something there even now." She lifted her hand and again touched my chest with gentle fingertips. A nervous energy rose from her. Her heartbeat quickened as she thought about it. My body responded again but I fought it down forcibly. We needed to talk.

Why lie? "I don't know."

"Will it go away when we leave here?" The curiosity blended with sadness, as though she already knew the answer.

"You're the first woman that I've let get this close during a full moon. I assume it has something to do with what I am. I've been with other women but it's never been like this."

That made her happy and she hugged me. Every woman wants to think that she's special. This time, it was the truth. There was a pause. It was filled with the clove scent of pride, the light tangerine of happiness, and determination mixed with a healthy dose of fear. She took a deep breath. My stomach clenched. I wasn't sure I wanted to hear what she was about to say.

"I've got this big house," she said abruptly and continued quickly so I couldn't interrupt, and probably so she wouldn't lose her nerve. "They put a full apartment in the basement. A real apartment with a kitchen and bath and a separate entrance. I can't put Mom down there because she can't handle the stairs. The door to the main floor can be locked so you can come and go and nobody can bother you. There's a

fenced estate and a pool." The fear faded as she finished the
speech she had prepared. It was said. The implication was
clear.

She didn't move even a muscle as she finished. She was
frozen against me, waiting, nervous. I let the silence grow
for a moment as I thought about all of the consequences.

"And geese," I said lightly. She let out a relieved breath.

"And geese." Humor edged her voice. Then she hurried
on. "Anyway, if I paid you in advance, I wouldn't want you
to wander off with my money and not do the job."

"Naturally."

"So I was thinking that maybe you could sort of, maybe, take
the apartment. It's huge. Really. It's the whole lower level."

I didn't know what to say. Her words echoed my thoughts
from a moment ago and I still didn't have an answer. "And
do what? I'm not the Ozzie and Harriet type, Sue. This has
been great. Incredible, even. But I don't want to move in
with anyone."

"I know you don't. Neither do I." Part truth, part lie. I
didn't know which was which.

"I was thinking more of . . . well, a bodyguard. There have
been some threatening calls. Mom stupidly promised some
man money to *protect* us. He said that no *accidents* would
happen as long as we paid every month. Even *I* know what
that means."

I laughed at that. "A combination bodyguard/assassin.
Sort of an oxymoron, don't you think?"

"You'd keep me safe until it was time. When the heat died
down. I could pay you a salary in addition to the fee. You
could help me with things around the house."

"Like keep your mom in line and the money suckers
away? Is that it? A hired gun?"

She looked up at me, hope plain on her face. The light,
dizzying scent of it made my head swim. "I'd let you poach
the geese. . . "

I smiled and leaned back into the sofa with a laugh.
"Couldn't be any worse than half-cooked turkey." She
laughed with me.

Then she looked at me very seriously. "Yes. I'll be here tomorrow."

I grinned without intending to and felt a little foolish in the darkness. I leaned over and kissed her deeply. I opened my senses and let the moon in. Power crawled over my skin but it wasn't strong enough yet to turn me. Maybe there was still time. If we hurried . . .

Chapter 10

Sue wasn't in the suite the next morning. I found a note from her saying she hoped I made it back okay.

Made it back from where?

There was a sack on the dresser with clothes. Khaki Dockers and a black T-shirt with a pocket. She even remembered socks. A second note in the bag said, "Look in the fridge." I went to the bar and opened the refrigerator door. I found a whole prime rib, bone in. It barely fit inside the small space. She had to remove the shelves and bend it nearly in two. I thought about eating it for breakfast, but no. That would be overkill. Still, her thoughtfulness really took me by surprise.

I started a pot of coffee while I took a shower and brushed my teeth and then settled down to read yesterday's newspaper—better than nothing. As always, room service knocked on my door without calling them promptly at 8:00. The trays filled with eggs over medium, toast, fried potatoes, and a rare t-bone were on a cart in the hallway. I wheeled it inside. I pay tips through my room account.

The day was starting grey and gloomy. It was a welcome change from the summer heat but I wasn't sorry that I was indoors. I closed the curtains and turned on a lamp after I saw rain pattering gently on the glass.

Several minutes went by before I heard footsteps moving down the carpeted hallway toward the suite. They stopped in front of the door. I couldn't smell through the thick oak so I grabbed my Sig and quietly stepped to where the door would hide me if it opened. There's a peephole but I never use one. That's a real good way to get a bullet in your brain. I know.

I heard paper rustling and the key card slip into the lock. Even though I was expecting Sue to return, I remained cautious. I'm not without enemies. The door opened fully and I saw the back of a black wig and Sue's well-shaped body. She looked terrific in a hot pink T-shirt tucked into tight blue jean shorts, but it wasn't exactly *incognito*. I sighed. We'd have to talk about the concept of low-key.

Her bare arms wore tiny droplets of water that shimmered and moved as she walked. The scent of her, dewy and laden with moss, mingled with the scent of the rain. It affected me like a drug. I would have a hard time pulling the trigger even if someone dangerous were with her. That's not a good thing.

I slammed the door behind her—just in case. It latched and locked with a sharp crack. Sue turned quickly, eyes wide and panicked. She saw the gun and the bags in her arms dropped to the floor with a soft thud.

One hand went over her chest and I felt her heart race for a moment. "Don't *do* that," she exclaimed. She smelled slightly annoyed but relieved. Tangerines blended with coffee and with the musty scent of anxiety.

"I'm really glad you're back. I was worried," she said.

We'd deal with that in a minute. I put the Sig in the waistband of my pants so it rested at the small of my back. I stepped closer and eased my hands around her waist. I couldn't seem to help it. I needed to touch her, run my hands along her bare skin, drink in the scent and taste of her. I raised a hand and took off Sue's dark sunglasses. Her eyes were greener than yesterday. I saw those eyes smile at me, comfortable, possessive. I ran the back of my hand down her cheek and she leaned into my touch with a sigh.

"Good morning," I said and pulled her the rest of the way into my arms. The sunglasses dropped to the carpet as I kissed her slow and easy. Her body was damp and warm against my artificial chill. The kiss deepened and her arms moved up my back and tightened. She was more aggressive this morning and took what she wanted. Her tongue found mine first. I moved my hands down her back to those tight shorts and lifted her up until her legs were wrapped around my waist. She dug her nails in again but it didn't sting. In fact, I hadn't realized it earlier in the shower but my back had healed completely. Very nice.

Even this morning, our bodies were charged with energy. It rolled across my skin and made me shiver. Whatever was between us wasn't temporary. I knew that if I took her now it would be as intense and fierce as yesterday.

I pulled back from the kiss, leaving her breathless. She let out a little laugh. "Good morning to you too!" she said as I gently lowered her feet to the floor.

"Now, what did you mean, you're glad I'm back?"

"I was worried." She stopped when she saw my expression. "You don't remember, do you?"

I shook my head with a frown. "What happened?"

She smelled embarrassed and couldn't meet my eyes. She stood and walked toward the fireplace. "I feel just horrible. I didn't mean to let you out. . ."

"Out?" A buzzing filled my ears. "What do you mean, out?"

She glanced at me, still anxious. She chewed on her lower lip for a moment. "Last night. I went downstairs after we . . . well, you know. While you were sleeping. I got back to the room a little after dark. I thought it would be okay. But when I got here, you'd already changed."

I was starting to feel butterflies in my stomach. "When I opened the door, you sprang past me, faster than I could move."

Oh, shit! I sat down heavily on the sofa. "You mean I was out all night?"

She turned then and looked at me. "I honestly don't know. When you bolted I tried to follow you. I swear I did. I thought that once you found that you were confined to this floor you'd come back to the room with me.

I had a flash of memory, just like yesterday. I stalked the hallway, feeling trapped. There were walls all around me. They led in a circle. I remember one man exiting the elevator as I walked past. I bared teeth at him and snarled. He backed into the elevator before the doors shut. I felt his fear as I passed and it was good. Fear was a good thing. Sour and sharp. It made me hungrier, though.

Sue's words sifted through the memories of grey walls and black carpet; where scents were visible in the air like faded watercolors. They were recollections of a world sharply focused and alien.

"You slowed down when you heard my voice," she continued. "But something else caught your attention. I don't know what. You headed toward the window at the end of the hall. It was almost faster than I could see. But I could feel it." There was an odd edge to her voice. I looked at her. She hugged herself and shivered.

"I could literally feel you move. Experience your anxiety. You felt trapped. Before I could react, you took a running leap and went . . ."

"Right through the window," I completed softly, distantly. I remembered it now. I saw the moon through the window and needed to reach it. Needed to touch it, let it touch me. I leapt and I soared through the air. The window glass felt like tissue paper. It was nothing to me.

Sue nodded. "I was terrified. We're nine stories up!" She walked toward me and drenched my senses in the clove-scent of pride with a healthy dose of fear. "I rushed to the window. I couldn't believe it. I saw you jump into space and then land on the roof of the hospital across the street. Across the street!" Her voice held amazement but her scent was still pride.

I knew that it should be a big deal. Really. But it didn't feel like I was straining at the time. It was just an average jump. Nothing special.

"I *felt* you jump, felt my muscles react and my breathing increase. It was incredible; wonderful. Like flying but better."

I nodded, still lost in the dream of it. I felt free. So trapped for so long and I was finally free. It was my turn to shiver.

"You ran to the other end of the roof and then I don't know where you went. I could feel you go but I lost sight of you."

I knew where I went. I needed trees. I needed meat. I picked up the story where Sue left off. I could hear my own voice from a distance as if I were narrating a movie. "I needed the night. Too trapped for too long," I heard myself say.

Sue nodded in agreement and hugged herself again. "I felt that too." She smiled suddenly and it was beautiful. "God, it felt so good to *run*. I could feel your muscles stretching, your body moving and it felt so incredibly . . . *incredible*." She looked at me then. Her smile was radiant. Tangerines blended with the cloves, buoyed by her own summer forest. As scents go it was a serious turn-on.

"Why do you coop yourself up in this room? You loved it out there. In the night. The fresh air, the scent of trees and rocks . . . I didn't even know that rocks had a smell until last night. But I stood there at the window after I couldn't see you anymore. I could feel you, sense you. Smell through your nose, see through your eyes. Well, actually, that's not quite true. I couldn't actually *see* but I could feel you react to what you *did* see. What kind of duck was it?"

I remembered that too. The image was so strong it sucked me back inside. The pond at the city park; the cattails where I lay in wait. Even now I could smell the musty scent of rotting vegetation. I saw the bloated body of a small-mouth bass float by as I watched the birds move closer. It was a male duck. He separated from the group and moved toward shore. I could feel a small line of saliva drip from my lower jaw as I watched.

I moved closer, each paw settling quietly into the moistened undergrowth. And I could feel Sue there. Knew she was with me. It felt *right*. My mate should be with me in the hunt.

"Pintail," I finally said.

"The taste exploded into my mouth when you caught it. I felt like I should bite down, like there was something there to chew on."

I didn't know what to say to that. It had never happened before. Not with anyone.

"Why did you leave the hotel?" I knew somehow that she had.

She shrugged. "I thought that if I could feel you I could

find you. But I couldn't. I knew that you couldn't get back into the hotel as a wolf and you wouldn't have any clothes if you woke up outside. So I went after you. I left the door ajar just in case you came back. I guess you got back in."

I tried to recall how I got back to the room. I had awakened on the bed. How did I get back upstairs? I felt my brow furrow as I fought to remember. Nope, not there.

"I have no idea. Maybe the same way I went out?" I suggested.

Sue shrugged. "Maybe. I didn't check to see if they fixed the window."

"And where have you been since then?"

"At the park mostly. But I had to buy some stuff too."

Sue told me that she drove to just outside the city and called her house to say she was staying out of town with a friend. She used a calling card so it would show up as a long-distance call. I nodded in approval and cloves dusted the air again.

She told her family that she wouldn't be back until the following day. Her mother and sister gave it to her with both barrels for leaving without a word. They apparently tag-teamed on two extensions in the house, accusing her of the fiasco in the lobby. She kept up the confused story, claiming to not understand what they meant. She looked at me hopefully, fishing for a compliment.

"I'm proud of you," I told her. "Good job."

"But I'm worried. When you move in, she'll know I was lying about not being in the hotel."

I looked at her sharply. I was afraid of this.

"I *might* be willing to *look* at the apartment, Sue." Her cheeks flushed with embarrassment and her scent changed to match. She nodded.

I'd never lived with anyone before. Not even a roommate. I like my privacy. But this . . . felt somehow natural. Like I was meant to be with this person. All by itself *that* made me tense.

"Let's go have some breakfast and we can talk about it some more."

The spring tightened in my gut again. Ever one to change the subject, I wiggled my eyebrows at her. "I actually had something else in mind. I've already eaten," I said, pointing toward the empty trays.

She pouted a little bit and it was cute. "But I really *am* hungry." She flashed a smile designed to melt me. It did, damn it.

"Okay. We'll order some more room service."

"Nah. I'm feeling restless. Let's go to the dining room."

I shook my head. She didn't understand. "I can't leave the room until tomorrow."

She cocked her head to the side, questioning. "Why not? In the daytime you're fine."

"No! I'm not. I *look* okay but I'm not fine. There's still shit inside of me boiling around. I can't be around other people. I tried it after I became—well, what I am. It doesn't work."

I turned from her and walked to the window. I looked around me as I stepped. The fireplace, the leather furniture, even the wall of tinted glass with its gorgeous view remind me that I'm a prisoner. Locked away from the rest of humanity. Caged like the animal I've become. A night in the park only reinforced that. I stood with legs spread slightly, arms crossed against my chest. Gazing at everything and seeing nothing.

"When it first happened. I didn't know what it was. I just felt real aggressive, plain mean for a couple of days a month. I thought I just woke up on the wrong side of the bed. Until I met you I'd never *remembered* turning into an animal. But I feel like one." Sue came to stand behind me. I caught the misty smell of sorrow, laced with an unknown spice. Concern, maybe? It's not one I've smelled often. She put her arms around my waist from the back and I hugged her. The memory was easier with her there.

"The third month, some guy cut me off on the road. Not intentionally. He just didn't see me. But I started to growl. Right there in the car. That sound coming out of my own mouth . . . it was eerie."

Sue's eyes were wide in the reflection of the window and her arms twitched as though she knew what I was going to say next. I could tell that she thought about pulling away but she didn't.

"I saw red—literally. My vision had this weird-ass pink haze and all I could think of was blood. His blood. It made my stomach growl if that's sick enough for you."

This story was hard to tell. I don't like how badly I lost control. Babs thought the story was funny. Big surprise. She thought killing me was funny too. It wasn't so funny to her when I showed up alive.

Babs is still around somewhere. That's a thorn in my side every day. I tried to kill her—twice. Put a bullet through her head once, but she got away. That was the first time she knew I'd survived. The second time I tracked her down, I blasted her chest open with two rounds from a twelve-gauge. She stayed down but by the time I got to my car, she was fully healed. She bent my shotgun into a pretzel. Tough lady. Supposedly, I'm just as tough, but I haven't had the occasion to test that theory. We made a brief truce that lasted until she betrayed me.

After the second attempt, Babs learned the identity of my client. Then she took him out. I had no sense of humor about that. I may still go after her again someday with some silver rounds I'm working on, but other things have concerned me more lately.

"Anyway, I tracked the guy down and ripped his throat out." Short, sweet and to the point.

She did pull away then and came around to face me. She watched my eyes as I spoke. I couldn't tell from her expression or her scent what she thought. She was sorting. I looked her squarely in the pupils. I wouldn't hide from what happened. I couldn't hide from it. But it still gives me nightmares sometimes.

"Again, literally. With my bare hands. But even that wasn't enough. I didn't just kill him, I mangled him. Bathed in his blood." I looked down at my open hands; palms up. It was too familiar, too close. My mind's eye saw the crimson blood, slick and shiny on my hands and arms. My shirt was soaked; my pants as well. I looked down and visualized again the face of the victim, eyes wide with surprise, mouth open in a scream that never reached air. My heart pounded like a caged animal and bile seared the back of my throat.

"Let's just say that I had a hell of a time cleaning it up." I turned from her and walked back to the bar and poured a glass of water. I downed it in one gulp. It chased the bile back down. "No, it's just not safe."

"Are you going to hurt me if I stay?" Fear now in her voice.

"No." My head shook as I said it. I knew the truth of the statement. I didn't understand why. "If I was going to hurt you it would have been last night. But your average jerk on the street? I can't say. Some months are worse than others. Someday I might get a handle on this and be able to control it but right now I can't."

She nodded her head, trying to grasp the concept.

"You can leave if you want." My hand tightened around the water glass. I stayed turned from her. "I'd understand. It's a bit much to start a relationship with."

I felt her eyes on me. She was startled, surprised. She walked toward me. She stopped just behind, not touching. I smelled her and it was like earlier, sweet enough to drown in. Parts of me tightened but the coil of fear remained. Except now the coil was a snake—writhing, sinking fangs inside my gut again and again.

"Do we have a relationship?" Hope mingled with fear in her scent.

I faced her. I wanted to see if there was horror in her eyes. The green eyes were just the same, warm with concern. There was no fear. No hate.

"I think we might have the beginnings of something," I replied quietly. "You tell me."

"Can I ask you a question first?"

I nodded, even though I didn't want to hear the question.

"Why are you so affected by this?" It was my turn to be

startled. I mean, how could I not be? My surprise must have shown on my face because she responded to the unasked question.

"You kill for a living. Why does this bother you so much? It's not his death." She touched her own chest and then mine. "I can feel it. There's something else inside you that is *horrified* by this."

I took a deep breath and let it out slowly. How could I explain it so it made sense? "I do a job. I'm not Scotty. I don't kill for pleasure." But I did. God help me but it made me happy while I was ripping his skin open. The bile returned, hot and burning.

I groped for the right words. "It comes down to standards. Humans don't eat their dead. It's what separates us from the real animals. We kill without remorse, torture without regret, but we aren't cannibals. We have standards."

I really believe that. Often personal standards, morals, are all we have against insanity. His death had been too . . . participatory. Sue nodded in agreement but still looked confused.

"Some things are still beneath us. It's why *Silence of the Lambs* scares us and Jeffrey Dahlmer was front-page news for weeks instead of hours."

"I understand that." She crossed her arms and shook her head. "So you lost control." She shrugged and gave a little laugh, meant to lighten the mood. "But it's not like you ate him afterwards."

I didn't answer. I just looked at her. Our eyes locked and I willed my eyes alone to tell the story. Some part of me didn't want to admit it. I couldn't quite voice the reality.

The look was enough. Her eyes went from confused to alarmed and then the slightest trace of horror set in. Her jaw dropped slightly and her arms dropped to her sides almost unconsciously.

"Did you?" It was a whisper.

I held her gaze for as long as I could but I broke eye contact first. "I don't know for sure." But I suspected.

"When I came to and started to clean up there were marks

on him. Marks that didn't match up with finger gouges; marks with ragged edges. I couldn't find some of the pieces." Ah. *Now* there was horror settling in at the back of those emerald eyes.

"When the smell got to me from the ruptured intestines, I threw up." I can't forget the smell. Rancid thick gas that churned into the air. The blood was sweet and coppery but when I laid open the gut... Half digested food, partially formed feces. My stomach threatened to repeat. I swallowed hard and forced the bitter acid back where it came from. I left the conclusion unspoken.

Her voice shook ever so slightly. "Did you find the rest of the pieces?"

I shrugged. I hadn't looked. I didn't want to know. But I could still remember the taste of sweet, warm blood that lingered on my tongue as I knelt over the body.

She nodded her head. I looked at her but she couldn't meet my eyes. She just kept nodding. Her gaze was on the carpet at my feet. I reached out to touch her shoulder and she flinched, pulling her arm back. I let her. I dropped my hand to my side and waited.

I started kicking myself almost immediately. Why did I tell her? What did I hope to accomplish except to chase her away? Then again, maybe that was it. I wanted to frighten her away. There was something about Sue that I wanted to keep near me. Maybe this was my subconscious way of making her leave. If my buddy, John-Boy, knew about the whole werewolf thing, he would probably tell me that I was exhibiting self-fulfilling behavior. I think I'm an animal and don't believe that anyone could want me so I'll tell her what an animal I am so she won't want me.

"Like I said, if you want to go I'll understand." I meant it.

"You'd just let me go? Even knowing what I do?"

"Well, actually, no. It'd just mean that I'll take the job you wanted to hire me for. But it would be hard. Know that. Really hard."

She almost smiled but she didn't come any closer, didn't touch me. Her scent was a blending of everything I knew and a few I couldn't sort out. "Can I think about it? This is all happening so fast. It's not what I planned."

I smiled. "If life was only what you planned, it'd be pretty dull."

She smiled back but it was shaky. "Maybe that's why my life has been dull. But I really need some time to assimilate all this."

Suddenly, I was annoyed. I didn't know why. Her reaction was what I expected. Then again, maybe not. I think a part of me hoped she would laugh and call me silly for worrying. Stupid and romantic. But it's what I hoped for even though reality isn't like that. Some things can't be gotten past.

Another part of me wanted her to run screaming from the room; leave me to my misery. Let me drown in my fears and my curse and never move on.

"Go then," I said harshly. I turned from her and walked to the couch. I sat and picked up the paper. "Come back if you want. Don't if you don't." The words sounded cold, unfeeling. I didn't look at her, couldn't watch the fear in her eyes. "If you don't come back, bring a case with fifty grand back here and leave it with Max to put in the safe. I'll see you in a year or so. I can find you."

I glanced at her briefly where she stood immobile. I could smell her discomfort. Her sympathy and fear were almost equal. She gestured with her hands helplessly not sure what to say. I certainly wasn't going to help. I don't need pity. I tried to concentrate on the front page story but the words only swam through my brain. They didn't form sentences.

"Can I take the key card with me?"

I let out a short, bitter laugh. "Might as well. *I* won't be needing it. If you decide not to come back turn it in at the desk. If it's there when I check out I'll have my answer."

She picked up the white, credit-card sized square of plastic and turned it slowly in her fingers. I tried to ignore her but she slipped into my peripheral vision. She opened her mouth and then shut it again. Tears were close to the surface. I could smell them. I didn't want her to cry. She was digging too far under my skin. I knew that if I saw tears I would go to her; hold her; try to make it better. I went back to staring blankly at the paper.

After a moment I felt her gather dignity around herself like a cloak. She took a deep breath, released it and then slipped the key into the pocket of her shorts. She picked up the bags that were on the floor. I tried not to watch. Tried not to think.

"I'll see you later." Tentative hope edged her voice.

I nodded without looking at her. "One way or another."

She left without saying good-bye.

Chapter 11

The longer I sat alone the easier it was to forget the look on her face when she left. Confused, helpless, scared. All rolled into a last lingering look that I knew that I would be regretting for years. The smell wasn't so easy to ignore. It stirred something deep in me and I wanted it back. Wanted her back. But I didn't expect it. If the tables were turned, I wouldn't. I know it's hypocritical but I expect more of other people than of myself. Isn't it always the way?

I needed a distraction so I turned on the boob tube. Daytime television is a joke. There isn't any football and the game shows have been replaced by what I call 'controversy shows'. Jerry Springer and the like—not talk but confrontation. Soaps are fiction, but the controversy shows rival them for content and are disturbingly real. Whoever said that "truth is stranger than fiction" knew their stuff.

I clicked through twenty-four channels before I finally stopped in the middle of *Casablanca*. I like old black-and-white movies. *African Queen*, *Ship of Fools* and *In Cold Blood* are favorites. I did watch the colorized versions that Turner did, but it's just not the same. Chocolate syrup that looks like real blood turns back into Hershey's finest even after they change the color.

I felt restless. I should be doing something. Usually when this is planned, I bring along my laptop or pay my bills. Last March I did my income tax returns after getting all the forms off the 'net.

I tried to think about work. I had three other jobs to plan; jobs that I've already been paid for. But all the detail—the maps, photographs, and itineraries were at my house. I also started cursing myself for not laundering a case of cash in Atlantic City before I screwed up my free pass. I'd decided to wait until after one more job. Just my luck that the next job happened to be Jeffrey. Now I wouldn't be able to use any of the casinos there friendly to my type of transaction.

I can run a lot of money through the security company, but I'd taken too many jobs in too short a time. The plan was to take a vacation for a year or so. I hadn't had one in awhile. I was swimming in cash and needed to have it appear legit, so I could bask in the sun in Hawaii or Monaco. A rigged gambling game is best for that. But it would mean I'd have to go to Vegas. Shit.

Thinking about some of my least favorite characters didn't improve my mood. I checked my broken watch, then shook my head in annoyance and finally took it off. Useless piece of crap. It was only 1:10 p.m. by the clock in the bedroom. I went to the fridge and removed the prime rib. I opened the package over the sink in the bathroom and left it to warm to room temperature. Dinner was ready. I supposed that I should eat lunch.

I called room service and ordered a Monte Cristo sandwich with raspberry jam and homecut fries. It's one of my favorites. I considered trying to get drunk, going so far as to pour a double Maker's Mark, neat, but then poured it back in the bottle. It wouldn't improve my mood. It'd probably make it worse. I can't seem to get drunk anymore and the effort makes me grumpy.

It shouldn't matter whether she came back. One night of fairly good sex and I get these lofty fucking ideas of some imaginary romance. Worse still is a romance that I don't have the time or the inclination for. I've had enough women in my life that it shouldn't matter.

I was probably just pissed that I'd gotten my calendar messed up and I was stuck here. On the plus side, though, now I could go to the poker game. I had cancelled because of the job. But with the job over and the change over . . .

That brightened my mood considerably. Yeah, getting together with the boys for an all-nighter would get my disposition back to normal. I started to call Carmine to tell him that I'd be at the game with bells on but remembered that the calls are tracked and put on my bill. No, tying this room number with Carmine's private line wouldn't do at all. I got my nerve together and went downstairs.

When the elevator door opened on the main floor I headed straight for the pay phones. I did my best to ignore the smell of people moving around, their blood flowing thick and heavy under paper-thin skin. I smelled their joys, their sorrows, their fears. It was too many smells. Too many emotions. Another reason I lock myself away—sensory overload.

Only one phone was working. I called and heard the sultry recording of Carmine's wife, Linda. I left a message and then called Jocko and asked him to check up on my car. I hadn't intended to leave it for days.

"I wondered why you hadn't come back," he said. "Found a new lady? I noticed the way the brunette was looking at you."

"Keep your mind out of the gutter," I snarled. "Is the car okay?"

He was silent for a moment. "Yeah. I let Sweetboy know it was yours and both gangs are keeping away from it. Unilateral decision. They know what you'd do to them. It's probably the only thing they've agreed on this year."

"Damn straight." For a moment my vision started to redden as I imagined pounding one of those street punks into a bloody pulp. The thought of his screams as I tore him apart made me smile. I could almost smell his sweat and mouth-watering fear. My stomach growled and I shivered.

"You okay?" Jocko asked quietly. "You sound rough."

I took a deep breath and let it out slowly. Calm. Stay calm. No bloody rampages in the lobby of the hotel. I felt a tap on my shoulder and I turned. A woman with dark hair and a tailored business suit looked impatient.

"Will you be long?" she asked. "I need the phone." She wore too much perfume and it masked her underlying scent.

I ignored her by turning back to look at the phone bank. "I'll be okay. Things haven't gone as planned this week."

"Okay." He sounded uncertain. The broad behind me tapped again and I fought back the urge to turn and grab her throat and slam the receiver into her face again and again and then lick the blood off the black plastic.

Whoa! Definitely time to get back upstairs.

I shook my head hard to clear it. "Hey, I've got to go. I'll be back in a day or so. Keep the word out that my car is off-limits." I turned and looked right into the eyes of the brunette when I allowed my voice to drop an octave and take on a heavy Italian accent. "Anyone touches my ride and I'll rip off their dick and feed it to them. *Capisce*?"

I smiled evilly and the brunette's eyes grew wide. I watched the pulse in her neck move faster. A light dew of sweat began to form on her upper lip. I wanted her pulse between my teeth. I scrutinized the prey intently. Her eyes darted back and forth quickly as she looked to escape. Fear turned quickly to ammonia panic. Excellent. I bared teeth at her, then brought my lips together and blew her a kiss. She backed slowly away, nearly tripping over her own feet. I struggled not to follow, not to pounce.

Jocko chuckled over the phone line. It startled me. I flinched abruptly and then laughed with him but for a different reason. There was a high edge to my laughter that I didn't like.

"I'll let them know," he promised.

I made it all the way back to the room before I remembered that Sue had the card key and I was locked out. I stood in the hallway fighting the beginnings of panic. I didn't need this shit today. I kicked the door hard and felt the force of it sing through my leg. The heavy oak cracked sharply and I watched a hairline fracture swim up the grain of the wood. Oops.

"Mr. Giodone?" came a voice from the hallway. I turned to see Tim, one of the kitchen staff, rolling a cart toward me.

A wave of relief passed through me. "I locked myself out."

He laughed and produced a pass key. He reached past me and opened the door. I entered and he wheeled the cart in after me. "Can I get you anything else?"

I shook my head, not trusting myself to speak. They'd miss him; I know they would. But I could smell him. His aftershave only partly masked the scent of his skin. My stomach growled agonizingly and I fought down a snarl as I looked at his smiling face and thought of him only as food. Another part of my brain questioned what kind of wine went with red meat and I almost laughed. Just call me Hannibal. My tongue slipped out to catch a thin line of saliva that was creeping down my jaw.

I shook my head, clearing the thoughts. He had to leave. Now! I reached into my pocket and removed my wallet. I peeled off a twenty and handed it to him.

He looked at the bill in surprise. "They'll put the food on your tab."

"As they should. Thanks for letting me in."

His smile was brilliant against his dark skin. "Hey, wow! You need anything else, you just let me know!" I nodded and turned my attention to the cart. It was his cue to leave.

Sadly, the build-up of the prey smells left the sandwich incapable of satisfying my hunger. My nose led me to the bathroom. The bathroom still smelled like Sue. Trees and musk and sex. My body reacted to the smell and I slapped the thought out of my mind.

The scent of the meat, warm and bleeding in the sink was too much. Everything was too much today. Fine. If not sex then blood. Sweet, metallic, heady. Even as my mind screamed its disapproval I bit a bloody hunk of prime rib and chewed it slowly. The tension dissipated as I chewed the raw beef and I accepted what I was for these three days.

A wolf. A carnivore. So be it.

At least for today I wasn't a cannibal.

Chapter 12

Darkness came and went. As I woke to the daylight the room was silent as a tomb. I toured the room and found the remains of a gnawed bone in the tub. One end of it was cracked and ragged. The marrow had been removed as far as, I presume, my tongue would reach. Maybe it's better that I don't remember the things I do.

I didn't find any sign that Sue had come back. Not unexpected but still disappointing. I took my shower and dressed again in the Dockers and T-shirt.

I called down and asked that a newspaper be brought to the room along with breakfast. After I finished eating I put the cart outside in the hallway along with the one from the afternoon before.

When I heard the lock release nearly an hour later I didn't even reach for my gun. I could sense who it was—thick moss, musk, and sex. I actually felt my heart stop as the door opened. I watched the silly sunglasses and wig enter the room ahead of Sue and fought back a grin. She could just be returning long enough to say good-bye. I wouldn't get my hopes up. Shouldn't even have hopes.

"Hi," she said softly. She was worried; nervous. She stood at the edge of the room but wanted to come closer.

"Hi. What's up?" Might as well get it over with.

"Can I come in?" Her expression made it clear that she didn't know the answer.

I couldn't seem to stop the reply. I even meant it. "Always."

She stepped into the room. She looked delectable in a purple cotton short set with pansies embroidered across the neck of the spaghetti-string top. Her breasts were unfettered and made the cloth tent out far enough that the bottom of the shirt didn't touch skin. Another pair of jelly sandals matched the outfit. She must be buying as she went. I wanted to take her right now whether or not she planned to leave me, and that scared the shit out of me.

She took off the wig and glasses. Her hair was damp and tightly curled from the heat and humidity. I smelled the sweat and it still smelled of herbs. I remained seated but leaned forward and rested my arms on my knees. I hoped I looked interested and not like I was waiting for the other boot to drop. Although I was.

She sat down across from me. She looked at me, then away, then back. Her polished nails tapped a nervous pattern on her bare legs. "I've been thinking."

"So have I."

"You first," she said quickly, anticipatory. Her whole body moved forward on the couch several inches.

I shook my head. "This is your decision, not mine."

She nodded and scooted back in the couch. Her eyes dropped again and she suddenly looked as she did when we first met, uncomfortable and set in stone. She couldn't meet my eyes. Her foot began to tap lightly on the thick carpet.

I jumped in with both feet. "You're leaving. Right?"

Her eyes shot up and locked with mine. She looked surprised. "No!"

The heady scent of spices rolled off of her. Too many to sort, but over the top, the comfort smell of baking bread reached me. Then why the nervousness?

She continued, a little flustered. "I mean, not unless you want me to." She looked at the floor. With her legs crossed, head bowed, and hands folded in her lap, she looked like a little girl waiting outside the principal's office. She expected to be rejected one more time. I could feel it in my chest. She didn't even dare hope that I might want her. Odd that we were both thinking the same thing.

"Look, let's just be open here. You said you've been thinking. Do you want to stay or go?"

She took a deep breath. "Stay. If you want me to."

I fought not to grin. I motioned with my hand. "Then why are you sitting over there?" I patted my knee. Sue looked up, watched my face, to see if I was mocking her. I did smile then. With my face and with my eyes.

She smiled shyly and stood. She walked around the coffee table, turned sideways and then sat down on my lap. I put my arms around her waist. She snuggled against my chest and laid her head on my shoulder. A small sigh eased out of her and her arms went around my neck. I felt her fingers glide over my scalp. I rested my face against her hair. The honey-colored curls smelled of salty sweat, soft musk, and herbs.

The scent did more than turn me on. If only it was that easy. I would kill, or die, for the scent of her. God, I shouldn't ever want anyone this much. It's too dangerous.

"You're sure about this?" I asked after a few moments of silence.

"I really did go stay at a friend's last night. I used to have lots of friends. We hadn't even spoken for over a year!" She moved her head so she could look at me. "I missed you. I spent the night wondering about you; wishing you were there, wishing I was here. I could feel you pace around the room looking for me. I felt you eat the prime rib. I laughed when you got frustrated that your tongue couldn't reach the marrow in the center of the bone. I wanted to be here to help." She was silent for a moment. "A part of me wanted you to come look for me. Find me. Take me. Another part of me was really scared that you would."

"I can't say that I missed you last night. But this morning was a bitch. Yesterday too." Tangerines dusted my nose and blended with the herbs.

"So? Now what? What's next? I've never done anything like this, felt anything like this before. I don't want to leave without you but I'm sure you've got a life. I don't even know if you're married. I don't even know your real name. Is it really Bob?"

I shook my head. "My friends call me Tony. Only clients call me Bob." I ignored the "real name" question. Too soon. "And no, I'm not married."

I paused as I thought briefly, then I nodded. "You're right. We do need to get to know one another. When are you due back at your house?"

She shrugged. "Whenever I get there. Bekki is staying until I get back. So Mom has someone around. I'm sure there'll be hell to pay but I told them I'd be gone a couple of days. I don't have a job so as long as Mom's covered . . ." She grinned suddenly, "Oh God, Bekki will be mad! Heaven forbid something should intrude on *her* life!"

I chuckled. My lady was starting to grow a backbone. Good. "Then let's check out and we'll go on a trip. When's the last time you were in Vegas?"

"Las Vegas? I've *never* been there. You mean that we're just going to pick up and leave town?" She seemed startled at the suggestion.

I shrugged, which rubbed my arms against her breasts. "Why not? I have some business, but it'll only take a few hours. We can take an afternoon flight and make it back in the morning. Hell, we can stay a week if you want."

"Oh! I can't be gone *that* long! I don't even have any clothes."

I shrugged again and felt the urging of the hunger under my skin as she pressed against me. "We'll buy new. I only need to stop at my place for a second to pick up some stuff." No need to bring up what sort of stuff I needed. Even if we were getting together, the less she knew, the better.

"We're going to be stopping by *your* house?" The question seemed loaded and I didn't know why.

"Is that a problem?" Her scent was suddenly tense.

"No. No, not at all. I'm just trying to imagine where you might live and I'm coming up blank."

"Well, in a little bit, you'll see. But for the next few minutes," I said and tightened my arms, "you won't be having any time to imagine much of anything."

She was smiling as I kissed her and our teeth clicked together for an instant. The thick, heady scent of her desire made thinking impossible. So I didn't bother to try. I just let the hunger have its way.

Chapter 13

After I checked out she drove me to Nick's so I could collect my car. It's a '67 Mustang Fastback. Black with white interior. It'll overtake almost any other car off the line or on the stretch. Not only had nobody bothered my car, they'd waxed it. I could smell residual sweat blended with the fresh paste wax. It's nice to be feared.

Sue was amazed that nobody had touched my car in that neighborhood so I told her about my conversation with Jocko.

"You'd really do it. Wouldn't you?" Burned coffee, burned water, with the slightest hint of cloves.

"Absolutely," I said firmly. "A threat has no teeth if you're not willing to follow through." It was a lesson she needed to learn if she wanted to be able to stand up to her family.

"Okay..." I couldn't smell her mood.

We stopped at her bank first. She was amazed when I suggested that she take about a quarter mil. She finally agreed to take five thousand. What a waste of a good gambling trip.

I took the lead and she followed to my house to drop off my car. I live in a large ranch-style in a quiet, suburban neighborhood. The house is huge. It's bigger than I need but I like space. The suite is half of the top floor of the hotel but even that feels cramped. As I parked the car I wondered again what was possessing me that I kept letting her further and further into my life. Only the boys have ever been to my place. We take turns hosting the poker game. It's only once every five months, so the neighbors don't bitch. Much. Bodyguards and unconcealed carrys make folks nervous.

I unlocked the door and ushered her inside. "Look

around," I said. "I'll just be a minute. I really want to get out of these clothes."

She smelled like I had hurt her feelings. "You don't like them?"

I smiled and gave her a quick kiss on the cheek. "Actually, I like them a lot. But I've been wearing them for two days."

"Oh!" came a relieved comment. Her fragrance was sunny again. I was going to have to watch what I said around her until her skin thickened a bit.

I went into the master bedroom and as I stripped, she called to me.

"This is really nice! Did you decorate it yourself?"

I turned on the shower for a quick rinse. "Mostly. Some of the paintings were gifts from my dad."

I turned to see her standing in the doorway of the bedroom. "I thought you said your dad died before you were born."

"No, I said my *father* died before I was born. My dad is the man who raised me."

She gave me a questioning glance.

"Dad was a bodyguard for the *Patrone*," I explained, using the Italian pronunciation. "You've probably heard him called the Godfather. *Patrone* doesn't actually translate to Godfather. Literally, it's 'patron'; figuratively, 'grandfather'. The head of the family, a protector. Anyway, Dad didn't have any family and when I moved into the big house, I didn't either. Dad felt sorry for me and he always wanted a kid. So he asked and *Patrone* let Dad raise me."

She smiled at me and smelled of warm cinnamon rolls. "That's nice. It's nice that you found each other."

I stepped into the shower. I spoke louder to be heard over the water. "It's a family of choice, rather than a family of blood. Both are important."

I heard her voice move closer. I could sense that she was standing just inside the doorway.

"Do you have any blood family left? Did your mother or father have any family?"

"If they did they've never come forward. I didn't know my mother's real name. She just called herself Amber."

I stepped out of the shower and joined her in the bedroom. The towel I wore around my waist was to finish drying off. I'm not real modest.

I could feel in my head that she was hoping I had a picture. I did, but it was old and tired-looking from riding in my wallet for years. Still, I sorted through receipts and business cards until I found it. I pulled it out so she could see it.

Sue stared at the photo as I scrubbed my hair with the towel. "She's beautiful!" she exclaimed in surprise. I glanced at the picture. I don't look at it often. Mom had thick black hair, which I inherited and sapphire blue eyes I didn't. Her pale skin and delicate features put her in the model category. The body matched the face. She could have been more than just a whore if she had tried, but I didn't know her long enough to ask her story. It's not something that a ten-year-old thinks of.

Sue pointed to the young boy smiling out of the cracked and faded wallet print. "Is that you in the photo with her?"

"Yeah. I was five when that was taken. It was right before she got the syphilis real bad. She didn't look so pretty when she died. It wasn't anything that a kid should watch."

She looked at me and watched the brief flash of pain appear then disappear from my eyes as the memory slipped through.

"I'm sorry." She really was. The feeling made my chest tight.

I shrugged. "Oh, well. Can't change the past. It's what happened."

"Yeah. I understand about pasts not going away." She stood there staring at the picture of a woman long dead, a person she didn't even know and felt sorrow. Hot tears shimmered just below the surface. She handed me back the photo without a word.

I wanted to go to her and hold her; make it better. But I couldn't. Instead, I hurriedly put on clothes suitable for Vegas. She watched me dress with a proprietary air. As I would walk from place to place she would reach out and touch a leg or an arm. Like it still wasn't quite real to her. I smiled at her once and she smiled back.

Once I was dressed and packed for a day or two, I reached into the closet behind the clothes and the shelves. My finger found a small indentation in the wall and I pulled sideways. A small panel opened and blind fingers found the handle of a briefcase. It was a typical hard-side case made of black leather, with twin dial locks set into the top. I didn't open it. There was no need. I knew what was in it. There was a handcuff attached and I snapped it closed around my wrist.

Sue watched with interest. Curiosity sparkled in the back of her eyes. "What's in the case?"

"Something I need to deliver to someone. It won't take long." My voice was light but neutral.

She shrugged but I could smell her curiosity. I was pleased that she didn't ask any questions I didn't want to answer.

We dropped off Sue's rental car at the airport lot. Plane tickets were easy to come by. The next flight boarded in only twenty minutes.

We went to the airport stores and found several outfits for Sue. I was a little surprised when she selected size fourteens. I'm usually better at guessing than that. We also bought her a travel case, new cosmetics and toiletries.

"I can't believe I'm doing this!" she exclaimed, as we paid the cashier. "This is so . . ."

"So . . . what?"

"I don't know! Wicked? Extravagant?"

Still that sense that she wasn't entitled to be happy. I turned her to face me right at the cash register. I put a hand on each shoulder and held her gaze. I repeated something I said the first day. "You're allowed to enjoy this, Sue."

Her eyes thanked me with words she couldn't say. A smile spoke the rest and she hugged me.

When we arrived at the security gate, I accompanied a guard to a separate room after flashing a card that identified me as a high-security courier. It hadn't been an easy I.D. to obtain and I was proud of it. I was fully bonded and could transport large sums of cash and jewels all over the country as carry-on. I had to check my gun but I could keep it as concealed carry when I landed. I just make sure that my carry piece isn't what I use for jobs. My carry piece is either the Sig or a snub nose Taurus .38. I had the Taurus today. Sweet shooting gun. It'll put five rounds in a one inch group right out of the box.

The drug dogs were a trip. They completely ignored the case and sniffed me all over. Then they went to their bellies in submission with tails flipping madly. A female beagle flipped on her back and howled. Apparently I'm a big dog now. I've seen it before, but the guards didn't know what to make of their reaction. They finally had to drag the dogs through the crowd of laughing passengers and then hand searched the bag.

Sue was waiting for me on the other side of the x-ray machine when I returned. My briefcase now had a security seal taped across the opening. She looked at it with undisguised curiosity but didn't ask any questions. Smart girl.

We had to scramble a bit to reach the gate, two concourses over. She was out of breath but laughing happily when we slid through the door and handed our boarding passes to the flight attendant.

The flight attendant tried to tell me that I had to stow the briefcase. When I showed her the handcuff and the security tape, she relented but wasn't happy. Oh, well. Her attitude wasn't my problem.

The weather was perfect for flying. I'm used to flying, but it was obvious that Sue wasn't. Her scent changed to nearly abject terror. Terror goes beyond the ammonia smell of panic. It's like a week-old cat box—it could peel paint off the wall if humans could smell it. Her knuckles were bloodless on the chair arms as we accelerated toward take-off. I could hear her heart beat faster and faster until it was hummingbird quick.

"Don't like to fly, love?"

"Never have before," she said, eyes closed. "The thought of being suspended in a tin box ten thousand feet in the air just came home to me. I think I might be sick."

I thought it best not to mention that we'd be significantly

higher than ten thousand. I tried to take one of her hands to hold it and comfort her, but she refused to let go of the armrest. So I settled for resting my hand over the top of hers, and stroking the skin gently. Take-offs are usually the worst for non-flyers. I could feel her pulse race where my fingers touched her wrist. She whimpered slightly. The sound made me want to nuzzle her, comfort her.

"It'll be over soon," I said instead, and patted her hand.

Her eyes opened suddenly, and she glanced at me in panic. "Why do you say that?"

I chuckled softly. "I didn't mean we were going to crash. Once we're at level flight, you'll see that it's not so bad."

The acceleration decreased, and I could feel the flight level off. The pilot came over the speaker to welcome us and tell us that weather conditions were perfect for the short hop to Vegas. It would only be an hour flight. The plane was packed, and the flight attendants were at a dead run. They came around and offered us coffee or sodas. Sue turned a little green when I ordered orange juice.

"This really doesn't bother you, does it?" she asked.

"I really like to fly," I admitted. "I've even got ground school under my belt, but never had the time to finish getting my pilot's license. There's lots of air time involved. Life has just been too busy."

The trip was nearly half over before Sue relaxed her hands on the chair arms. I suggested that she might want to get some blood back into them. They were stiff and rigid at first, and I helped rub them to get the circulation going again.

"You must think that I'm some sort of wimp," she said ruefully.

"Not at all," I said with a gentle smile. "Thousands of people don't like to fly. You're not the first. You won't be the last. I've known some real tough guys that turn into jello in an airplane. We all have our phobias."

"What are yours?" she asked. Curiosity filled the pressured air and then disappeared through a vent.

I chuckled. "You wouldn't believe me."

"Please?" she pleaded. "It'll make me feel better to hear about someone else's."

"Okay," I said, "But it's stupid. I'm afraid of needles."

Her eyebrows raised. "Needles? Like shots, or sewing?"

"Like shots," I repeated. "Now, understand. I know that they have beneficial uses, but all the stuff inside looks the same to me. Could be medicine, could be poison. Get a needle near me, and I'll beat the person holding it senseless. I almost got tetanus once because I wouldn't go to the hospital. Dad finally had to hold me down—with the help of three interns, so they didn't have to cut off my foot."

She gave a crow of laughter. "Needles! That's wonderful! A big, strong . . . ," I could sense that she nearly said the word, *assassin*, but stopped short. "man, like you."

I gave her a sarcastic smile. "Glad I could amuse you. I didn't laugh at you, ya know."

That sobered her right up. "I'm sorry," she said, with humor still in her voice. "I guess you don't get flu shots, huh?

"No," I responded, "That's not high on my priority list. I figure if everyone around me gets one, I should be safe. But tell you what, I'll roll up my sleeve for you if you'll go flying with me. Just you and me in the wild blue. We can do barrel rolls and Immelmans." There was a sparkle of teasing in my eyes. At that precise moment, the plane hit an air pocket, and we dropped a foot or two. She went slightly white and her panic tickled my nose.

"Okay, I give," she said quickly. "Sorry I laughed. Really, really sorry." I laughed, loud and hard until she finally joined in.

We talked more about our likes. It turned out that we both could live on Italian food forever, but that neither of us liked veggies on our pizza. She doesn't like scallops, but enjoys calamari—which I detest, and we both adore shrimp.

"You will *love* the shrimp cocktails at the casinos," I commented.

"Good, huh?" she asked.

"Even better. Free."

Her eyebrows disappeared under her bangs. "They *give away* shrimp cocktails? Cool!"

"Food's cheap," I said with a shrug. "Free food keeps people spending money at the tables."

Sue kept glancing out of the window nervously so I reached over and shut the blind. She smelled startled but it really did calm her down. We talked about books. Turned out that we had major differences in taste.

"Mostly I like real life stuff," she said. "Not biographies, but like true crime."

"Ah. Joseph Wambaugh and such?"

She nodded her head. "Yeah, that sort. And drama about people who have done interesting things. What about you?"

"Nope. I like escapism. I've already got enough drama in my life, thank you. Real events are traumatic enough without borrowing other people's problems. Sci-fi, good mysteries—the ones that make you think about whodunit—and thrillers are good, too. I read a lot of Asimov, Cussler and Clancy."

All in all, I managed to distract her enough with conversation that she didn't even remember most of the flight.

But when we started to descend into Vegas, we ran into turbulance. We were racing down the runway before I could forcibly remove her bloodless knuckles from my arm. If she'd lost much more circulation we'd have had to amputate.

After we arrived I had to check in with Security to get my piece back, have the tape removed and get the money counted a second time. I snapped the case around my wrist and locked my fingers around the handle.

Sue was waiting for me at the luggage carousel. The bags were on the floor next to her and she was smiling broadly.

"Happy?" I asked, even though it was obvious from her scent.

"I've never done anything like this. I am having so much fun."

"The fun hasn't started yet."

She opened her mouth to speak when my cell phone rang. I have it set to actually *ring*. It sets it apart from all of the chirps and inane songs from other phones. I glanced at the display. Damn it. I might as well take the call. Sara would dial constantly until she reached me. I held a finger up to stop Sue's reply, pressed a button and held the phone to my ear.

"Tony here."

"Tony, it's Sara. I've been trying to reach you!"

"I've been in a plane, Sara."

Panic suffused through her voice. "Does that mean you're out of town?"

"Yes, Sara. I'm out of town for a few days. What's the problem?"

"But I need you to come over. The security system isn't working."

I sighed. The security system is *never* working when Sara is managing the store. I don't think machines like her.

"What's it doing?"

"It's those damn door sensors! They beep at the customers every time someone goes out the door."

"*Every* time, Sara?" It helped to get enough information about the problem to be able to fix it.

"Well, no, not every time. But it's gone off six times in the past hour! See, there it goes again!" She was right. In the background I heard the characteristic tones of the shoplifting sensor.

"Did a customer go through? Or an employee? Tell me what's happening, Sara."

"It was a customer. The man had just gone through the register line and it still beeped at him."

"Did he buy something that needed to be nullified? Did the clerk remove the tag?"

"Yes, Tom's the clerk on that register."

Okay. I know him. He's pretty careful. So, maybe it was the sensors. "Is the customer still in the store?"

Her voice sounded hurt. "Of course. I'm standing right here next to him. What do I do?" I heard her cover the mouthpiece with her hand and explain to the customer that she was talking to the security repair company. Then she started chatting with the customer and forgot I was on the phone.

I didn't have the time or inclination to play with her today. "Sara? Sara!"

"Oh! Sorry, Tony. What do I do?"

"Take the customer's bag and stand away from the sensors. Then swing the bag through the sensor and tell me what happens."

"Okay. Hold on." I could hear her set down the receiver and ask the customer for the bag. The male customer objected, which perked my ears. I listened closer, focusing in with my wolf hearing.

"This is stupid!" said the man. "I don't have time to help you fix your equipment. Now, give me my bag. I have other things to do."

Ah, ha. I got an idea.

"Sara! Pick up the phone!"

There was a scrambling sound and then I heard her voice. "Yes, Tony?"

"Do you have the bag?"

"Yep. Right here." Her voice muffled again. "I'm sorry, sir. This will only take a moment. I get a reprimand in my file if I don't report these errors when they happen."

"Sara? Did you wave the bag through?"

"Yes. It didn't do it this time."

"Do me a favor and ask the man to walk through the sensor again. But this time, *you* hold the bag until after he goes through."

"But . . ."

"Just do it, Sara. Trust me." The customer didn't want to walk through and I knew why.

"Tony? He doesn't want to walk through. I can't force him to. What do I do?"

"Call security, Sara. The guy's shoplifting."

"No, really, Tony. I've got the bag right here. I watched him check out."

Sue was watching me closely with furrowed brows. I knew that she was listening. Even if she could only hear part of the conversation, she found it interesting.

"He bought some things. He just didn't buy *every* thing.

Don't let go of that bag, Sara. If the guy bolts, follow him out to his car and get a plate number. I'll bet that whatever is hidden in his pocket or under his shirt is worth a lot more than what's in the bag. But he probably won't leave without what he paid for. Call me back after security's checked him out."

I hung up without waiting for a reply.

I held up one finger aloft for Sue to wait and didn't even look at the display when the phone rang a second time.

"Tony here."

"Oh, my God! Tony, you were right. The guy had pockets sewed all up and down the inside of his pants. There were those real expensive cell phone batteries, some pricey women's perfume and a couple of CDs. Do you think that all of the other beeps were thefts, too?

"Maybe a couple of them. But the unit probably does need to be adjusted. I'll swing by when I get back. Until then, have a couple of the stockers stand at the exit and carry people's bags through. Then you'll know if it's the person or the bag. It'll get you by until I get back."

"Thank you *so* much, Tony! No wonder Carol insists on using your company!"

"No problem, Sara. I'll be by in a couple of days."

I hung up to find Sue looking at me curiously. The thick, sweet scent of antifreeze filled the air. At least that's how it smells to me.

"How could you know the customer was shoplifting over the phone?"

I shrugged. "Most people consider the security devices annoying, but they're pretty good about understanding the need for them. When he didn't want to give up the bag, I figured that there was something wrong. It takes one to know one."

"So, you run a security company? Is that what you do for a living?"

I chuckled. "It's what I do to keep busy. You already know what I do for a *living.*"

But, having the phone out reminded me of something. I picked up my bag and motioned for Sue to do the same. I punched the menu button on the phone and scanned down the list of names. When I reached Sal's number, I dialed.

"Talk to me." It's how Sal always answers.

"Sal? Tony. How's business?"

"Hey, Tony! 'Sup, buddy? You in town?"

"Yeah. I'm hoping we can do business. I've got money burning a hole in my pocket." It's the truth and it's also innocuous enough that it didn't matter if anyone overheard. Sal knew what I needed to do.

We'd reached the car rental booth and I handed them my membership card with all the pertinent information, so I didn't need to talk to the girl.

I was disappointed at Sal's response. "Sorry, Ton. It's audit week. Can't help you out."

Shit. "Any suggestions?"

"Not really. The gaming inspectors are running all over the city. Oh, wait! They've already finished at the Lucky Strike. You can probably take care of it there."

I grimaced. "Not my first choice, Sal."

"It's the *only* choice right now, Tony. Unless you want to come back next week."

No. I'd already screwed this up once. If I didn't take care of it this time, I was going to be stuck with the cash. That damn cop has been watching me like a hawk. I wouldn't be able to run it through the business. Without the cash, I couldn't afford the vacation I wanted.

But truthfully, I wasn't really looking forward to going to the Lucky Strike. Leo Scapolo may be Family, but isn't a friend. He *is* high on my list of enemies. But it was necessary.

"Okay. Well, thanks anyway, Sal."

"Stop by anyway, Tony. I'll comp you a room. That much I *can* do."

"I'll take you up on that. We'll be by in a few."

"Ah. You have a guest." He chuckled. "I can guess the gender. Mixing business with pleasure, are we? I'll get you set up in a nice suite."

"Always a pleasure working with you, Sal." I hung up

and grabbed the keys that the clerk had slid across the counter with a smile.

"Where are we going? Sue asked.

"Down to the strip for the night. But then we're going to have to spend some time downtown. Is that okay?"

She shrugged and the bright scent of tangerines filled the air. "I don't care where we go. I'm along for the ride."

Once we arrived at the hotel, I suggested that we do some touring of the strip casinos since the car was already parked. Sue was suitably awe-struck staring at the lights of the strip. They're impressive even in the daytime.

We checked in. Sal greeted us warmly and then personally delivered my case to the safe for the night. I didn't worry about it. Las Vegas casinos have some of the tightest security in the world. If a hotel ever got a reputation for valuables disappearing, it would go out of business in a heartbeat.

The lobby had been all muted light and quiet conversation. But I was completely unprepared for the assault on my senses when we walked through the doors of the casino.

I'd been in crowds since the change. I'd even been in bars with live music. But the high pitched tones of the bells and buzzers that only a year ago were a pleasant background became a frenzied cacophony that gave me a splitting headache almost immediately. I also hadn't planned on the variety of extreme emotions that put my nose on overload. Joy. Fury. Grief. They were all too intense and each one was penetrating and thick as liquid hanging in the air. For a moment my heart raced and I couldn't breathe. I couldn't think; couldn't move. I needed to leave. I wanted to run from away the emotional bedlam. Sue watched me with near panic on her face. Her eyes darted this way and that, trying to find the source of my discomfort but it wasn't from one source.

I fought back into control and slowed the pounding of my heart. I stood quietly and took deep careful breaths. I let the smells pass by me and didn't fight to sort or categorize them. That was the trouble. I was trying to identify everything and I couldn't. The sounds were still too loud so I reached in my pocket and stuffed in a pair of earplugs. Better. Much better. The high end of the noise muted. The din faded and I could think again. I gave Sue a shaky smile but she continued to watch me like a dog watches a nervous master.

We walked around but didn't play much. The headache was still right behind my eyes. My nerves were starting to get edgy the more places we went and Sue was beginning to notice.

"You feel tense," she said. I *feel* tense? That was a strange way to phrase it but I couldn't disagree.

"Let's get out in the sun for awhile. Maybe that'll help. I thought we'd go see Hoover Dam," I said, when she finally turned back around.

"That would be fun," she said and we headed for the parking garage. Once outside, I could remove the earplugs. The further we got from the center of the Strip, the easier it was to relax. The dam is a ways out of town. We started to talk again about whatever struck our minds. Movies, into politics, and then religion. Our views were more alike than not, but there were some significant differences. We disagreed on the ethics and legality of photo radar that the cops are using now, since we saw one parked on the side of the road on the way out of town. I generally travel the speed limit so it's not an issue, but I think that the inability to confront your accuser violates certain personal rights.

Sue believed that the deterrent is the visibility to *other* drivers of the pulled over car. Hence the bright, multi-colored lights that can be seen for miles.

"So you think that the flashing lights aren't just about safety and visibility for the stopped car, but for the sheer spectacle to others?"

"Exactly." she replied with a burst of citrus and clove scent. "So the photo van's strobe is the same deterrent, or even better. People always "resume illegal speed" when a parked police car doesn't follow, but with photo radar, you aren't sure whether you got hit until you get the ticket in the mail. They stay slow because they're nervous."

I thought about it and then waggled my head slightly.

"Sorry, not good enough. That may be the rationale they try to push, but the whole concept still reeks of constitutional violations on a number of fronts. It's just revenue enhancement to me." I said with a shake of my head.

A smile played across my face as the beginnings of burnt metal frustration drifted to me. A glance told me I was right. Her jaw had set slightly and her arms were crossed tight.

When she noted my smile, she rolled her eyes and tangerines replaced her frustration. She laughed and I soon followed. We agreed to disagree, since both viewpoints had merit. She proved that she had a mind, and was willing to stretch it, which is real important to me. Debates, as long as they don't degrade into personal attacks, are a lot of fun.

We had to wait for a few minutes for the first tour to start. It occurred to both of us that we had forgotten to eat lunch. We had only gotten a snack on the plane. No matter. After the lecture, we'd go back into town. I've been on the tour several times. It was as informative and interesting as always. Sue was fascinated by the tunnels under the dam, and asked some real intelligent questions about the construction. Like I said, she's got a mind.

It was nearly sunset when we arrived back at the strip and Sue got to see the full spectacle of daylight at night. When the moon rose through the warm desert air, I could feel the pull of it, but it was only a tease. A few times, though, I found myself standing motionless, staring at the sky. Sue touched my arm and warm tingles flowed through me. God, that sensation was addicting.

We spent the night wallowing in each other's bodies. I couldn't get enough of the taste of her, the scent of rich soil and growing things—the feel of magic as it flowed between us. The sound of her cries as I brought her to climax over and over took my breath away.

But even so, the next morning I woke really early, tense and fidgety. I had planned on this being a nice relaxing trip.

Visiting Leo's place would keep me watching my back for the rest of the visit.

"Are you okay?" asked Sue as she stepped out of the bath-room from her morning routine. I'd given her first shot. Her scent changed to the sharp, tangy scent of worry.

I grabbed my travel case and headed in to shower and brush my teeth. "I just need to get my business taken care of. I didn't mean to ruin your mood."

She shrugged and smiled. "Then let's get your delivery made so we can go back to having fun. I returned the smile.

It was only about 6:00 a.m. when we drove downtown and parked in the Lucky Strike's lot. Downtown isn't as brazenly flashy as the strip but there's still plenty of lights and activity. The cowgirl and cowboy neon signs are still there and the old Union Plaza still has the huge canopy of lights with the train in the background.

I thought seriously about putting the earplugs back in. But no, they'd be viewed as a sign of weakness by Leo. I needed to be on top of my game to see him. I knew he'd be awake and already working. He only sleeps a couple of hours a night and sometimes not at all. He calls people who sleep a full eight hours "wusses." I only sleep about six myself, so I partially agree.

I took a deep breath and braced myself but my head was pounding by the time we walked up to the desk. The brief-case was once again attached to my wrist.

The clerk was a kid. Lately everyone seems like a kid. Thirty-seven years into life and I'm already feeling old. I took an instant dislike to him. I had to fight not to growl. He smelled like blood and death and worse things. It didn't fit with the boyish face.

"Could you ask Leo to come to the desk? I need to speak to him." I used my best polite voice. Sugar might be better than vinegar. We'd see.

His back went up immediately. The smell of black coffee and dry heat rose from him in a cloud. Pissed him off, I did. Touchy little shit.

"The General Manager is very busy right now. I can't interrupt him."

That was bull and I knew it. No business is more important to Leo than money. I was in no mood to have a snot-nosed kid tell me whether or not I could see him.

"Sue, wait here. His office still in the same place?" I glanced at the clerk as I headed for the hallway next to the front desk.

The clerk moved to step in front of me. "You can't go back there, sir. It's for employees only."

I started to push him to the side when Sue touched my arm. "Tony, please," she said. "Let's just go somewhere else. It's not a big deal."

I would have loved to comply. But I turned to her and put a finger to her lips. "It's okay. I don't plan to make a scene." I turned and scanned the room and my eyes fell upon a tall black man that I knew. He wore a white shirt with a name badge. I smiled.

I walked toward him. "Bobby," I said jovially. He turned and when his eyes focused on me his dark face lit up with a smile. It was brilliantly white against his dark skin. Bobby is from somewhere in South Africa. His skin is almost a blue black. He smelled of expensive cologne, Chapstick, and old cigarette smoke—not his. But as for his underlying smell, the cologne overpowered any sense of it. His hand shot out and I shook it. He still had a grip like a full-grown bear, but this time I was able to give as good as I got.

His eyes flickered oddly for a second when we shook, but it passed quickly. I guess I surprised him.

"Hey, there, you old reprobate!" he said heartily, "How you doin', man? You've been working out! What are you going by now-a-days?"

"Still Tony. Life's so-so right now," I fingered the white shirt. "Pit Boss? Getting up in the world."

He pursed his lips and shrugged. "It's more trouble than it's worth most days. But the money's good."

The smile dropped off my face. "I need to see Leo."

Bobby's smile also faded and took on a look that was similar to my own. Blank, expressionless.

"You sure that's a good idea?" His face showed a level of discomfort that I couldn't smell.

"It's business. I've got no choice."

He turned and walked back toward the desk with me. "There are always choices in life, Tony. Always." I could tell he believed it.

"Obligations frequently overpower choices, Bobbo. You above all people know that."

He stopped and glanced at me. He licked his lips, a quick flash of pink on his dark skin. A cloud passed over his face and pain slid through his eyes. Bobby and I had a history that involved some pretty nasty things done in the name of obligation. Maybe I had lied to Sue when I said I had never been used. He nodded briefly.

The clerk smelled surprised as Bobby walked toward the desk. "It's okay, Ben," he said on his way down the hall. "Leo will want to see these folks." The clerk shot me a dark look. His anger hit me like a hot breeze. I blew him a kiss.

Sue smelled nervous, so I took her hand and pressed it to my lips. "Just let me lead," I instructed her.

Bobby came out of a door down the hall and a second man followed. Leo Scapolo is a big man. Most of it is muscle but a little has turned to fat around the waist. A lot of people mistake him for Jewish because of his dark curly hair. Over the years, the hair has become just a fringe around a bald pate. He has a big nose and small nearly black button eyes. They're always shifting, always thinking. Always dangerous.

As he approached the counter I got a whiff of him. Not surprisingly, Leo smells like someone else's pain. It was a wet thick smell that oozed out of his pores. He smelled of lies and hate and menace. He reeked of dead things, like raw meat that's sat out for too long. One particular odor made me look at him sharply. He smelled of fur. Fur like mine. It made me want to growl. Sue could feel the tension between us. Her fingers trembled on my arm.

Bobby's tongue flicked out over his upper lip again. He looked a little nervous too.

The smile that was on Leo's face was for show only. It never reached his eyes. He stared at me with a dangerous look that made me think somehow he knew who I was— *what* I was.

"Tony, good to see you." Yeah, right. And I believe in the tooth fairy.

"Leo," I said with a false smile of my own. "How's business?"

"Good, good," he said, nodding. His voice warmed a notch for a flickering moment. "How's your dad?"

That question was actually an honest one. They really did like each other. "Dad's doing well. He's retired now. Living the life down in Florida. Whiling away the hours playing boccie and canasta."

"He always was a sucker for a good boccie game." Leo's laugh was deep and genuine. He sobered so suddenly it was like someone hit pause on a video. "What can I do for you?"

I raised the briefcase slightly and it caught his eye. "I've got some business with you."

He stared at me menacingly for long seconds. I didn't flinch. Sue looked back and forth from me to Leo. She nibbled her lips nervously. Without a word, he turned and walked down the hallway. I started to follow when she grabbed my arm in a panic.

"I've got a bad feeling about this, Tony."

I touched her arm lightly and winked. "Don't worry. Everything's fine. Why don't you wait for me in the restaurant? Order me a beer and a steak. Rare. I'll meet you in a couple of minutes. Bobby, would you show her the way?"

Bobby nodded and moved to stand next to Sue. "Okay," she said hesitantly but followed Bobby. She looked back to me more than once.

Leo was standing at the door of his office waiting. I followed. He opened a door at the end of the hall. A placard on the door read, 'Private—No Admittance'. Leo's inner sanctum.

I entered the room, scanned for bodyguards and cameras

and then closed the door behind me. He was a confident little asshole. Nobody was in sight. I listened for a moment with my wolf hearing but I didn't hear any mechanical sounds other than the slight hiss from the blower. I shifted my leg and felt the ankle holster press into my skin. Good enough.

He went behind a carved oak desk and sat down on a black leather executive-style chair.

"Well, well," he said snidely after he was seated. "Tony the Nose. You realize that I'm only seeing you out of deference to your dad."

I reached into my pocket and withdrew the key to the cuff. "Yeah, I know. It's the only reason that I'd set eyes on your ugly puss too."

All hints of the polite smile were erased. "What do you want, *sazee*?"

Huh? Must be new slang for something really bad. Leo wouldn't address me with anything less. "I've got business. You want it or should I go elsewhere?"

I opened the case and turned it to show him the neatly stacked bills.

"How much?" he asked.

"A million. What's the house cut?"

He pursed his lips and I could see his beady eyes sparkle. "Ten percent."

My eyebrows shot to the roof and I snorted. I closed the case again with a shake of my head. "You've got to be kidding. Fuck this. I *will* go somewhere else." Audit or no, someone else in town had to be doing business.

I closed the case, set the locks, and was just about to snap the cuff around my wrist. He tapped all of the fingers of his left hand on the desk. It sounded like a muted woodpecker. Finally, he spoke.

"Fine. Five percent. Plus an hour with your lady."

Whoa! Where the hell did that come from? I didn't think he'd even glanced Sue's way.

"The hell you say!" The cuff snapped closed. I wanted to reach across the desk and rip out his throat. But I didn't. Say 'thanks', Dad.

"No dice. You don't want my money? Fine. But you even *talk* to my lady and you'll be breathing out of a new hole in your skull."

He quavered his hands in front of me. "Ooo! I'm so scared." He wasn't. His eyes were cold and dead.

His mistake. He should be.

I flipped him a one-finger salute and pocketed the key. He exhaled a sharp breath and I could hear him counting slowly under his breath. I walked toward the door. The knob was in my hand when he said with annoyed acceptance, "Six percent. It's the best offer you'll get in town."

I stopped where I was and thought about it. Yeah, six percent was at least equal to what I'd get elsewhere and it'd make me points with Dad. God, the things I do for family. I turned to face the piece of scum.

"Done." I repeated the performance of unsnapping the cuff and handed him the case. "I'd like a receipt."

"Don't trust me?" he asked with a sneer. The sharp, unpleasant smell of his hate oozed through my brain.

"Not as far as I can throw you and I can't even pick you up."

He wrote a house receipt for the cash and accepted the case. He told me what table to be at and who the dealer would be.

I was surprised that he never mentioned that he could smell my fur like I could his. But then again, I didn't mention it to him. Maybe that's the way it works. But I learned I could smell others like me. Or, maybe I'm nuts.

I left Leo's office with the receipt and no case. I had some cash to get coins and the table would be set up for me soon. So I joined Sue in the restaurant. I raised my eyebrows as I saw her digging into a half-eaten rare steak. Another rested on a plate across from her.

"I thought you like your steaks well done."

She raised her eyes to me in confusion. "I do. Why?"

I motioned to her plate. She looked at the piece on her fork as though she had seen it for the first time. Horror filled her eyes and she set the utensil down shakily. "That's weird."

I shrugged my shoulders. "Ask the waitress to send it back."

"But it's half eaten!"

"So? It's none of their business. You're not asking for a new one."

I was almost done with my steak when hers returned. But she had a hard time eating the thoroughly cooked slice of meat. I got the distinct impression that she preferred it rare. The wolf inside me was pleased but I didn't say anything.

We went downstairs and while she was looking at the quarter slots I set her up on a machine.

I called to her and she sat where I directed. She looked up at me as I started to leave. "Aren't you staying?"

"I'm going to go play the tables for a bit. Gambling is kind of a solitary activity. You won't be real social when you get involved in the machine in front of you."

"Okay," she said with a shrug, "If you say so. Where will you be?"

I directed her attention to the blackjack table at the edge of the pit. "See the table with the red-headed woman dealer? That's where I'll be. If you run out of money or want to leave, just come get me." I pressed the button to start her reels spinning for the first time. A single cherry came up and she won two credits.

"Ooh, look! I already won! This is fun!" She pressed the button again but nothing hit. She was engrossed but twenty credits down by the time I left.

I knew the dealer at my table. A single chair was open and waiting when I arrived. Marge smiled at me and I smiled back. "Good to see you again, Mr. Giodone," she said softly, as she removed the small placard labeled 'Reserved' from the spot in front of my seat.

Marge smells nice. Sweet and soft, like a fluffy blanket just out of the dryer. She's sort of the 'Mom' on the floor. She's older than she looks and smells. Meaner too.

"New hairdo?"

She smiled and smelled warm and fuzzy. "Nice of you to notice. Are you in for this hand?" I nodded.

An hour later, I was ten thousand up and going strong but I needed a break. The table had attracted a crowd while I played and there were groans from the group when I stood and stretched. "I'm going to take a break, Marge. Cash me out."

She handed me a tray and I stacked the multi-colored, paper wrapped tokens in it. I glanced toward where Sue had been playing and she was still sitting at the same machine. When I came up behind her, she started in surprise. "You scared me," she said with a giggle.

I looked at the display. It read 407. Not bad. Two hundred up from when I left her.

"You're doing well." I nodded in approval.

"Okay, I guess." She smelled a little disappointed. "I was higher earlier. It'd be more fun if it was *big* money." I looked at her and my brow furrowed. She didn't consider this big money? Then I realized what the confusion was and I smiled.

"Sue, what's 500 multiplied by two?"

She looked at me and shrugged. "A thousand. Why?"

"Then 200 times five is the same?"

"Duh," was her reply. "So?"

I pointed toward the number on the face of the machine. "Then I guess that you've won about a thousand dollars, huh?"

The look on her face was worth the wait. I didn't need a smell to know her thoughts. She looked again at the front of the machine and then to the machines to the side of her. "This is a *nickel* machine, right?"

I shook my head. "A five dollar machine." There was no dollar sign in front of the large number on the face of the machine. She had thought she was playing nickels.

"Five dollars a pull!?" She looked at the display once more. "Oh, my God! I won a thousand dollars! Aahh!"

I chuckled as she exploded into laughter. Her happiness gave way to delight and citrus burst into my nose. She leapt up and hugged me hard enough that I almost dropped the tray in my hands. The tingles were even headier from her excitement. I had to smile. All of her millions and she's still enthused by this small win. She stood in front of the machine just looking at it, not sure what to do next.

"Do you want to cash out?" I asked. "I thought about taking a break."

She looked at the machine again. "I don't know how." She appealed to me with glittering but confused eyes and I grinned. I reached across her and pressed the 'Cash/Credit' button. The machine began to ding wildly as the oversized, copper-colored coins exited into the tray noisily. I winced slightly. The headache was back.

We took a break and walked around the casino watching the other players. We stood back from the gaming tables while I explained each game in a whisper so we wouldn't distract the participants.

"Are you going to play again?" she asked, after she thought she understood how the games worked.

Well, I sort of have to. I didn't want to be here for days to "win" back my money. "I had planned to. Want to watch?"

She nodded eagerly and she started to pull out a stool at the table where we stood. I shook my head and steered her back toward Marge's table.

Sue leaned in to me and whispered, "Why this table?"

I shrugged. "I was winning here. Call me superstitious." She mused about that for a moment and then smiled. She believed me.

"Are you both in?" asked Marge with a calm face. Her question actually was, "Are you both supposed to win here?" I thought about it for a second. It would look better overall for both of us to win but I didn't want Sue to get sucked into this too far. She's a bright girl. I figured she'd understand the concept and why I needed to launder the money, but I didn't think she'd want to be involved in the process.

Money laundering is a necessary part of my business. Large amounts of cash are hard to account for, even with a couple of businesses to run it through. Capone and Gotti never got busted for murder or racketeering. They got hammered on tax evasion. So I dutifully pay my taxes even if I have to break secondary laws to do it. But the less people involved in deals like this the better. I don't know how the casino works it into their books. Nor do I care.

I shook my head. "Just me." Sue looked at me in dismay. "Oohh," she said with a pout. I probably should have let her in on the plan, but it was too late now.

I lifted her hand to my mouth and kissing it gently. "You're my good luck charm. I don't want to play against you and risk losing."

She smiled. "Flatterer." Cookie spice and citrus licked at my nose. She tucked an arm through mine.

I anted and the game began. Sue watched the game and the people as well. She tried to whisper things to me but it was sort of distracting. Even when the odds are stacked to win, I still have to pay attention to the game. I put a finger to my lips and she shushed. I could tell that she wanted to play. After about an hour she started to get bored. She shifted in her seat constantly and kept looking around her.

"Can I go play the machines again?" Frustration edged her voice.

I nodded. "Don't go far. I don't want to have to track you down later. Try playing the keno machines. I think you'll like them." She nodded happily and wandered off toward the slots again.

Another hour passed and I looked up from my game and stretched. Marge took a sip of water from a glass, which was my cue to lose the next hand. Can't win every hand. It would be noticed. But I was already thirty thousand ahead. The crowd around the table was sizable. I glanced around the room to find where Sue was sitting. She should be very visible considering she was wearing bright yellow. I didn't see her. Oh, well.

There was a smattering of annoyed sounds from the crowd when I lost the hand and Marge gathered the chips from the table. I jumped slightly when a heavy hand landed on my shoulder. What now?

"We need to talk, Giodone," Bobby's voice hissed in my ear. "You've got trouble."

I glanced at Marge without giving any reaction to Bobby's warning. I stood up smoothly.

"I've got a call, Marge. Hold my chair." She nodded and raised one finger. A guard moved over to her side. She whispered to him and he sat in my place to keep the crowd honest. Another grey suit widened his coverage of the area in response.

I moved away with Bobby and said in a low voice, "What's up?"

"Like I said, you've got trouble." His voice was still low and strained. I couldn't catch his scent to see if he was lying or if he was worried. He *looked* worried. He kept scanning around us and checking the mirrors on the walls to make sure that we weren't followed.

When we reached a semi-private spot—not that there are many in a casino—I stopped him. "I'm not going any further until you tell me what's going on."

He crossed his arms over his chest and stared at me with angry eyes. "Does the name Jeffrey Prezza ring a bell?"

Ah, shit! "You heard about that, huh?"

"Hell, Tony! *Everybody's* heard about that. Well, anyone who matters. Anyway, I just overheard a conversation. Leo's setting you up. He called Vito Prezza and a couple of his boys are on their way over to collect you. That's why you haven't been winning so fast this time. They're stalling you. You need to get out of here."

Yeah. I did. But I started to wonder who was setting up *who*. Was I going to run right into their arms if I went with Bobby?

"Why would you care?" I asked with narrowed eyes. My instinct told me not to trust anyone I couldn't smell. I'd worked with Bobby before, so I knew he was capable of a double-cross.

He let out an exasperated noise. "Christ, Tony. I'm the good guy here. I still owe you my life from Panama. Other than that, you're right. I don't care. Granted it took a big pair of *cajones* to off the kid right at the precinct steps, but it was pretty stupid, too."

He was right about Panama. That had been another really bad week. "Okay, let's say I believe you. How long do I have?"

"Not long. Leo's getting ready to leave for a meeting so that he's not here when it goes down. I know a back way out. But you'll have to get your lady and get moving."

"Not before I get my money back, Bobby. Leo's got a case full of it."

"Leave the money, Tony. Let it go. I'll get it for you if I can, but you need to high-tail it out of here right now."

I saw Bobby's face harden as he looked over my shoulder. I turned to see one of Vito's goons walking toward the table where I used to be. Shit! How long ago did Leo call them? How could they be here already?

I was trying to figure out how to find Sue when she found us. The hallway where we stood wasn't on the way to anywhere. It couldn't been easily seen. But that damn wolf intuition told me it was how it was supposed to work.

"What are you doing here?" asked Bobby with a startled look.

She shrugged her shoulders and a confused blend of scents rose from her. "I don't really know. I just got the feeling that I should come over this direction, so I cleared out my machine. But here you are! Wasn't that lucky?"

Yeah. Lucky. That weird, eerie sort of lucky.

"We have to go." I grabbed her hand and started to lead her in the direction that Bobby and I had started.

She pulled her hand back and soured milk disbelief burst from her skin. "But we just got here! Where are we going?"

Good question. I turned my attention to Bobby. "Where *are* we going?"

"The garage. Let's go! Now!"

I followed without a word pulling Sue along behind me by the hand. When we reached a doorway near the end of a hall, Bobby used his keys to open it. Inside was a stairwell that was narrow and steep. This wasn't for the public to use. That was obvious.

"What's going on, Tony? I don't want to go down there." Her fear was back and it struck me in the face like a brick.

I had to tell her. I hoped she could handle it. "Look, Sue. There are some men back there that are looking for me. If they catch me, I'm toast. We have to leave. You have to trust me."

Her breathing stilled and her voice was quiet. Her scent was a rising anger that caramelized the tiny room. "Are the police after you?"

I snorted as Bobby darted down the stairs to try to find a vehicle for us. "I wish! No, I won't have to worry about the police if *these* guys catch me. And they've seen me with you. You can't afford to stay, either." I stared at her long and hard. "What's it going to be, Sue? What am I worth to you?"

Her jaw set as she made her decision. "Let's go. But what about our stuff?"

"Leave it. We'll buy new." I turned and headed down the stairway with Sue at my heels. I quickly pulled away from her so I could get to Bobby to help him find a car. I bounded down two flights of stairs at a good clip. I was halfway across the garage level when I heard a commotion behind me. I turned to see that a doorway had opened on the next landing up and the kid from the desk had emerged behind Sue. He grabbed at her and was trying to cover her mouth with a cloth. She pulled away and swung her denim purse at him. It hit the side of his face with a thud and staggered him. Good purse. I started toward them with a burst of supernatural speed.

He quickly grabbed her arm and ripped the purse from it. It dropped to the stairway like lead. She screamed once as he pulled her through a doorway, the cloth once again over her face. I felt fuzz try to cover my brain and I stumbled against the wall for a moment. What the hell? I shook my head and blinked a few times as the door latched behind them.

Bobby only caught a glimpse of me as I growled and headed back upstairs.

Chapter 14

I opened the door where the kid had gone. I dropped to the ground and sniffed. Bingo! Dead things in a summer forest. Something inside me went berserk. It ripped away the last shreds of haze clouding my mind. Bobby had reached me and tried to slow me down. He grabbed my arm with a grip of iron. I knew in that instant that he was like me, like Leo, but I didn't have time to dwell on it. I moved through the door with supernatural speed. I heard the sleeve of my silk shirt rip with a wet sucking sound. I left Bobby holding a swatch of cloth.

I followed the trail of Sue's scent, nose up, nostrils flared. Her fragrance hung in the musty hallway like mist, laced heavily with ammonia panic and the chemical scent of whatever drug the kid had used. I could feel something building inside of me as I tracked her down. Something dangerous. When I heard her first moan I re-doubled my speed and found the shaft of dim yellow light from the doorway at the end of the third hallway. I smelled gun oil and the kid's confidence. I smelled Sue.

He stood inside the small room with gun aimed at the door. He held a semi-auto 9mm in a comfortable knowledgeable grip. So young, so self-assured. So stupid. A single, bare bulb hung from the ceiling of the grey concrete chamber. The room had the scent of multiple deaths. Too many to sort. Some had been quick, some slow and tortured. The scent hung like a pall and made the room seem small and close.

Sue was in and out of consciousness, crumpled on the floor in the corner. She hadn't gotten a full dose of whatever the drug had been and was trying to shake it off.

I smelled Ben's pride at catching Sue; his lust, sweat and then his terror as he saw me race toward him. He moved quickly, tried to get a shot off but I leapt at him before he could fire. I ripped the gun away from him. It skittered across the floor to disappear into the shadows. New muscles flexed and I felt him raise off the floor. My fingers convulsed around his neck. He flailed at me with fists and got me with a kick between the legs that would have dropped me to the floor a year ago. I hardly felt it.

I casually held him before me by the throat for a moment. I tightened my hand until I could feel the elastic skin start to give. He clawed at my fist, gasping for air. While I held him I saw his thoughts. Heard his conversation with Leo where they nonchalantly decided how to torture Sue once Vito's boys had taken me. Decided what acts would hurt me the most. I was supposed to die but not until after I knew what they'd done to her.

It didn't win him any points. I might have only hurt him. Not now. With one violent movement I snapped his neck. Sue didn't see what I had done. But I felt her tolerance of my act as well as a dark pleasure that surprised and frightened her. I saw the light in his eyes go out with a final surprised look. It pleased me.

"Jesus!" exclaimed Bobby from the doorway. He was breathing hard and stared with open horror at the scene. I held Ben's limp weight with one hand. His legs dangled above the floor. I turned and looked at Bobby. My lips were pulled back from my teeth and a nasty snarl erupted from me.

My stomach growled angrily and I battled the hunger again. What the hell was wrong with me? The moon was long gone. Why did I have the urge to rip out his throat?

Bobby swallowed hard but didn't back up. I had to give him credit.

"What the fuck *are* you, Tony? Ben was one of the best I've ever known."

My eyes flashed blue. "Better than me?"

He paused and considered. "Better than you *used* to be. What's happened to you? You're scaring the shit out of me here." He looked scared but didn't smell scared. In fact, he didn't smell at all, which was still confusing.

I dropped the kid to the floor with a thud. I turned and got a flash from Bobby as I brushed by him on my way out the door with Sue in my arms. I figured that he would be worried about Leo's wrath when he came back and found his plan ruined, whether or not Leo thought that Bobby helped. But that wasn't it. I sensed something else instead. A strength that was new to me. He wasn't afraid of Leo. He was higher somehow, more dominant. Dark images. Anger. Bobby had plans but they now must be changed. That was the worry. Everything was spoiled. Because of me.

"We've got to get you out of here," said Bobby, the anger rising into his voice. "Before they find us."

"I *want* Leo, Bobby." I had plans for him. I wasn't going to run anymore.

He was suddenly in front of me. His determination bit at my nose. His eyes were cold and hard. He stood right in my face. "No! That's not your decision."

I growled but he didn't back down. He sighed in frustration. "Look, Tony. I know he's got it coming. But there's shit going on that *you* don't know about. Don't get involved in this mess. Just take your lady and go. I'm serious here. Just go."

Sue was coming around. She rose to her hands and knees and shook her head.

"No! I want my money and I want Leo's head. He was going to hurt my lady!"

"I told you before. Walk away from the money, Ton," he said quietly. "I'll get it back to you if I can. But you've got to trust me on this. I'll clean up this *mess* you've left as best I can. Don't start a war you can't win. Let us take care of Leo. I promise you that he'll pay for this. I swear to you, man. My word."

I stared at him. There was something that Bobby was withholding. But then I looked at Leo's protégée lying at wrong angles on the floor, his eyes still open and startled. I sighed and Bobby took a deep shaky breath.

"Get us out of here in one piece and we'll call it square. But if you don't do him I *will* come back."

He nodded curtly. "I owe you nothing as of now. Right?"

I returned the nod.

"The only vehicle I could find is Leo's private limo. I took care of the driver. It's running. I was going to drive you, but now I've got to clean this up. Do me a favor and find another car before you get out of the city. I don't want to give him any reason to chase you."

I nodded. Sue could stand on her own. She shook her head again and blinked her eyes.

"What happened?"

"Let's get going. I'll explain on the way."

Chapter 15

I picked up Sue's purse at a run. Jeez! The thing must weigh twenty pounds! I handed it to her and she slung it over her shoulder with considerable effort as we flew down the stairs to the waiting car. I put on the chauffeur's cap and sunglasses that were lying on the dashboard. I couldn't hide the torn sleeve on my right arm. I had to hope that the guard wouldn't notice. Sue ducked down in the back. I put a finger to my cap as the gate raised, kept my arm tight to my body and smiled. The attendant did the same. The dark windows hid Sue's form in the back. Boy, would he hear about it for letting me out!

"It was nice of Bobby to give you back your case." Sue said after a few minutes. I glanced into the back in surprise, almost hitting another car in the next lane.

"He did?" Sue held up the case and damned if it didn't look like mine.

"See if you can open it up for me, will ya? The combination is 2192." I heard metallic clicking as she moved the dials and a snap as the latches opened.

"Is it all there?" I asked.

"I guess I don't know what *all* is," she replied.

"There should be about a million dollars in there. It's mostly twenties and hundreds."

Her scent from the back seat was surprise and disbelief. "No. There's no money here. It's all just documents and maps." I heard rustling paper.

I was getting annoyed that I kept hitting green lights. There was nowhere to park but I couldn't afford to anyway. I needed to ditch this car quick. I headed toward the suburbs to try to pick up a car from a grocery store lot. I really hate stealing cars. It's beneath me. And the second time in a month! Poor planning like this is a serious blow to my pride.

"There's a blueprint of a house and a bunch of things about some guy named Carmine Leone."

"What?" I turned my head again but snapped it forward when a horn blared beside me. I reached out my right hand. "Give me that blueprint."

"You can't look at it while you're driving!" Her voice matched the shock of soured milk.

"Just do it, Sue. This could be important."

She handed me the blueprint and I glanced at it while I drove. It didn't take much concentration. I knew the design immediately. It was the schematic of Carmine's house, all right, down to the security system. I had helped design it. What the hell was Leo doing with it? And why was it in my case?

The sound of screeching tires returned me to the car. I glanced in the rearview and found a black sedan quickly pulling up on our tail. Damn! There's nothing as conspicuous as a black limo in this town. They're *meant* to be noticed. I hit the gas hard and winced a bit as I heard Sue get thrown onto the floor from the force.

"Ow." She moved her head from side to side and I heard the joints crack back into place.

No time for sympathy right now. "Put everything back in that case and lock it up!" I ordered. "I need to look at everything in it. And see if there's any other paperwork back there, too."

"We can't take this!" Her anger bit at my nose. I'm getting really sick of the smell of burnt coffee. But at this point, I didn't care if she was angry or not.

"It's my case, Sue. There's got to be a reason why *my* case with *my* fingerprints all over it is holding documents showing how to break into *my* boss's house. Doesn't that seem a little suspicious to you?"

Her eyes widened in the mirror and she looked down at the papers in her hand. "Do you mean this Leo person is trying to frame you for something?"

"Looks that way. But I won't know *what* until I look everything over."

The anger scent slowly dissolved, to be replaced by thoughtful confusion. I glanced back at her in the rearview. She slipped inside herself. I didn't go with her. I was too busy weaving through traffic. I ducked through a cold red light before the oncoming traffic made it past the crosswalk. That did it! The black sedan did a nosedive as the brakes locked up to avoid getting creamed. I turned a wide corner and then pulled into the nearest alley. I just about had to hit the car on the other side of the street to make the turn. The doors barely opened far enough to exit in the narrow space between dumpsters. I removed the key and bent it in two. Then I tossed it on the seat. Like Bobby said, no reasons to follow. Leo probably has another key somewhere. I took the case from Sue's grasp and tugged her hand. She had a death grip on her purse with her other.

"Let's go!"

Her voice had a thoughtful edge and she stubbornly held her ground. "Why does Leo hate you enough to do all this?"

We didn't have time for this! I could hear squealing tires not too far away. "If I promise to tell you later will you get a move on?"

She nodded and we took off at a run.

We entered the next block and found ourselves in the middle of a group of elderly tourists. We tried to get around them, but they wouldn't be hurried. We tried to turn around to find another group of gamblers filling in behind. The casino in front of us was likewise packed with people. We were stopped cold. I looked back down the alley. With the limo in the way and the key useless, the pair of thugs had to struggle to get around to reach us. We had only a few seconds of respite. I sneezed suddenly as multiple scents assaulted my nose from the crowd. The primary scent was pineapple. God only knows why. I sneezed a second time and tried to edge us through the group.

"Slow down and enjoy the day, you two!" said a smiling woman with a cane and a bright pink sun visor that read, "Born to Gamble!" over thinning silver hair.

"Oh, look, Leonard!" said another elderly lady. "Let's take the shuttle." I glanced at the goons again. One of them was crawling over the roof. I turned at the old woman's words. Perfect! No grand theft auto for us today!

We waited in the crowd as the bus slowed and then stopped. When the bus door opened with a hiss, I noted that another one was just about to depart across the street. That's the one! It was heading in the direction I wanted to go. I grabbed at Sue's hand and pointed. She took another look behind at the commotion from Vito's boys. Her eyes got wide and we darted across the street. The bus was just pulling away from the curb and I had to rush to bang on the door with the briefcase. It stopped with a lurch and the doors opened. Fortunately, they hadn't gotten back into traffic yet. Sue was breathing hard as we stepped up the stairs. I was reaching for my wallet, hoping I had a couple of singles when Sue produced a bus pass from her bag. She handed to the driver with a flourish.

I glanced at her in surprise. She shrugged. "They were for sale in the casino store. I thought it would be easier to get around."

I grabbed her face with both hands and planted a kiss on her lips. "Good job!" She beamed at me as the driver handed her back the card with a shake of his head at our antics.

I turned to look behind as Sue settled into a seat beside me. Her heart was still beating fast and I realized that the pineapple scent was coming from her. I don't know that particular emotion yet. Or maybe it was the drugs. I looked at her closely. The edges of her nostrils were red and she was squinting a little.

"You doing okay? I don't know what the kid gave you. You look a little rough."

She turned to me. "I'm fine. I didn't get much more than a whiff," she replied. "I've got a little headache, but it'll be gone soon." I couldn't detect any pepper. Just pineapples.

The two men had finally reached the street and watched as our bus pulled out into traffic. One of them took off his baseball cap and threw it against the wall in frustration.

Sue was busily tucking the bus pass back into her purse.

"What the hell's in that thing?" I asked. "It weighs a ton!"

She looked sheepish. The scent of hot sand was edged with cloves. It blended with tangerine and the remaining pineapple. Fruit salad in the desert. Weird.

"I didn't have a chance to turn them all in." She reached into her bag and pulled out a large stack of oversized copper coins. I remembered her heaving it into the kid's head. I laughed—a sudden burst of sound that caused people around me to turn.

"You're a dangerous woman, Sue." My eyes sparkled with humor and pride.

It wasn't funny for long, unfortunately. I was angry with myself for going to the Lucky Strike. I'd nearly gotten Sue captured and I'd lost the whole damn million. Still, I'd replaced it with a case of dynamite. I just didn't know what the package was going to blow up.

Chapter 16

Renting a car didn't take much time. We used Sue's name for it. Leo probably wouldn't be able to trace us that way and she had more cash than I did right now. We didn't dare take a flight. Leo would already have someone posted at the airport.

By the time we reached the outskirts, Sue was finally relaxing. Ozone filled the rental from both of us as relief replaced adrenaline in our system. Hmm. Maybe pineapple is a rush of adrenaline. I'd have to do some investigating. I would have thought it would smell more bitter.

"So, are you going to tell me about Leo now?"

"Hadn't planned to." I said flatly. The question reminded me that I was still pissed at myself.

She looked at me with confusion at the strength of my statement. Her head cocked sideways a bit and she turned in her seat. The seatbelt cut into her neck.

"I want to know. Why does he loathe you enough to want to frame you?"

A burst of brittle laughter escaped me. "He isn't trying to frame me, Sue. He's trying to kill me. Whether Carmine does the job, or Vito's boys do it instead. He wants me dead."

"But *why*?"

"It's a long story." My voice went cold and empty. I stared at the road.

"It's a long drive," she replied tentatively, a small attempt at a joke to lighten the mood. When it failed, she shrugged. Emotions bled from her. Soured milk, just-burning

coffee, burned metal and antifreeze. Annoyance edged her
voice. Not quite anger. "If you don't want to tell me, fine.
It's your business. But I think I've sort of earned the right
to know."

True. More true than she knew. This wasn't over yet. I'd
had a chance to look through the case while we were waiting for the rental to be brought around. I didn't know
where he'd gotten them, but the papers documented a
series of intended hits on Carmine's various businesses.
There were names, addresses, as well as photographs and
schematics. The case held payrolls for Carmine's legit
businesses, along with schedules for material shipment for
the under the table stuff.

The problem was, I didn't know what the hell was being
planned or who was planning it. Was Leo planning a take-
over of our town? Was the case intended to go to Vito—or
to the unnamed person Leo was planning to meet? Or was it
even more sinister? Was the case going to be delivered to
Carmine along with photos of me walking through the
casino with it? My prints were all over the outside and
inside. I just didn't know. But I knew that Leo would want
it back. I just had to get it to Carmine before that happened.
I was hoping that someone's fingerprints, other than mine
and Sue's, were still on it. It wouldn't do much good to just
tell Carmine that the papers *smelled* of Leo.

Sue was sitting with her arms crossed. The nose-tickling
scent of her annoyance filled the car. I sighed. I *had* promised.

My hands flexed rhythmically on the steering wheel more
than once. Where could I start? I leaned back in my seat, trying to get comfortable. A little tough, given the circumstances. "Leo wanted my mom."

Sue smelled surprised, like she hadn't expected me to tell
her. Hadn't expected her appeal to matter to me. It sort of
annoyed me that it did.

"He wanted her bad. Rumor was that he went so far as to
actually court her. She couldn't stand him. *That* was from
her own mouth." I looked sideways. Sue was watching my

every movement, hanging on my every word. I looked back at the road. "He was a little perverted even then. Wanted to do strange things and my mom said no. Repeatedly. At first. he'd just back off and go. But over the years he got more insistent." I never saw Mom and Leo together. She'd always send me to my room when he would show up at the door. But I wasn't deaf.

"Early on, he never went so far as to beat her or rape her but he was loud. She had to threaten to call the police more than once." Sue continued to watch me intently as I drove. She really was interested in Leo's rationale.

"When Mom hooked up with my father," I said, then interrupted myself to add a disclaimer, "Keep in mind that most of this information is third hand since I wasn't born yet." I glanced at Sue and she nodded.

"Anyway, Mom told Leo that she wasn't on the market anymore. She really went for my father and he for her. She started tapering off her clients and intended that by the time she married him, she would be a proper wife." She always phrased it that way whenever she talked about it. "A proper wife." My hands tightened on the steering wheel. Part of me is glad that I never witnessed most of this. Part of me wishes that I had been there at my present age to break Leo's skull open.

"Leo went insane when she told him that she was going to get married. Leo called my father a lot of names—then he started calling her names. Joseph—that was my father's name—got to her place just as Leo had started to slap her around. He really believed that hitting her would change her mind. Joseph jumped Leo and pulled him off. Then he punched Leo in the face. Leo threatened them both. Said they'd never reach the altar." I paused, letting the hate wash over me. "They didn't."

My fingers started to drum on the wheel as I remembered the story I was told by Jocko. He was around for the end, a teenager when it happened. "Only a couple of months after that, Joseph was killed. There was gossip that Leo had a hand in his death. Mom suspected it. She told me as much when I was about the age in the picture you saw. She could never prove it, though."

I'll always wonder if anyone tried to help her pin the murder on him. Leo's an asshole but he's got a lot of pull.

"After Joseph died and Mom started to show with me, Leo came sniffing around again. He tried to convince her that she needed a man around if she was going to be a mother. Mom told him to shove off. Said she knew he had Joseph killed. Said she hated him and would die before she would ever let him touch her." I flipped on the left blinker and switched lanes to go around a slow-moving car. Sue's eyes were focused on me. I knew that she was creating a picture in her head to go with my story.

"If the Family hadn't been at her back, I think Leo would have just killed her right there. But they were being real attentive and apologetic to her for Joseph's death. There were flowers all around the house months later from the top dogs in the Family." Mom had always been proud of that. Proud that Joseph had been respected. That's a big deal in the Family. She kept all of the cards they sent. I found them after she died.

"Leo couldn't have helped but notice. So he left her alone. But I'm a constant reminder of what he couldn't have. What he never had."

I laughed, a harsh sound in the closed car. Sue flinched at the ugly sound. I heard a snarl in my voice as I continued. "And he's a constant reminder of what he deprived me of. I could have had a real family if not for him, instead of a whore with a broken heart for a mom and no father. It was only luck that I ended up with a dad. It's the only reason that I've never killed him outright."

Sue was silent for a moment. I could feel her discomfort, smell her concern and sympathy. "Wow. That's quite a story. I see now why you reacted like you did." Her voice continued with a note of confusion. "But is that all there is?"

I looked at her sharply. "Isn't that *enough*?"

"For you to hate *him*, sure," she said. "But for him to try to kill *you* all these years later? Just because your mom wouldn't sleep with him? That is just really out there." Her eyes blinked and a blend of confused scents muddied the air.

"People are strange, Sue. Look at Bosnia and Serbia. Those guys are fighting for things that happened *centuries* ago, between people that are long dead. This isn't nearly as strange. All I know is that the first time he saw me at Dad's house, when I was eight, he swore that he would see me dead."

Sue was open-mouthed. So was I when it happened. He had laughed at my expression and walked out. I never told Dad what he said. Leo was my battle, not his. I paused for a second, and then amended.

"But first he has to ruin me. Those were his words. *I'll ruin you, kid. Then I'll dance on your grave like I danced on Joseph's.*"

As soon as I said the words, it hit me. I knew which scenario he was planning. I shook my head angrily as the picture cleared.

Vito's boys would take me back to New Jersey and rough me up for a few days. Then Leo would hand over the case to Carmine, saying he "found it in my room." Sal would be able to back up that I'd gone to see Leo. Vito would turn me over to Carmine as a gesture of good faith. It would be Carmine who would finish the job. Like I said, *nobody* crosses him—not even me. Vito would be satisfied, Leo would be satisfied and both would have clean hands. I would be the bad guy. Torturing Sue was probably just a pleasant bonus to him. Clever. Very clever.

"I'm having a hard time even imagining that level of hate," Sue said with still-wide eyes. "I guess you're right. I've heard of things like that. I've just never encountered it first hand."

I shook the scene out of my mind. Fortunately, Leo's plan was blown out of the water now. I had the case. I was in control. Carmine would be able to do a little housecleaning—find out the leak in his organization. I was confident he would think of a suitable demise for Leo.

I just wished I could have *thanked* Leo personally for his clever plan. Hell, the whole thing had to have been on impulse. He couldn't have known I decided to go to Vegas or that I'd end up at his place. Or could he? When's the last time I checked the hotel room for bugs?

A jackrabbit hopped across the road and I blinked suddenly. I swerved to avoid it and just barely succeeded. It brought me back to myself and threw a question into my mind. Now there's a segue for you—from a nearly squished rabbit to a purse full of copper.

"By the way," I said. "Why did you fight so hard against the kid? He would have killed you just fine and you wouldn't have owed me a dime."

The question startled Sue. She stared at me open-mouthed and her jaw worked noiselessly for a moment. "I—I don't know." Her eyes darted from side to side as she tried to think through the logic.

"Why did *you* save me?" The best defense is a good offense. Fortunately, I was expecting it.

"For the money. I lost a million bucks today." I left my voice flat and looked at her with raised brows. Then I returned to looking at the road.

She studied the side of my face for a long moment. I kept it straight. No good. I heard her mind whispering doubts.

She raised her nose in the air and tried to appear haughty—baiting me. "Well, I hired *you* to do it clean and neat. I didn't know him at all. He probably would have messed it up and left me alive."

Okay, good one. A chuckle escaped me. I looked at her, with her eyes sparkling humor, and then made a quick decision. I flipped on the right blinker and pulled over to the side of the road. The tires locked and skidded slightly in the thick blown sand. The road was nearly deserted; not surprising considering the heat and the fact that it was the middle of a workday.

I unhooked my seatbelt and turned to face her. The intensity of my gaze made her suddenly nervous.

"I couldn't turn anyone over to Leo. *Especially* not you.

You've become surprisingly important to me in a real short time." Scary but true. I picked up her hand and held it in both of mine. The rush of power grew with each passing second. Sound roared in my head.

"God knows I didn't plan it. There's something between us that I don't understand. It's deep and overwhelming and scary as hell." I felt her thoughts swim by me as I touched her. Scary. But I want it; need it.

"I'll promise you something." I said.

I became very serious. Because this was serious. I released her hand and she drew it back. I didn't want to be distracted. I locked my eyes on hers and spoke to the person behind them. "I don't make promises lightly and I keep them." She sat quietly, hands in her lap, listening to my words.

"I'll keep you safe. And I'll try to keep you out of the bad parts of my life. But, Sue, it's who I am. I won't change for you. I'll shield you from the danger and from the law as much as I can. But, it may not be enough. So if you want to walk away, do it now."

I could feel the fear rise off her like heat. Yet there was something else there too. An affection, more than desire but less than love. She shook her head. Then she reached out for my hand and I let her take it.

"I've never known anyone like you, Tony. Your life scares me. I can't deny it. But *you* make me happy." She smiled more brilliantly than the sun. Warm, baking bread filled the car. "Even when I was terrified in the garage I was happy 'cause I was with you. So if I have to live in your life to have you then I'll do it."

I sighed. The snake coiled tight inside me relaxed. It was what I had hoped she'd say. Funny, I didn't realize it was what I wanted until she said it.

A semi drove by at top speed and the wash of air rocked the car. It moved me forward slightly and I kept moving on my own after it passed.

I closed my mouth over hers gently. I braced a hand on her door. A pulsing warmth passed through me along with the familiar tingles. This close, I could hear her heart beat and heard it speed up until the beat matched mine. We stayed like that for a time, mouths together, jaws still and quiet. Tongues dancing together in warm wetness. Just tasting each other. I loved the taste of her. I wanted to be near her. Wanted to drown in the scent of her.

My right arm was balanced on the top of her seat and I moved my left arm until it rested on her lap. My bare forearm and hand pressed against the skin of Sue's thighs. Nerves tingled where they touched her skin. I moved my hand slightly and caressed her skin. Her reaction was strong enough to that brief touch that I felt a frantic surging in my groin. It didn't start out to be sex but I wasn't adverse to it progressing that way. Her scent changed to the deep musk I was getting addicted to.

I eased my hand underneath her cotton shorts, then inside the second layer of silky cloth until my fingers rested against her. Her breathing increased and I felt her heart skip a beat as another semi passed by, sending us swaying. I twisted my body until I could get my right hand behind her head and bury it in her soft curls. A roll of power grew between us. It raised every hair on my body. The longing inside of me wanted to pull on it but I fought it down and concentrated on her pleasure. I thrust the silvered power back into her and felt her whole body tense as it swept through her.

My mouth locked over hers as I rubbed her slowly. Her arms were trapped between our bodies and the seatbelt kept her tight against the bucket seat. The only part of her that could move was her hips and she wriggled and squirmed under my touch. My jaw ate against her mouth in time to my hand motions. My tongue teased her as well. Slow then fast, until she could take no more.

A startled sound escaped her when she fell over the edge. I felt her body tense under mine and then go slack as she floated on a hazy cloud. I moved back from her to watch her face. Her eyes were in that half-closed position that only occurs after. Not quite sleep but not truly awake.

She laughed shakily after a moment while I feather-kissed her cheeks and lips.

"On the side of a highway in Nevada! Life is never dull with you."

I chuckled.

She never opened her eyes before she drifted to sleep.

Chapter 17

It took almost eight hours to drive to an airport big enough to have a direct flight to our town. It had been a long day at the end of a long week.

I can't sleep in a car so I was nearly dead when we arrived. I offered to let Sue stay to sleep off the trip but she wanted to get home. I thought I should probably go into the office, or stop by to see Sara, but screw it. I needed rest. However, I did try to call Carmine about the case. He wouldn't be home until the game. I told Marvin I'd see him then. It wasn't something to be discussed with an employee.

I gave Sue my home number and she gave me hers. I suggested maybe doing lunch the next day or something similar. I remember mumbling something like "See you later. Love you." I wasn't sure that I was in love with her yet but I was definitely in lust. They're different things.

The shrill ring of the phone woke me up with a start. I squinted at the clock across the room through sleep-filled eyes. It said 7:10. The bedroom curtains weren't quite closed and a shaft of fading sunlight highlighted my feet, lumpy under the covers. It wasn't even night yet. Ooh, boy. A whole two hours sleep.

I picked up the receiver on the second ring. Only a few people know the number at my house.

"'Lo?"

"Tony?!" Sue's voice was shrill and panicked. "Oh, thank God. I've got to see you! Right now! It's worse. Oh God, it's so much worse. Damn it!" I felt her anger like it was my own. All that was missing was the scent.

"Hey, hey," I said soothingly, now fully awake. "Slow down. What's the problem?"

"She's in a wheelchair, Tony. She's really gone over the top this time. There's a nurse and equipment and . . . Oh God! I just can't deal with this!"

I kicked off the covers and rolled to a sitting position. Her voice faded slightly and I knew that someone had tapped into our conversation. Probably on an extension.

"Listen carefully, Sue. Can you meet me at the place where you first saw me?" I was hoping she would take the hint to give as little information as possible.

She didn't even slow down. "Please come here. I really need to see you! Please, Tony."

I sighed. About half an hour later, I found myself driving the Mustang slowly down an older paved road. I'd at least taken the time for a shower, but I was feeling pissy. It probably wasn't the best day to meet her family. Oh, well.

I didn't recognize the address when she first gave it to me so I looked it up. 10522 Vivian Drive. It was way out in the country. I finally found the number on a brick gate post. I turned into the cutoff and found a gate. Luckily, Sue remembered that she had a security fence so I had the code. Out of habit, I glanced at the fence as I pulled up. It needed serious work. As it was, it was pretty useless for keeping people out.

I pulled up to the little box and opened my window. I entered four digits—4628. I shook my head again. A clear pattern that anyone with a lick of sense could guess.

A green light flashed and the wrought iron gates clicked open and swung haltingly inward. Hmm. Maybe a loose connection. Or they could just need oil.

Large trees blocked my view for more than a few feet as I entered the drive. Not good. When I could finally see the house I had to stop the car and stare. It was impressive enough for two stares.

The house stood slightly elevated on a hill. The graceful wrap-around front porch beckoned and the white paint gleamed in the sunlight. Jesus H. Christ! It was Tara! An exact replica of the Tara plantation from *Gone With the Wind*.

It's one of Linda's favorite movies. She loves sitting in front of that damn television with a box of tissues and a big bowl of ice cream. I can't imagine why—the battle scenes are almost laughable. I really don't get the attraction of watching something for the sole purpose of weeping uncontrollably.

I drove the Mustang around the circle drive and parked right in front. A Geo Metro painted English Racing Green was parked just in front of me. That had to be Sue's real car. It suited her.

Sue must have been waiting for me to arrive because the door opened just then and she ran out. She was crying, but from anger, not hurt or pain. Her fury caught me in the chest. It was hard to breathe past the flood. I was barely out of my car when she threw herself into my arms. I hugged her for a moment, nearly sneezing in the process from the scents that engulfed me, and then convinced her to walk with me outside. I didn't need anyone to overhear.

When we were a sufficient distance from the house and blocked by the trees, I turned to face her. "Okay, what's up?"

She snuffled and wiped at her eyes with a bare arm. "It's happened again. This time it's her other hip."

I felt my brow wrinkle in amazement. "She threw herself off the balcony again?" Wow! Now that's just impressive.

"No, no. The doctor said it's because of stress. But she can't walk. What am I going to do with her, Tony? I can't take this anymore." She sounded about ready to scream. No doubt.

Uh, wait. Stress related hip failure? What a load of b.s.

"Who's in the house right now?" I crossed my arms and settled my stance, body centered and solid.

She took a deep, calming breath. When she spoke, it was a little steadier. "Mom and the nurse."

"Where'd the nurse come from?"

"Bekki. Apparently, it's okay for *Bekki* to hire a nurse." The burnt coffee bit at my nose. "Of course. *Bekki* can't afford to lose her job. *Bekki* has a family to help support; a *husband* to take care of. *I* have no reason to be running off and imposing on poor Bekki's family. I have nothing better to do and should have the *simple courtesy* to stay around."

She was trying hard not to believe the words but part of it was a lie. She *did* believe it.

I didn't comment on the discourse. "What doctor told you it was stress?"

She shrugged her shoulders, but her scent was a little confused. "Mom's doctor, of course. Where else would she get the wheelchair and the other stuff?"

Yes. Finally, the light was dawning.

"Supply houses deliver." I let her assimilate that information, open-mouthed. The emotions rode over each other until all that was left was scorched coffee.

Her eyes narrowed and her arms crossed over her chest. "That little BITCH!" she exclaimed ferociously. I like anger. It's a damn sight better than depression. Maybe it would make Sue take a leap to get out of this hell hole.

I looked in her eyes and saw the pain of all the disappointments and intentional cruelties that had been her life. Even angry, her eyes had a haunted look. But wrapped around it all was an innocence, pure and real. Sue still couldn't comprehend betrayal or pettiness. She wasn't jaded. Yet.

She deserved better than to get that way.

As much as I wanted to make the hurt go away, I wasn't ready to get in the middle of a family battle. Now that the immediate crisis was over I could work with her.

"Look, Sue, it won't do any good to confront her. She'll just deny it. Let's do something constructive and help you cool off a bit."

I led her back to my car and removed a metal clipboard. "I'm your security consultant as of now. There are some things you need to fix around here. I can't be here twenty-four/seven. It won't take long before people know we're an item."

My jaw clenched at the scent of the beginnings of fear. She'd made her choice, but the scene in the garage had shaken her a little more than she's like to let on. I tried not to notice.

"Let's just keep honest people honest and make the job a little harder for the rest, huh?"

Her eyes grew wide and slightly panicked.

"Look," I said quickly with cold fire in my voice. "Sometimes danger finds you. It sucks. But there's no reason to live in fear if we fix a few things." I reached out and touched her face with the back of my hand. "I'll keep you safe. I promised you that."

She stared into my eyes and believed the promise. I hoped I could live up to it. She nodded, determination growing through my touch. "What do we need to do?"

The first thing we did was change the passcode to the gate. Sue admitted that it had never been changed since she moved in. God knows how many people had the combination at this point. I picked a number that was uncommon. Random, without a pattern, is best. Then we walked around the perimeter of the brick wall surrounding the "plantation." The barbed wire was old and hung limply from its guides. We'd need to replace it. Next, I pointed out several trees towering overhead. Sue trailed along behind me as I made notes, nodding somewhat uselessly. I knew most of it wasn't sinking in, but the point was to get her mind off her mom.

"These will need to be trimmed. A person with a ladder could reach up, grab these branches and go right over the top of the wall."

We toured the grounds. It was obvious she was trying to make the place the showcase it had once been. The grass had been cut and aerated. Years of pine needles and leaves had been removed and new sod had been laid. She was proud of the work that she had done. I could smell it. She pointed out her room on the second floor. The window was surrounded by a cloud of multi-colored roses climbing on trellises. I'd have to take a close look at those from inside.

Next she showed me the swimming pool. She had been right about the geese. There were droppings everywhere. The large birds ignored Sue completely as we approached, but when I got closer, they milled nervously. I tried to speed up the process and barked like a dog. Except it didn't come out like I intended. I planned on it just being a funny moment. But the sound came from deep in my chest. Low and threatening and just like a wolf. Funny thing. The sound ended with a vicious snarl and I felt my lips pull back from my teeth. Sue looked at me a bit alarmed when the geese suddenly took to the air in a panic. Loud honking accompanied their flight and soon the ground was clear of unwanted visitors. A part of me wanted to go after them. Chase them down until the hunt was over. Fortunately, the moon was far enough past full that I could fight it down.

I must have looked as startled as Sue. Her voice was filled with amazement, "I felt that! How do you live every day feeling those things?"

She felt it? I tried to shrug it off. "I've gotten used to it. Fortunately, I don't like goose. Too greasy." Her eyes widened for a moment. Then I smiled. Once she realized that I was teasing her she laughed.

She hesitated when we stepped onto the wide front porch—no, more a veranda.

"What's up?" I asked.

"I'm just a little nervous. I've given you such a negative build-up of Mom that I'm afraid when you meet her you might not want to stay with me."

"I haven't exactly said I would yet, remember? But why wouldn't I?"

She struggled to find the words. "So many people believe her. I'm afraid that maybe I *am* the one who's nuts and you'll believe her instead of me. Or that you'll see her just like she is and won't want to stay with me with her around." She glanced up at me nervously and then lowered her eyes. She was embarrassed again.

I reached out to her, put a finger under her chin and raised her face. "I've spent a lifetime learning how to read people. It's a necessary skill in my trade." She opened her mouth to speak and I shushed her with a finger to her lips.

"I promise I won't judge you by what I think of her. Okay?"

She got an amazed look on her face. "Every time I think I've got you figured out, you surprise me. You have such strong opinions that it's hard for me to believe that you could sit by and keep quiet if you didn't like something."

That brought a dark smile to my face. "Well frankly, if I dislike her enough I'll probably try to scare her."

She looked alarmed. She grasped my arm frantically. "No, that won't work. If you scare her, she'll call the police. She's done it before. I don't want you to risk that."

I removed her clutching hand with a smile. "I know, Sue. It's okay. I was kidding. No scare tactics. It usually backfires. No, I'll kill her with kindness. It's one of my specialties."

She grimaced. "She'll see right through that."

I chuckled. "Doesn't matter. All she'll have are suspicions. I'll be sweet and thoughtful and very, *very* patronizing."

"And I'll do my best to keep a straight face." Sue gave me a weak smile and turned toward the door. I stopped her by touching her arm. Then I pulled her back and led her out to near the parked cars.

I made my face serious. I'd met people like Sue's mom before. "You should know that she's going to try to put a wedge between us. She'll make wild accusations. Without knowing a thing about me other than what's printed on my business card, she'll say that I'll put you in danger or that I'm just after your money. She'll tell you anything to scare you off from me. Some of it may even be true. Can you stand up to that kind of pressure? If you can't then it's better for us not to even start this. It'll only get worse if I move in."

"If?" Her voice was several notes higher as she said it. Her scent was a mixture of thick dew and tang.

I sighed. "I gotta tell you, Sue. I have a house and I like it. It might be better to just see each other on the side and not live in the same place. We'll have to see. Especially if you can't handle the pressure."

She listened and while I was speaking her jaw set. The hot metal determination nearly made me smile. She had decided and she would stick by it. "No. I want this. I'll do my best to handle it. If I can't, then we'll make other decisions."

I smiled at her. She would try but I wasn't sure she could do it. "Let's go in and greet the lion, then. But let me do the talking." She nodded.

"Let's start with me as the "security consultant," not your lover. We'll tour the house and I'll let you know what you need to have done. We won't mention the monitors out loud but I'll look them over as we go. Afterward, we'll go to my office to sign the paperwork."

"And where will we go instead?" she asked with a knowing smile.

I looked at her seriously and raised my brows. "To my office to sign the paperwork. So I can get started on repairs."

"Really? I mean . . . I thought . . ." I understood her confusion. I reached into my back pocket and withdrew my card case. I don't always carry it with me, but I'd grabbed it for today's visit. I opened it and handed her a white business card with black lettering and a swirl logo.

She took the card and read it out loud. "Specialty Services, Inc., Security Consulting, Anthony Giodone, President. You have a whole *corporation*?"

I chuckled. "Of course. I really do handle security systems. I rent out an executive suite downtown. Most of my clients are Family but a few are legit. It gives me something to do during working hours. It's also useful to have the run of the town after dark for my *other* job. Anything I install has a back door built in for my use."

"If you have an office, why did I meet you at that awful bar?" The sourness of her distaste drifted on the breeze.

"I'll tell Jocko you said that." The insult in my voice wasn't all faked. My face probably showed it.

She blushed and fidgeted. Embarrassment and shame replaced the distaste. She keeps forgetting these people are my friends.

"Hey, I'm kidding." But by the flat tone of my voice, she could tell I wasn't and flinched. "I meet clients at the bar to put them at a disadvantage. Keeps them nervous. It worked, didn't it?"

She nodded several times—vigorously.

"My office is in a high-rise downtown. I pay rent to the owner. He hired my company to install and maintain the security system in the building. So if you want me for *future services*, and we agree on terms, the transaction will be nice and clean."

Normally, I don't work for clients—because of that whole "known to associate" thing. But this one had a built-in cover. *Gee, Lieutenant. She was a rich client who paid her bills. Why would I want her dead?*

Her eyes grew a little wide right then. "Oh. About that." Her eyes shifted away from me.

My voice took on a sharp edge. "Getting cold feet?"

"Well, actually . . . I mean . . ." She looked up at me then and her expression grew warm. There was fear in her eyes along with something else. Something deeper. "I think I might be falling in love with you, Tony."

I recognized the smell. But I couldn't accept it for what my nose told me it was. She looked at me hoping for a reaction. She got one, but probably not the one she wanted.

I shook my head. "Please don't. It's not love you're feeling. It's lust. Or crisis bonding. It's intense but it doesn't stick. Doesn't last through day-to-day life. We can't possibly be in love yet. Not yet." The cold knot of fear that thought put in my stomach made me realize things may have already gone too far. Shit.

"Look." I put hands on her shoulders, deliberately keeping her at arm's length. "Even if there's something there, I'm keeping distance intentionally. I'd never be able to pull the trigger if I let it go too far."

Sadness filled her eyes and my voice softened a bit. "I decided when we first were together that if you wanted to get away from life bad enough to hire someone like me, it would be wrong to deny you. I'd be using you. Just like everyone else. Keeping you around because *I* wanted something. Do you see?"

She nodded. "But what if there comes a time when I decide I *want* to live?"

I felt a surge of hope and immediately crushed it like a bug. "Aren't we getting a little ahead of ourselves?" I deliberately injected a note of dark humor in my voice. "You haven't paid me and I haven't agreed to do the job."

She smiled shakily. I returned the smile, but my next words were serious. "Let's take it a little slower and see, okay? You may decide that you don't like me all that much."

She put one hand over mine on her shoulder. "I won't change my mind. Are you ready to go inside?"

I watched as she steeled herself. A buzzing began overhead and I glanced up to see that the old mercury vapor lamps dotting the yard were just coming on. My brow furrowed slightly as I looked at her. I lifted her chin with one hand and turned her head from side to side slowly in the flat white light. She gave me a puzzled look and I sensed her confusion.

"What are you doing?" she asked when I released her chin. I sighed and shook my head.

"We're not going to do this tonight, Sue. I'm going to go home now."

"What! I mean . . ."

"You've got dark circles under your eyes and your skin is sagging. Neither of us has gotten a good night's sleep for days." *I* hadn't slept soundly for almost a week. "If we go in there now and get started, it's going to be hours. I get grumpy when I'm sleep deprived, so I'm going to go home and you need to go to bed, too."

"But what about Mom? I can't go back in there alone, Tony. I just *can't*!"

"Sure you can. You just walk right in, ignore her, and go upstairs and go to bed."

"But she'll follow me, yelling. I'll never get a wink of sleep."

I smiled darkly. "Your mom's got hold of a double-edged sword this time, Sue. It cuts both ways. If she follows you to your room, she'll have to get out of that wheelchair, won't she? The nurse will back you up on it to your family. If she stays in the wheelchair, she's stuck downstairs, and you get to sleep. See?"

A shock of scent rose from her and her eyes looked startled in the growing circle of light. "But I don't know if Bekki paid the nurse to stay overnight."

"It's well past 5:00. If the nurse is still here, I'm pretty sure she intends to stay. She must have at least stayed last night, so she's already got a room in there somewhere."

"But I'll still hear Mom. The entryway echoes through the whole house."

"What? You don't have a stereo in your room?" I rolled my eyes. "Please." Then I fished in my front pocket and removed a small plastic packet containing orange pieces of foam. "But if it'll make you feel better, put in earplugs."

She looked at the plugs with delight and squished them through the plastic. She watched as they returned to their original shape and then did it again. I tore open the package and showed her how to compress and roll them and then insert them into her ears. I made her tap lightly until they expanded. One ear took a couple of tries to get it seated correctly. When she took them out and tucked them in her pocket, I continued.

"The plugs don't completely remove sound. They just dull it. You'll still be able to hear muffled loud sounds, but it won't be enough to keep you awake."

She reached forward suddenly and planted a whopping kiss on my lips. A hot wave of need flowed through me. My body was suddenly as hard and ready as the first time I touched her. I wanted more and I reached for her hungrily. But my brain fought the need. I balled my hands into fists before I could wrap her in my arms. No. I was *not* going to start again. I forced my hands to reach for her shoulders and I gently pushed her away.

"Get some sleep, Sue. I'll stop by first thing in the morning when we're both feeling better."

She backed up and nodded. She was feeling too many things for my nose to sort. I could relate.

Chapter 18

Where is he? He should be here by now.

I opened my eyes slowly and blinked several times. The words that I heard in my mind weren't a dream. I could feel tension and anxiety pushing at me, but distantly. I glanced at the clock and swore. It was already 9:00 in the morning! Damn! The last time I'd slept for twelve hours straight was—well, the last time I'd been *awake* for a week.

I started a pot of my favorite coffee. *French Market* blended with flavored fresh ground. Irish Creme works best. The scent of it brewing rode over the steam of the shower. I struggled to free my head of restlessness. I just knew it was Sue's frustration I was feeling. I didn't get why it was happening, but it feels the same as when I touch her and get her thoughts. Maybe I was spending too much time with her.

I booted the computer to check my e-mails and began to pick up the pots and pans scattered around the living room and bedroom. I'd been so exhausted last night that I was afraid that I'd miss the burglar alarm if someone broke in. So, I used a low-tech solution—I stacked three metal pans underneath each of the windows and turned out the lights. Anyone defeating the security system would make a bunch of noise. It's enough to wake the dead.

I was sipping an oversize mug of java and reveling in the scent. It never tastes very good after mint toothpaste, so I just enjoyed the scent for the time being as I sat down at my desk. The software informed me that it was downloading 32 messages. Well, there went my morning! Against my better judgment, I decided to check my voice mail. Let's see, with the Atlantic City job, the moon change, and the trip to

Vegas, I'd been gone for nine days. There were probably fifty messages waiting for me. I grabbed a pen and pad and started to work.

After I'd had to re-write a message to a customer for the third time because it sounded arrogant and condescending, I was sick of Sue's frustration pushing at me. I picked up the phone and dialed the number that I'd already memorized.

"Hello?" Sue's voice sounded like she felt in my head. All that was missing was the burnt metal scent of her frustration.

"Would you chill?" I snarled. "I've got to get some work done here. Go read a book or take a hot bath or something. I'll be by when I get business taken care of!"

I could feel her start in my head and then embarrassment washed through me. I hung up without waiting for her to reply into the receiver.

I'd probably been too harsh, but I had a life, damn it! I couldn't be there to hold her hand every second.

Once I listened to all the voice mails—I'd guessed high, there were only twenty-seven—I had a list of clients that I had to visit. But first, I needed to work off the rest of the tension in my shoulders.

I changed quickly into shorts, T-shirt and sneakers. Once again, I set the alarm, even though I wouldn't be gone for long. Atlantic City and Vegas still stuck in the back of my mind. Paranoia keeps me alive.

I checked my mailbox on the way out. No surprise that there was nothing in the box except a yellow card informing me that I would have to go to the Post Office to pick up my mail. It had sat too long.

"Mr. Giodone!" came a voice from across the street as I started to take the note back to the porch. "Tony?"

I turned to see Mary Stickey, my long-time neighbor. She doesn't like me much, but tolerates me because I'm quiet and I keep the lawn mowed. She was holding a box.

"Yes, Mary?" I asked tolerantly. The frustration I still felt made it hard to be civil. Mary always smells like Dr. Pepper. I'm not sure if that's her base scent, but she is always prying into everyone's business, so maybe it's antifreeze. It's not a trait I like in a person. Still, it keeps me on my guard, so she's useful.

"The UPS man was here yesterday. He's been by several times and asked if he could leave a package for you with me. Well, of course, I told him he could."

"Of course you did." The words came out a little sarcastic. Damn busybody. But I put on a smile when she started a bit and smelled disapproving. She handed the box over without another word. I glanced at the address and recognized it. Fortunately, the company doesn't advertise on shipping boxes, and it hadn't been tampered with, so she didn't know what was in the package. Mary also didn't know that she'd just made my day.

"Hey, great!" I said sunnily. "I've been waiting for this."

"It's so heavy," she said and the potent antifreeze scent of her curiosity overpowered the vinegar of her earlier disapproval. "And what a strange size."

The narrow box was about seventeen inches long. Yep. Just enough for packing material around it.

I didn't comment on her implied question. "Thanks, Mary." I turned and walked back to the house. From the corner of my eye, I saw her stamp her foot before grudgingly turning to go home.

On the porch, I noted what I had apparently missed in my exhausted state yesterday. Three gummed notes—all from UPS, telling me that they had tried to deliver a package on different days, and now it was waiting at their office. I guess after I didn't show up there, they tried one more time. I punched in my code to turn off the system and put the messages and box on the kitchen table next to the pad of clients to visit.

That done, I turned off the coffee pot, set the alarm a second time, and left once more for a run. I resisted the urge to open the box. I knew what was in it and I could play with my new toy later. First I would need to deal with business and Sue.

It was hours later when I finally got to her house. "What took you so long?" she asked.

I shook my head wearily. "You would not *believe* the day I've had. God, but people are idiots some times!" Even a long run and a couple of sets on the bench press in my gym hadn't prepared me. Usually a run will keep the wolf at bay and I can be professional and courteous. Today it had been a chore.

Sue's scent had started as embarrassed but frustrated. She'd kept her distance when I arrived and I could tell that part of her was annoyed with me for being late. She was also annoyed with herself for needing me to be there at all. But the air around was slowly turning to curious. I took off my wrap-around mirrored sunglasses as we walked into the shade. I joined her on an ornate, wrought-iron bench and tucked them in the pocket of my grey polo shirt.

"What happened? Was it that Sara woman again?"

I gave a little wave of my hand. "Yeah, her and others."

"Were you able to fix the sensors in her shop?" Sue was honestly curious. I could feel it and smell it. Okay, sure. I could let off a little steam.

"There's nothing wrong with the sensors, Sue. There never is at that store. It's always employee error or actual thefts. I had to give *yet another* demonstration on how to nullify the magnetic strips. The check-out clerks hadn't read the memo that said hardback novels are now carrying sensors in the center of the book, near the spine. They were just scanning the bar code but not running them over the demagnetizer. Every book that went out of the store beeped. But that was easy. At least I was in and out of the place in under thirty minutes."

And I'd decided that Humphries' Department Store was about to get a whopping increase in their annual maintenance charge. I figured that if I tripled their fee, maybe they would move their business, or at least hire someone with a lick of sense to manage. I had made more than twenty service calls in a single quarter. That's just ridiculous.

"You figured it out and gave a demonstration that quickly?" The clove scent of her pride blended with surprise.

"It didn't take a brain surgeon. All I had to do was watch

the clerks for a few minutes. I *wrote* the memo. It was obvious that they hadn't read it."

"You must have had a lot of calls to handle after being away for so long." She was trying to give me the benefit of the doubt.

I shrugged and shook my head. "Not too many, really. Most of the calls were billing questions. Bookkeepers always complain about my bills until I show them an itemization. I just had a lot of things to do."

I didn't want to make excuses by blaming my clients. I wanted to prove that I could continue on with my regular life, despite her existence. But whether or not I wanted to admit it, I had to struggle constantly all day not to come over and be in her arms. I really hated how tough it had been.

"Do you bill every time you go somewhere?"

I chuckled. "Only when they're idiots. Fortunately for my pocketbook, that's pretty often. The annual fee covers quarterly check-ups on the equipment and routine maintenance. If it's employee error, it gets billed."

I could feel that she didn't understand. It'd be easier to illustrate. "Take this doctor's office I went to. Just after I left to go to the east coast—before I met you—the last person out of the office forgot to lock the front door, but set the alarm. The wind kicked up, opened the door and the alarm went off." I glanced at her and saw that I had her full attention, so I continued. "The security monitoring company called the police. They checked it out and found nothing wrong."

I leaned back then and stretched my legs. I arched over the back of the bench and heard a couple of satisfying pops as my spine slid back into place.

"But why would they call *you*?" she asked.

"You've got me. The monitoring company turned off the siren by remote after the false alarm. On most systems, all the lights blink after a reset until you enter a three or four digit code. It's all explained on a sheet that I give customers when I install the system. I even wrote down the name and number of the monitoring company supervisor. There's a copy for each person with a key to the building. But did they even glance at the instructions?"

"No?"

I shook my head with a patronizing look. "No, they didn't even try. So, I'm gone for, like, nine days. This whole time, the system has been down. It's just merrily blinking away on the wall. They're just damn lucky that nobody walked in and cleaned out the place."

I shook my head as I remembered the rage of the two doctors who owned the building when they'd found out. Of course, they're *never* the last to leave, so they didn't know about the alarm until I presented my invoice. Several of the front desk girls had been terrified they'd be fired. The scent of their fear had made me ravenous enough to stop and pig out on a triple decker burger on the way to the next call.

"And, as always, there are the employees who forget their codes and can't get in the building, or can't remember their codes so they write them down on paper and lose them. Then I have to pull out the laptop and assign a new passcode in the master computer. It was all typical stuff. It was just annoying and tiring."

I saw Sue flinch at one point during my tirade and it reminded me.

"By the way, what was the emergency this morning? You seem fine now, but you were really antsy earlier."

She looked at me and the dry dusty heat that spoke of embarrassment and shame burst from her. "I guess I'm one of your idiots. I forgot the code for the gate and nobody could get in or out of the estate today."

I stared at her for a moment, open-mouthed. I shut my jaw and tried to think of something to say that wouldn't be interpreted as an insult. "But you wrote it down. You asked for a sheet of paper, and then tucked it in your pocket. It can't have gone far."

"I did?" Her look of alarm was blending with the anger. She thought for a moment. "You're right! I did." Burning coffee and dust seeped off her, slowly intensifying until it filled the air. "Then I must have lost it. I can't believe that I was that stupid!"

I reached out and put a comforting hand on her arm. I moved it up until it rested on her neck and then rubbed the muscles gently.

"Hey, don't be too hard on yourself, Sue. You were exhausted. It's why we both went to bed last night. It's no big deal. Really. What did you do all day?"

Her mood began to lighten as I rubbed and she relaxed into the massage. "Actually, it was a pretty good day. I got the whole upstairs cleaned! Then I read a book and relaxed in a long bubble bath for the first time in months."

I forgot to rub for a moment. "You don't have a house-keeper? You clean this place by yourself?" She'd already explained why baths were impossible. Every time she would try, her mother kept interrupting, asking for stuff and being generally annoying.

This time, I earned the patronizing look. "No, of course not. I have a housekeeper that comes in once a week—today. But she can barely keep up with the kids. Fortunately, *none* of them could get here today."

"Kids?" I'd never thought to ask, but that could be an issue in a long-term relationship. I don't *dislike* them, precisely.

She caught the tone of my voice and shook her head. "No, not mine. Bekki's. And frankly, after dealing with them for the past two months, I may *never* have kids."

"So you babysit every day?" That would explain why she'd gotten beat down enough to want to kill herself.

She nodded angrily. "You might as well say that. Actually it was *Mom* who agreed to watch the kids for the summer. It just ends up being me because Mom never does the things that need to be done."

"Such as?"

"Mike has T-Ball, and Cindy has swimming lessons at the Y."

"But your mom doesn't drive. Why would she agree to take them? And why would *Bekki* set it up to fail?"

"I told you. I'm supposed to be attached at the hip. What

Mom agrees to, I'm part of. It's the way it is. I'm usually happy to take them somewhere, though, because otherwise they destroy the house. They play tag and knock something over, or leave the kitchen a disaster because they "made cookies" when I went to the store. Last week, Mike dropped a crystal punch bowl from the top of the stairs because he wanted to see whether it would explode. Big surprise—it did. Mom never makes them clean up. That's *my* job."

I suppressed a smile when Sue mentioned the punch bowl. I did a similar thing when I was a kid. Of course, I *did* have to clean it up and got grounded for a week to boot. "Well, the timing's good for us to do this today, if the kids aren't here. Remember what we talked about, though—"security consultant", right?"

She looked at me and winced. Then she smiled bravely. Tangerines filled the air. She leaned over and gave me a hug. I returned it with interest. "I'm glad you're here," she said.

Chapter 19

A moment later, we walked through the massive oak doors and I was greeted by my first sight of Sue's mother. I had to admit that she was truly pathetic looking. I almost laughed but that probably wouldn't set the right tone. Sue glanced at me but couldn't read my expression. Blank is one of my best expressions—I've had lots of practice.

Myra Quentin sat in a wheelchair with a nurse standing primly at her back. Her face looked pained and her eyes were dark with a sunken appearance. She hunched slightly in the chair and rested heavily on one armrest. She made herself as small as possible by scooting in the seat. Her legs shook visibly from the strain.

The problem was, she smelled of deceit. Lies upon lies until the black pepper smell made my nose burn. She also smelled like that buzzard daughter of hers. Not Sue. The blonde witch. That made me immediately more wary than I might otherwise have been. Well, that and the sharp smell of vodka that hit me like a wind. Odd that Sue hadn't mentioned mom was a drunk.

Myra's eyes were bright with suspicion and anger. That's not a real common trait in someone truly sick or injured. Pain dulls the eyes. If she had an injured hip she would favor it and keep weight off it. Sue told me it was her left hip that had been replaced. She should be leaning on the left hip, instead of the right, supposedly injured one.

When I looked closely, I could see that the pale face and sunken eyes were make-up. The dark circles from truly sunken eyes are actually blue from irritated blood vessels under the skin. Her "sunken" eyes were created by brown eyeliner. I could smell the waxy cosmetic. The dark wasn't uniform, meaning it had been applied somewhat hurriedly. Her nose was slightly more pale than the rest. Tsk. A bit too much facial powder. She probably pays better attention to detail when she's sober.

I glanced at Sue to see if she noticed. I could feel in my head her embarrassment and frustration at her mother's transparent ploy. What I couldn't figure out is why Sue had never called her on it. Part of me wanted to reach out and rub a finger through the liner and say, "Oops. Missed a spot." But again, not the right tone.

I could tell Sue's mother had once been a pretty woman. Now she was unattractive. It was intentional, which made it worse.

I decided to try a soft approach. I squatted down in front of the chair. I wanted to be eye to eye with her to watch her reaction. The smell of vodka nearly knocked me over. I had to breathe through my mouth to stay in character.

"Mrs. Quentin," I said loud and slow, "my name is Tony Giodone. How are you today?"

Her eyes flashed with anger and her voice was filled with venom. I pretended not to notice. "I'm in pain, not deaf. Idiot!" Hmm. I'd have thought she would try nice first. Try to swing me over to her side. Okay, Giodone. Time to pour on the charm.

Keeping in character, I raised my eyebrows and appeared apologetic. I lowered my voice to conciliatory. "I'm very sorry, Mrs. Quentin. Sue mentioned that you hurt your hip. Can you stand at all?"

Her eyes lightened and her head rose slightly. The sweet, cloying, black peppery scent of deceit and dark glee overpowered the alcohol for a moment.

Her sigh was heavy and faked. "No." She was pleased that she was apparently fooling me. She smelled more like Leo than I'd care to think.

"It's just the stress of everything lately. I do wish that I wasn't such a *burden* on dear Suzi." I glanced at Sue, who smelled hurt and angry again. "I'm sure that an old, crippled woman cramps her style." The words ended with a knife edge.

My response was saccharine sweet. "Well, that's about to change, Mrs. Quentin. May I call you Myra? I'll be around more to help Sue take care of you."

I smelled Sue's surge of hope and I flinched internally. Jeez! Why did I say that? The logical part of me knew I needed to keep my distance but I just couldn't seem to stop myself. I managed to keep the pleasant, professional look despite being startled.

I saw Myra's eyes light up with distrust and a healthy edge of foreboding. Still, she tried for the soft sell. "I prefer Mrs. Quentin, thank you. I'm afraid I don't understand, Mr.—Giodone, is it? Why would you be around more?"

I glanced at Sue as though in surprise. It wasn't all faked. She kept a straight calm face. Attagirl! I looked back at her mother and said, "Didn't Sue tell you? I'll be moving in to the basement." My voice dropped at the end. It held a note of finality that disturbed me a little. Meeting Myra decided it. I didn't like the smell of her. She smelled like a threat to my mate.

That stopped me cold. Mate? It's not a word that I've *ever* used to describe a girlfriend, but I didn't have time to think about it now. Not with Myra right in front of me.

My voice was cold but calm as I continued. The threat needed to be *very* visible.

"I've been hired to handle the security for the estate and be a bodyguard. You won't ever take another fall like you did." I smiled and it was probably the same smile the snake gave Eve. "I'll make sure that you're taken care of in the *exact* way you need to be."

I was hit by a blast of scorched coffee scent. Honest shock and anger shattered the act. She could sense I was on to her so she changed her tactics. She didn't bother to be subtle.

"We don't need any help here! So you won't be moving in. Get out!"

"Mother!" exclaimed Sue. "You said you didn't want the nurse, and what about that horrible man who called? We need to have someone around. It's my house and I've made the decision. Tony stays."

I was getting a headache. The burnt metal of Sue's determination and frustration overpowered the carmelized coffee from her mother.

Myra's eyes narrowed for a second before they returned to schooled innocence. The coffee scent did go away. "But, Suzi dear, that will be so expensive."

Sue's jaw thrust forward and her voice was steady. "I've got the money, Mom. Remember? Aren't you the one who told me I should reimburse Bekki for the nurse since it was *my fault* that she had to be hired. You said that I've been frivolously wasting my money and I should be spending it on something useful. Well, this is useful. And you won't take it away from me!"

Ooh, bad move. We probably should have discussed the script a little more. I could already hear the reply. A new wave of anger exploded into my nose, cranking my headache up another notch and tickling my nose enough that I had to fight not to sneeze.

Myra pointed a shaking finger at Sue. "Don't you dare use that tone with me, Suzi Lynette Quentin! I don't want some strange man living in my basement. We don't know anything about him. He could be an axe murderer for all you know!"

Yup, that was the next line.

Sue turned to me with an expression of stubbornness. "Are you an axe murderer?" Her voice quavered with anger.

I thought for a moment and then smiled darkly. "Nope. Never used an axe before. I could try it if you like."

Myra's eyebrows shot up and her hand went to her mouth in shock and disapproval.

"*Tony!*" Sue spoke through clenched teeth. There was a brief blast of annoyance. I guess I wasn't helping.

I fought not to grin. "Sorry. Mrs. Quentin, I've been hired to *protect* you. I've been in this line of work for years. I'll do my best not to intrude on your life. You'll hardly know I'm here. But I will be here. For your benefit and for Sue's." There was a trace of warmth in my voice. It was intentional.

"Bedded her already, have you?" Myra turned and glared at Sue. "You've always been weak. Your father hated that about you." I didn't react but Sue jumped like she was struck. Hot wetness filled the air and tightened my throat.

"I tried to raise you to take some pride in yourself." She shook her head in disgust. "But look how you've let yourself go. It's disgraceful." Myra reached out slapped Sue's thigh with stinging force. She winced as a red handprint blossomed on her skin. "Look at that flab. No wonder you have to whore yourself. You know he's only after your money. What *decent* man would want you?"

My eyes narrowed and I struggled to hold my temper in check. "What you believe," I said coldly, "doesn't concern me. But understand that the decision has been made. Whether or not you approve."

Myra glared at me. Her arms tensed on the chair and I thought that she was going to rise out of the chair and strike me. God, I could hope! I wouldn't hold myself responsible if she did. But no. She turned her fury to Sue who visibly flinched. I stepped closer. I didn't give a shit who she was. No way was she going to attack my lady.

"You are going to regret this, Suzi. Mark my words. This decision will cause you no end of grief." From the look on her face, I could tell who would be at the giving end of that grief. I turned to face my new adversary. I let my eyes grow cold and deadly. White anger flared between us.

"I hope that we can work together, Mrs. Quentin. Sue needs both of us to keep her healthy and happy. I'd rather work with you than against you to achieve that goal." That at least was the truth.

"Her name is *Suzi*," Myra said sarcastically. She addressed Sue: "I'm sorry that you don't like your given name enough to use it. It was your father's favorite. But I guess that doesn't matter to you, you stupid ungrateful slut."

Sue was near tears. We needed to end this confrontation.

I looked down at the middle-aged actress in the chair. My words were steel. "I'll be moving in by week's end."

I moved a fraction of an inch closer, invading the hell out of her personal space. She leaned back in the chair in response. Good. The blast of alcohol scent was nauseating. "Understand that *Sue* hired me. I will report to her and her alone. About *any* threat to her." With that promise I stood and turned toward Sue. Myra's anger and indignation beat at my back. I didn't need to smell it.

"Are you implying that I am a threat to my own daughter?" Myra asked loudly. Her offense was genuine but there was guilt there, as well. "Well, I don't need to sit here and be insulted!"

I didn't give her the satisfaction of looking at her. "No. You certainly don't. You're welcome to leave any time you wish." Sue got an alarmed look on her face but I shook my head the smallest bit. She bit her lip and kept silent.

"Suzi, aren't you going to say anything." The tone was an order not a question.

Sue swallowed hard and closed her eyes. "Only that I think it's time I showed Tony where he'll be staying." I blew a kiss at her as a congratulations. She let out a slow tense breath that Myra couldn't see through my body.

"I *see*," said Myra. She glared daggers at my back. I could smell the roasting jalapeños of her hate over the stench of alcohol. "Well, I wouldn't get too comfortable. If you manage to move in at all you won't be staying long!"

I could afford to ignore her so I did. I took Sue's arm and led her away. I glanced at the nurse as we left. Her eyes rolled and she let out a disgusted breath. Personally, I wouldn't stoop to earning a living by catering to whining hypochondriacs. But to each their own.

Sue's steps were shaky at first but she gained confidence the further away we walked from her Mother.

We toured the upstairs and Sue pointed out the location of the hidden monitors. No good. The coverage was too sketchy. Luckily, I have a friend in the business.

Entering Sue's room was an experience. The smell of flowers was overpowering; the pollen in the air thick enough to walk on. Twin trellises overflowed with climbing roses just outside the open windows. Pink on one side, yellow on the other. Only a screen kept out the dozen bees flitting back and forth.

The trellises had to go.

Sue scowled when I told her that. "No! Those trellises are the only reason I took this room. I love them right next to my window!"

I was surprised at the strength of her response. I glanced at the positioning again. "Well, I guess we can trim the trellis below the window."

"Absolutely not." Her arms crossed over her chest and her stance was final. The hot metal of her determination bit at my nose. I could see she wasn't going to budge on this one.

"Okay," I amended, opening the screen and looking outside to get a feel for the construction, "How about we move it off to the side where it can't be used as a ladder?" I brought my head back inside before the bees could follow. "Or we can install windows that can't be entered. Those are the only choices that won't get you killed."

"The roses are wonderful in the summer." She was lost in thought. "They're the best part about the house. I'd rather fix the windows."

"It'll cost you. But . . . if it's that important to you." She beamed a smile at me. It made me sigh again. I was turning into a softy for that smile. Bad plan.

However, her mood made it a good time to bring up a sore subject. I closed the door and heard it latch. Arms over my chest and I centered my stance. I kept my voice low and locked eyes with Sue. "How long has your Mom been an alcoholic?"

Her expression was dumbfounded. "What are you talking about? Mom doesn't drink! Why would you think that?"

A harsh laugh exploded from me before I could stop it. She continued to look confused. Wow! That level of denial was more than *I* would be able to fix, but I had to at least try.

"Remember I can smell things other people don't, Sue. The woman *reeks* of vodka."

The wheels started spinning in her head and she paced the room for a moment. I could hear her thoughts as she moved around the room. It can't be possible. He must be wrong. But Grace at work was and you didn't notice that until she went into treatment. Oh, my God! What if he's right?

She didn't comment one way or the other, but when we walked back into the hallway, she was shaking. She tried to talk normally, but it was a lie.

She showed me the basement next.

It really was a full basement—nearly the size of my whole house. It was decorated in dark walnut paneling and burgundy carpets. The paneling could stay but the carpet had to go. It was too somber with both. I said as much to Sue.

"Pick any color you want. Buy new furniture if you don't like this. But please stay." Sue was almost frantic, thinking I might change my mind after meeting her mom. Especially after learning about the vodka. I could smell it, feel it inside me.

I looked from the full kitchen to the huge bathroom that dwarfed mine. A regulation pool table sat in the den, balls racked for the next game. A pinball machine rested against the wall. Sue would be just upstairs. Always. She could come downstairs or I could go up.

"I'll probably regret this . . . "

Sue grinned broadly and threw herself into my arms with an exclamation of joy. Citrus and baking and spices galore.

I hugged her in return. "Remember what you said, though. Come and go as I please. Right?"

There was a flash of fear and jealousy that didn't bode well. I decided to keep the feeling warm so I steered her toward the bedroom with the king size bed. She tried to pull back.

"I can't!" Her loud whisper echoed the frantic pounding of her heart. "Mom's upstairs!"

"We're not fourteen." My smile was both gentle and

amused. "We're allowed." I pushed her backwards and she ended up lying down on the bed after a gentle bounce.

"Besides, I take my job as bodyguard very seriously. If I see the slightest hint of danger," I said, as I fell on top of her, "I'll throw my body on you."

She giggled. I kissed her.

"What's the danger?" Her voice was thick with amusement and the beginnings of desire. I tried to focus on her words, but my body wanted to control. I pointed to the ground. Her eyes followed my finger to a small black cricket making short hops across the floor. "It could be poisonous." I ruined the serious words by grinning. She laughed.

The doorbell rang and it echoed through speakers in the downstairs living room. Good engineering. I approve.

"Mom will get it." She kissed me deeply.

The realization hit me and I pulled upward sharply. I scrambled off the bed and headed toward the stairs.

"What's wrong?"

"We changed the code at the gate. Who could have gotten to the door?"

Her hand flew to her mouth. "Oh, God! Mom!" The musk of her desire was suddenly replaced by sourness.

She moved quickly enough that she beat me to the stairs. I grabbed her arm roughly and pulled her back behind me.

The Sig came out from where it hid in a holster underneath the polo shirt. In one quick motion, I jacked a cartridge into the chamber. I heard voices as I entered the main floor. The nurse was unconscious on the floor. An old acquaintance, Vinny Coblentz, stood over Myra's wheelchair. Vinny is Family on his mom's side. His dad doesn't really approve of his career choice.

One beefy hand rested on each arm of the chair. His Baretta 9mm was visible in a shoulder rig under his sport coat.

"We can make this easy or hard, old lady." He smelled like wet clay. I'm not real sure what emotion that is. Maybe it's just him.

Myra Quentin was sputtering angrily. "Why, you . . . you bastard!" Vinny smiled. He always did like that term. He works hard to live down to it. "You can't just barge in here and threaten me. I'll call the police!"

He shook her wheelchair roughly and she shrieked. I glanced down as an amber pill bottle dropped to the floor. My eyes focused in on the tiny print. Interesting! Generic oxycodone, commonly known as Percocet®. Well, well. Not just a drunk.

Vinny laughed just then. He knew the old lady wasn't a threat, so he was toying with her.

Maybe she's not. *But I am.*

Sue tried to push past me but I held her back firmly and used a sharp look to command her to stay put. Her expression was frantic, her scent ammonia with panic, but she did as I asked. She moved to where she could see the scene and still remain protected by the thick walls.

I pointed the Sig at him at hip level as I stepped out from the stairwell. "Back off, Vinny," I said.

He looked up and reached for his piece at the same time. "Don't even think it!" I brought the gun up into a two-handed grip with preternatural speed and stared down the barrel at him.

His hands froze. He raised them away from his body and then backed away from the wheelchair. A greasy lock of sandy-colored hair fell across his eyes. His voice was condescending. "Well, well, Tony the Nose. Haven't seen you in a long time."

"Likewise." I walked toward him. I stretched forward while holding the gun steady and took his Baretta from the holster. He didn't try to stop me.

"This ain't your turf," he growled after I stuck his gun in my belt. Myra was actually too surprised to speak. Sue had entered the room and stood by her mother's side, watchful.

"It is now. These ladies are under *my* protection."

"Thought that wasn't your thing." His eyes narrowed slightly and he smelled suspicious.

"I've been hired as their bodyguard." The truth is always simpler than a lie.

He lowered his arms slowly, watching my body language as he did. In a moment his grey eyes cleared. "Bodyguard, huh?" He accepted the statement with a nod. Then, as is the proper way, he began to address me as the protector, the head of the family.

"The old lady made a deal with me, Tony. She owes me money. She's been avoiding my calls. I feel insulted." He put his hand over his heart to show his sincerity. He actually *did* smell offended. "I gotta collect. You know that. It's the only way to make amends."

I shook my head. "She hasn't got any money, Vinny. She promised you money that ain't hers to give."

"I don't care where the money comes from. Promises have been made. I offered her services. She accepted. If she's hired you now, fine. I'm willing to negotiate." The statement was flat but he kept his eyes locked on mine. I had the upper hand. He had no choice but to negotiate, but he would be stubborn. Trouble was, I agreed with him. That wasn't to Sue's benefit. Damn it.

I motioned at him with my gun. "Let's discuss this outside." I wanted to know how he got into the estate. Vinny wasn't one to climb trees. Also, I wanted him away from the ladies in case the "negotiations" got ugly.

He walked toward the door. I didn't like the way he was moving. His scent changed. Like he was getting ready to pounce. I slapped him on the back of the head with the Sig. "Don't try it, Vinny. Blood's tough to get out of hardwood." He stopped, nodded without turning and opened the front door.

I followed him out and we walked toward the gate. There were no additional cars in the drive. "How'd you get in, Vinny? You're not a climber."

He shrugged. "It's an old system. Cut the electric feed and the gates pop right open."

That was annoying. "You don't have to cut the power to the whole estate?"

He stopped walking, turned and looked at me. "Why should I tell you? What's in it for me?"

We were out of sight of the main house. I removed his 9mm from my waistband and popped the clip with my thumb so that it dropped on the ground. I handed him back the unloaded gun butt first. He looked surprised but took the gun.

"Open the chamber," I held the Sig nice and steady in a one handed grip against my body.

He jacked back the slide and a single bullet jumped into the air and landed near the clip on the ground.

"Happy?" he asked sarcastically.

"Don't bitch. I didn't have to give it back."

He followed the logic. "Yeah, okay. So, anyway, what's your piece of this? You're a bodyguard like I'm Santa Claus."

I thought about lying, but questions were going to be asked anyway. It's a surprisingly small Family despite the number of people. I shrugged. "The daughter's my new lady. She hired me to bodyguard her and the mother. It'll even be on paper."

"Shit. Well, that sucks! I'm going to have to go through you to get the money I'm owed?"

I shook my head. "There won't be any money, Vinny. Not for protection. How much the old bat promise you a month?"

"Ten grand," he said sullenly.

I whistled. "Protection's gone up a little since I was in the biz."

He pursed his lips and shrugged one shoulder. "I'd have done a good job. Kept all the other vultures away."

"No vultures will get past me, either. It's time to leave, Vinny." I reholstered my Sig. I could handle him without it. I walked him to the gate and could smell that he was annoyed. He turned and faced me and I thought he might take a dive for me.

Violent anger suddenly flashed through my body, charging my muscles with adrenaline. It wasn't mine. Somehow I

knew that but it affected me the same way. I fixed Vinny
with a look and saw his eyes go wide. I could see the glow
in my eyes reflected in his. Well, that's a first this far from
the moon. I'd have to work on that. I forced myself to calm.
The wolf inside me settled down. Like it was a separate
thing. A dog on a leash.

"Yeah sure, Tony. Whatever you say." Ammonia replaced
the burnt coffee. I *wanted* him to run, hoped he would run
so I could chase. He left carefully. Slowly. Damn.

I waited at the gate until he drove off. My muscles were
trembling with energy. My eyes twitched. I'd never had this
strong a response so far from the moon. Deep down I knew
it was because of Sue. The pleasure, the bonding—it was all
making the other qualities that I'd been repressing come to
the front. The wolf inside waited with confident anticipation. I was being led by my instincts toward an end I couldn't
see or understand. I didn't like that I couldn't look around
the next bend.

With Vinny taken care of for the moment, I went to check
the fence. I saw what he meant. There was a separate feed to
the fence, direct from the pole. There was no need for him
to cut the house. I walked back up the drive, musing on how
to secure the electricity. I caught the tail end of a discussion
that appeared to have been going since I went outside. It was
mostly one sided. Myra was raging at Sue, trying to drive in
that wedge. It was Sue's anger I'd felt. I listened outside the
door for a few minutes.

"For God's sake, Suzi!" I heard Myra shrill. "He knew the
man's *name*."

Oh, please! So did she.

Sue's voice was conciliatory, despite her anger. She was
trying to appease her mom. That wouldn't be my choice. I'd
scream right back at her.

"That only proves that he's talked to him, Mother. You
knew his name too." There was a pause. "Besides, what
good is a bodyguard who doesn't know which people are a
threat?"

"They had *guns*, Suzi! Is that the kind of people that you want in this house? What about Bekki's children?"

That was Myra's problem, not Sue's. And it was the old bat's own fault for agreeing to Vinny's terms. It was lucky for her that Vinny respects me or he would have hurt them.

I almost felt it as Sue released an exasperated breath. I was taken aback when the words from her mouth nearly mirrored mine. Maybe the connection was working both ways.

There was anger in her voice. "You started this, Mom. Vinny came here because *you* made promises. You had *no right* to commit to things that involve me. And as for guns, you should be *happy* that Tony has a gun. What would we have done if that man came here and Tony *wasn't* here or didn't have a gun?" Sue's voice got louder, harsher. "Do you want to spend the rest of your life in a *real* wheelchair? He could have beat us, raped us, or even killed us!"

Silence stretched long seconds. I could hear the bitterness in Myra's voice along with surprise that Sue was talking back to her. "A *real* wheelchair. Just what are you implying?"

I opened the door just then and they both turned toward the movement. The nurse was no longer on the floor. I didn't know where she was. "Nothing, Mom. Just nothing, okay?"

She walked toward me and was going to put her arms around me but I gave a slight shake of my head. She stopped in front of me and smelled strongly of disappointment. Her breathing was fast. I could see the pulse in her neck beating furiously. These confrontations weren't doing anything good for her blood pressure.

"All taken care of," I said.

"Did you call the police?" asked Myra. "Has he been arrested?"

"No. He was merely trying to collect something he had been promised. I convinced him that it wasn't a good idea. He left. I'll call a friend I know to fix the fence. By the time I get back, the gate and the walls will be secure."

A blast of fear roiled into my nose. Both Myra and Sue looked nervous. "You're going somewhere?" There was an edge to Sue's voice I was coming to recognize. A combination of fear and jealousy.

You're *leaving?*" exclaimed Myra. "What kind of body-guard are you?" From the expression on Sue's face she agreed with her mother on that point. Uh, oh.

I took a deep breath. "Look, Sue. We need to go to my office, fill out the paperwork, and plan a schedule that works for both of us."

Sue hesitantly agreed. The nurse came out then. She was sporting a black eye that touched the edge of her greying blonde hair. Vinny must have decked her when he first arrived. She had her purse on her arm and was ready to leave. It was hard to tell with all of the other emotions floating in the room but I think she was afraid and angry.

I sighed. Sue wouldn't leave her mother unless someone stayed. One look at the nurse convinced me that she had quit whether or not she had actually said the words.

I pulled the nurse to the next room so we could talk privately. I took my wallet from my pocket and peeled off three hundreds. Then I wrote a phone number on one of my business cards. I handed them to the nurse as a single package and said, "Can you stay for a few hours more? I'd really appreciate it. We need to sign some papers just a few minutes from here. The number is my cell phone. Call it immediately if there are any problems. I'll can get here before the police. Deal?"

She glanced at the door. Her voice was a hiss. "I will *not* be responsible for that woman! She specifically requested a nurse practitioner so I could load her up with Meperidine. Her arms are so full of scar tissue that the injection had to go in her hip! She also pops Percocets like candy and washes them down with vodka. I will *not* participate in that abuse!"

I raised my brows. I couldn't disbelieve the nurse. No wonder Sue was messed up. I've seen others riding on that particular roller coaster. The nurse smelled angry and afraid. I smiled hopefully and peeled off two more hundreds. Her eyes followed the movement and greed added to her scent. I added a little flattery for good measure. "I really don't trust anyone else at this point . . ."

A sigh told me I had won. She held up a pair of fingers. "Two hours. No more. But if just one thing goes wrong, I will call 911 and wash my hands of her." She folded the bills neatly and put them in her purse. Then she turned and went back where she came from.

I decided that the money would come out of Vinny's pocket or his hide. The nurse wasn't even part of this. I just hoped she was the same one that treated him after I was done with him. It'd serve him right to get patched up with no pain killers.

Chapter 20

I went over the details of the bodyguard agreement as we drove to my office. It would cover all contingencies but have a specific exclusion for suicide. That's standard. You can protect a person from the world but not from themselves. So her death would appear to be a suicide. She nodded nervously. Worry and fear surrounded her like a cloud.

"How much?" she asked when I had finished the conditions.

I sighed. It had been tough to imagine watching her die. I could do it—I'd seen others I cared for go away—but I didn't like it much.

"A million." I didn't watch her face as I said it. I kept them squarely on the road. The resulting silence in the car seemed endless.

I finally glanced at her but it wasn't long enough to read her eyes. When I looked back again, tears were streaming down her face. I couldn't tell whether she was happy, sad or angry. The smells were all mixed. So I waited to hear it from her own lips.

"Deal." She started to cry into her hands. Great. I still didn't know what she was feeling. I guess I shouldn't be surprised at the tears. She's an emotional wreck right now. She could use someone to talk to who wasn't so *involved*.

Ah. I knew just the person.

I placed another call using the speaker phone attached to the cell. I really hate people who drive with a phone glued to their ear. A woman answered, "Good afternoon, Dr. Corbin's office."

"Hey, Karen!" I said. "Is John-Boy in?"

A deep-throated chuckle escaped her, but then she must

have heard Sue crying in the background. Her voice grew more serious, concerned. "Can I tell him who's calling?"

"Yeah. Father Guido Sarducci." I tried to ignore Sue sobbing beside me. She was exploding with anger and gratitude and pain. I started sneezing and nearly ran off the road. Damn, what a cocktail. I didn't even know if it had anything to do with me. I acknowledged her tears by handing her a tissue from a box tucked under my seat. She accepted it with a glance in my direction and I heard her blow her nose. I turned on the first road east toward the 'burbs.

"This is Dr. Corbin," said a pleasant tenor. "Who is this?"

"Trouble. With a capital T. How you doin', John-Boy?"

There was a sigh deep enough that it came over the speaker. "I really hate it when you call me that, Tony."

"Hey." I shrugged automatically even though I knew he couldn't see me. "You started it."

"We were kids! *I* grew up."

We could continue bantering all day but I had other issues. "Yeah, well . . . anyway, I need an appointment for a new patient."

Dr. John Corbin is one of the top psychiatrists in the city. He's also a childhood friend. I trusted him to help Sue get through some of her problems. I hadn't been lying. I wasn't a therapist or a social worker. John is. Sue needed someone to help her work through stuff—with her mom *and* with me. If she could heal some of her pain maybe there wouldn't have to be a final act to the play.

I really wanted to believe that.

"Finally decided to get your head examined after all these years, huh? About time." John knows full well what I do for a living. He's Family too.

"My head is just fine," I replied. "I'm perfectly well adjusted."

There was a pause. His voice grew deadly serious. "I wish I could believe that, Tony."

I didn't respond to that comment. Well-adjusted is a state of mind. Anyone—mother, hooker, teacher, accountant, killer—can be comfortable in their roles. I am.

"This is for a friend. She needs someone to talk to."

"Fine." A small sound that might have been a tired laugh came from the speaker. There was a pause and shuffling of papers. "I can fit her in next month, around the 20th."

"I'm about one minute from your office, John-Boy." Only a trace of humor remained.

"Tony! Jeez, buddy. I was about to walk out for the day."

I pulled into the parking lot and drove to the opposite end. "And I'm about to walk in." Sue watched me with amazement. "Let's see, the black Mercedes is yours?"

"Yeah . . ." he responded slowly. "Why?"

It was the only car at the north end of the parking lot. I parked cross-ways behind it. "I just blocked you in. Now you have time to see us." Sue laughed but the tears were still near the surface, hot and salty.

There was another long-suffering sigh. I have that effect on him. "I take it my patient is in the car with you?"

"Suzi Lynette Quentin. Have Karen make a file."

"Whoa, whoa. I know that name. Wasn't she on the front page last year? The Lotto winner?"

"The same. See, I even bring clients who can afford you. Am I a pal or what?"

He was laughing when I hung up. Sue got out of the car. When she looked at me, her face was etched with sorrow. I could feel her betrayal and hurt. "Even you think I'm crazy?"

I smiled at her and thought warm fuzzies that I hoped would reach her. "You're not crazy. You've just some stuff in your head that I can't help you with. I want you to make an informed choice on whether or not you want to end it. John will help you make that choice." She smelled surprised. Nothing more.

We walked into the building and checked in with the guard. I flashed my carry license and showed him my piece. He didn't ask to keep it but he did write down my name and permit number.

"Why do you call him John-Boy if he doesn't like it?" she asked as we entered the elevator.

I smiled at her. "His name is John Walton Corbin. The middle name is his mother's maiden name. Keeps the family heritage going, you know? So, John Walton? John-Boy Walton?" I smiled hopefully.

She got the joke but it wasn't as funny to her as it still is to me. I shrugged. "What can I say? It was a hot show when we were kids. Besides, he started it."

"You said that. How did he start it?" A little humor was finally reaching her voice as we stopped at the seventh floor.

It was nice to know that she listened well. "You heard what Vinny called me when I got the drop on him?"

She got an embarrassed look. "Actually, no. I was a little preoccupied."

"Tony the Nose. I've been saddled with that moniker for nearly thirty years."

She stared at me briefly and then laughed. "Tony the *Nose*?" Dr. Corbin gave you that name?"

I shrugged but grinned. "Hey, I had a big nose as a kid. I grew into it but nicknames stick."

"Tony the Nose . . ." she repeated and tried, without success, to fight back a grin. She smelled nervous but it was blending with amusement. Good. Nervous is better than hurt.

We reached John's office. The door had been propped open. I pushed it open carefully, shielding Sue with my body. She'd agreed to the fee. I might as well earn it.

John Walton Corbin, M.D., Ph.D., was sitting at the receptionist desk playing solitaire on the computer. The sugary smell of semi-sweet chocolate wafted to me. It's not an emotion. John just smells like chocolate.

"I think holding a doctor hostage is a felony in some states," he remarked as a greeting. His eyes were twinkling when he said it.

"I'll remember that."

He closed down the computer. "I told Laura that you were buying next time since you canceled our dinner reservations."

I snorted. "I have to buy every time. You're so damn cheap!"

He grinned and then turned to greet Sue. "Hello, Sue. I'm

Dr. Corbin. It's a pleasure to meet any friend of Tony's. His friends are some of my best customers. He's not insane but I've suspected for years that he's a carrier."

Sue smiled broadly and citrus blended with the chocolate. Nice. "Well, he's not dull." She glanced at me and I smiled. John's always been good at putting people at ease.

John led Sue into his office and I cooled my heels in the waiting room. I was glad that he introduced himself as "Dr. Corbin". I wanted to keep their relationship professional. I know I shouldn't be jealous, but damned if I didn't feel a twinge.

Now, I expected to hear their conversation. It's normal, considering my ears. It's why I stayed. I like to know things. But the other, that was just weird.

I didn't expect to experience her every emotion. All of the emotions that I know and a few I didn't blasted at me for over an hour. Not just smells, actual feelings. I fought through tears, laughter, lows, highs. I didn't know what to think when she told him about me.

She wasn't going to at first. But then he interrupted her as she stumbled along trying *not* to use the word, "Assassin."

I could hear the smile in his voice as he replied. "It's okay, Sue. I know that Tony kills people for a living."

Her voice was small, a tiny squeak of noise. "Oh."

Then she started to open up. She didn't tell him about the wolf part. It hadn't even occurred to me when we arrived, but it should have, damn it. I'll have to mention that subject is taboo. I'm not sure if John would believe her or not. He might, and that could be a problem.

But she *had* felt betrayed when I actually named a price to do the job. I sensed it, smelled it. Had she expected me to refuse the job? Wouldn't that have gotten the same reaction? I wish I knew what she wanted from me.

John considered what she said for a few moments and the silence stretched. Finally, he asked in a soft voice. "Do you understand why he did that, Sue?"

Her admission followed snuffling and blowing her nose. "No."

I had to agree. I *thought* I'd just picked a number out of the air. A high one, admittedly, but random.

"I know Tony's normal price for a job, Sue. The fact that it's so unusually high means two things: One—he cares for you a great deal. He doesn't want to see you dead, but he's a businessman. You asked for his services. He'll do it—make no mistake. But he set the price high enough to try to force *you* to refuse."

Sue's emotions soared. I could hear her heart skip a beat. Or maybe it was mine. Damn. I hate it when he's got me pegged.

"And two—he needs enough money to disappear somewhere for a good long time afterward. Somewhere where he can drown himself in a bottle, or at the tables, or be around so many people that he doesn't have time to think. He knows what he needs to get past losing you. He's smart, Sue. He understands psychology at an almost savant level." He added with a note of chagrin. "He certainly got better grades in college."

"He has a *degree*?" She sounded surprised. I was a little offended. She just doesn't get that this is a career choice, not merely the only thing I'm capable of doing.

"Yes, indeed—in business, with a psychology minor. It should have been his major, as talented as he was. I just kept going into grad school. He went . . . well, in a different direction. Still, I wouldn't suggest trying any manipulation on him. Ever. Be straight with him and he'll be straight with you. Provided he isn't lying to you, which he *also* does better than anyone I know."

No. Lying's reserved for business. Personal life gets too complicated. I'll keep my mouth shut, but I won't lie. John should know that, but I suppose this is a rare exception. I normally don't mix the two.

When the door opened finally, John motioned for me to step in. Sue passed me on the way. She watched the floor intently. She knew I had been a part of the session. She smelled guilty and a little afraid. I touched her shoulder as I walked by and she jumped a foot. She looked at me with startled eyes. I kept my hand on her arm and winked. A shy smile appeared but the guilt didn't go away.

John closed the door behind me. I sat down in a guest chair and noted his wall of fame. He has some very impressive pedigrees: Past-president of the National Psychiatric Council, Johns Hopkins, Notre Dame. All real; each one earned. I like having intelligent friends. Keeps my mind sharp.

He sat and stared silently at me for some time. I ogled him back. I crossed one leg over the other knee and leaned back in the chair. If we were going to have a stare-down, I might as well be comfortable. He smelled puzzled and a little annoyed.

"I'm not sure why you brought Sue to see me," he said. "I originally thought that you were looking for a trumped-up diagnosis . . ."

I gave a little sniff. "I wouldn't ask you to lie, John. I never have. And I don't think you're going to have to fake anything. What did you find?"

He tapped his fingers on the desk and took a deep breath. Then he leaned back in his high-back chair and laced his fingers behind his head. The springs creaked, sounding loud in the room. He stopped just inches before the balance would have pulled him over backwards. He took a second deep breath and let it out slow.

"You know I can't tell you that, Tony. However, I can say that she is very likely clinically depressed."

"No shit. I could tell you that."

"In short," he concluded seriously. "She's bordering on suicidal."

Oh, way beyond *bordering*. "I know." I nodded again to confirm it.

He dropped back to a sitting position abruptly, palms landing flat on the smooth wood with a sharp sound. His scent was mildew and burned coffee. Mildew must be amazed. Hey, I learned a new one!

Annoyance edged his voice. "Then why haven't you brought her in before now?"

I laughed and he frowned. "I just met the woman, John. This is the first chance I've had."

His anger reminded me that I needed to let him in on why I'd brought her in. I didn't want him to get the wrong impression, and assume I wanted her to be *treated*.

"The goal here isn't like your regular ones, John. She probably didn't mention how very suicidal she is." Although I knew she had. My voice flattened with edges of warning tones. John and I have a few philosophical differences. "Understand that she gets to die if she wants to, John. That's her choice. Your only job is to find out if she really *wants* to. I don't want her to spend years struggling from appointment to appointment with little hope of ever being happy. If she's ready, I'll do my job."

After a moment of internal sorting where his scent changed to thoughtful, he asked, "So what is she to you then, Tony? Why are you trying to help her, instead of just hunt her?"

"That's my business." My smile disappeared. He was fishing for confirmation on his guess to Sue. No dice. My words had a tone of finality. But he would have none of it.

"I've known you for years, Tony. I've seen that look before. You only think that your face is blank. But I can read you like a book."

I settled in. "Give me your best shot."

"You're in love with her." His face was serene.

"No, I'm not!" My temper flared.

He shook his head with amusement. "You always did fall for people with problems."

"Hey! Not always. What about Linda? She's normal."

"Linda?" He guffawed. "You think Carmine's wife is *normal*?" He rolled his eyes. "Wow!"

His face showed that he was feeling in control. He was wrong. I changed the subject. I didn't admit or deny his earlier statement. "Did she mention her mom's a junkie?" I knew she hadn't so John's raised brows didn't phase me.

He picked up his pen and cocked his head. "How would you know?"

I shrugged. "The nurse told me. Prescription painkillers, mostly—pops Percocets like candy". I raised my hands to add in the quotation marks. "Plus, she has track marks all over her arms." I raised one finger as I remembered, "Also, she's a heavy drinker. I smelled it on her breath."

He added the words "enabler" and "co-dependent" to the list on his pad.

When he was done I leaned back once more. I fixed him with a stare to bring him back to the subject. "So, can you make her happy? Or do I need to start making plans?"

He hedged just like a doctor. He grimaced so slightly that most people wouldn't have noticed. He leaned forward and rested his forearms on the desk, hands clasped in front of him. The body language and the scent said sincere and concerned.

"You know better than anyone that nobody is happy 24/7, Tony. We all have our doubts, our fears, our bouts of depression. I *do* think that I can help her make an informed decision. I think I can help her want to live."

See, there's that philosophical difference again. The concept that dying isn't an *informed* decision. Still, John's good. If I keep him on track, he'll end up doing the job I want.

I pointed a finger at him. "Without drugs." I'd met too many people that ended up more screwed up after they started taking medication. Then it really wouldn't be an informed decision.

"I won't prescribe them." His hands raised in a placating gesture. "I deal with behavioral problems. Sue is missing tools that most people are born with. She calls it backbone."

He waggled his hands. "As a tag, it'll do. She needs reassurance that she has value. She thinks she's worthless, ugly, unlovable. For a while, constant encouragement couldn't hurt. Congratulate her when she does something firm where her family is concerned."

He wasn't telling me anything I didn't already know. I wouldn't have even bothered to sit down with him except I didn't want him to know that I'd heard the whole session.

"Oh, I think I'll get plenty of opportunity for that after I move in. I'll be all alone with her and her mother."

"Move in?" I could tell from his scent that he had found a bone to chew on. That's right. Sue hadn't mentioned it. Interesting. He sat with his mouth open just an inch, the question trembling on his lips. Then he dropped it. He blinked but his face gave nothing away. His scent did, though. He'd just realized that Sue wasn't being completely open. It was a pretty big thing to leave out of the session. His words were quiet and calm.

"Well, that will help. Really, though, she needs to be somewhere far from her immediate family. I suggested that but she didn't feel capable. With you there, she can learn how to deal with her mother and family one issue at a time with space enough not to feel trapped. If you can keep even a little professional distance and not get sucked into the mess, I know we can set the right wheels in motion."

Right is relative. My final diagnosis might end up being different than John's. If the tricks of the trade don't show a turn-around in her death wish in a reasonable time, I'd make my plans without telling him. Still, I nodded.

We talked for a bit longer, catching up on mutual friends. When we finished, I joined Sue in the waiting room. She spoke cheerily but it was a lie. "Am I a total fruitcake? You were in there a long time."

I smiled. "John didn't tell me anything I didn't already know. He says you need a buffer between you and your family. He also says that he wants to keep meeting with you. Would that be okay?"

She looked from me to John, then nodded shyly and a little embarrassed. "I enjoyed talking with you, Dr. Corbin. I'd like to meet with you again."

"I enjoyed it as well, Sue." His smile was warm and genuine. "Why don't we meet tomorrow, around the same time."

"Will Laura get pissy?" I asked

He shook his head. Just chocolate, no black pepper. "Nah. She's got some monthly meeting to attend. I was on my own anyway. I think this is important." He looked at Sue very pointedly. "I think *you're* important." She smiled but dropped her eyes. I guess I need to work with her on how to take a compliment.

We drove to my office next and signed the security consultant and bodyguard agreements. We agreed that a lease for my space in the basement would be a good idea. Sue read each document entirely and then initialed each page before she finally signed them. She even corrected a typo in the form.

"Do you really have to leave town?" she asked nervously after all the paperwork was signed. I gave a copy to her and kept one for my file. "What about the gate? And Vinny?"

"Yeah, I've got to go. They're expecting me. I wouldn't worry about Vinny. He won't come back for awhile. But if it'll make you feel better I can leave my car at your place. I'll take a cab. Vinny knows my car. But I don't think he'll risk his life for such a small amount of money."

I didn't want to alarm Sue, but I *was* a little worried. I called Gary right then and there and explained the problem. He agreed to fix the fence as an emergency call that day.

Chapter 21

Sue sat on the bed at my house. We drove there after the office so I could pack. The poker game sometimes lasts more than a day so I usually take spare clothes.

"Can I go with you?"

I shook my head and stuck a couple of shirts and a few pairs of underwear in a bag. "No ladies. No exceptions."

Sue hugged her knees to her chest. She looked miserable. Sad and embarrassed about Myra; about everything. "I'm sorry," she said, for the tenth time.

I sat down next to her on the bed. "Look, this doesn't have anything to do with you. This is something that I do every month. I'm not running out. But I told you—I won't change my life."

She smiled but it was sad. I hated seeing her sad when I was going somewhere to have fun. An idea occurred to me.

"Say, tell you what!" I sat down next to her and slipped my arms around her shoulders. "All of the wives and ladies of us guys will get together tonight while we're playing. Why don't I see if you can go along with them? I've heard they have a great time. They use a limo and everything!"

Her eyes lit up with equal amounts of excitement and fear. "Do you think they might? I don't know any of them."

"Hey, they're great gals. Lots of fun! I'm sure they won't mind."

I picked up my cell phone and dialed a number. Carmine answered and I explained my brilliant thought. He put Linda on the line. A few minutes later, it was all set up; Linda was real curious to meet anyone who had caught me, and she'd come to pick Sue up on the way to get the other women.

Linda suggested that Sue dress up, since they were going "clubbing." My brows raised. I've been clubbing with Linda before. It's an event. I chuckled and hung up.

I suggested that Sue not tell Myra that she was going out. We both knew the old bat would try to spoil it. Sue flat refused.

"No. I should be able to go out once in awhile. I should be able to have friends. Plus, I can't exactly *sneak* out with a limo sitting in the drive. I'll just have to ignore Mom's reaction. I hope it won't embarrass Linda too much, though."

I nodded, but added. "Don't worry. Linda will make sure you get out the door. She can handle Myra without even sweating."

I drove her home. When I kissed her goodbye, it took longer than I planned. I was hot and bothered by the time I left, and she was pleased and proprietary about that reaction.

Chapter 22

I arrived at Carmine's with a few minutes to spare. I stopped by the bank first. Then I remembered I had forgotten the briefcase from Vegas and had to go back to the house. I knew the case wouldn't make it past the guards, so I put it in the trunk after sliding the papers into an envelope using my gloves to keep any prints intact. The guards met me at the door. I handed them my Sig and the Colt derringer back-up. I pulled a wad of money from my pocket and turned that over, as well. The game is cash only. No checks. No house credit.

They still patted me down and ran a metal detector wand over me. Hey, it's a lot of money. I can put up with certain indignities. They got to look in the envelope without touching, but didn't get to read the contents. When I was cleared, I was given a tray of chips. They're normal plastic chips like you buy at the discount stores but they're assigned much higher values than dimes, nickels, and quarters. More like fives, tens and hundreds.

Carmine has a great house. It's a rambling ranch-style with a separate enclosed poker room where we can lock ourselves away from the world. If you can think of a debauched activity, you can find it at Carmine's. Drinking, smoking, gambling; as much and as often as you want. No sex or drugs, though. At least, not on poker night. The poker games are guys only and drugs are out.

Five of us play each month. Me, Carmine Leone, Joey "The Snake" Karasiuk, Ira Hillyard, and last but not least, Louis—pronounced "Louie"—Perricone. The five of us grew up together in the Family.

The drill is that you arrive, pay the guards the buy-in of

ten thousand, plus a grand each for their fee. It's the same guards every time, so no surprises. The fee from each of us keeps them neutral. They clear you, hand you a rack of chips, and keep your weapons. We play until there is one winner, and the winner always takes home the fifty thousand. It either pays the rent or lays you low. On a good month the game lasts a couple of days

Carmine was at the bar fixing a drink when I was ushered in the room. Carmine smells like whiskey, cigar tobacco, and recent sex. Carmine always smells like recent sex. Today he smelled specifically like Linda.

It took awhile for me to find something that smells like Linda. When I did, I had to laugh. She smells like a *sarracenia rubra*. I didn't take much botany, but when I smelled one in a little flower shop back east, I looked it up. The common name is the Sweet Trumpet Pitcher. It's carnivorous, like a venus fly trap, but the flowers smell like roses. That's her, all right. Sweet but deadly.

"Hey, Tony! Glad you could make it!" His hearty words were tinged with curiosity. He motioned to the bulky envelope I carried.

I lowered my chin to acknowledge his unspoken question.

"Wouldn't miss it. Do you have a second? We need to talk."

He nodded and motioned with his head for me to follow him to the back. On the way past, I said my hellos to Ira, who's an accountant, and Louis, who handles protection gigs like Vinny. Ira smells like fresh cut lemon grass with overtones of cherry cough drops. Louis reminds me of the desert. Sort of dry and sandy.

Carmine closed the door behind me as I entered a small conference room off the back of the bar. He sat down at the table and motioned me into a chair.

"What's up?" His face was serious. I could smell his anger. I had invaded a "play" night with work.

I told him about the whole Vegas trip as quickly as I could. He kept his eyes on me and listened with his whole body. He didn't interrupt me once; he just waited until I finished.

I handed him the envelope. I watched his face and scent flow from concerned to angry to outright fury.

"Any ideas who's been telling tales?"

I was sitting back in my chair with my arms crossed over my chest while he looked over the papers. I shook my head. "Not one. I'm just the bearer of bad tidings, I'm afraid. They wanted you to think it was *me*."

His scent muddied—too many things to sort.

"I'll take care of this," he said flatly. "I hate to say it, but I'm glad you brought this with you. Nothing can be done today, but I'll start the wheels in motion. You just keep doing what you're doing—and watch your back," he added.

"Always do. Let me know when you find out anything. I want a piece of it." My voice was flat and cold. I don't like being set up.

He nodded his head once. "Let's go play some poker. It'll help me think."

Joey the Snake arrived just as we sat down at the table. Joey probably has a scent, but he always smells like Vick's Vapo-Rub. I don't know why he uses it so much, but the eucalyptus overpowers everything else.

Carmine was the host so he dealt first. After that the deal goes around the table, clockwise. We were six deals in when the phone rang. Carmine turned to watch one of the guards answer it. It didn't slow down the conversation for the rest of us. We were discussing the state of affairs in the Middle East. No business talk; sports or current events only.

"Tony?" Marvin was holding the receiver out to me. "Phone call. It's Linda."

Carmine looked at me sharply. It's amazing—and flattering—that after all these years he's still jealous of me. He crossed the room, took the phone and the guard backed off.

"What's up, baby?" I didn't watch him. I went back to my hand. I had four out of five for a straight flush. The odds of drawing into it were hopeless but what's life without risk? I put one card on the table. It wouldn't be dealt until Carmine returned.

"Hell no!" Carmine growled. "No way."

I could hear Linda's voice over the receiver. If I focused I could listen. Linda has a real penetrating voice. Not shrill or sharp, but it carries. If you want to save your eardrums when you're talking to her, hold the receiver away a few inches. In fact, Linda's whole personality carries. Her essence. You can walk into a room and you just know that she's there or has been there.

Linda is lovely. That's not a word that you can use to describe most people but she is. She's not beautiful, or hot, she's lovely. She looks delicate and fragile, but she's as tough as nails.

She's probably about 5'6" with straight, blonde hair. Her piercing eyes are ice blue. Her body will stop traffic but only because she works at it. She knows her assets and her faults and plays them right. Linda's bubbly and outrageous and intelligent. If she hadn't been so damn avaricious, we probably would have stayed together. Still, you can't help but like her. I figured that she and Sue would hit it off.

The table conversation had moved on to sports. The Broncos were having an undefeated season but the puppy quarterback was hurt. The discussion was whether he would play the next game. Since Carmine was the dealer, we couldn't play without him. The bet was six hundred to him. Joey folded when I only wanted one card. Ira was hanging in there. He doesn't bluff, so I was in for some stiff competition.

Carmine came over, the portable phone to his ear. He said, "Yeah, hang on," and handed the phone to me. "Your lady needs a sitter."

I nearly spit out a sip of beer. "Oh, shit. Don't *even* tell me!" I took the phone. "What's up, Lin?"

I could hear loud voices in the background. Someone was arguing. "Hang on, Tony, let me get outside." I could hear her staccato steps on the polished hardwood. A door opened, then closed and then there was blessed silence.

"Tony, baby, you there?" She calls everyone baby, and everyone hates it.

"I got here about half an hour ago. Ohmagawd! Did you see this place! It's *Tara*! I didn't know this place even existed. I really like Sue, Tony. She suits you." There was static and she faded out for a second.

"You're breaking up, Linda," I said. Carmine dealt me a card. It wasn't what I needed so I folded. Then I told Joey to deal me out of the next hand and backed up my chair so the others could play.

"I've got a situation."

I moved to the other end of the room and sat on a bar stool. The static cleared on the phone and I heard Linda's voice again. "Can you hear me now?"

"Yeah. Go ahead."

There was silence for a moment. "Eeww, there's goose poop all over the ground! I just got it on my new shoes. Just a second." I heard movement again.

"Come on, Linda," Frustration edged my voice, "Pick a spot." I spoke loud since the phone wasn't by her ear.

I repeated the words several times. Finally there was a response. "Okay. I got in the limo. Anyway, here's the deal. I get here and Sue is dressed, but not good enough, you know? All she's got is really dowdy office stuff."

I twirled my hand, hoping she would speed up. The one thing you can't get Linda to do is go faster than she wants to. And it's questionable whether you want her to. Once she gets going it's like a runaway freight train.

"But she's got the greatest hair, Tony! You ought to see it up like I did it!"

"Linda . . ." I said pleadingly. "The game?"

She remembered where I was. "Oh yeah, sorry. Anyway, I told her that the clothes just had to go! I had to dig through her whole closet and then chop up a silk shirt with sissors. But we found her something to wear. You ought to see her, Tony. She's hot! She'll make the guys go crazy at the clubs."

My eyes narrowed and my voice grew flat. I've seen Linda's version of 'hot'. "I'm not sure I like the sound of that."

She blew out an annoyed breath. "Oh please! We're going to Carmine's clubs. We don't have a *hope* of getting hit on."

I had to agree with her. Carmine is the jealous sort. Everyone knows it. Nobody would want that kind of trouble.

"So what's the problem?"

"Oh yeah! Anyway, we're all set to go and jeez—that mother of hers. She's like the bitch from hell!"

I let out an exasperated breath. I was wrong. Linda's a runaway freight train with multiple spurs. "No shit. But can we move this along a little, Linda? I've got to get back."

I could imagine her placating hand movements. "Okay. So anyway, we were just about to leave when the front door opens and in comes this little yuppie family. Dad, Mom, and two rugrats." She paused and then sighed. "Actually, that was mean. The kids are cute. It's the parents who are jerks. The mom is Sue's sister."

Yep. I knew it.

"They started in on Sue, saying that *Mommy dearest* had promised that Sue would watch the kids 'cause of how Sis was *inconvenienced* last week, whatever that means."

I rolled my eyes. "Sue and I went to Vegas together— without *permission*."

There was a pause before her incredulous voice. "You're *joking*. I hope."

"'Fraid not."

There was a slow exhale of air. "Ooookay, then. So we've established that Mom and Sis have it in for Sue. Problem is, Sue's trying to cancel. She says she feels guilty."

I shrugged. "No surprise. She's seeing John Corbin for that very thing."

I could hear a smile in Linda's voice. "John-Boy? No kidding! I haven't seen him for ages. How is he?"

I glanced at the poker table longingly. Another hand was starting without me. "Stick to the subject, Linda. I want Sue to go out tonight. Any ideas?"

"Well, I actually did have an idea but Carmine shot it down. If you can get him to bend we'll be home free."

Carmine glanced at me just then like he knew what Linda was saying. "Go ahead."

"Mike and Jerry are our bodyguards tonight. You know how Mike adores kids. Got four and a bun in the oven. He hates clubbing but Carmine insists on sticking him with it 'cause he's big and mean looking. We're not going to *do* anything tonight, Tony. We'll stick to Carmine's clubs. Word of honor." I could see her in my head, holding up her hand like in a Girl Scout salute.

"So . . . what? You're suggesting that *Mike* watch the kids? Why not tell the parents to get screwed and just leave with Sue?"

"Easier said than done. We're in the limo. It's Carmine's new baby—this year's model. We're blocked in by the other car. We'll have to satisfy them or ram the car out of the way. Carmine wouldn't like that." I had to agree with that. God knows how much insurance costs on one of those beasts.

"I asked him, Tony. Mike, I mean. He'd rather stay here with the rugrats than go with us. Carmine said he won't pay for Mike's time to babysit. I suggested it to Sue and she said she would pay. Thing is, I don't think she should be responsible for it. I mean, it's not like she said she would and *forgot*. Someone else promised her time. That just isn't right. The kids already adore Mike. You know how kids are around him. He's playing some board game with them in the next room while we're working this out. So what do you say? Carmine will okay it if you pay. I still think the parents should pay. I'll try to push for that on this end. But Carmine will want *your* word."

I thought about it for a moment, and as soon as I thought of Sue I could feel her. Angry and hurt. She wanted so badly to go have fun. She liked Linda. But she felt guilty even though she knew she had no reason. That decided it. I held the phone away from my ear without covering the speaker.

"Yo! Carmine." He turned to my voice. I could see his hand. Unless someone could beat a full house, Queen high, he had the pot. It made me glad I wasn't sitting in this hand. It was a pretty big pile, with mostly blue chips.

He raised his chin slightly in acknowledgment.

"I'll pony up for Mike if you'll okay Linda's idea. What do you say? My lady needs a night out. Her family are assholes."

He snorted lightly. "From what Linda says, they beat out Joey's family." He let out a slow thoughtful breath as I walked closer to the table.

Joey responded to that statement with raised eyebrows. "Gawd, I hope not! I feel for your goil if they do."

His people are serious jerks. Talk about dysfunctional. Unfortunately, I had to agree with Linda.

"C'mon, Carmine, what say? You know that Mike would rather be with kids. I'll pay his fee."

He tapped his finger on the table. "It's not just that, Tony. I'm just not sure that I want the girls going out with just *Jerry* watching them."

I knew that he'd been having trouble with Jerry for a while now. Had it gotten worse? Was I sending Sue into danger?

I could hear the edge in my voice. "Yeah? What's up?"

He moved his head in tiny little shakes. He was trying to fight off a bad feeling. He smelled a little angry and worried. He set his cards on the table face down while he thought.

"He's been real pissy lately. He asked for a promotion and I turned him down."

"What did he want a promotion to?" Carmine doesn't usually hold a guy back if he wants to move up in the world.

He looked at me pointedly. "To *your* job." Well, I'll be damned. I didn't know he was interested in my line of work.

"I told him I was satisfied with your work for me and we didn't need two in this region. Not anymore. The work's just not there. He knows that he can't freelance without my support but he's not happy." He shrugged. "But, I guess it's not the end of the world. He'd never hurt the girls. He knows what I'd do."

He thought for a moment while I held the phone at my side. I could hear Linda trying to get my attention. I pressed the mouthpiece more firmly against my thigh, muffling the words.

"Mike got a raise last year. Think you're up to it?"

He named a figure and I let out a slow whistle. "Guess I'll have to win tonight."

"So you'll pay? Up front?"

I reached into my stack of chips and sadly removed most of my blue chips from the pile and dropped them into his stack.

"Agreed?" He grimaced for a second but nodded reluctantly. I started to put the phone back to my ear. I stopped when he suddenly snapped his fingers. He raised an index finger in the air and shook it slightly.

"Wait. Have them stop at Carlin's first. They can pick up Jake to take along. Yeah. That'll work." He smiled the smallest bit, then went back to his hand without a word. His scent calmed immediately. He was no longer worried. That relieved my own unease.

"You catch all that, Lin?" I asked.

"Thanks, Tony! I'll make sure that Sue has a real good time tonight." She paused and then added, "Did you know they call her *Suzi*? Makes her sound like a Barbie doll. Blech!"

"Well, it *is* her name."

"So? Damn it, when you know that someone doesn't like the name and she said so right in front of them, you ought to call them what they want. Hell, she could want to be called Carmen Miranda and they should respect that, you know?"

I couldn't disagree.

"And her mom! God, that woman's attitude sets my teeth on edge, you know? She started complaining about how she was so *helpless* 'cause she's in that chair." Linda's voice was bitter and sarcastic.

I spit the words angrily. "She's faking!"

"Hey, doesn't matter! *My* mom's in a wheelchair too! She does just fine."

Shit. That's right. I'd forgotten that. Once upon a time, I thought Lissell was going to be my mother-in-law. She's great; got a real zest for life. Linda inherited that from her.

"You remember. It was such a stupid thing," said Linda with equal parts of anger and sadness. "She got drunk and fell down a flight of stairs. Broke up her back real bad. She's paralyzed below the waist. Won't ever walk again." The words ended flat but I knew Linda. She was near tears thinking about it.

"How's she doing, anyway?"

Her voice firmed up. In my mind, I could see her chin raise high defiantly. "Mom didn't take it lying down. Shit happens. Carmine bought her one of those motorized wheelchairs. You know, the ones with the buttons to move around? She buzzes around her place like a madwoman. It's solar powered and everything. Mom insists on living by herself. She even does her own shopping with a little cart that she drags behind. Last month, she went to Hawaii with her cronies. They fixed the wheelchair so the back laid down."

She hooted with laughter for a moment. "She did the limbo! *and* won the contest! Got a trophy and everything." She snickered. "Although I think they probably *let* her win."

I laughed. That sounded like Lissell. "Glad she's doing well."

"So I don't have any sympathy for someone that doesn't even *try*."

"Did you say that?" My grin was a mile wide.

"Damn straight I did! Didn't win me any friends. Except maybe Sue. Oh! I forgot to tell you. Mom asked me if Carmine might buy her one of those special wheelchairs with the tilted-in wheels. She wants to enter races! Can you believe it? She lost all of the fat on her upper arms when she had a regular chair and doesn't want to go soft." Her voice was proud, happy.

I laughed.

"Hey, I've got to get back before they bum Sue out for the whole night. Catch you later! Give Carmine a big smooch from me! He's great!"

"How about I let you—" But she hung up.

I clicked off the phone and handed it back to the guard.

"Everything kosher?" asked Ira when I returned to my seat. There was a new pot and a big stack of chips in front of Joey. Well, I'll be damned! He beat Carmine's hand.

I nodded. "Yeah." I turned to Carmine. "Linda said to give you a big smooch. Want it on the lips?"

He looked at me and I made kissing motions. His broad face split in a smile and he reached for his belt. "Yeah, baby. I'll show you what I want you to kiss. Pucker up."

Chapter 23

It was about 4:00 in the morning when Mike and Jerry were admitted to the poker game. Verbal reports won't do for Carmine when it comes to the girls. People can be bought or tortured. Carmine wants to see their faces. He's really good at spotting lies. He was better than me before I got my new nose.

Ira lost his money early and was snoring away on the couch in the corner. Louis had just lost his last chip and was sulking at the bar. If I didn't win the next hand, I was out too. Joey and Carmine were about even so it looked to be a long game in front of us.

See, once a person is out he can't just leave. We have certain rules. Fifty grand is a chunk of change and it's all cash. So all the games are on weeknights. That way there's a bank open the next day.

Then, to prevent any "accidents" as the winner is leaving, one of the guards escorts the winner directly to his bank. The rest of the players are stuck in the house with the other guard until the winner makes his deposit. Anything happens to the winner or the guard, the rest of us are held until we determine who's responsible. Then that person is eliminated from the game. Permanently. It's how Louis got his seat and Marvin his job.

Louis's predecessor had a turn of bad luck. He decided he needed the money. He should have asked for a loan. His problems were taken care of the hard way. Pity. Harry was a nice guy, but he let his problems get in the way of his ethics.

When Mike and Jerry came in, Joey took a bathroom break so Carmine could talk to them. Mike stepped over to the table while Jerry grabbed a beer from the fridge. Mike smells like good quality Italian spice—probably from Marie's cooking, like fresh basil and garlic.

"Everything okay?" Carmine asked.

"Yeah. The girls are all home safe."

"You get paid?" I asked Mike. "Or does Carmine owe you?"

"Nah." He gestured casually. "They paid. I cut 'em a break. They were nice kids."

"How much did you charge?" Carmine's voice had an edge to it. I wasn't sure what it was. Sort of a mix of stuff.

He shrugged. "Five hundred. Like I said, Cindy and Mike were real well behaved. Good kids. They just need a firm hand. Shame they're saddled with those parents. Little Mike—that's what I called him, has a real interest in shooting. Parents won't let him." He shook his head. "Shame to waste potential talent."

I chuckled under my breath when I thought about it. Bekki and hubby probably didn't plan on a five hundred dollar sitter bill.

"You charged them five hundred? What the hell am I paying you twenty-five hundred for?"

I replied before Mike could. I knew that he wouldn't speak his mind to the boss. He'd come up with something that would satisfy Carmine, but it wouldn't be the truth.

"You got him doing something he doesn't like doing, Carmine. You know as well as I do that costs more."

Carmine looked steadily at Mike. He smelled suspicious and a little angry. "You don't like going with the girls?"

Mike shrugged again. No big deal. "I can take it or leave it. I do what you tell me to do."

"Do you like it?" he asked slower, and a little dangerous.

Mike never lies to Carmine. Nobody does. "Truthfully? I'd rather be home with Marie and the kids. But the girls only get together once a month. I'll do it. No sweat." Carmine nodded, satisfied.

Mike turned to me. He smelled warm. "That's a real nice lady you've got, Tony. She's a keeper. Settling down material."

Carmine interrupted. "You and Tony can talk when you've finished reporting." Carmine doesn't take a back seat to anybody.

Then he turned to Jerry. Carmine's scent was suddenly different than when he talked to Mike. More aggressive, more heavily musky.

"Where did the girls go?" Carmine asked.

Jerry sat his tall frame in the chair that Ira vacated. Even sitting, he's a head above everyone else at the table. Jerry and Mike are both big guys but Mike has more upper body build. Jerry is slender but it's deceiving. He's actually the meaner of the two. Jerry brought a closed fist to his mouth and coughed. It's a nasty hack, from years of smoking.

Jerry smells like infection. Something's really wrong with him but he refuses to go get it checked out. It's a pervasive, thick smell. It's not the scent of death, like Leo, but close.

When Jerry got control of the cough, he replied, "We went to the usual places. Carlin's first for dinner. Then the Blue Velvet Room and finally Margarita's for dancing."

Carmine got a look on his face that I couldn't place. He smelled like anticipation; lust. "Anything *interesting* happen?"

Jerry leered, showing uneven yellow teeth. "Yeah. Linda hit on the new stripper."

Carmine's face lit up with a smile filled to brimming with triumph and lust. He smelled heavily of fresh sex. "Which one?"

"The little redhead at the Blue Velvet."

Carmine closed a fist and brought it down once sharply in front of his chest, victorious. "Yeah! I was hoping she'd see that one. I've been looking forward to doing that pretty little number ever since I hired her."

I shook my head with a smile. Carmine and Linda are quite a pair. They've agreed that it's not cheating if they're both doing the same person.

"She respond to Linda?"

Jerry smiled and it was a touch sinister. Made me look twice. Now he really did smell like Leo. Not good.

"What do *you* think?"

While Carmine was savoring his victory, I took the chance to ask, "How did Sue get along with the other girls?"

Jerry turned my direction. Jalapeños dusted my nose. No big surprise, I guess. But his words were polite. Good thing.

"She was real shy at first but Linda drew her out. By the end of the night, they were both wild. The only downer of the group was Carol."

Louis heard Carol's name and turned from his drink. "What did you say about Carol?"

"Just that she's out of sorts," said Jerry. "Real bitter right now. I think it had something to do with that kid she was seeing. She said you offed him. She was warning Sue to stay away from Tony, 'cause Sue would end up *property*, just like she was."

"Fuck!" Louis exploded with a level of anger and hurt that surprised me. He slammed his drink onto the bar hard enough that most of it spilled out over his hand. "She starts screwing around with some punk kid and just because he disappears, she assumes I did it? It never occurred to her that he might have just walked out on her?" Louis smelled betrayed; wounded.

"You tell her that you didn't help him disappear?" I asked.

"I never even confronted her with the affair! I figured it was a passing thing. Thought it might spice her up a little bit to hang around with a kid. She's been feeling old lately."

There was a sadness with that last. He stared off into space for a moment. I knew he was remembering better days. They've been together for almost six years. A record for Louis.

I almost didn't want to interrupt his meditation. "You might mention that you didn't do it. Maybe even help find him to prove it. She'd think better of you. It'd make points. Just don't rough him up when you find him. Tell her that you hope that she'll stay with you. That you want her to."

Damn! I sounded like John-Boy again. Every month it's the same. Maybe John needs to sit in on the next game and give me a break.

"Yeahhh," he said slowly, thinking. Hope rose from him

like a balloon. It lifted the edges of his lips into a smile. "I'll find the kid, give him back to her as a present. I'll be the good guy for a change. Yeah. I like that." The air became thick with citrus.

He pulled a cell phone from his pocket but J.R. tapped his shoulder before he could dial. J.R. held out his hand for the phone without a single word. Louis sighed with annoyance and embarrassment, flipped it closed and handed it to him. "Forgot. No calls out." He turned to Carmine. "Sorry."

Carmine shrugged like he hadn't even noticed. But I knew how intently he had been watching Louis out of the corner of his eye. "It's a joint rule, not a house rule. Nobody else cares, I don't."

I shrugged. "I don't care. You, Joey?"

Joey was just sitting down again. His scent was determined but not quite hostile. His face was blank. "We've got rules for a reason. I had to give up *my* phone. No calls. You'll be home in a few hours. Deal with it then."

I stood and walked to the bar to get another drink. Louis was still behind the bar so he passed me a beer in a green bottle. I like some of the imports. Others taste like boot polish.

Jerry sidled over to me. His smell preceded him and I had to turn my nose away. It's like standing next to someone who hasn't bathed for a year or so. "I hear that you've been referring out some of your jobs lately."

I glanced at him suspiciously. Where had he learned that? "Yeah. So?"

He was trying way too hard to appear nonchalant. It didn't wash. "So I'm available if you ever need a back-up. I'm sort of trying to break into the business. If you're thinking of easing up on your schedule ... " He didn't finish the thought. He shrugged. "I could use a referral from you. It would carry weight."

"I'm not retiring, Jerry." I stood and walked around the end of the bar. I needed to find something to take the near-death smell out of my nose. Something strong. Peppers, maybe. Or garlic. Salsa! Yeah, that would work. I leaned under the bar, searching for an unopened bottle.

"How do you know that I've been turning down jobs?" I asked without looking up.

He didn't answer right away but his smell changed. He was thinking that I had stepped away because I was afraid of him. It raised my hackles. Okay, bad term, but it did. I looked at him sharply and abandoned my search for picante sauce to come around the bar and stand up close and personal. If he wanted a challenge, I was up for it.

Carmine was suddenly next to Jerry as well. Like me, he was standing a little too close. Jerry's eyes darted quickly between us and I could hear his heart beat faster. The blood in his veins was close to the surface and he smelled of fear and anger. Good. My senses now alert, I could hear a slight rattle each time Jerry breathed. He would be slow; an easy kill. A part of me wondered whether his blood would taste bitter. Would it be a taste I would enjoy? A little shiver raised the hairs on my skin. I let the thought rise to my eyes. I let him see exactly who he was dealing with.

"What the *fuck* do you think you're doing, Jerry?" Carmine asked forcefully before I could get a word out.

"Just chatting with Tony here." He tried to focus on Carmine but couldn't take his eyes off me. I knew my eyes were still human. No tell-tale glow. But they were the eyes of a hunter. In either form I was one.

He didn't immediately give Carmine his undivided attention. It was not appreciated. Carmine reached up and grabbed his chin. He twisted Jerry's face sharply until their eyes met. His voice was soft but had the weight of lead. "I said no, didn't I? Didn't I tell you that I don't want you doin' jobs? What, you deaf or something?"

Jerry swivelled on his chair to face Carmine. Satisfied, Carmine let go of his chin but not before he nearly took off a chunk of skin. Carmine was *really* in no mood tonight to have people go against his orders. Jerry had to look down to meet Carmine's angry gaze. Carmine isn't real tall, but that doesn't matter when you're the boss.

Jerry didn't look happy. He was much more hostile than he could afford to be. It made me wonder what he was hiding. "You said that as long as Tony was in the biz, I wasn't needed. If he's stepping down, I want a shot at it."

Something about the way he said that . . . "Did I say I was stepping down?" I moved a fraction of an inch closer. My voice was cold and heated at the same time. "When I'm feeling old enough to retire I'll let you know. And you better *hope* I never hear you were thinking of speeding along the process."

Carmine's face took on a wary look when I suggested advancement by assassination and his glare could bore holes. Jerry's eyes darted back and forth between us and his tongue flicked out nervously. "I didn't say nothing like that. I'm just asking for a chance to show my stuff."

Carmine poked a finger into Jerry's big chest, nearly pushing him backwards off the chair. You forget how strong Carmine is until he needs to prove it. "You'll show the stuff *I* want you to show, Jerry! Got it? I don't want you going behind my back talking to Tony or anybody else. You go through me and me alone. *I'll* decide when I think you're ready to try something different. *Capisce?*"

Jerry nodded, eyes flashing. But he didn't talk back.

"You and Mike head home. We'll discuss this tomorrow. Carlin's, nine sharp."

"Sure, Carmine, whatever you say." The words were cautious, not angry or sarcastic. Good plan. Carmine's got a short fuse. Mike had wisely stayed out of the fray and quietly followed Jerry out the door.

I sat back down and Carmine followed. He visibly smoothed himself out like a bird settling ruffled feathers. The table was empty of chips, so Joey must have won the last hand. Carmine picked up the deck and began to shuffle. Joey had taken in the whole scene without a word. Carmine responded to Joey's earlier comment about the turning off the cell phones as though he had never been interrupted.

"A few hours, my ass. You'll be cooling your heels until I get back from the bank, my friend."

Joey snorted and picked up the cards as Carmine dealt. When he had finished the deal, I remembered something. I held out my hand toward Carmine. "By the way, I think I have a refund coming?"

"Yeah, yeah." He dropped a stack of blue chips into my hand. I asked for smaller chips instead. It might keep me in the game long enough to win a hand.

Chapter 24

I got back home around noon the following day. Joey won the game. First time in months.

I went directly to bed. I called Sue, telling her to stop over if she wanted to. I must have been totally zonked because I didn't even hear when she unlocked the door with the key I had given her. Fortunately, she remembered the alarm code. I'm not positive giving her a key and the code were good things, but I did it.

I woke to warm hands rubbing my back. I was annoyed that I hadn't heard her but sighed contentedly anyway. I could smell her perfume, but underneath the artificial mask was her own scent. Sweet and musky. It made me feel warm inside. I glanced sideways and watched her hand squeezing the knots out of my muscles.

A part of me really resents that I'm getting this attached to her. But it isn't her fault. It's my problem. I need to pull back from her. I know it, but I don't want to. I also know that John was right. It's going to hurt to pull the trigger; hurt to see those hands lying lifeless on the ground. I'll dream about it. I know that, too. Maybe I'll end up needing to pull the trigger again to stop the dreams.

I fought my way back through the dark images to the feeling and scent of her very alive body. "Did you have fun?" I asked sleepily and then yawned.

I could hear a smile in Sue's voice. "I had a wonderful time! Thank you so much for setting it up. Linda and Ellen are great. Carol's a little odd, though." There was a tenseness in her voice that made me roll over to see her face.

I stared into her startled eyes and shook my head. "I heard about that. He didn't do it."

Her breathing increased. "Carol swears that he did. Just up and killed him. She feels trapped and scared for her life." Sue actually seemed afraid for her.

I frowned a bit. "Carol talks too much. But Louis is nuts for her. Always has been. He wouldn't do that to her. Jerry told him what Carol said at the club. He's going to try to find the kid and hook him back up with Carol if that's what she wants."

Astonishment passed over her face and wafted into my nose. She dropped her jaw. "He'd do that? She made him sound like such an ogre."

"Don't get me wrong," I replied seriously. "Louis *is* an ogre. If he didn't love Carol he *would* have offed the kid. It's not like it's beneath him."

"Oh." Her voice was small and quiet. Then she looked at me with a trace of annoyance and punched me lightly on the chest. "*You* didn't tell me that you and Linda used to date!"

That took me by surprise. I guess it never occurred to me. But now that I thought about it, it probably should have. "You know, it didn't even cross my mind. Is it a big deal?"

"It was so strange. When she first arrived, she looked around the house and was just in awe. She had to look in every room. She kept muttering under her breath, "It's Tara. Oh my gawd! It's Tara!" Then she said to me, 'Wow, Tony's doing well by you!'"

I laughed. It hadn't occurred to me that Linda would think I bought the house for Sue. I *did* expect the house to be a hit with her.

"I tried to explain that it was my house and she just nodded her head in that certain way. You know, the one that says, '*Sure* it is'. Then she said that you must really like me because you haven't spent this much for anyone *since her*."

I winced. Again, the truth was best. "Okay, I get the point. Linda and I were an item for a couple of years. But we broke up." I shrugged like it was no big deal. Truthfully, though, it had been a hard decision. One I regretted for months.

"We had different values. She wanted money and power

and I wanted someone to kick back with. They were mutually exclusive goals. She and Carmine hooked up. They're better suited."

"She's so pretty and fun. Do you ever regret not staying with her?"

I gave her a warm smile. Still self-conscious. "Feeling like a sparrow in a flock of peacocks?"

She nodded. "All of them are just gorgeous." I had no doubt she felt envious. I could smell the odor—it's pepper, but closer to cayenne flakes and seeds, like the ones you sprinkle on pizza.

I reached up and touched her face. She leaned into my hand. "They're trophies and they know it, love." I pulled her against my chest and spoke into her hair.

"If I wanted a trophy, I'd be with one of them. I want brains—and personality. Looks only last so long. One of these days Carmine, Louis, and Ira are going to want to trade in last year's model." Sad but true.

I tightened my arms around her in a hug. The scent of her this close stirred something inside of me. Something that made me think of home, safety—eternity. I fought it down with effort. I *like* to be alone. Unfortunately, the more I tried to convince myself that I wanted to remain alone, the more I smelled my own lie.

"What do *you* want?" she asked in something close to a whisper.

I thought about Mike's words—a keeper. Did I want one? I just didn't know. I kissed her hair. "You."

It slipped out, just like the 'love'. Warm sugar and cinnamon wafted through the summer forest. I breathed it in deep and had to shake myself to come back to my senses. I changed the subject back to the evening. "Other than Carol, did you have fun?"

She smiled and I could smell her happiness. "Linda is so wonderful! We spent the whole night talking. We probably bored the other girls. We have so much in common! I feel like I've known her my entire life after just a couple of hours."

Then she moved her head a little, amending with a bit of chagrin, "Actually, more than a couple of hours. We dropped off Ellen and Carol around 1 a.m. and sat in the back of the limo drinking wine and talking until almost 3." She started laughing suddenly and her chest bounced on mine.

"It was so funny! When we went to a club called the Blue Velvet Room, Linda was pretending to hit on female strippers! I swear I've never laughed so hard!"

She couldn't see my face. I bit back a laugh. I didn't quite know how to tell her. I wasn't sure she could wrap her white-bread middle class values around Linda.

I raised my hand to scratch an imaginary itch on my upper lip. It hid the smile. I don't think I hid the twinkle of amusement. "Um, she wasn't pretending."

Sue raised her head and looked at me curiously. All she could see was my hand scratching. "What do you mean?"

I removed my hand and the smile peeked out. "Linda swings both ways."

Sue continued to look confused, shaking her head to indicate that she didn't understand. I tried again. "Linda is bisexual. You understand that term, right?"

Her face was a case study in amazement. Her jaw dropped. "She *has* sex with *women*?"

"As well as men." I waggled my hand. "Actually only one man—Carmine."

Her voice was incredulous. "And he doesn't mind?"

I shrugged. "Not a bit. He likes to watch." I watched her take in that bit of information. Her eyes stayed wide long enough that I had to ask, "Are you okay? You look a little weird."

"Well . . . it's just that Linda was in the room when I was changing. And she was so attentive to everything I had to say in the limo! I mean . . ." she stammered.

I understood immediately but her assumption wasn't correct. "Did Linda *hit* on you?"

She cocked her head a tiny bit. "Well, no."

"Then don't presume she's interested in you." She couldn't quite seem to get past shocked. A small laugh escaped me.

Probably rude but I couldn't help it. "Haven't you ever had any gay friends?"

"Yeah, in college. But only guys. I've never had any female friends that were—well, like Linda."

I hoped that she realized that I wasn't laughing at her but I couldn't keep the grin off my face. "Sue, do you leap into the lap of every man that walks in the room?"

"God, no!"

I looked at her pointedly. "And Linda doesn't leap into the lap of every woman that walks in the room."

She still seemed nervous so I turned off the smile and looked at her with as much seriousness as I could muster. "Look, Linda knows that you're with me. That means that she knows you're straight. She also knows I don't share so she would never approach you. Would you think less of her if she only dated Hispanic men? Or black men?"

She shook her head.

"Of course you wouldn't." I shrugged. "So what if she likes both men and women? Big deal. You can still be friends with her. She won't try to seduce you. Unless you want her to . . ." I added cautiously. I didn't really know all that much about Sue's tastes. I shouldn't automatically assume.

Her face immediately panicked. "No! No, that's not my thing." All of a sudden, though, she looked pensive and then blushed. She smelled of something just short of desire laced heavily with embarrassment.

"Thinking about it?" I asked slyly.

She shook her head. "Not really. I'm just not sure whether to be grateful or insulted that she wasn't interested in me."

I laughed loud enough that she finally broke into a smile. I hugged her against me tight. We laughed and rolled in a contented glow. I wanted to stay like that forever, just being happy; being together. Trouble was, I knew someday the other boot would drop.

Chapter 25

A couple of days passed. Things were going well with Sue. I was gradually spending more time with her, getting to know her. We went out to dinner last night with Carmine and Linda. Carlin's has the best Italian in town. Big surprise. We all ate more than we should have and then stayed up late playing poker back at my place. You'd think I would have had enough of the game, but nah, I love playing. My favorite is Texas Hold'em.

I find that I'm not sleeping at Sue's house much. I had tried. I'd spent a few nights there, locked away in the downstairs. But Sue could never get comfortable enough to do more than snuggle. She was too antsy for sex and couldn't sleep. That doesn't work for me. It left me frustrated beyond belief. I've put a couple of changes of clothes there, and some toiletries, but nothing permanent. I don't trust Myra enough to store my guns there. And where I go, my guns go. I know it bothers Sue, but there's no helping it.

Speaking of guns—I had finally assembled my new toy. The Thompson Center Arms Encore pistol was gleaming softly in the fluorescent over my reloading bench. I'd just finished wiping it down with the last coat of oil. The package Mary had given me contained the final custom piece. It was a 15" stainless steel barrel, chambered in 6mm PPC, with a black chromium oxide finish. You can't buy a black chrome stainless steel barrel off the shelf. After all, who'd want to blue a stainless finish? Me. I like the weather resistance of the stainless, but they're way too visible at night.

I'd debated long and hard about the scope, but finally

settled on a Burris Black Diamond Titanium 4X-16X-50mm ballistic. It's a little big for a pistol, but Encores are adaptable. They're intended to be either pistols *or* rifles. The frame holds the scope and it can be fitted with any number of barrel calibers and lengths. I was still doubting Burris' claim of a true "scratch-*proof*" lens, not just scratch resistant. Supposedly, you don't even have to use a clean, dry cloth on it. If it's true, it will be hugely useful in the field. And I like Burris scopes. People will say that there are better foreign optics available. Maybe. But any guy who would quit his job as a top designer and start his own company just because his old firm was cutting corners earns my respect.

I was looking forward to taking it to the range to sight it in, but not today. I'd gotten an interesting message on my cell phone while I was in the shower. It was the second odd call in the same number of days. The first one had been from Leo. I'm not sure how he got my number. I wasn't surprised at the call when his spy failed to retrieve the papers. The day after the poker game, I'd remembered about the briefcase in the back of my car and went to retrieve it. The trunk had been popped and the case forced open. It could only have been one of Carmine's people—or, more precisely, one of Leo's people.

Leo's snarl came over the tape. "I want my property back, Giodone. You give it up or things will start getting messy."

Things were *already* messy. I was pissed that I had to take the Mustang in to get the trunk latch fixed. I told Carmine about the call over dinner. He cut off any speculation by Linda with one sharp word—"Enough!"—and then went back to eating dinner. Conversation was a bit tense after that, but I managed to lighten the mood after a few minutes.

I called Leo back when we got home and left a voice mail of my own. "Screw you."

Today's message *was* a surprise. I'd recognized the voice, but only because I'd spent some time following him. He apparently knew it, which bothered me a little. The little shit really *is* good.

"We need to meet," Scotty had said. "I have some information you'll want. Southside Mall, in front of the pretzel stand. 12:00."

I didn't really trust the kid, but he'd never called me before. He piqued my curiosity. But I wasn't going to meet him in public. He'll understand if it's not a set-up.

I dropped by a store on the way. I got to the mall early and wandered around some, stopping in the gift shop to pick up a card and some candy for Sue. Holding a bag made me look more inconspicuous. I couldn't spot any plain-clothes cops, and none of the mall guards even glanced my way. No surprise. Today I was a blonde with a mustache wearing a ball cap.

When Scotty arrived, I followed behind him at a distance. He was nervous—that much was obvious. I wasn't close enough to smell his emotions, but his body language was definitely edgy.

I got lucky. He stopped to tie the lace on his running shoe, raising his foot onto a bench. I had been wondering how to work my plan. He stood in line at the pretzel stand, ordered a hot salted one, and then drenched it with mustard after he sat down.

I walked right up to him and tapped his shoulder. He jumped a foot.

"Hey, kid. You left your cell phone back there." I placed the prepaid cell phone that I'd bought across town face down on the table. I could suddenly smell him—the painfully raw fear blended with cloves when he recognized my voice. The shock of surprise was enough to tell me that he was nervous not because of any set-up, but because he was scared to meet me in person. He was just that impressed with me. Okay, that was a little flattering.

I didn't wait for a reply. I just walked away as he stared at the phone in shock. In the reflection of one of the store windows as I walked away, I saw him pick it up and turn it over. He saw the yellow sticky with three words printed. "Go. Five minutes."

I exited the mall. He's a bright boy. I figured he would

understand. We're both in the same field. We can't afford to meet.

I went to the Camaro I'd borrowed from Carmine and sat down to wait. When the sweep hand reached the last second of the five minute mark, I hit the speed dial that would ring his phone.

His voice was cautious when he answered. "Hello?"

"What's so important that we have to talk, Scotty?" I could hear a roaring sound in the background that grew and faded at intervals. I listened closely for a minute. Ah. He was at the skateboard park. Good choice. He should be able to spot any undercovers without sweat.

I pulled out of my parking space and headed onto the freeway. "Man, that was sweet, Mr. Giodone!" he exclaimed. "I didn't even recognize you at first! And I like the cell phone idea."

"Glad you approve. When we're done, destroy the phone. I'll do the same." I said flatly, but it pleased me that he didn't call me "Tony." He hadn't earned the right yet. "What's the scoop?"

He went business on me. That's Scotty—he can turn it on or off like a switch. "There's some new talent in town. Word is that your boss is under contract."

That got my attention. How the hell would *Scotty* hear about a new assassin in town who was after Carmine?

My silence must have been interpreted as disbelief, because he continued. "I've got a friend who works the streets. This new guy likes them young—and she looks it, so he's been spending some time with her. I spend time with her, too. The guy talks in his sleep and she listened in."

"Why would *she* care if something happens to Carmine? And why would *you*?"

"She doesn't care. She told me because she knows what I do and he was competition to me. I guess she's sort of sweet on me."

He tried to pass that off as an explanation. No good. "What's in it for *you*?"

There was silence for a moment. I could hear him

breathing. I wished I could smell him. His voice lowered to a whisper. "I got made the other day. The mark took off running because he got nervous. Kids aren't supposed to make people nervous." He sounded annoyed, and a little scared of the truth.

He isn't a kid anymore. Teenagers absolutely make people nervous. Scotty was entering a new phase of his life.

"So, anyway," he continued, "I'm hoping that if the info is useful, you'll teach me stuff. New methods."

Ah. He wanted to learn about guns. He was going to have to stop doing close-in work.

"And?" I pressed.

"And . . ." he grudgingly admitted. "If Leone is dead, he can't put me to work. He's the only game left in town, other than the crappy whiners who really don't want it done *right*."

Good. The kid's got some pride in his work. He's right. Most people don't want to let an assassin do his job. They want *input*. That leads to mistakes.

"Let's say I believe you," I said, as I turned randomly onto a residential street. "Can your friend ID the guy for us?"

"Um, I took a few liberties," he said nervously. "I was going to just . . . well, but no go. I can't do the guy. He's too good. He made me in a heartbeat. I just barely got out. But I've got him *set up* to do. Sally's already got a date with him for tomorrow. He'd wanted it earlier, but she stalled. He's coming to her place, or what he *thinks* is her place. There's a parking garage across the street that closes at 10:00. Her appointment is at midnight." He paused and when I didn't respond, he hurried on. "It'll check out. I promise. Put in a good word for me. I know you can find me if you're willing to show me a thing or two. Thanks."

He hung up. I thought about calling him back, but if he'd followed instructions, his phone was already dead. I pulled off the battery from the unit in my hand—it would work on my regular cell. Then I closed my fist around the phone. I felt the plastic begin to give as I applied pressure. I squeezed harder. A moment later, it shattered in my grip. So much for that hundred bucks. These new muscles are occasionally damned useful. I dropped the shards of plastic in the trash bag hanging from the gear shift. I'd dump them at a couple of different car washes around town. I swung the car around at the intersection. Carmine's house was my next stop.

I wasn't there long. He wouldn't believe the tip without talking to Scotty, "up close and personal." I couldn't blame him. There hadn't been a peep on the street about Carmine. We'd checked. So now I was driving a black sedan with Mike in the passenger seat next to me and Carmine in the back.

Normally, Nico would be in the car beside me instead of Mike, but Nico was . . . unavailable. His current residence was at the bottom of a lake. Carmine's boys had lifted some nice prints off one of the papers in the briefcase. Nico shouldn't have had any access to the document to have a print on it. After some prompting, he'd admitted to searching my car.

Carmine still wasn't satisfied that he had plugged all the leaks. He was taking the whole thing very personally, and very seriously. We were in the bulletproof rig today and he was packing in a couple of places.

I had to admit, I was surprised about Nico. I would have bet my favorite body part that Jerry was the leak. But Carmine swears that he's had no opportunity. I guess I have to believe him. But if I were Carmine, I'd be watching my back with that guy.

We'd been following Scotty for a couple of blocks, looking for an opening. I saw him start to cross the street to reach an arcade when I made my move. He looked both ways and darted into the street between two parked cars. I stomped on the gas and felt the car leap forward. Then I screeched to a halt in the middle of the road right in front of him. Carmine opened the door of the sedan on the fly, just barely missing his leg. I turned in my seat and lowered my sunglasses so he could see my face.

"Get in, kid."

Scotty's face was surprised, but he did what he was told. He slammed the door behind him and we took off again. I could hear Scotty's heart beating like a triphammer. He was good, but he knew he was out of his league. I'm sure he recognized Carmine. He's been in the papers a lot—mostly in the society column. Carlin's is a favorite of the "in" crowd.

The air was suddenly awash with hot and sour soup. It made my jaw clench and I felt a trickle of spittle at the edge of my mouth. I wiped it away before anyone noticed. Damn it. I should have eaten before I went to Carmine's. My stomach was going to start growling any second.

I kept my attention on my driving while Carmine talked to Scotty. Mike and I both pretended we were deaf.

"So you're Scotty," he said. Carmine's voice gave nothing away.

"Yeah . . . I mean—uh, yes sir, Mr. Leone." Good boy. Make some points.

"Tell me what you told Tony. I want some more detail."

Scotty cleared his throat. "Okay. Well, I've got this friend named Sally, and she . . ."

Carmine interrupted. "Define *friend*."

I could see him shrug in the rearview mirror. "We hang out. Sometimes we have sex."

Mike shook his head and sighed. The kid's pretty young, but he wouldn't be the first.

I asked a question from the front seat. "I thought girls made you nervous. And how do you see her when you still live with your folks?" I'd told Carmine I would only butt in if it was something important. His relationship with the girl could be.

"Well, I mean, Sally's not a *girl*. She's a hooker. And I don't live with my folks anymore. I got bored and took off. I live with another guy." He shrugged. "He doesn't care what I do as long as I pay him rent."

Carmine was the one to ask the next question. His voice was sharp and intended to frighten. "What is this "Sally", some sort of drag queen?"

"No, no. Nothing like that," replied Scotty, who was starting to smell confused. "I mean that she's not a girl you *date*. She's just a hooker."

Ah. Mike gave me a knowing look. It's a common attitude. They've even got a name for it: the *Madonna complex*. Either a girl is a *good girl* that you date and marry, or she's a *whore* and not even seen as a person. That attitude wouldn't win any points with Carmine. He's very equal opportunity. Of course, he has little choice with Linda around.

"So tell me what Sally told you." Carmine's voice wasn't warm and fluffy, but he kept on point.

"Just that there was this guy that picked her up. She got him off and he fell asleep. He started mumbling your name and some other stuff. She really didn't know what to think. The next day he picked her up again."

Carmine was listening intently. He was leaning against the locked door, watching the kid's face. I was doing the same in the mirror when I could spare a second.

"So anyway, the next time he fell asleep, she checked out the room. She found a case and opened it. I guess there was a gun inside that breaks down and fits into foam. She put two and two together. She told me because she thought he might be competition. She doesn't like the guy much and wants to help get rid of him. She said she can set him up. Get him wherever in the room you want him. The apartment belongs to a friend of hers. You'll have to pay for anything you break, though."

Carmine sat silently for a long moment, just watching the kid. He was sorting. Without taking his eyes off Scotty, he said, "Tony? Mike?" I knew he was asking our opinion.

On the way to Carmine's, I'd driven by the only apartment building in town that's across the street from a parking garage. Each unit had a balcony overlooking the street that is accessed by a sliding glass door. It wasn't a *bad* set-up, but it was obvious that Scotty didn't understand how to plan a job using a firearm. The garage was too close to get away after a gunshot sounded. The complex has a full-time security guard. He would recognize the sound and either investigate or call the police.

But I did like the idea of using *a* garage. Fortunately, there was another parking structure about a block and a half away with a clear line of sight to that side of the building. The Thompson with the 50mm scope would work fine so long as I loaded the shells a little hot and she could get that glass door open. The Thompson is a single shot, not a semi-auto. I could use one shot to take out the window, but couldn't reload before he took cover.

"The girl will need to get him out on the balcony," I said flatly, implying to Scotty that I already knew where the job would take place. "Or at least get the sliding door open. I'll only have one shot. The mark will be paranoid— especially since *you* already made one try for him. He won't want to be in the open like that. I sure as hell wouldn't if I was on a job."

I conceded a point. "Of course, if the girl flubs it and he kills her, I can probably still pop him when he comes out on Vine Street. It's the only exit he can use. The back one has a dead bolt. Killing her would be an impulse. He wouldn't have time to get a key."

Scotty started when I said all that, because he knew that he hadn't said anything about the location. Once again, the cloves and fear returned, blended with amazement.

"Yeah, he might be paranoid like you, Tony," said Mike, "But *you* wouldn't visit a hooker during a job and let her see your piece." said Mike. "The guy sounds pretty dim. It should be an easy hit. I say we believe the kid."

Good point. I took a deep breath, trying to sort out which scents belonged to Scotty. He smelled mostly like mustard—probably his underlying scent, but there was no deceit. I'd say he was possibly being used by the girl, but he hadn't smelled particularly warm or concerned when he talked about her, or when I suggested she might die. And he already tried to take the guy out. No, if Scotty said the guy was a pro, he probably was. He seems to know his limitations.

Carmine watched me in the mirror and then turned his attention back to Scotty when I gave a brief nod. I was nearly back to the spot where we'd picked him up. I stopped the car just a little up the street.

"I'll be in touch, kid," said Carmine as Scotty left the car. It was the closest Scotty would ever get to a "thank you." If it played out, I'd check with Carmine about some apprenticing.

When I left Carmine's after the meeting, he said that he would do some checking and get back to me, one way or the other. It would be at least hours, maybe even days. I might as well take the card and the now melted candy over to Sue.

Chapter 26

"Tony! Wait!"

Sue's plaintive call was cut off sharply as the door slammed shut behind me. I stalked to my car. I was more furious than I'd been before in my life. The sun was just setting, creating long shadows as I walked. As I reached the car, the pole lights around the circle drive blinked on and chased my shadow away.

The other boot I had worried about had dropped, all right. Right on my frigging head.

I got the car keys out of my pocket and promptly dropped them. I just barely stopped myself from kicking the car door. I'd be really pissed if I had to take the Mustang to a body shop because I couldn't control my temper.

One tall oak door opened as I reached down to pick up the key ring. Sue raced out, leaving the door open. "Tony, please! Don't go. I'm sorry. It'll never happen again."

I looked up at her, furiously. "Damn straight it won't!"

I could hear Myra's shrill voice through the open door. "Just let him go, Suzi. He *must* have something to hide if he got so angry over an honest mistake."

I glared at the voice behind the triangle of yellow light and bit back a smart-ass reply with gritted teeth. She wasn't worth the effort. I should have trusted my first instinct and dusted her when I met her.

Sue was in tears as she ran around the car. I stepped back. I didn't want her to touch me right now. I was entitled to my anger and I would be damned if I would let it roll away in that silvery glow.

She stopped when I backed up, not coming any closer.

Her chin was quavering and salty tears rolled down her cheeks. I felt her embarrassment and pain. Fear and sorrow tightened my chest and all I wanted to do was wrap her in my arms. No, damn it! I'd been careless enough.

"I'm so sorry," she whispered.

"Not your fault." It wasn't. But it didn't calm me down any. I unlocked the car door and she let me.

Her voice remained soft and guarded. She didn't want to be overheard. "Where are you going?"

"Out."

"Are you coming back?" Her fear hit me full in the nose. She didn't include the word, "ever" but it was implied.

"Probably not tonight."

She nodded, miserable. The fear was a little less but only a little. "Can I come with you?"

"I'm not real good company right now, Sue. I need some time alone." The tension was still in my voice. Big surprise. "If you don't want to stay here with *her*, go to a motel, order some room service and veg out in front of the television. Or go out somewhere."

Her arms were wrapped around her body, hugging tight against the world. Her head dropped and glittering tears fell to the pavement. "I don't know anyone to go out *with*. And I don't want to stay in a motel. I don't like motel rooms when I'm alone."

I stopped as some of my anger was defeated in her pain. I leaned against the car, hands resting on the open window jamb. I bowed my head and took a deep breath. "Why don't you call John? I'm sure he wouldn't mind."

She shook her head. "It's almost seven. He's probably already left."

I opened the car door, leaned inside and grabbed a pen and paper. I wrote a number and handed the sheet to her, being careful not to touch her skin. "This is his home number. Call him." When she wouldn't meet my gaze, I touched her shoulder. I fought off the familiar pulling in my groin. She looked up suddenly and gasped at the contact. "Call him, Sue. Please."

She took strength from me gratefully and nodded. It was shaky but she nodded.

I drove off with a roar, leaving her standing alone and forlorn in a circle of light.

I went to Nick's. I needed somewhere where I felt at home. The band was up and running as I stalked in the place. The joint was packed. A gust of wind caught the door and slammed it shut behind me, rattling the windows.

"Hey, easy on the building," Jocko exclaimed as I grabbed the only available stool and pulled up to the bar, "It's not paid for yet."

Not funny. I glared at him. One look at my face made him utter a low whistle. He grabbed a shot glass with one hand and an unopened bottle of Maker's Mark with the other. He broke the thick red wax seal and poured the caramel-colored liquor into the shot glass, stopping just short of spilling.

Without a word I grabbed the glass and carefully lifted the whiskey to my lips. I threw it down my throat but forgot to inhale first. The liquid seared and nearly went down the wrong pipe. I refused to cough. A shudder passed through me, and I closed my eyes and took a deep breath. Warmth spread through my chest as it flowed toward my stomach. When I opened my eyes again, the glass was full. A small smile played at the corner of my mouth and I gladly downed the second shot. I couldn't get drunk anymore, but the effort made me feel better.

After a third shot, Jocko finally said, "What's got you so lathered up?"

I snorted and pushed the glass toward him a fourth time. He tilted his head and shook it a little with a sigh. He smelled nervous. A bartender really doesn't like to get an angry guy drunk. But he poured.

My voice reflected my irritation. "I got a visit from Bob Sommers today." I sipped the whiskey this time to make him feel better.

"That homicide dick from the Fourth? Shit. He's so Ivory Soap that he squeaks."

I was sipping when he said that and I laughed abruptly,

spraying whiskey on the marble bar. It wasn't all that funny but it just occurred to me that Sommers really *does* smell like Ivory Soap. I hadn't realized it until that moment.

Detective Robert Sommers is tall with greying blonde hair. Blonde hair doesn't grey well. It makes him look jaundiced. He has a perpetually rumpled look that always reminds me of Columbo. They'd have been pals.

Jocko wiped up the spray of whiskey from his prized bar top. When I didn't elaborate further, "And . . .?"

I noticed that the person at the next stool was unusually interested in our conversation. He didn't look at us but he stared too studiously ahead and smelled anticipatory. I motioned with my eyes alone to Jocko that we were being overheard. He caught the look and without a word looked up and glanced around the bar.

He raised a huge arm and caught the eye of one of the waitresses. She moved through the crowd toward him. When she reached the bar she waited.

"Watch the bar, Marni, I've got business."

She nodded her head and moved behind the bar, sparing me a smile. I returned it with a nod.

We wound through the crowd. The smells and sounds were nearly overpowering. Not as bad as the casino but it didn't help my frayed nerves any. When we got to the edge of the dance floor, I almost laughed. Wall to wall people and my booth in the corner sat eerily empty.

We sat and I noticed for the first time that he had brought the bottle and two glasses. I must be really messed up.

He poured some whiskey in my glass and then in his own. He took a sip, but you could hardly tell the difference after. I knew Jocko. He could nurse a shotglass all night and nobody would know it was his first.

We sipped, me silently, him with a quiet slurp. He set the glass on the table in front of him and rested forearms on the chipped and scarred wood. He smelled patient. There is no hurry to Jocko, no rushing. He's the perfect bartender. Wait long enough and you'll find out everything.

"Like I said, Bobby-boy dropped in." He nodded. He

glanced at the crowd as I took another sip, watching for any signs of trouble. I didn't begrudge him. He's the boss. His eyes darted from group to group, picking out voices a little too loud, movements a little too sloppy. He lighted specifically on one group of boys just out of their teens. As we watched, one of the kids lifted a mixed drink from a neighboring table when the people left and started to sip it. Jocko stood. "Hold that thought."

He never took his eyes off the table as he wove through the throng like smoke. Quite a trick for someone his size. He reached the table and descended on them like a storm. Angry energy crackled around him, almost enough to see. He plucked the drink out of the kid's hand and spoke quietly enough for only that table and my wolf ears. "Out."

One of the boys started to argue. Jocko simply crossed his arms over his massive chest. Muscles strained and rippled under the short sleeved white T-shirt, the product of years of training.

No argument would be sufficient. He could lose the business, lose everything. He has no humor for that. The kids swallowed their pride before they started swallowing their teeth. The kid with the drink didn't even look at him. He just picked up his stuff and tried to slip out while his friends were blustering. Jocko reached out a beefy hand and tapped his shoulder. He froze and turned nervous eyes to Jocko.

Jocko studied his face for a moment. I knew he was committing every feature—the color of his eyes and the slope of his nose to permanent memory. "You're 86ed."

The boy opened his mouth but Jocko just turned away and walked back to my table. Trusted that they would leave as instructed. They did.

The people descended on the suddenly empty table like vultures. Hands reached for chairs almost before the bodies were completely out.

By the time Jocko returned to the table there was a new party in the same spot as though the previous group never existed.

"Sommers bothering you again?" he asked me like we were never interrupted.

I took another slug of whiskey. "He was investigating a grand theft."

Jocko leaned forward, eyes intent on me, his whole energy engrossed. "You don't steal and that's not his turf."

He's right. I don't steal. My next words were bitter. The anger returned full force. "Apparently, *anything* is his turf if it involves me."

"What happened?" Antifreeze seeped from his pores.

"Myra," I replied with biting intensity, as though the word was enough. It wasn't.

"Myra?" He paused. All of a sudden he thought he understood. I knew it from his smell. A new lady. A new problem. Partially right.

"Sue's mother." Then I realized that he doesn't even know about Sue. It felt like we'd been together years, but it had only been a little over a week. "The brunette I was in here with last."

Jocko nodded knowingly. Cloves drifted to my nose. Right again.

I told him the whole sordid story. How I got to Sue's house earlier to find Sommers' car. I didn't tell him about the panic that pounded my heart when I saw he and Myra in earnest conversation inside. If he had a search warrant, I was screwed. I'd slept down there at least two nights. He's never had any way to get my fingerprints or DNA before, and I wanted to keep it that way. Shit.

But he didn't have a warrant. He had merely intercepted a phone call. Myra was missing a brooch—a Tiffany's special. Compliments of Sue and the millions of gamblers in the state. Cost more money than my car, which made it grand theft. He heard my name mentioned when the call went out and dropped by himself. He'd sell a good chunk of his soul to get some samples.

Sommers isn't stupid, though. When I'd gotten there, he stepped back from the whole deal a bit. I could tell he was suspicious. Myra seemed to know too much about the crime.

"Do you mind if I have a look around down there?" he had asked Myra.

"I mind," I replied hotly. "There isn't any way that I could have gotten upstairs to get any brooch, Lieutenant. I come through a separate entrance in the back. I don't even have a key for the stairwell door." I'd made certain of that.

He turned to Myra. "Is that true, Mrs. Quentin?"

"Absolutely not! He comes and goes in this house as he damned well pleases, Detective. Don't believe him! I know he took my pin."

Sue spoke up, to my surprise—and certainly to Myra's. "It is true, Lieutenant. And I would appreciate it if you would address your questions to *me*. I'm the owner of this house and I'm the one who wrote the lease with Mr. Giodone."

Wow! I was surprised, but pleased, at the force of her words. One word had perked up Sommers' ears. His scent was suddenly a blend of odors. His face looked suspicious and frustrated. "Lease? I wasn't aware that the basement was a separate dwelling." That one word changed the whole complexion of the investigation.

I shrugged. "It didn't used to be before I hired on with Ms. Quentin to help her install some new security components. You can see the state of the fence outside, Lieutenant. She wanted the work done quickly and I've stayed a few nights to write up plans."

I thanked my lucky stars that Sue and I *had* written up a lease when we did the bodyguard agreement. Without permission from me, Sommers wouldn't touch the case. He once told me that if he ever caught me he wanted it so clean you could eat off it. He was ready to leave. Hat in hand.

But then I had a brilliant thought. I remembered the monitors. When my buddy Gary had come in to repair the fence, Sue had him change the tapes in the monitors. Just yesterday, I'd set up a machine in a back room to review the tapes. There had been nothing of interest, but that was before Myra called the cops. Every camera doesn't overlap perfectly, but there *is* one hidden right over the stairwell doorway.

Myra probably had never noticed it.

"Lieutenant, I think you might want to see something." I had led Bob to the room and shut the door behind him. Then I rewound the tapes for the day.

"What did they show?" Jocko asked. He was smiling wickedly as I related the story to him. Sweet thick antifreeze hung in the air and his eyes glittered with unconcealed glee.

The lights blacked out just then and my heart rose to my throat. The strobes began to flash, the glittering ball smoothly turned and the music slowed. The male lead's voice lowered to a seductive whisper, the stuff of frantic hearts and satin sheets.

I returned my gaze to Jocko and saw him in snatches and flashes through the darkness. Multi-colored light played across his face. The drumbeat was in time to the strobe. I felt each beat in my chest. I closed my eyes to block out the input. Everything became surreal. I started to speak, to answer his question. Then I was free-falling. I was weightless; breathless.

The channel changed. My voice was a thready alto and I was telling the same story all over again. As I opened my eyes I was staring at a ceiling. The colors were warm, the air smelled of cinnamon.

I heard John-Boy's voice. "How did it make you feel when your mother set up Tony?"

I knew the answer before the sound reached air but it wasn't my voice. They weren't my thoughts. "Horrible. Terrible. I was embarrassed, angry, guilty. You name it. She had no right!"

"Could she be worried about you? Worried that you've made a mistake by getting involved with him?" Always playing devil's advocate, huh, John?

Hell, no! But that wasn't what I said, what We said. "Maybe. I like to believe that sometimes she cares. But probably it's because she doesn't like Tony. He stands up to her. She can't bear that. She always has to be the strongest. Has to be the *only*. I spend time with him. That's not allowed. If I spend time with him, it's being taken away from her. They can't co-exist."

"So, what else did they show?" The warm tones and cinnamon were still there but John had Jocko's voice, a scratchy baritone. I felt an awareness. A knowledge of who and what we were. Then blackness again.

I was back in the bar. The lights were up, the song long over. Had I been speaking? I couldn't remember.

"What?" I asked hazily.

"The tapes, Tony. You said you rewound the tapes and showed them to Sommers. The tape showed Myra walking. You said it like it was a big deal. Then you just blanked out on me. You was there but you wasn't. Ya know?"

I tried to focus on him. Really. I wanted to tell him what was happening to me. I wanted to tell someone. Anyone.

No. Stick to the subject. Angry was better than confused right now. The tapes. Yeah.

The tapes showed Myra getting out of her chair. No surprise to me, but it was to Sommers. He was angry. I could see it, smell it. There was Myra, in living black and white, unlocking the door to the downstairs with a key. I wondered where the hell she got it. I heard a sound from Sommers that was amazingly like a growl as we rewound a second tape near the wet bar downstairs. It showed Myra's right side as she snuck into my bedroom and stashed the pin under my mattress. Oh, real smooth.

He gritted his teeth and I heard a slight grinding as he spoke. He grudgingly asked me whether I wanted to press charges. I could. Breaking and entering, false accusations. Sommers hated asking, hated that I was the good guy for a change. But he's right wing law and order. It's his job.

I declined gracefully, but I thoroughly enjoyed watching him dress Myra down on his way out. Threatened to prosecute her for false reporting. That's a crime too. The best part was, he'd never again believe her. That made me a little less pissed about the whole thing. Only a little.

"Damn!" Jocko let out a slow breath and finished his whiskey with a fast swallow. "You sure you want to get involved with that one?" He shook his head. "It's not starting out real well."

"Myra's been at my throat ever since I moved some stuff in." I tipped over the shot glass on the table and busied myself rolling it in circles. "I swear to God, if she ever pulls . . ."

"Whoa, whoa!" interrupted Jocko quickly, "Back up. Since you *moved in?*"

I tried to dismiss it quickly. "Moved *some stuff* in. I've still got my place. I just keep a few things over there."

"Even so . . ." He suddenly smelled a little worried and slightly happy. "You never even left a toothbrush at Linda's and you *proposed* to her."

I didn't know how to explain it. It's not like I had a choice. It sort of happened without much input from me. I can't just make the feelings go away. The need to be with Sue. A part of me doesn't *want* it to go away. I feel things I've never felt before and it's incredible! But it's scary and annoying and frustrating too. That much I told Jocko. He nodded sagely like he'd been there before.

Then it happened again. Free-falling; frozen in place. Again I was in two places at once. I could see Jocko. See the bar, feel the table under my hand—but I was somewhere else too. I felt happy. Heard a second heartbeat that wasn't my own. There were hands on my shoulders rubbing gently and it was nice. I saw light and polished wood superimposed over the bar. I heard a loud crash, like wood breaking but hard and fast. There was female laughter. I smelled Linda's signature perfume.

I looked around me. She wasn't anywhere close that I could see. Wherever Sue was, I was with her again. I felt her surprise when she felt me with her and the shock broke the connection. I was myself again. It was like a brick wall was suddenly constructed in my head, shutting out the sensations. The wall smelled like fur.

"You okay?" I heard Jocko ask as though in a dream. "You disappeared again."

I sounded as shaky as I felt. "Yeah. I'm fine."

I stayed at Nick's all night. Jocko let me stay in my booth even after he closed up. He did take the bottle away from me. It's the law.

I got back to Sue's place around dawn. She was still up.

When I walked in the door I could smell her. Soft and musky, worried and remorseful. She had fun but would rather have been with me. I wanted to hold her, touch her. But I knew that if I laid a single finger on her, all would be forgiven. I couldn't seem to help it. I didn't have to like it, though.

We went downstairs so we could have some privacy.

"Did you have fun?" I asked casually as I stripped off my shoes, emptied my pockets and checked my piece.

"You know I did." She gave an amused sniff that was not quite a chuckle. "You were there for part of it."

I couldn't acknowledge that. It was too weird. *Way* too weird. I kept moving, kept the hell away from her. "Where were you?"

"I saw John but you know that. He didn't think I should drive. So I called Linda. I couldn't think of anyone else. She came and got me. We bowled."

"Bowled?" It would explain the images. Bright lights, pins falling.

"They've got a bowling alley in their basement." Bright citrus blended with some other emotions that I don't know yet. "I like Carmine. He reminds me of you."

He should. We grew up together.

Sue smiled happily. "He's decided that Linda and I were twins separated at birth."

"How so?" I sat down on the couch and patted the seat next to me. She sat down with a little bounce.

Her smile remained. She turned in her seat and moved one bent leg onto the cushion. She put her left hand on the back of the couch, not quite touching me. "We are so much alike! We have the same views on politics. We like the same movies, the same foods." She smelled sad suddenly yet still happy. Wet tangerines. Weird.

"It's how I always thought having a sister would be. But how can I be so close to someone that I barely know? It was like . . . okay, she told a story about when she was a kid. Her older brother stole a candy bar and then blamed her. That happened to me all the time. But I knew what she would say next. I knew how her parents punished her, as though I remembered hearing the story before. But I just met her! Is that strange?"

It's strange all right. *Scary* to be more accurate. I knew that story. Sue was picking up on my memories. Feeling the warm fuzzies I still have for Linda.

I shook my head, trying to break that image and at the same time remembering something else. "Who else was there? There was someone else."

"Oh!" She blushed. "Barbara was there too."

"Barbara?"

The blush remained. "She's the woman from the Blue Velvet Room. The one that Linda was . . . well, *interested in*." I smiled knowingly. I reached up and touched her arm to ease her embarrassment. I ran fingers along her skin. I couldn't help but admit that I enjoyed the electricity as it played over my hand.

She tipped her head like a bird. "That was strange too. Their relationship doesn't seem to bother me anymore. Once I saw them together . . . it's like they're a couple and so are she and Carmine. We talked about how odd I felt at first. Linda was real open and honest about why she's the way she is. She made it seem so absolutely *normal*. We talked about everything and nothing. Carmine took Barbara home about one and then went to close one of the clubs. Linda and I stayed up all night and told dirty jokes and laughed about stupid crooks, the television and people we both know. God! Just everything. I just got home a few minutes ago myself."

So, not waiting up after all. She stopped suddenly and looked at me as though she just remembered something. "Oh! That reminds me. Barbara says hi."

I shook my head. "I don't know anyone named Barbara."

"She knew a lot about you. It was definitely you." She tried another approach. "About 5'2", long, reddish-gold hair? Has a body that would stop traffic?"

She saw my confusion and tried to think of something that would get a response. "She has the most incredible eyes. They're almost golden, with a darker ring around the pupil. It's a real startling effect."

Golden eyes. Wolf eyes. That did it. My voice was awestruck and horrified. "B*abs*! Linda and *Babs*?" I couldn't even fathom Linda sleeping with my mentor/attacker.

Sue seemed startled at my reaction. "Is there something wrong? You suddenly smell scared."

Linda and Babs. Wow . . . Carmine would have his hands full with those two. It sunk into my brain slowly, from a distance. I apparently wasn't hitting on all cylinders. "What did you say?"

"I asked if there was something wrong," she repeated, confused. "You look nervous."

I shook my head, quick and tense, standing up and backing away. "No. That's not what you said. You said I *smell scared*."

She shrugged and stood as well. "I might have, I guess. It's the same thing."

I felt my heartbeat increase and there was a whole flock of butterflies or maybe bats in my stomach. She was smelling emotions like I could. It wasn't a big deal to her. That was worse. Yeah, definitely bats. Clawing and churning and making me nauseated. Scared didn't cover it. The connection between us was getting tighter. The circle growing smaller. Ever closer. Like a noose. If she was getting my wolf traits and I was seeing things through her eyes, where would it end?

"Are you all right?" Sue seemed truly concerned. She moved closer to me and I backed away almost unconsciously. I could smell her. Smell her worry; concern; affection. Sweet musk. Trees and dew and moss. As she stepped closer I could smell the thick sweet beginnings of her desire. She stopped suddenly and her nostrils flared. Like she caught my scent too.

Now closer still. I could see the desire and hunger flare out from her eyes. They grew darker and more electric. I stopped abruptly as my back hit the wall. Why should I be afraid of this? Why was I terrified that she would touch me?

As soon as the questions appeared in my mind, I knew the answer. The feeling that I get when I'm with Sue, even without sex, is like an addiction. There's a high when she's there and a dark and bottomless low when she's not. Like any addiction, it's out of control. Out of my hands. I *need to* be with her.

Sex is one thing. I know people who are addicted to sex. It's the physical sensation, the carnal need. That's the addiction. Not the person. This addiction was to *Sue*, not what we did in bed.

I realized that if she were in danger I would kill for her. I *had* killed for her. I would drop everything in my life to be with her. With a shudder I realized that I'd die for her. I would willingly lose my entire personality. Thirty-seven years of individuality . . . gone.

She took one more pace. We were almost touching. I was shaking but couldn't seem to tell her no. I couldn't convince my muscles to move away. She touched my cheek with her hand and it felt so incredibly good. I closed my eyes and savored the tingling contact.

She moved that last fraction of an inch and I let her. I kept my eyes closed and breathed in the scent of her. I balled my hands into fists to keep from reaching out to pull her against me. I desperately wanted to wallow in her scent, in her body. But I couldn't stop her from touching me. God help me. She ran hands down my cheeks, down my neck and ended up by resting them on my shoulders. She leaned forward and pressed her body the full length of mine. My hands were shaking now. They wanted to do something that I refused to let them do. I could feel my teeth clenched tight together. All of the muscles in my body were rigid, fighting the need. I could beat this. I would have control of my own life!

Her words were a whisper, hurt, confused. "You don't want me . . . Why?"

She moved back from me. I could feel the electricity between us lengthen and stretch like a rubber band. It danced along my body and made me open my eyes to look at her. She stood in the middle of the living room, her eyes were wounded. She wouldn't meet my gaze. But even through all of that she smelled like warmth and desire. She smelled like something that belonged to me. Just me. Like a favorite sweatshirt or a child's blanket.

I spoke softly but it was loud to my ears. Being around her seemed to bring out the wolf qualities more strongly. "I'm losing myself, Sue. Getting lost inside of you." I walked toward her even though I knew it was a bad idea. The current strengthened; sweet tingles. I stopped.

"Any more I don't know whether I'm feeling my own emotions or yours. I don't want to lose my identity; my sense of self."

She looked at me then. Then she nodded. "I know. Like running with you when you were a wolf or seeing the bar when I was at Linda's."

She saw the bar? I didn't realize it went both ways!

"But I'm not as afraid of it as you are." She moved a little closer to me. "It's not bad. It's just different. I sort of like some of the stuff, like the running. And the sex! You can't deny that it's incredible." She smiled and it made my stomach pull.

I was actually trembling. "No, I can't deny it. But don't you see? That's the problem. It's *too* good."

She slipped her arms around my waist. She smiled at me. "For the first time, Tony, I think that there might be a reason to live. It's because of you—because of whatever is happening to us. Maybe if I try real hard, I can have a life. Who knows? I might even stand up to Bekki and Mitzi."

My body didn't listen to my brain. It did nothing to protect itself. My arms reached for her and pulled her against me. I swallowed hard. She slid her hands underneath my shirt. The tingles made me shudder. It could be so good. But the thoughts of danger kept rising from the depths of my mind like creatures from a Lovecraft novel. She had already been used against me once. My enemies were becoming her enemies, and I couldn't be with her twenty-four hours a day.

The bottomless emerald of her eyes sucked me inside them once more. The pleasure raced across my mind, smothering the doubts. All I could think about was her body against mine; her skin touching me; her lips; her scent, and I was lost again. Drowning in her, basking in the warmth of the electric tide that crashed over me. I kissed her slowly, deeply. Like I would crawl inside her body.

When it ended, she took my hand and led *me* into the bedroom. I gave in. Damn! what a wimp I am. I didn't stop her when she opened my shirt one button at a time. She planted gentle kisses on my skin in a downward path. She was kneeling in front of me when she pulled down my pants to expose a part of me so dense with blood it was almost painful.

She took me in completely and it was at once both velvet soft and cutting sharp. My head fell back of its own accord and my eyes closed. I was beyond breathless. It was even more intense than I had imagined. Her teeth scraped me lightly and it was my turn to cry out; pleasure and pain. She only took a taste; a slow, lingering sample that ended with a quick pull that weakened my knees and shut out coherent thought. She stood and pushed me back on the bed. If I bounced, I don't remember.

I watched her with animal hunger as she slipped off the silken panties she wore. When she sheathed me and straddled me I couldn't think. I just let it happen and enjoyed the rush.

She moved over me and instinct took over. I ran my hands along the curves of her body, kneaded her breasts as she rocked over me. I grabbed her forearms and pushed her backwards to change the angle while she moved. She cried out as her back arched. It pleased me. When she finished trembling from the climax, she leaned over me and kissed my neck. She murmured in my ear. "I love you, Tony."

It touched something in the deepest center of the wolf inside. Sparked something that reached out to her. When it pulled, she went. She followed the lure through a door that I didn't know was there. I rolled her over, still in her. Her legs wrapped around me and we moved together like we were one body. I could see the edge. I could have it all if only I'd let go. I just had to let it happen.

I kissed her neck then bit her softly. I gripped her skin and ran frantic hands over her body. Her clothing defeated my need to touch all of her. I needed more, even more than the first time I was with her. She clung to me, bit me with abandon. She moved against me with a fury and passion that made my last shred of willpower break.

My arms tightened around her until I finally had to let go and clutch the bed for fear of hurting her. Every thrust built power. It flowed between us and grew to white hot intensity.

The orgasm caught me unaware. It centered nowhere and everywhere. Every nerve, every muscle achieved the absolute height of ecstasy. It was unlike anything in my experience. Sort of like living your life with only the moon; and suddenly seeing the sun for the first time. No other woman would ever be enough. No other sensation could fulfill.

I wanted to say so much but I didn't have the words. It wasn't love. It was more and less. I couldn't think of anything to say to her words except, "I know, baby. I know." And I did know. I could smell it, feel it like a pulse against my brain. I felt another barrier break inside me. A little one but still . . .

Tighter and tighter squeezes the noose.

Chapter 27

I was sitting on the floor in Humphries' two days later, tearing apart the security sensors for regular maintenance when my phone rang. I was going to let the voice mail pick up, but when I glanced at the display, I answered it.

"Tony here."

Carmine's voice hissed over the line. "It's on. Find the kid. He's got the details. Your usual fee." He must have finished the arrangements. I sighed. Tonight wasn't the best night. I'd paid a bunch of money for tickets for a traveling Broadway show. They were second row center, and Sue had been ecstatic. But there was no way I could attend the play and still make the hit and this job was more important.

"This one's on the house," I said with a dark smile. I'd been thinking about the new hitter in town. The only ones who could have sent him were Vito or Leo—probably Leo. It was his style.

Carmine and I had been very busy boys for the past forty-eight hours. I hadn't seen much of Sue, but that was okay. She's been spending a couple of hours a day with John in therapy. Linda and Babs have been keeping her busy in the evening playing pool and bowling. Anything to keep her away from her family. I'd have to thank Linda for that. Of course, it helped that she'd met them.

I could feel in my head that both John and Linda were helping. It made my life easier. I could continue on with the plan without worrying about Sue. She was in safe company.

Carmine's been real low-key about the whole operation. He's been having Marvin pose as Nico when calls come in. Nico's contact has been getting fed bad info. In the meantime,

Carmine has been changing schedules and locations of materials like mad, so that the paperwork is no longer valid.

I hung up with Carmine and immediately dialed in the number to the theater box office. There was one more showing the following night. I was able to switch the tickets, but not for the same seats. Oh, well. Sue would just have to understand that I had to work. I couldn't tell her what sort of job I had to do. I'd already changed some things in the past couple of days so I could work on systems after business hours.

One of the systems had been at Carmine's house. We rerouted a bunch of his security sensors and feeds so that if you cut the wiring, the lights on the panel will go out, but a silent alarm trips in Carmine's war room in the basement. That's where he's been spending most of his time. Linda hasn't said anything, but she goes around armed for bear. I can't tell her that there's no need. The wolf bitch living with them can protect her just fine.

Babs tried to talk to me again when I was working on the alarms, but I wouldn't listen to her. I just kept asking Carmine to remove her so I could work. Fortunately, he complied. I know I'll have to deal with her eventually, especially if they were going to stay a trio—and it looks like they are. It's not just lust I've been smelling.

I'd be happier if I never had to see Babs's face again. Every time I do, the nightmares come back.

It's as much a memory as a dream. I'm lying on my stomach, wearing black. I'd been studying the redhead for a week, watching her every move. I knew she would be walking this path, at this time. When she reaches the top of the rise, I raise my weapon.

She stops halfway down the other side of the small hill. I see her head raise. Her nose points into the air and she turns in a circle in the light of the moon. She gazes directly at me, as though she can see me through the dense trees.

I pull the trigger.

It's impossible, but she moves out of the way. I couldn't possibly have missed from that range. There's a blur of motion and she's suddenly next to me.

"You have no idea what you're dealing with!" I was too surprised to ask what the hell that meant.

She reaches up in a blur of speed. I feel her fingernails grip my throat and dig in. She lifts me into the air like a toy doll as blood pours over her upraised arm.

I clutch at her hand but her fingers are like iron bars. I kick out with my legs, but it's useless. With a sudden movement, she flings me to the ground and my throat tears away in her fist. The pain was immediate and intense. White waves of light shoot through my brain. My scream was cut short when the equipment necessary to make sound falls where she threw it to the ground beside me. The only sound I can make is a gurgle that I've heard before. I try to use my hands to stem the flow of blood, but found that the hole was too big. I was going to die.

"Don't worry," she says coldly as I lay bleeding to death on the ground, wiping her hands on my shirt to clean them. "It will only hurt for a few minutes. It's more than you deserve, assassin. I should tear you apart and feast on your bones for hunting me."

My life flashes before my eyes. No regrets. I've always known I'd come to a violent end. Someone out there would be faster or meaner. I was just surprised at how much it hurt. I'd always expected a bullet in the brain.

Mercifully I blacked out, expecting to die.

I hadn't died. I'd woken up screaming the next morning—and every morning after for nearly a year. This morning, I felt Sue in the back of my mind, trying to grasp what had happened. She felt nauseous from the images and I knew when she threw up on the floor beside her bed.

God, I hate Babs. Someday I'll see that bitch dead, but not while she's with Carmine. Whether I like it or not, he feels something for her.

I put the sensors back together quickly and tested them to make sure they functioned. Then I cleaned up my tools and headed home to prepare. Carmine has given no indication to anyone that he even knows the briefcase exists. It's intentional. When I kill the hitter, the body will get misplaced in the morgue. Then we'll wait for Leo's, or Vito's, boys to come into town to investigate.

We hoped that by not letting on, the person behind it might make another grab for the case. The hit on Carmine was the start. I figured that someone would probably show up on my doorstep next. I was taking extra precautions with security at home and in my car, but not letting on that I was expecting anything. The only ones in Carmine's organization who know the whole scoop are me, Mike and Marvin. Even the regular guys were out of the loop for this deal until Carmine is certain of their loyalty.

I glanced at my new watch, a Timex SeAL model with an Indiglo face. I cancelled the rest of my maintenance calls for the day and spent the remainder of the time preparing myself. I met with Scotty and he gave me the details. Sally had stalled again and set the meeting for tonight. The girl would try to get him to bend her over the bed so that he was in position. She wasn't sure it would work. Neither was I.

The next time I'd glanced at the lighted dial, it read 12:01 a.m. I released the button, and the darkness closed around me again, cool and silent. I leaned against the concrete wall, feeling a mild chill seep through my coat. I always wear a coat on jobs.

The night was warm, but the dimly lit garage held an air of the approaching fall. The window that I watched remained dark. The girl had assured me that he would come to the room before 12:00.

I waited.

And watched.

A distant rumble warned of an approaching car, even before I saw headlights scan the wall. Damn it! The place was supposed to be deserted. The car turned the corner to the next level. My level. I stepped behind a massive pillar. The floor moved under me as the car neared, then passed me without notice. I observed with mild interest as the car parked, and the engine shut off.

The door of the car opened, and a high heeled pump attached to a nylon-clad leg appeared. The woman stood.

She reached into the car and removed her shoulder bag. She was attractive in an elegant way. Her vivid blue business skirt and patterned shirt set off her dark hair. She was intent on her own business, not even caring to look around her. Stupid. If I were a rapist, I could take her now. She started to walk toward the elevators, across the darkened garage, her heels clicking on the concrete floor. She stopped briefly to point the remote lock toward the car. I heard the familiar 'beep, beep, boop' as the door locks latched.

Isn't that the way with people? Protect the car, but ignore their own safety. The car can be replaced. Oh, well.

She took no notice of me. No surprise. I'm never noticed unless I want to be.

A flash of light caught my attention, and I turned away from the woman. Back toward the apartment. I reached under my leather duster and carefully drew my weapon. The drapes in the room were open slightly and the door had been blocked open by inserting a screw into the guide. The mark wouldn't be able to close them. The man came to the sliding door and fought it for a few minutes before giving up.

He looked out into the darkness, right toward me. I knew he couldn't see me over a block away. I could see him without much strain of my supernatural eyes, although not clearly enough to use the gun without a scope.

I recognized his face from the packet that I had taken from Scotty. It was a shame that I had insisted on using the Thompson tonight. With a semi-auto, I could take him right now.

Through the open curtain, I saw the girl, Sally, enter the room. She *was* young, not more than seventeen, although she looked fifteen. She was wearing a halter and shorts, and had her long blonde hair tied in pigtails. She had a fringe of bangs, and wide blue eyes.

They wasted no time. The mark walked past her and locked the door. She was waiting for him when he turned, and stepped into his embrace. Their clothing disappeared in moments, and I watched as he lifted her onto the bed and they began to have sex. Not make love. There was no feeling, no emotion. The parted drape gave me a clear view of their act, and I raised my gun in front of me.

Sally ran her hands through his hair and whispered to him. She smiled brightly—convincingly. He pulled out of her and she scrambled off the bed. She bent over the mattress and I saw him stand up behind her. It was now or never.

It was then that I realized that Sue was with me, feeling what I felt—the weight of the gun through tight leather gloves, the cool air blowing strands of hair back from my forehead. She knew what I was doing, and she was appalled.

That made me angry. She had no right. I had no time to feel her emotions as I stared through the scope at the target. I cut the tie to her abruptly, using my mind. It was the first time I'd ever been able to do so.

When the mark raised his head the next time, I pulled the trigger. He was thrown forward by the impact and landed heavily on the bed with Sally pinned beneath him. She scrambled from under his dead weight, covered with blood. She backed away from the body with a scream that cut the night. Panic filling her face. She hadn't understood the reality of what she'd agreed to—what she started. She grabbed her clothes and ran from the room. I watched for a few seconds more to make sure that the mark didn't breathe or move.

I turned back to the darkness of the garage. It was time for me to leave now—before anyone could decide what to do. I placed the Thompson back in its shoulder holster, and buttoned my coat. It had been a trick to find a holster to fit. Usually, I keep my weapon in a secret compartment in my tool kit. I have two identical repair kits, down to the nicks and dents, with one difference. The black electrical tape that winds around the handle in a seemingly haphazard fashion—isn't. My *day* case is wound clockwise, while my *night* case is counter-clockwise. I can tell the difference by touch. Unfortunately, the scope on the Thompson wouldn't fit in the case. I'd had to search all over town for a holster to fit it. It weighs about the same as a hunting rifle under my arm and has an extra strap around my waist to keep it at a decent drawing angle. Another reason for the coat.

I picked up the grappling hook and rope that waited on the floor beside me, and strode toward the center of the garage. I was parked on the first floor, but a man walking down the stairs or leaving the elevator might be noticed even this far away.

I had taken care to file off the barbs from each of the five hooks. I gently placed two of the hooks over the railing that guarded the opening in the center of the garage. The core was open from the first floor all the way up to the fifth, where I was. The rope had been painted grey to match the concrete. I flipped the rope over the railing and watched it spiral down. When it stopped swinging, I climbed carefully over the railing.

That's when I heard a woman's muffled scream. I had no time for curiosity, but I silently climbed back over and moved toward the sound.

The woman in blue was pressed against the wall. A fat white man with long black hair, and clad in a dirty T-shirt, was fondling her with one hand. The other hand was tight over her mouth. Apparently, I had not been the only predator in the garage this night. The woman was no concern of mine, and she had been careless. I turned back to my own business.

Then I started to think. I hate it when I do that. Sue was becoming a bad influence, even when she's not in my head.

Did the woman deserve to suffer this man's touch, his penetration? What she had endured so far would teach her to be more careful.

I sighed and reached under my coat again. I was close enough that I didn't even need the sight. In fact, it wouldn't work at this distance. I opened the action to remove the spent shell and insert another from my pocket. The shell wasn't supposed to, but it popped out of the action and flew through the air. It landed in the darkness, and I could hear it roll down the concrete ramp. I followed it as quickly as I could without being noticed. The pair at the elevator didn't hear the tiny metallic sound or my movements. I caught sight of it again, just as it was rolling into a sealed drain. Damn it! I'd have to leave it.

Now I was angry, which made it simpler. I inserted another bullet and slowly worked the barrel up the man's back, to his neck, and then to his head. He didn't notice. His breathing was heavy, and he moaned as he pressed his body against her. The sound was louder than the woman's smothered protests.

Her eyes were closed. She had stopped struggling, becoming passive. She was no match for the big man's strength, and so had given in to the inevitable.

But she didn't want to see what her attacker was doing, so she didn't see me.

I felt a certain satisfaction as the bullet erupted from the muzzle.

The man dropped to the ground wordlessly. His stringy hair covered the entry hole nicely. The woman stood there startled for a moment, and then screamed. The sound bounced off the low ceiling and filled the garage.

She gathered her ripped and ruined blouse around her and ran toward the elevator, and safety. She was missing one of her pumps. It didn't occur to her to take the other one off, so she limped toward the protection of humanity. I really need to get out of here fast now. Damn it to hell! I should have left her to her fate.

I hurried back to my task, since the attempted rape would bring the curious quicker than the murder down the block. I slid down the rope faster than normal, the rough nylon stinging my hands even through the black leather gloves. My suede duster billowed around me like a cape as I descended.

When I reached the bottom, I made a sudden movement of the rope, and the hook detached from the railing, falling into my arms. Just the way it's supposed to work. I practice. A lot.

I quickly, but not hurriedly, walked toward the rental car. I opened the trunk and put the hook inside, underneath the

spare tire. I took off my gloves and my coat and put them in
the back seat under a blanket, along with my holster. I was
wearing a business shirt underneath, complete with a tie. I
got in the car and drove out of the garage, making sure I fed
the proper amount into the machine at the gate before I left.

My work here was done.

The next night when I called to tell Sue to get ready, she
abruptly cancelled. She said Myra was sick. I hadn't been
able to feel her in my head all day. It was sort of pleasant,
but unnerved me a little. When I figured out that we weren't
going anywhere and all that money was wasted, I was roy-
ally pissed.

I decided I might as well take care of my equipment. I
always clean my piece after I use it. Then I clean all the others—in case I forgot one last time. It's relaxing. I heard her
unlock the front door, and I breathed in the scent of her summer forest. It was made bitter by the boiling coffee that surrounded her like a cloud.

Something inside of her was enraged that I *needed* to
clean the Thompson.

"You did it, didn't you!?" She slammed the door behind
her. She was trying to make me jump. It didn't work.

I shrugged noncommittally. "Did what?" Pieces of the
Thompson lay on newspaper on the coffee table. I had
removed the barrel and it was soaking in cleaner. I was
preparing to run the rod through. The frame had already
been oiled. The Taurus and Sig waited their turns on the
floor.

"*Killed that man*," she whispered tersely.

"Yeah. It's what I do. Your point?"

She didn't reply. She just stood there, ammonia horrified,
burnt coffee angry and thick, wet betrayal. She must not
have known whether or not I completed the job.

"You don't feel anything, do you? Some person is dead—
lying in a gutter and you just don't give a shit!" She was
more angry than I had ever seen her. Getting my temper too.
A small part of me was pleased.

"He wasn't in a gutter. He was on a bed. And I really don't

want to discuss this, Sue." I pushed cleaner through the barrel with a wire scrubber.

"Afraid someone will *overhear?* Feeling a little guilty?" Her words were sarcastic, biting.

"No." I stopped my cleaning to look at her. "The place is soundproof. If you want to blast the place, knock yourself out. But it's none of your business. It's my job; my life. I explained that."

I returned to the gun. Over and over, I scrubbed the cleaner through the barrel. Like I could clean away the sour smell of her disapproval if I just kept working.

I decided to take the bull by the horns but I kept my cool. "What's the *real* reason you cancelled? I know damn well it's not your mom." I didn't look at her. I already knew the answer but I wanted to hear it from her lips.

"Fine." She walked toward me and stood over me with hands on hips, "You want to know? I could *never* enjoy watching a play knowing that someone had lost their life."

That's what I was afraid of. She could have left her mom for the evening, but she wouldn't sit with a killer.

Goddamn it! No! No matter what bound us, it was none of her business. I'd just have to find a way to keep her out of my head during jobs—control her involvement.

I stopped cleaning and carefully placed the Thompson, cleaning rod still in the barrel, on the newspapers. The pungent smell of the chemicals gave me a headache, which was annoying. It didn't improve my mood. I stared at her and she stared back. My eyes were as angry as hers. She looked away first.

"No! Don't look away," I said harshly. "Look at me!" I paused and repeated softly but still with force, "Look at me, Sue." She did. Her gaze was both angry and pained.

"I am an *assassin*. I kill for a living." She looked away again.

"*Look at me!*" Her head snapped back. "Don't start this holier than thou shit, Sue! You sought me out because of my profession. Wanted to hire me to *end your life*. This is no surprise. No big secret that I've kept from you." I stood and walked toward her. She stood her ground without flinching. I wouldn't hurt her. I *couldn't* hurt her. The tricky part was, she knew it. It made me wonder whether I'd be able to do the job.

"When I met you I had three jobs to do. Three jobs that I had already accepted, had already been paid for. This one was a surprise. But I told you about the others." I put a hand on her shoulder. Even angry, the tingles were still there. Her gaze was on the floor. She wouldn't meet my eyes.

"Since I agreed to be your bodyguard I've had nine calls on my pager. Nine prospective jobs." I let the words sink in. "I *turned all of them down*." Surprise showed on her face as she glanced into my eyes.

"A bodyguard," I said, "Is a lifestyle. I guard your body. Only yours. Nobody gets near you. Nobody hurts you. I will kill for you. I will take a bullet for you."

There was tense silence for a moment. "But what about the others? You said three jobs. What about the people who are going to die—who you're going to *kill*? How can I live with that?"

I shrugged. "I don't know how you're going to make peace with yourself, Sue. All I know is that I have. Three people were scheduled to die. If not by my hand, then by someone else's. But understand that they *will die*."

I put my hands on her waist. She let me, but only just. "If it will make you feel any better, this guy was a killer. He was sent here to assassinate Carmine. Linda probably would have been eliminated, too. As for the rest, they've done enough crimes to get them life in prison. One would probably get the chair. None of them are disgruntled spouses or ex-lovers. These jobs are just business. But understand that even if they weren't, I've made commitments and I *will* fulfill them."

She had smelled startled when I revealed the nature of my job last night. I could feel her anger and hurt disappear in a flurry of worry about Linda and Carmine.

I tilted her chin with one hand, lifting her eyes to mine. I spoke softly, but with conviction. "I don't want to lose you over this, Sue, but my promises are important to me. Can you understand that?"

She nodded but didn't speak. She was near tears. I couldn't help that. I pulled her into my arms. Eventually, she held me back. We stayed like that for some time, while she tried to sort things out in her mind. By the time she went home, she was better. Still tense and skittish, but better.

I knew this was going to be a sticking point. A make or break. One of us would have to bend.

It wouldn't be me.

Chapter 28

The moon was nearing. I could feel it like a shadowy presence just behind the sun. From now until it's full, when I look into the vivid blue sky, I'll feel the pull. Soon, said the wolf. Soon we'll be free.

Sue had been spending more time in appointments with John since the hit the other night. She was keeping herself consciously closed off. It annoyed me that I was sorry she didn't want to be inside my head, while at the same time I didn't want to be in hers. She seemed to be more proficient at cutting the ties than I was. Maybe it's because she accepts it as real, and can therefore deal with it better.

I felt it when she left this morning. I slept in for a change, and after a slow and leisurely shower, I decided to have lunch at Nick's. John-Boy's office is on the way. As I was driving past, I got caught at the light. I noticed Sue's little green car in the parking lot. No surprise.

But as I thought about her it happened. Not like last time. This was different. I started hearing her voice as though on the radio.

I was just sitting there in traffic when suddenly the conversation was clear as a bell. It was odd because John's office is soundproof—and I was seven stories down, on the street.

I should have just driven on but I didn't. I turned into the parking lot and found a space. Then I sat there and listened. I put the newspaper that I had planned to read at lunch on the steering wheel so it looked a little more normal.

"Thanks again for seeing me, Doctor Corbin. Really. I'm sorry I'm so much trouble."

"You've said that five times now. You don't need to keep apologizing. Go ahead with what you were saying."

"I just keep going back to the fight we had. I can't seem to get past it. I don't understand why I was so angry with him. He was absolutely right. I know what he is."

John said nothing. He knows his biz.

Sue paused. "Before I met Tony my life was so . . . sensible. But I hated everything about it. I wanted to die. Now, I've met gangsters and their wives, strippers, killers, and detectives. Those kind of people are normal for Tony. But it's all new to me."

I got sucked inside again. I heard the smile in her voice. "I've never met anyone as wonderful as Linda. I never imagined that there could be people as twisted as Leo." I felt a wave of fear race through her. I couldn't quite smell it.

"I've been places and done things most people only read about." She stopped for a moment, lost in thought.

"Mom set up Tony, but what if it had been real? What if Mom had found evidence on something he's *actually done*? I know what Tony does. He would go to jail and that scares me. But a part of me believes that he should be in jail."

Well, this was interesting! I turned a page of the paper by instinct. Nobody reads a paper without moving pages.

"But *another* part of me agrees with him. The people would die anyway. People die every day. Why should I feel sorry for them? I really don't want Tony to change. At least I don't think I do."

She paused. "No. I don't. What he does makes him what he is. He's smart and funny and affectionate. But he can also be cold and ruthless. He's got this sense of . . . completeness." Her words were soft and warm. "I don't understand it, but I think I like who he is more than I like myself."

Then she stopped. Her voice sounded odd. "He told me once that I'm not really in love with him. That it's just the excitement, the constant intensity."

A part of me never really believed that.

"Is it?" asked John.

She must have shaken her head. I felt soft hair brush my

neck. This is too weird. "No. He's wrong. I'm drawn to him. He's a part of me that I didn't know was missing. Does that make any sense?"

There was a moment of silence. "Sue, what you're feeling is very common. Not that Tony is common, mind you. Tony marches to music that only he hears. But your confusion between your duty to yourself and your role as a human is absolutely normal. Should you stop death or pain when you can?" I knew John. He would be shrugging about now. We'd had this discussion before.

"It's a question I've asked myself more than once. Where a person draws the line on their involvement with the rest of the world is something that each of us deals with. Some people choose to be activists. They make their role as a human more important than themselves. Other people travel the opposite direction. They let the world handle itself and concentrate only on their own lives. Neither is wrong."

Another pause. "In other circumstances I would advise someone like you not to get involved with someone like Tony . . . "

Gee, thanks, John. I love you too.

"But we *are* talking about Tony. I understand Tony. He has value. I grew up in the same world he did. He's ruthless, but he has morals. He wouldn't kill a child, for example. He has the ability to love. Most killers don't. I won't say that he *can be saved* because he doesn't need saving. If I thought that, or thought that locking him away would help him, I would have done it myself years ago. You need to decide whether or not you can let go of what you consider to be your role in the world and love Tony."

"I can't have it both ways, can I?"

John laughed. "Not without becoming a split personality. What Tony does for a living isn't 'right' as mankind defines it in religious writings. That's where you seem to be having the conflict. But it also isn't evil if you look at intent."

I felt it again when Sue nodded. "He doesn't *wish* death on others. He said that once."

"Correct. What he does has always existed. Tony wasn't

kidding when he said that if he didn't do it someone else would. I know several that would like to take his job right now."

"Will he ever stop? What would he be like if he did?"

"When he gets tired of the running, and the smoke and mirrors he deals with every day, he'll stop. Tony doesn't run on adrenaline like some do. It's a job to him. Someday he'll quit. His Dad did just fine when he retired. I understand he's an upstanding citizen down in Florida." I heard Sue chuckle.

"A lot of 'upstanding citizens' throughout history were scoundrels early in their life. Can you wait Tony out? Or if he never changes, is he worth it?" There was another pause.

"I have to decide that, don't I?"

"Yes, and you *can* decide it. You're capable of it. Don't think about your mother or what she wants. Don't think about your sisters or their children. Don't even think about Tony. Think about Sue. What is best for *you*?"

"I'll think about it. I either have to accept him and love him, or . . ."

"Or not. But even without him, *you* have value. You don't need to die, Sue. You only need to find your place." I felt her accept that, believe it. It pleased me.

"But what if my place makes *me* a different person? What if Tony only stays with me because I'm like I am now? Will he leave me if my place is somewhere different?"

Hmm. Good one. I had to think about that for a minute. Do I only want her as she is now? Or am I trying to raise her to become a vision of I want her to be? I think it's both. Why would I be helping her get her head on straight if I wanted her to stay the way she is now? And if her place is somewhere else, then so be it. I'd already steeled my emotions to lose her anyway.

"I wish I could answer that, Sue. I don't know what's in Tony's head right now. But I can tell you how he's responded to similar situations in the past. He appreciates— even demands growth in himself and in others. He challenges his mind daily. Reads constantly. He's annoyed by stupidity and laziness. He wouldn't even put up with you unless you were bright. I think the more you grow the more supportive he'll be."

His voice changed slightly and I could imagine him shrugging. "I could be wrong, of course. I have been before."

Then he changed the subject. "But what about your meeting with your sister today? Why are you seeing her? I thought after the fight you had . . ."

I folded up the paper and started the car. They'd be going on for a few minutes. I'd heard what I wanted to. She was slowly healing. But I wished I hadn't gotten a knot in my gut when John suggested "without him." Shit.

I flipped on the turn signal and entered traffic. As I drove away I expected that the conversation would fade. It didn't. I couldn't seem to shake the voices. It was like they were in the car with me or talking on the radio. It was sensory input, not mental.

"You remember the fight?" Sue sounded surprised.

There was a distinctly male chuckle. "I have a good memory, Sue. Yes, I remember the fight. It was about riding lessons."

"I still can't believe her *nerve*! Where does Bekki get off thinking that just because I have money I should support her family for the rest of my life? It's *my* money. *I* bought the ticket. Bekki called the Lotto a waste of money. A tax on the stupid. Now suddenly she deserves to share in my fortune?" Spite and bitterness rushed through my head.

I chuckled. I could almost see her gesturing with her hands. She and Linda have that in common.

"I set up the trust, tried to be nice about it. Now that they've become *nouveau riche*—because of me—they suddenly 'can't live on' what the trust gives them. Bekki and Robert are set for life and *I'm* supposed to pay for riding lessons for Cindy and Mike? Because their new friends at the country club are laughing at them and they 'just can't afford the extra expense'? I don't understand that. How could she have the gall to even ask? Why do they feel entitled to things that I have? I just don't understand!"

"It's not unusual, Sue. I know you're having a hard time

grasping it but it's a common way of thought. You have more money than you need. You should share happily because they're your family."

There was a exasperated release of breath from Sue.

"I can only explain them, Sue. I can't change them. So why do you want to talk to her again? Why are you setting yourself up for more pain?"

"I did something before I came here. I want to tell her in person." There was determination in Sue's voice and just a hint of fear.

When I opened the car door and stepped onto the sidewalk, the voices suddenly disappeared. It was as though the car was some sort of antenna and when I moved away from it the reception dissolved. I was suddenly by myself again. Why did it bother me that I missed it?

I almost walked back to the car to see if it would start again but I didn't. As curious as I might be about what Sue had done, if she wanted me to know she'd tell me.

I walked in the tavern and sat down on a stool at the bar. I heard a cheep on my hip and realized that my pager had been going off for some time and I hadn't heard it. I unclipped it from my belt and read the display. Three new calls. I didn't understand this sudden increase in business. I used to go for days without a single page. Now it felt like I was getting one every hour.

I spent the next ninety minutes on the pay phone in the hallway. That's twelve jobs I've refused. I think it's a new record. I sent them Scotty's way. What the hell. None went to Jerry. Not until Carmine asks me to.

I was waiting for a double order of fried shrimp and chips. When Jocko took out the kitchen in favor of a dance floor, he kept the deep fryer. It's in a small room off the walk-in fridge. It's not much, but you can cook a lot of stuff in a deep fryer. As a bonus, fried foods coat the stomach so people don't get drunk as fast, and teenagers can come in to buy sodas and listen to the live music.

Jocko was making a run to the bank which left Marni tending bar. She was just setting the basket of butterfly shrimp in front of me when Jocko came through the front door. I could smell him and watched his reflection move in the mirror behind the bar. He got a startled look when he saw me. His scent changed to anxious; fearful.

He stopped next to me and looked around him nervously. "What are you doing here, Tony?"

I looked at him in the mirror. I felt my brow furrow in confusion. "Eating lunch. Why?"

"Sommers was in here looking for you earlier." That gave him my full attention!

The bats were back in my gut. "Any idea what for?"

He motioned me to the back booth and I followed him with my shrimp and beer. If I was going to be bolting fast, I wanted it to be on a full stomach.

When I was seated he leaned toward me. "I don't know for certain but he was looking real cocky. Janice heard Sommers's partner mention on the way out that he was looking forward to nailing your ass."

Yep, definitely bats.

"They have a warrant? What'd you tell them?" I bit one shrimp off at the tail. No time for sauce.

Jocko shrugged. "I told 'em the truth—that I hadn't seen you in days. They waited for a while and talked to some of the customers before they left. They questioned Janice on the way out. She asked what they wanted you for. They wouldn't tell her anything but she overheard something about some lady who had picked you out of a photo line-up."

Shit. I knew I shouldn't have let that woman leave. I should have eliminated them both.

I heard tires screech outside and glanced out the window to see Sommers' car, followed by three squad cars. Doors opened. They had weapons drawn.

"You got a back door?" I already knew the answer.

He nodded. I gulped down the last of the shrimp, burning my tongue in the process. I took a final swallow of beer as I stood.

Thoughts not my own overwhelmed me just then. Who are you? What do you want?

The sheer power of Sue's terror engulfed me. I was suddenly on my knees and couldn't remember how I got there. I couldn't breathe past the fear.

Jocko turned when he heard the thud. I looked at him as though through gauze. I was in two places again. I was Sue. Rough hands pulled at me. There were walls around Us. Metal. A van. I heard a female scream in the background and knew it was Bekki. Sue was being abducted and I was along for the ride. I smelled a familiar scent but couldn't place it. The connection wasn't perfect yet. I was only getting pieces. Sweat. Fear. Menace. Something else. Nope. Can't remember.

Jocko was shaking me. "They're out front, Tony. Sommers! What's wrong with you?"

I tried to focus. I realized that I hadn't been breathing while I was with Sue. I filled my lungs and it burned. Panic of my own now. I had to get out of the bar. The connection dimmed for a moment.

I pulled my Sig from the waistband as the door to the bar opened. "You'll thank me later." Then I stood and moved slightly behind him and grabbed his ponytail to put him off balance. I put the gun to his head.

"What are you, nuts?" He didn't move. Probably a good plan. I had one in the chamber. "Drop it, Giodone!" exclaimed Sommers as he and three of his men entered the bar and fanned out. All guns were pointed at me.

"I will pull the trigger, Bob," I said calmly. I wasn't in my body completely. Nothing really mattered yet. "Put them down."

No officer likes a hostage situation. The bar patrons had either dived for cover or were too scared to move. One of the uniforms—he looked like a rookie—moved his thumb toward the hammer of his revolver. I put a bullet into the wall next to his head with preternatural speed. The gun immediately returned to Jocko's head.

Everybody froze.

"I *said* to put them down." I was still amazingly calm, but that's because I was too spacey to be scared. I hoped they wouldn't realize that I couldn't kill Jocko. It was best to let them think I was unstable. Hell, maybe I was unstable.

Sommers lowered his gun first and raised his opposite hand to order the others to follow suit. "I've got a warrant, Giodone. Even if you make it out of here, one call will put up roadblocks for fifty miles in every direction. Put the gun down now and we'll forget about you resisting arrest."

I smiled and it wasn't pleasant. I didn't have time for this shit. I had to get to Sue. I started to back away and pulled Jocko with me. To his credit, he followed smoothly. He didn't trip or dive. Others might have.

"We're leaving here," I said. "If you follow, you'll be picking up a body along the way. Maybe more than one. I've got nothing to lose."

Jocko blocked me as I backed behind the bar, through the employee break room and to the back door. I poked my head out to check for guards and then we slipped out the door into the adjoining building. It's not truly a dead-end inside the other part of the building—there's a locked door. Jocko has a key. I doubt the cops know about it. We were suddenly inside the upholstery shop. Faces looked at us but I wouldn't remember them later. I normally would, but I was with Sue again.

Her emergency was *not* helping right now. A wave of recognition hit me with a leaden thud. Oh, *shit*! Leo had her. Not good. Really, *really*, not good! I had to get to her.

I tried to focus on where I was there in her head. Tried to impress how important it was to give me some clue. Some way to find her.

I felt her mind center slowly as she understood. She opened herself to me and I followed, setting my fear aside. She looked around her slowly. Tried to fix names to people. She didn't know most of them. She did know Leo. He was in the front of the van. Bobby was there too. Damn it! I trusted him! I should have known better.

What direction? I asked in my head. There were no windows in the back of the van. She looked out the front, just as Jocko and I exited the upholstery shop. Nobody was waiting out front for us. I tried to position the sun that I could sense in Sue's mind with the sun that I was seeing. I pivoted my head until there was a spark of recognition. East. Yes! East but slightly north. She was traveling in a van—a black van—heading northeast.

"You with me, Tony?" Jocko asked. Again I was faced with one thing at a time.

"Northeast." I cleared my throat and then strengthened my voice. "We have to go northeast. Sue's in danger." I looked at Jocko in panic. "Can you drive me northeast?"

I was glad that Jocko has a reserved space. I opened the passenger door of his powder blue Lincoln Towncar and got inside. I automatically reached for a shoulder belt but remembered that it was old enough it only had a lap belt. He got in the driver's seat and started the engine. He glared at me with a mixture of confusion and anger. "What the hell was that about? I would have helped you. Why the gun?"

I tried to focus on his question. I blinked repeatedly. My tongue was thick and hard to move. "Hostage." I stared at him, willing him to understand my train of thought. "You're a hostage now, not an accessory. They won't do anything to you after you get me to Sue."

His brows rose and his jaw dropped. "You can barely walk, much less talk and you thought all that through while they were coming through the door? I mean, I know it's what you do, but wow!"

He pulled away from the curb and then hit the gas. He checked the rearview mirror more than once. "They'll tail us, you know."

"Then we'll have to lose them. You know Leo Scapolo?" He looked at me like I was whacked.

"Only by reputation. It's not a particularly rosy one."

"He's got my lady. I have to get her back."

"Your lady? The one you told me about? Shit." He thought for a moment and shook his head with a worried look. "Man! Leo Scapolo." He muttered under his breath. "Damn straight I'm a hostage. *Nobody* shoot the hostage."

Another glance in the rearview brought a string of curses.

He turned sharply down an alley. "Where do you need to go? You know where she is?"

I shook my head. I didn't know. Road? I asked. What kind of road? Highway? Dirt?

I felt her raise her body so she could see out the window. Highway. I heard as though she was in the car with us. Then fear stirred the adrenaline in my blood. For a brief flash, I saw through her eyes. I recognized another of the men. So did Sue. Vinny was back, and pleased to be there. I'd put odds that when Leo had looked for local talent, Vinny had jumped at the chance. Vinny is such a whore for money. I saw him through her eyes. He looked at her warily when he realized that she was being too aware. Noticing too much.

"Leo," I heard him say. "I think we ought to put her out." I felt Sue's panic as We watched Leo turn his ugly head and fix beady eyes on her.

One of the other men in the van spoke up. "Not yet. I want that case back. Where is it?"

Sue shook her head and I could see through her eyes as Leo raised his nose to sniff. "I don't know. Tony has it."

"I don't want the girl hurt until we get back those papers, Scapolo."

Leo snarled. "Don't tell me how to run my job. This is as much your fault as it is mine."

"Mr. Prezza is not pleased with your work so far, Scapolo. I've been sent to make *sure* you don't mess this up, too."

He growled low and deep and I could see Vito's boy blanch a bit. "Fine. We'll give her a little shot that will make her *talk* instead. Will that make your boss happy?"

The goon's eyes were still wide. He swallowed hard and nodded.

Leo motioned to Vinny. Sue turned as Vinny removed a syringe from a black bag. Oh no! Not a needle. No way! He removed the cap as though in slow motion. Hands grabbed Sue. One pair of hands was Bobby's. Traitorous bastard!

"No problem, pretty lady. We'll get the case back from your boyfriend. But until then, we'll have a little *fun.*"

Someone's hand pushed up her sleeve to expose bare skin. My panic added to hers. I couldn't let the needle near her—I needed her awake and alert if I was going to find her.

We started to struggle and the hands holding her tightened. Fingers dug in hard enough to bruise. I didn't care. No needles! I was panting, hyperventilating. Adrenaline rushed through muscles that weren't mine and supernatural strength followed. I felt the connection between us blow open another locked door.

My power added to hers and Sue broke free from her attackers. She kicked and punched and fought like a wildcat while I pushed her on. She knocked the needle from Vinny's hand and she punched Bobby hard enough that I felt the bone in her middle finger crack in a flash of pain.

The van swerved to knock her off balance. Leo shouted instructions, keeping out of her way all the while. Bobby re-entered the fray but I got the feeling that his heart wasn't in it. He grabbed for her and missed. It was Vinny who got fed up after she clawed manicured fingernails across his cheek. Blood dripped down and landed on his clean white shirt. He reached a hand up and it came away red.

"Fucking bitch!" he yelled. We watched as he hauled a fist back. My skills couldn't move her out of the way in time to avoid taking the punch full in the face. Her body wasn't trained to fight.

Pain erupted in Our brain. Her head snapped back and then hit the wall of the van. She sunk into unconsciousness; the connection broke.

I was in Jocko's car again, shaking and sweating. He was driving intently and trying not to watch me.

"You having some sort of seizure, man? Do we need to get you to a doctor?"

I could breathe again with Sue unconscious. I shook my head and tried to center where I was. "Is anyone following?" I asked shakily. "How long was I out?"

"I've been watching. I'm pretty sure I lost them." He glanced at me. He smelled curious and a little nervous. "You were 'out', as you call it, for about five minutes. What's up with you? I've known you for years and I've never seen you like this."

No doubt. *I'd* never seen me like this. Trouble was, I couldn't explain it without going into detail.

My cell phone rang. The abrupt sound startled us both. I stared at the number on the screen. I knew that area code, but I couldn't give away my hand.

"Tony here." I forced my voice to sound normal for those first words.

"Hey, Tony!" said Leo jovially. "I've got a friend of yours here in the car with me. I'd let her talk to you, but she's a little *unconscious* right now. If you want to see her wake up again, you bring me back my property."

"Where are you, bastard?" I could yell now. He would know it was bluster.

"I'll let you know." He hung up.

I stared at the phone long and hard for a moment and then turned to Jocko.

"Things are too complicated to explain. Can you live with that?"

I was concentrating on waking Sue. For the first time I was *trying* to start the connection.

Annoyance edged his voice and scent. "Fine. I'll keep my mouth shut and drive. But when this is over, I want to know what the fuck you've been up to."

I didn't respond. I didn't know whether I could ever tell him. I wasn't even sure I could explain it.

Whisper. Nudge. I reached out to Sue and tried to jump start the link. I pushed harder, then harder still.

Suddenly I began to feel her heart beat. Like it was part of me. I felt each throb in her body as though it were my own. As though I could control it. Then I saw it in my mind's eye. A thread, no thicker than a spiderweb, floating in the blackness. It glowed softly, like a tiny fluorescent tube and pulsed with each beat of her heart. Her heart beat slowly. She was safe. Not drugged. I was happy for that but felt guilty that my personal phobia caused her injury.

I could feel her blood flow, feel the pain in her hand. It was abstract. I knew that it wasn't my body hurting but it felt like it. My right hand started to throb as though I'd been in a bar brawl.

I whispered into her mind but it wasn't enough. I couldn't wake her. I pushed just a little more and was suddenly aware. There in the van, smelling blood from Vinny and surprise from Bobby. I was in her head and I was alone there. She was still out.

I couldn't move her. I simply had one or two of her senses. I could see and smell but I couldn't hear.

"Take the Interstate," I instructed Jocko. My own voice came to my ears from a distance. Vaguely I knew that he was still in the car and had heard me.

He glanced in the side mirror. "The cops are behind us, Tony. I'll have to lose them first. Hold on!" He accelerated the Lincoln hard enough that it threw me back into the seat.

At the same time, there was a sudden jolt in Sue's body as the van turned off onto a dirt road. The road was deeply rutted. The van slowed and swerved to avoid the deeper potholes. But which dirt road? There are a thousand of them outside of town. I closed my eyes to limit the input from where *my* body was. I felt Sue start to wake and she knew I was there. I begged her with a thought to stay quiet, to let me concentrate.

Now fully awake, she added her senses to mine. Input flooded my brain. Sounds. I could hear now. Scents were stronger. Vinny was flat pissed and smelled like blood and pain. He smelled like *food*. Sue was startled as that thought swirled into her mind. I fought back the need and she settled. I smelled Bobby react abruptly, felt his surprise, his pleasure. Pleasure?

I heard something through Sue's ears. "Pull over."

"Can't right now. I haven't lost 'em yet." We took the next corner on two wheels. A part of me wanted to watch and make sure that they were gone but I had to trust Jocko for that. I felt the car slow suddenly and move at a more sedately speed.

"Lost them." Part of my brain heard him. Part was still with Sue. My eyes opened there in the car and Sue was with me. She hadn't been in my body before other than the night at Linda's and she didn't know how to react.

I saw as we got on the ramp to the Interstate and headed north.

I removed Sue with a thought and stared into space. Jocko started to open his mouth but I held up a hand to silence him. He closed his jaw without a word. I listened through two brains and could hear sounds from both. One sound was a high pitched intermittent pulse. I knew that sound immediately. We had a tracker. The cops had *let* us go, but why did they follow in the first place? Maybe they figured that we'd get careless if we thought we lost them.

Jocko switched lanes abruptly to go around a semi. I opened the door of the car and leaned out. Wind blew back my hair as I strained against my belt to reach under the car.

Jocko glanced my way when he heard the door open. "What in the *hell* are you doing?!"

I ignored him. I had to lean out even farther to get my arm under the car. The seatbelt was cutting into my gut. My knuckles hit the speeding pavement briefly. I felt the pebbles embed into my skin. Jocko moved to the far left of the lane and one hand reached out to grab my waistband.

Damn it! I could hear the signal but where was the transmitter? I patted my hand all around the underside of the car and finally found it. The powerful glue was no match for my strength. I leaned back in the car and shut the door.

Jocko glared at me. "Are you *nuts!* You trying to get us both killed?"

I held out my prize. He looked at the small electronic tracker held in my fingers and swore. "Okay. Never mind. Get rid of that damn thing!"

I crushed the tracker in my fist, rolled down the window and tossed it over the car into the opposite lanes. With that distraction gone, I returned to finding Sue. I closed my eyes once more and pushed into her head.

I fought to place a new sound. Rumbling, whining. A

motor. But what kind? I closed my eyes again and let instinct take over. I breathed slow and deep and just let the sound filter into my head. Let my mind recognize it, place it.

It was more work than I thought as I tried to filter other sounds from both places. Speeding cars along the Interstate, rattling metal from the bouncing van. I calmed and drifted. Sue relaxed along with me and let me lead. I heard the sound again. Thup, thup, thup, then a vibrating rattle that grew to a roar. Propeller! Airplane!

I snapped my head to Jocko, who was staring at me out of the corner of his eye and looking nervous. "The old airport! At the edge of town. Can you get there from here?"

Somehow he was starting to figure out what I was doing and he could grasp it. Just. He kept muttering to himself, "This is weirder than shit! Nobody is *ever* going to believe this!"

I didn't comment on his discourse. I was concentrating on my own. I'm afraid, Tony, came a plaintive voice inside my mind.

I know you are, Sue. I'll be with you soon.

I tried to soothe her so they wouldn't know she was awake but her heart was beating faster. I could smell Bobby. He realized that she was awake. I felt him put a hand on her shoulder. He pushed down slightly. He'd done it to me more than once. Stay down, I commanded.

Sue slid along the floor slightly as the van came to a jarring stop in a swirl of dust. I could smell the dust irritate Sue's nose, irritate my heightened senses, and she sneezed before I could stop her.

"Good." said Leo's smooth oily voice before she opened her eyes. "You're awake. I want you awake. I want you *afraid*." He got out of the van and opened the sliding side door. Sue's eyes opened and I could see his face. His black eyes glittered brightly as he stared at her.

"You're going to tell me everything you know, little lady. And then *I'm* going to tell you everything I plan to do to you. Before I do it." He leaned over Sue. He ran his nose from her hair down her body and ended near her crotch. I felt her shudder.

He sneered. "You smell like that bastard Tony. I'll take care of that." He leaned over and licked slowly up the side of her face. She screamed and he laughed.

My vision bled red and I growled low and deep as we turned onto the road to the abandoned airport. Jocko's hands were fidgeting on the steering wheel, not sure whether to stop the car or drive faster.

Deep furrows had been cut into the dirt by the last heavy rain. Jocko was forced to slow the car to nearly a crawl to avoid ripping off his oil pan. I felt Leo lift Sue out of the van. She struggled but even with my added strength it wasn't enough. Leo held her effortlessly, then set her down. He released her and just stood there waiting. His eyes were smiling; amused. The other guards started to move in closer but he waved them back.

Run! I screamed in her head. She obeyed—she turned and ran at top speed—but it was a futile effort. Leo just stood there for a moment and then suddenly was in front of her. Like magic. She ran right into his outstretched arms. He had moved faster than the eye could follow.

"Hi there, baby!" He slapped her hard across the face with the back of his hand. She dropped to the ground, stunned. "Ready to play? I've got the knives all sharpened."

He bent down and touched her nose with each word. "Just . . . for . . you." He smiled evilly.

I could feel heat on my cheek from where Leo slapped Sue. Anger coursed through my veins.

"Move this damn car!" I exclaimed viciously to Jocko. "He's going to kill her!"

I could see the airport in the distance but we weren't going to get there in time if he didn't speed up.

It was Jocko's turn to be angry. "If I move this *damn car* any faster, we'll break an axle. Then we won't get there at all. You think you can do better, get out and walk."

I knew that I shouldn't be taking it out on him. This mess

wasn't his fault. He was trying to help. But that didn't rescue Sue. I felt her being dragged along the ground by her feet. She kicked and squirmed but Leo just kept on pulling her closer and closer to a metal shack at the edge of the runway. Her head hit a rock and We saw stars.

"Don't wait up, boys," Leo called over his shoulder as he pulled her along the ground. Through Sue's eyes, I saw the other men. Bobby looked positively pissed, and the rest just looked nervous—but nobody moved to stop Leo. Nobody wanted to get involved.

I wasn't going to be in time. I was going to lose her. Feel her torture. My leg was tapping nervously on the floor of the car. I couldn't concentrate on anything but the buildings in the distance.

Right about then, my tapping leg started to spasm. Twitch uncontrollably. I felt hot; feverish. It was a familiar sensation. But the full moon wasn't for more than a week yet! And it was the middle of the day!

I had to get out of the car. "Stop the car!" I screamed, but Jocko just kept driving, concentrating on avoiding the next huge hole. From my side of the car you couldn't see the bottom of it.

In a panic, I reached out and turned the key. The engine died and the steering wheel locked. Jocko didn't even have time to bitch at me. The left front tire immediately dropped into the hole that he was trying to avoid. Clear up to the axle. Metal screamed against unforgiving ground as irresistible force met immovable object. I heard the oil pan go and felt the frame twist as the axle bent. The scent of hot oil filled my nose. No gas, though.

Jocko slammed forward into the steering wheel. His head bounced backwards once against the headrest and then he slumped forward heavily, unconscious. He wasn't wearing a seat belt. I was. He's always been against the concept of belts. This is what that gets you.

With what I knew would be my last remaining thought before I turned, I reached out to make sure he wasn't dead. I didn't want to have his death on my conscience along with everything else. His pulse was steady. He did have the beginnings of a lump forming on his forehead. Good thing we hadn't been driving any faster.

Jocko was going to be pissed when he woke. The car was his baby; the only thing big enough to fit him. Finding parts would be a bitch.

I threw open the door and fell to the ground, thrashing in pain. I wouldn't scream. They couldn't know I was coming. White flowers erupted in my vision as I felt Leo and the goon stop dragging Sue long enough to open the door to the shack. Sue was terrified now, and unable to convince her muscles to move.

She felt cloth rip as my old body disappeared and new muscles appeared that didn't fit the shape of the shirt. For the first time I was *aware* during the change. I watched as color bled away from the world, to be replaced by brilliant whites and blacks and all shades of grey. I felt a thousand pinpoints of light and heat explode through my skin and watched long thick fur appear over my skin.

The change took only moments. Then I was running full out. I ran so fast that I couldn't even see the scenery. It whizzed by in a blur. I was to the airport and across the runway before Leo's hand left the doorknob. He looked at Sue and his confident look was replaced by a startled one.

He looked up just as I leapt into the air, not soon enough to get away. I crushed him into the wall of the shed. The corrugated metal screamed and bent from the impact.

Voices erupted around me as I tore at him with my mouth. Hot blood gushed from his arm where my teeth sank to the bone. He snarled, and it sounded like an animal. He grabbed my ear and pulled until I released his arm. Then he threw me aside long enough to get behind the shed. I followed, intending to finish the job. From the corner of my eye, I saw Bobby knock Vito's goon over the head. He dropped to the ground like a stone.

Vinny reached Sue before she could get away. She remained motionless on the ground. She was in the fight with me and couldn't seem to move her body at the same time.

Her anger and loathing fueled me as I stepped carefully around the shed. I fought to not let my heart lead my head.

I'd never before had human thoughts as a wolf. I could strategize, plan my next move. I stepped lightly and poked my head around the metal wall.

Leo wasn't there. In his place was a four legged animal. He wasn't a wolf. I'd seen a picture of what he was but it took a minute to place the picture with a word. Leo bared jagged yellowed teeth and it looked like a smile. It clicked the name into my brain.

A hyena! Leo was a carrion eating scavenger.

It fit.

The wound on his arm, now a foreleg, was healed. Only a rapidly fading scar showed where I bit him. He sidled sideways. I could tell that he had fought in this form before. He had a fluid movement to his muscles that I didn't. I felt gangly and clumsy, and I couldn't afford to be clumsy in battle.

A hot breeze cut across the sand. The airplane in the background was idling.

We moved back around the building. Leo was in reverse. I followed slowly. His blood dripped from my muzzle and I liked the taste of it. I licked it from my lips and Leo snarled at me.

I could see his black eyes dart from side to side, looking for an advantage. When we cleared the edge of the shack we were in sight of the others again. Nobody seemed surprised. Did everyone know what he was? Well, maybe he only brought people who knew. That made sense.

I rushed him abruptly but he dodged. People backed up quickly to avoid getting caught in the middle. Vinny had Sue's arm. He jerked it nearly out of the socket to avoid our fight. I felt a sharp pain in the same arm and I stumbled for an instant. Leo gave me that sickly smile again. His glittering eyes looked thoughtful and canny.

He jumped me and I only managed to get out of the way by a split second. He was aiming for a leg but only came up with a mouthful of fur. I took a bite at him on the way past and drew blood on his left flank. He yelped. I felt Sue smile darkly. She was getting a sample of vengeance. It tasted sweet.

Leo and I circled each other in the hot sand. The propeller on the waiting plane spun faster and faster, raising a sandstorm around us.

The men formed a circle. Vinny drew his revolver and tried to find an opening. I didn't have time to concentrate on him much but I managed to keep Leo between us. I saw a flash of light across the landscape, near the old control tower. My brief attention shift was what Leo was waiting for. He rushed me and I ended up on my back, holding his snapping jaws away from my neck with my legs.

What I had seen in the distance was the glint of light off a camera lens. I kicked Leo off of me and rolled over to gain my footing. A Channel 7 Action News van was parked near the control tower. Smile! You're on Candid Camera!

Leo dodged then and charged. But he wasn't aiming for me. He went past me. He ran full out past Vinny and then beyond Sue. He wasn't the type to cut and run but it happened so fast, I couldn't figure out what he was doing.

In the blink of an eye, he turned in a skid of dust. He aimed right for Sue. There was no way she could move out of the way in time. He went for her legs and bowled her over. Her body flew into the air. She landed on her back with a dull thud. The breath was knocked out of me so suddenly I staggered. Leo never took his eyes off me. When I reacted as I did, he gave me that sick smile again. He had figured out that hurting Sue hurt me. It hurt to breathe and I realized that he might have cracked one of her ribs. As he stalked toward me I tried to convince myself that I wasn't really injured.

Vinny was ignoring Sue now. He was concentrating on the fight. I felt Sue's pain, her anger and outrage. Leo had hurt my mate and he would pay for it.

With a deep-throated snarl I threw myself at him. I bit him; clawed him in a frenzy. He was unprepared for the ferocity of my attack and went down on his side.

I heard Leo's voice come out of that toothy muzzle and it startled me.

"Shoot the girl!" he ordered. Sue reacted in panic. Everything after that was in slow motion. Vinny turned to her. I felt her run, sluggish with an injured leg from the earlier fall. It wouldn't be enough. I tried to reach Vinny. Take him down. At least knock the gun out of his hand. Leo lunged at me and backed me away. I saw the gun raise and watched him aim. The gun barked as Vinny pulled the trigger.

Chapter 29

The bullet caught Sue in the right shoulder blade and spun her around. She was knocked off her feet. The shock and the pain made me stumble. I skidded on the ground in a tumble of dust and fur. I felt the wound as though it were my own. The smell of copper filled the air. Leo's lips pulled back from his gums in a predatory smile. He strutted toward me, lifting his nose to the scent. His tongue darted out and flipped across his muzzle. He knew he could take me now. It was just a matter of time.

I couldn't catch my breath. Sue's pain forced everything else from my mind. Blood. I could see blood when she looked down at her chest. There was a hole the size of a fist in the shoulder of her shirt, the flesh blown away by the Glaser round. She struggled to stay conscious. I struggled with her. Her heart was slowing down from shock. The scent of it was overpowering; nauseating.

"End of the line, Tony," came Leo's voice from the foam flecked muzzle. Stiff hairs rose from behind ears set back far on his head. His heavily muscled, brown striped body was sweaty from effort. God, he was ugly. "All you would have had to do was return the case, Giodone."

I'd never spoken as a wolf. But I had to reply. "What? So you could *ruin* me and then have someone else kill me off—like you did to my father? You haven't even got the guts to do the job yourself, you goddamn *scavenger*!"

His eyes filled with hate and the fiery scent of jalapeños filled the air. He bared teeth. This was the end of the line all right. I tried to move, straining to raise myself to my feet. I wouldn't go down like this. I couldn't let Sue die unavenged.

I knew I was going to die with her—I knew my heart would stop when hers did. The connection was too tight.

It was actually okay. Better to die with her than live without her. But, by damn, he would go down with me.

He lunged at me before I was ready, always one to take unfair advantage. What's a fair fight to a hyena, after all? He was in mid-air when I heard the first gunshot and smelled fresh gunpowder. His body jerked sideways. He screamed and landed on his side. I could see the wound where the bullet entered him. The flesh was charred around the edges. It wasn't healing like the bites had.

Bloody bubbles rose from the wound and I knew the bullet had opened a lung. Fitting. He raised his head and the burning coffee of his anger filled my nose, stronger than the blood. He started to rise. Even mortally wounded he was in better shape than me. A second sharp crack split the air and his head slammed into the ground. His left eye disappeared in an explosion of fur and darker things.

I turned my head to see smoke still rising from the muzzle of Bobby's stainless steel 9mm.

Vinny looked as shocked as I felt. He raised his Browning .357 and started firing. Bobby moved like quicksilver and took cover. He returned fire and Vinny's body twitched with each bullet that entered him.

With bullets sizzling through the air over my head, I dragged my body to Sue's side. She was nearly unconscious. I couldn't feel her in my head.

I closed my eyes and felt for that little thread. That shining glowing line of energy that was Sue. I found it but it was dull and limp. It glowed weakly.

"Sue?" She fluttered her eyes open and looked at me. A weak smile warmed my heart.

"Guess . . . it wasn't meant to be, huh?" Her voice was a husky whisper.

"You're going to be fine." We both knew I was lying.

The air was suddenly still. The absence of sound startled me. When I looked up, only Bobby was still standing. He walked toward us. I turned to him and growled. I wouldn't let him have her. Not even though he had killed Leo.

Bobby was bleeding from a bullet to the shoulder. It was healing before my eyes like time-lapse. There were bodies on the ground. All of Leo's enforcers. All with multiple bullet wounds —one or more in the chest plus a head shot.

Even if he was involved with hurting Sue, I still owed him for getting us out of Vegas. He seemed to know who I was and it didn't appear to matter to him.

I coughed up blood. That worried me. "Camera crew—by the tower. All of this . . . on film." I couldn't stand anymore. I dropped to the ground and felt my heart slow as Sue's life slipped away. I smelled his surprise and saw him move in a blur when he spotted the television van and reporters. Two more bodies would soon be in the dust. I didn't care. I only cared for the woman on the ground in front of me. My mate was dying.

"Don't go." I felt my eyes beginning to water. "I don't want you to go."

Sue whispered with eyes still shut. "I hoped that we could go somewhere exotic." Her voice was breathy and her body shuddered as she fought to get each word out. "Somewhere with white sand and palm trees."

I rubbed my hand against her skin in frantic gesture. "We'll go there! I promise I'll take you. Just don't leave!"

She smiled brilliantly and opened her eyes for a brief moment. "I love you." Then her eyes shut again and I couldn't feel her anymore.

I reached inside my mind. Felt for the thread. I tentatively reached out to touch it, to feel what was wrong.

It was as though a zoom lens focused. I was suddenly standing next to the thread. Except it wasn't a thread. It was a cord as big around as my hand with smaller cords connected and twisted to make up the whole. It was a living thing. You could tell. But it was injured. I could see that strands of the larger cord were snapped and broken. As I watched, more threads snapped. The glow faded even more.

I didn't know what to do. I hesitated to touch it, to make it worse. Her wounded heart beat slower and slower.

Suddenly it snapped fully. Instinct took over. I reached out lightning fast and grabbed one end before it disappeared into the darkness.

A wind rose up that became a hurricane-level gale in milliseconds. The cord I held tried to pull away from me. There was a weight to it like it was caught in the storm. It whipped back and forth and started to drag me toward the darkness with it. I looked for something to hang onto and saw the other end of the cord.

The moment I reached out and grabbed the other side, it happened. The force of the contact blew me away. It raised every hair on my body. I felt electricity, power, whatever it was, accelerate between us. Lightning bolts of energy raced from me to her.

I was part of her. I felt my power tear through her body. I think I screamed. The magic touched every cell, every neuron, seeking . . . something. Each time the energy found what it was looking for, it tripped a switch. Surprised light blazed in long-darkened rooms. I saw strands of the cord expand and lengthen. They re-connected with their counterpart on the other side of my body. I felt her body heal. Felt flesh rebuild itself.

"Don't leave me." The wind caught the words and threw them into the darkness, tried to rip the mended strands apart. The whisper became a howl that cut through the cold night and warmed it. I felt her pain and helplessness as the wind got stronger. I fought back by sending more energy, more warmth, more . . . love . . . to her. More switches were thrown. More receptors turned on with each new burst of energy.

Every human has dormant DNA. Strands of us have been unused since the dawn of time. Some believe that people who have certain receptors turned on have psychic abilities—telepathy, empathy, and other stuff. I don't know if I believe that. I know that studies have shown that some of that dormant DNA has to do with human sexuality.

Rather, not sex precisely, but mating. Marriage rituals are

fairly recent developments. What happened before rituals to bond people? Was it body language or body chemistry? Can we smell and sense things that can't be seen?

Each switch that flipped brought Sue closer to me. I could feel it. 'And the two shall become one.' What if those aren't just words?

I pressed harder and faster. The energy found each piece of the puzzle and put it together. When the last piece slammed home, I felt it. My eyes were closed, both in real life and in my mind. The wind died at last.

Suddenly it was absolutely still. Absolutely peaceful.

When I opened my eyes in my mind, the cord in front of me was whole. It glowed softly in my hands. I released the strand and it instantly dimmed. I touched it and it glowed— released it and it faded. She was still in danger. She needed my strength to *make* her live. I moved myself closer to the strand; it reached out to me, and wrapped itself around me.

I opened my eyes in the real world and looked down at her pale, drawn face. I tried not to look at the wound in her chest. It was a killing injury, and I didn't want to think about that.

Long dark lashes lay against those pale cheeks and her hair stirred in the hot breeze. Her mouth was open slightly and even the lips were pale. She was unconscious from loss of blood. She couldn't hear me, but she knew I was there. I touched that cool porcelain skin and was surprised that I was human again. I didn't remember changing back.

Tingles raced through me, just like always. Even now I couldn't bear not to touch her.

I heard a noise and I turned my head. I knelt, naked, by Sue's side. My head was foggy. I could only manage to keep Sue alive. A man dropped to one knee beside me and I recognized him. Carl Jenkins. *Dr.* Carl Jenkins, a noted neurologist and an old Family friend.

"Jesus!" He opened a black satchel and removed instruments and bandages. "She's lost at least half her blood supply. I can't imagine what's keeping her alive! She should be gone."

I would have answered but I was too tired. All I could get out was, "Can you fix her up?"

"The wound's bad." The thick fog of worry added to his seriousness. "But if she'll stay alive long enough to get through surgery, I think I can save her. It's a miracle she's still with us."

Nice to know I'm a miracle. But he voiced the trick. Could I keep her "with us" long enough for Carl to stitch her back together?

I looked at her again as Carl started to clean her shoulder enough to see the internal damage. Carl's a terrific surgeon but I didn't know if he was good enough to save her in a field setting. We didn't have time for a hospital.

The smell of ozone found me and a low clap of thunder filled the air. A wind came from nowhere. Carl looked up in a panic and stripped off his shirt suddenly, using it to cover Sue's wound as sand began to swirl.

"We need to get her somewhere protected. God, I hate to move her, but . . . Carmine!" He draped his body over Sue, trying to keep the wound clean. I saw Carmine, Jerry and Mike head our way. Where had they come from? Who called them?

"We need to move her into the hanger," instructed Carl. "Gently. She's in bad shape."

I watched from where I was as the sand blasted my bare skin. Jerry and Mike each took one of Sue's legs and Carmine eased large gentle hands under her spine. Carmine's face was level with mine when he looked at me for the first time. "Christ, Tony, you look like hell! What did Leo do to you?"

I didn't respond. I couldn't respond. He stared at me long and hard. "We'll take care of your lady. Carl will fix her up." He reached into his pants pocket and dropped a set of car keys on the ground in front of me. The movement registered in my brain but I didn't stretch to pick them up. It was too much effort.

"I've got some coveralls in my trunk," he said. "They won't be the best fit but you need something. That storm's going to be here any minute."

I glanced down at myself. I looked like shit, but I felt worse. I was nearly catatonic. All I could concentrate on was internal CPR. Beat, beat, breathe. Beat, beat, breathe. Nothing else mattered. Just keep oxygen pumping to her brain—keep her alive long enough to doctor her. It was a conscious effort.

They lifted her in one smooth motion as though it was practiced. I was breathliss and panicked as they moved her. I felt the blood drain from my face from the effort of keeping her calm. She could feel it and it hurt. God Almighty, it hurt. She shouldn't be able to feel. But if I could feel her, what was she getting from me?

"She's waking up," I whispered. I looked to Carl with pleading with my eyes. "Give her something for the pain before you start, huh?" His eyes grew wide and he flicked a light across her pupils and swore. He took off for the hanger at a dead run.

As they moved her, I was forced to ask a question. It slipped through my mind before I could stop it. Was I willing to risk my life for this woman? Because that's what I was doing. If Carl couldn't heal her, she would drain me dry. Take me into that black nothingness with her. I was breathing for her, making her heart beat as though I were a life support machine in a hospital. The effort would exhaust me little by little. It already was.

I barely knew her. All I had to do was let go. Just hold my breath and not make her heart beat. A few minutes is all it would take. I could go back to my life if I survived.

No. I didn't want to make this decision right now. Not until Carl had a chance to look at her.

I stayed where I was on my knees as they moved away with her. I could only concentrate on the beating of her heart. I didn't want to distract myself with any additional movement. But as she moved further from me the effort became more; having her near made the life support easier. I stood in the hot sand. My legs were shaky and I felt stings of pain as the superheated quartz blasted my body. It didn't matter.

Bobby watched silently as I dragged my weary body toward the hanger, following like a dog on a lead.

The boys laid Sue down on a table that Carl cleared off with a sweep of his arm. It was dusty in the metal framed building, but it was also cooler and out of the weather. It seemed odd it was cool. There must be some insulation in the walls—it should have been an oven.

Carl immediately went to work. He ripped the tatters of Sue's shirt away from the wound and turned to the waiting men. Scarlet blood stained her snow white bra. Nobody looked. It was somehow too personal.

"Jerry, congratulations! You've been promoted to nurse." He kicked the black bag on the floor toward the men. "Carmine, you get some water. Clean, please. Find some way to heat it up. Mike, get the rest of my stuff out of the car. Jerry," he continued, as I slumped to the floor in the corner. "Get two pairs of latex gloves out of the bag and one of the large alcohol pads." None of the men argued. Carl's the doc. He's in charge. Otherwise, the next time one of *them* needed patching he'd just watch them die. His Hippocratic Oath has a vindictive streak.

Carl dropped to his knees and pulled a small glass vial from the black bag. He inserted a syringe into the top. He inverted the works and slowly drew the clear liquid into the needle. My heart beat faster and Sue reacted to my panic by moving towards consciousness. I watched Carl remove the air from the syringe by squirting out a small amount of the fluid. One hand held the needle while the other reached out expectantly for the foil square that was about twice the size of a condom. Jerry put it in his hand just like a nurse. He ripped the packet open with his teeth and I could smell alcohol in a sudden wave. He grabbed the towelette and shook off the wrapper. When he swabbed the crook of Sue's arm I couldn't look anymore. I kept telling myself that this was *good* clear liquid. I knew and trusted Carl. But my fists were closed tight and my legs drew closer to my chest.

I felt when the needle pierced her skin. I could feel everything with her now. The connection was locked tight.

I concentrated on keeping Sue's heart beating, keeping her breathing, while the needle spilled its contents into her body. I felt a warm soothing wave sweep through me as whatever drug Carl had injected started to work. No more pain. Sleep lapped at my consciousness and I had to struggle to stay awake.

A tap on my shoulder made me jump. I had turned to face the wall. Curled in a ball in the corner. Oh yeah. Big strong tough guy, that's me. I turned to find Mike staring at me. He was holding an armload of equipment.

Breathing was still an effort and Mike noticed. "You're not looking too good. Let Carl give you something to sleep." I had to admit that sleep would be a good thing right now. But not by needle.

"No!" came a harsh exclamation to my right. I turned to see Bobby walking toward me. He held a video camera in his hand with a 7 News logo on the side.

Bobby set the camera on the floor under the table where Sue lay. "No drugs for Tony." He looked me over as though seeing me for the first time. His brow furrowed as he looked from me to Sue and then back again. He gave an amazed shake of his head. "You need coffee," he said to me. "I've got some in the car. Let's go."

I shook my head. "I can't leave. I *really* can't leave." I didn't know if he would understand the reason but I knew that he would smell the truth of my words.

Mike saw the look on Bobby's face and shrugged. He dropped off his load and walked back out into the wind.

Carl turned from his efforts and looked at me for a brief second. "Do you know your lady's blood type? We've got to get some replacement into her or she won't make it. I've got plasma with me, but whole blood would be better."

I shrugged. I really didn't know. I couldn't ask Sue even in my mind. She was out. But he was right. She would die. "I'm O negative—universal donor." I held out my bare arm to him. "Just promise not to be mad if I hit you when you stick in the needle."

Bobby grabbed my arm suddenly and pulled me to my feet

in a burst. He dragged me off to the side. "Are you insane?" he said in a terse whisper. "You can't donate blood!"

"Why not? I'm universal. She'll die without blood!" Fine. If he could be angry so could I.

He gave a sharp exasperated exhale of breath. He hissed the words at me. "You aren't type O negative, stupid. You're W positive—if you get my meaning." He glanced at Carl who was ignoring us and starting to clean instruments. I had nearly forgotten. Beat, beat, breathe. Beat, beat, breathe.

Wolf positive. It hadn't even occurred to me. Hope surged through me. My blood could save her life. I glanced at her. Tried to imagine her awake and laughing again.

But then she'd be just like me. Sub-human. I really believe that. I'm not more than human, I'm less. Could I let her die when I could save her? Would saving her like that be a curse or a cure?

Curse or cure? Curse or cure? I shook my head while Bobby watched my internal struggle. No, I couldn't do that. Not even to save her life. Given the choice again, I'd rather have died. It's a curse.

There was pain in my voice. "Then she'll die. I won't do that to her. I won't make her an animal." It made me sad. Without the blood and unless by some miracle one of the others was universal Sue would die. I sat down on the floor right where I was, still naked. I brought my knees to my chest once more. She would die and I couldn't save her.

Fine. Then I'd go with her. We'll travel down the black tunnel hand in hand. I *could* live without her, but I didn't want to.

I understood suddenly. It was like sight. As if all your life you'd been able to see but had never seen color. Black and white had always served you until you got a taste of red and yellow and green. Then grey was never again enough. No sunsets, no Christmas lights. Sue was like that now. I'd had a taste of something incredible in my head. A never-ending technicolor sunset. Some magical something that I knew was special. One of a kind.

I ignored Bobby and concentrated only on keeping Sue

alive. I'd do what I could. Give Carl whatever chance he needed to save her. Right to the end. Bobby clenched and unclenched his large fists, but it wasn't his problem. This was mine alone. My decision. My choice.

Mike came in again. His arms were loaded with supplies. He paused nearby and juggled boxes. Then he tossed a pair of blue coveralls my direction.

"Get some clothes on, Giodone. There are ladies present." He beamed a confident smile at me. I forced a small one in return.

Bobby watched me, took a deep breath, and sighed. He left me on the floor. I made no move to put on the coveralls. It was too much effort. Beat, beat, breathe.

Out of the corner of my eye, I watched him walk over to Carl. He spoke softly but I still heard his words. Guess the ears were still working fine. It was just everything else that was slowing down. Grinding down with exertion. Beat, beat, breathe.

Carl was busy unpacking boxes and giving direction to Jerry and Mike. They were setting up tables and instruments like they knew what they were doing. Maybe they did. Carmine stood off to the side. He looked normal. Not anxious; not fretting. Just calm. Apparently he had found hot water. He was waiting for his next assignment.

"Do you believe in miracles, Carl?" asked Bobby.

Carl turned to him and gave him a long look. I brought my head up from where it rested on my knees and watched them. Jerry and Mike seemed to sense something was going on and moved a little further away.

"Let's just say that I've seen some things that can't be readily explained by modern science. If they were miracles, then so be it."

"Did any of them happen when you were actually *present?*" Where was he leading?

Carl gave him a brief smile, never stopping his work on prepping Sue for surgery. "I've noticed that miracles don't like an audience."

"Do me a favor then." His cold calm unnerved me a little.

"Leave the room. Go take a leak. Get a cup of coffee. Come back in five minutes."

That stopped Carl cold. "She'll die, Bobby. I need those five minutes." He continued working. He shook his head. "No. I can't."

"One minute then, Carl, just one minute for a miracle." He put a large dark hand on the doctor's shoulder, "Please."

Carl looked down at Sue, then at Bobby. He looked at me last but longest. I returned the look. He appealed to me with panicked eyes. Asking my permission. I was Sue's protector. It was my choice. Bobby didn't look at me, he just kept staring at Carl.

It was Carl's choice. He was the doctor. I gave a brief nod and then returned my chin to where it rested on my knees. One minute wouldn't matter but Carl didn't know that. I could probably last another ten minutes before my own strength gave out. Beat, beat, breathe.

I closed my eyes. So tired. Beat, beat, breathe. I heard but didn't see Carl, Jerry, Mike and Carmine leave the hanger. Bobby and I were alone with Sue. Whatever he was going to do, I wouldn't let him end her life. I would prevent that.

In my mind's eye I focused again on the spider thread that I held. I felt each beat of her heart. I breathed each breath with her. The cable continued to glow but only because of what I fed it. She lived because I allowed it.

It didn't make me feel cocky. I didn't feel like God. I felt very alone. Very tense. I concentrated but couldn't reach her mind because of the drugs. It was like a door was closed. Not locked. She slept behind that closed door. She felt no pain and that was good.

I felt Bobby. It was like standing next to a bonfire. Or a live high-tension wire. I concentrated on Sue's lifethread. I stood guard against whatever he would do. I didn't have the physical strength to fight him but I would watch over her life like Cerberus himself at the gates of Hell.

I heard a dark chuckle from Bobby. "Only *you* could manage to screw things up this bad, Giodone." He spoke softly but knew I could hear. He sighed and it spoke volumes.

"Mated to a *human*. Fiona will have a strip of my hide for this. I should not be doing this. Gawd! I should not even be *involved*. You'd *better* appreciate it."

I had no idea who or what he was talking about so I didn't respond. Bobby touched Sue. Me. Us. Placed his hands right over her wound and sealed it. I felt pressure but no pain. I held her life in my hands and guarded it. I mentally became a wolf.

Then the gloves came off. It was like Bobby had been holding himself in check. Not letting on who—or what—he really was. Power sang through the room and raised every hair on my body. I looked up with a gasp. Bobby was bathed in a silvery glow that came from within him. I blinked my eyes suddenly. Just for a moment I thought I saw him shift. Saw the form underneath his skin peek out and then slip back in. I couldn't tell what he was. It was just a flash. But whatever it was, whatever *he* was, didn't have fur.

The light that pulsed around him was too bright. I had to shut my eyes. Even after I shut them I could see echoes of the glow in the blackness. The image was burned onto my retinas.

Sue's lifethread began to shine brighter. Brighter even than when I first touched it. It pulsed more radiant with each passing second until it was as bright as a captive star. A tidal wave of power churned over us both. It enveloped my virtual body until I gleamed like a nova. I felt refreshed, energized. I felt Sue's body start to heal. He was going to heal her! He was doing what I *could* do, but his effort was like a bulldozer next to my ant.

Then it stopped and the silence was deafening. I looked up, startled. Sue was still bleeding on the table. But she was a little closer. She'd make it now. Her heart was beating on its own. She was breathing on her own. I could think for myself without that strain. But I didn't feel gratitude—I felt anger.

I stood in a flash and stalked toward him. He was standing over her, looking healthy and not the least tired.

I grabbed his shirt with both fists and pulled his face close to mine. "Goddamn you! Why didn't you finish? You could heal her. Why did you stop?"

He reached around me fast as a snake and grabbed my neck. He turned it sharply. Carl and the boys were entering the room. "That's why," he whispered sharply. "What I've done is bad enough! Now get your clothes on and meet me outside. She'll survive."

He pulled out of my best grip as though it were nothing and walked away. He spoke without turning. "Don't make me come and get you."

I looked down at Sue. She had color again. There was a pool of blood in her chest where there was none before. Her chest rose and fell on its own and she felt confident in my head.

Go. I'll be all right now. Then she drifted off to sleep again.

I didn't know if she'd be okay but at least she had a chance.

Chapter 30

I pulled on the blue coveralls. They were a little short and far too wide. But they covered me. Just as I was leaving the hanger to join Bobby outside, I heard the exclamation of amazement and delight from Carl as he reached the table. I could smell his astonishment.

"A one-minute miracle. Shit." There was a hint of anger from someone. I couldn't tell who. Carl and the others stared after me as I walked out. A miracle indeed—and I was walking outside to meet that miracle now.

The heavy metal door protested noisily as I exited the hanger. It slammed behind me with a bang. Bobby was leaning against the wall lighting a cigarette. He didn't look at me until I joined him. He walked away from me and expected me to follow.

I could think again. I felt almost like myself again. For that I'd follow.

We walked toward the plane. The bodies were all gone. The boys must have made them disappear. I didn't know to where, nor did I care. The sun was bright on the baked earth. I had to blink a few times to get my eyes to adjust. The coveralls were already making me sweat but it didn't matter. Nothing mattered except that Sue had a chance.

Bobby stopped suddenly when he felt that we were a sufficient distance from the hanger. He turned to me, his face cut in angry lines.

"Are you completely insane? What you just did is an automatic death sentence!" Smoke billowed out of his mouth as he spoke and the wind blew it right in my face.

I presumed that he meant attacking Leo. "He was going to kill Sue," I said in a quiet, equally angry voice.

The cigarette smoke was irritating my nose and I sneezed.

He pointed a finger at my chest. "And that is the *only thing* that is saving your ass right now!"

He plucked the nearly whole cigarette out of his mouth. He dropped it on the ground and pressed it into the dirt with a twisting motion of his foot.

"Mated to a human!" He smelled burnt metal annoyed and mildew amazed at that same time. "I'm going to have to inform your pack leader of these indiscretions." He crossed arms across his broad chest. "Which pack are you attached to?"

I furrowed my brow and felt a pressure on my chest at the same time. Carl was starting to work. He must be using a rib spreader. It was a very strange feeling. Not pain exactly, just odd.

"I have no idea what you're talking about."

He gave a little exasperated movement of his hand. It remained tucked under his other arm. "Okay, fine. Maybe you don't have a formal pack structure around here. Who do you hunt with?"

When I continued to look confused he twirled his hand, "You know, on the moon?" He waited expectantly but I had nothing to offer him. I shrugged.

"No one."

He suddenly looked startled again. "You really don't, do you?"

"Nope."

His expression grew both suspicious and tense. He licked his lips more than once. "If I said I was with Wolven, what would you say?"

"Who or what is Wolven?"

He closed his eyes and dropped his head. "Oh, shit! At least tell me you're a family member."

I shrugged. "You know I am. I grew up in the Patrone's house."

He gave a nervous chuckle with his head still bowed. One

hand reached up and covered his eyes. "Oh, this is not good at all." Bobby was no longer angry. He was worried.

He shook his finger in the air, thinking and murmuring to himself. I continued to look confused because I was still in both places at once. It was hard enough to concentrate on this conversation when I should be in the hangar with Sue. I knew there was nothing I could do but I needed to be close to her. It felt just *wrong* not to be near her. I reached for her, a tentative touch along the mental connection and felt her warm and loving in the background.

Loving. It's not something I ever thought I needed. Absolute acceptance and warmth. That was what I got when I touched her. Even this, having Leo take her, hurt her—it was all accepted as part of being with me. That was so completely unexpected and amazing.

Bobby's hand was waving in front of my face and I returned to myself.

"I'm sorry," I said. "Were you talking to me?"

He rolled his eyes. "Apparently not. Okay, fine. I accept that you're not all here. You're with your mate. But try to stay with me. I have to ask you some questions."

I felt my back go up. I don't willingly give information. "You can *ask*." He caught the meaning.

"I have the right to ask." He looked confident. I couldn't see any deceit in his eyes. I was starting to get a little sense of frustration, with the slight coffee smell of anger from him for the first time.

"Fine. I can tell you believe that. Now make *me* believe it. And while we're on smells, why can't I smell you? I'm picking up some emotions now but nothing else. What are you?"

That brought a sudden frown to his face. "Hmm. Must be wearing off." He reached up with both hands and used the fingers of one hand to pull down his lower eyelid. Then he bent his head slightly and removed a contact lens. When he looked at me again I actually gasped. His right eye was a solid dark brown with a black pupil. Perfectly normal for a South African male. The other eye, though . . . it was reddish-gold. Not just the iris. I could almost have handled that.

But his whole eye, including where the white should be, was reddish-gold. The pupil was a small black vertical slit. Then he blinked. I hadn't noticed it before. His eyelids blinked up! The lower lid covered the eye, not the upper.

He licked his lip just like always but now the movement seemed foreign; alien. What was he?

It suddenly occurred to me what I had seen in that flash as he stood over Sue. "You're a snake?" I asked, a little startled. "Are there other kinds of . . . creatures too?"

Lions and tigers and bears. Oh my!

He gave me a little smile. "You really are new at this, aren't you?"

I opened my mouth but no words came out. I tried again. "Apparently."

He looked suddenly amused. "Okay then. I'll give you the quick course. You know some of it already."

He bowed slightly. "My name is Robart Mbutu. I'm from Mozambique, South Africa. I am a Reticulated Python. I am the last of my kind." There was sadness and fierce pride in that statement.

"Collectively, we are Sazi. Your kind, the wolves of America, descend from the Anasazi of the Four Corners."

"The cliff dwellers?" I asked. It *would* explain why archaeologists never found many bodies. Werewolves stay in whatever form they die in.

Bobby smiled slightly. "Actually that isn't quite accurate. It properly translates to, *cave* dwellers."

That made even more sense.

Bobby lit another cigarette and took a long draw. "This is a pretty truncated version of our history, but you'll learn more later. For the moment, know that hundreds of years ago, a representative of each of the known were-species came together from all over the world. Humans were encroaching on our land and attempting genocide of our kind. We overcame our language barriers and our prejudices.

The first meeting was chaired by Inteque, the youngest son of the Great White Wolf. He, a powerful jaguar named Colecos and Sasha, a polar bear, used both reason and force.

By the end of the gathering, the delegates had formed a government and created a Council comprised of the greatest among us. We chose a name, Sazi, to include all of our kind. We remain hidden from the humans to protect us all."

I suddenly felt Carl working on Sue again. It seemed to come in flashes. I was with Bobby one minute and in Sue's body the next. He was cutting high on her thigh. Maybe a graft? There was a lot of flesh gone. Bobby must have seen my attention disappear because he put a hand on my shoulder. I tried to focus on him but it split my attention between the two realities and made me dizzy.

"You're making it difficult to carry on a conversation here. Let me help." I felt his power flow from his hand into my shoulder and up my shoulder into my head. It flowed like water and like steel. A wall grew up between Sue and me; his doing.

"Whoa."

"You need to learn to shield." His voice held a slight amount of reproach. "Many things will get easier after you learn how." He released my shoulder but the power remained like a tether between us. It was really strange, and it was making me nervous.

"You're scared of me," He flicked his tongue between his lips like a snake. He didn't even attempt to make it look like a human movement. I suddenly realized that the reason for all of his lip licking wasn't a human one. Snakes sense things with their tongues. I stepped back, a little weirded out.

He shrugged. "Probably not a bad thing. Most are. I am an agent of Wolven, the law enforcement branch of our government."

"So you're . . . a creature cop?"

He let out a low hiss. "Of a sort, and I really prefer Sazi. We're not *creatures*. I've been working undercover for a couple of years, investigating Leo."

Wait. Sazi. *That's* what Leo said when I visited his office. He called me Sazi. Then I focused on what Bobby had said. He's been undercover for years? I was forced to voice my surprise and outrage.

"Years? Jesus, Bobby, everybody knew he was killing people. It took you *years* to figure it out?"

He gave me a dirty look and crossed his arms disdainfully. "No, it didn't take me years to figure it out. It took years to get proof enough to convict him. He kept eating the evidence. It's hard to establish a murder without the body."

I grimaced involuntarily. "He ate the evidence? That is *sick*." But I suppose that would be a problem with a scavenger.

The warm sun beat down on us. It felt kind of nice standing there without feeling the pull of Sue's needs. But it was lonely too. I glanced at the hangar. I hoped things were going well.

Bobby noticed and rolled his eyes. "So now I'm going to lose your attention because you're *not* connected? Give me a break, Giodone!" I felt the wall he constructed thin in my head. It wavered until it was an invisible barrier. If I reached across I could touch her. It was enough. Bobby had such absolute control over his abilities. I was both envious and curious.

His tongue flicked again. He nodded. "Curious. That's good. Are you ready to answer some questions yet?"

My eyes narrowed. Friend or not, he's a cop. "I'll let you know when I hear the questions."

"Always on the defensive." He gave an amused shake of his head. "Probably why I like you. Pity you aren't more powerful— we could use you in Wolven." I wouldn't comment on that. But I had to admit that if Bobby was typical of the others in this organization, I wasn't up to snuff.

Carmine and Mike stepped outside. They ignored us and started to drag bodies toward the second hangar.

Bobby smelled nervous at their presence. He turned and quickly put his contact back in. He walked toward the plane, and twitched a finger for me to follow. He sat on the lowered steps where it was shady. The white nylon cord stretched with a high-pitched creak as the steps came to rest on the runway. I sat in the dust. It wouldn't hurt the oil stained coveralls.

He started. "If you aren't family, I presume you were randomly attacked." The tone implied a question.

Okay, I figured out that "family", as he meant it, were other Sazi. I had no problem telling him what happened. "It was an attack, but it wasn't random. She fully intended to kill me."

"You know who she was?" His voice was all business.

I nodded my head. "I do. Her name is Barbara Herrera, although you'd never guess the surname from looking at her. She's a green-eyed redhead. But she wasn't a wolf when she attacked me. She was just a woman I was hired to take out."

His jaw dropped slightly. I didn't think I could surprise him any more. "She attacked you in *human form*?"

I nodded again. The hot wind churned sand into my eyes; I blinked several times to shift the grains to the edge, then turned my body so the wind was at my back. The sand didn't seem to bother Bobby. I glanced at the sky. It appeared that the storm was going to miss us. Good. We'd probably need the plane soon.

"After she turned you, did she train you? Introduce you to a pack?" I shook my head each time. "Did she at least teach you to hunt?"

"I know how to hunt," I replied with a shrug. He just blinked. I leaned back onto my arms, extended my legs, and crossed one ankle over the other. The sand was cooler in the shade, but not by much.

"You were hired to kill her. Were you given specific instructions on the way to do it?"

"I don't take instruction. You know that."

He shook his head and moved his body so his long legs rested on the edges of the steps. "We can only be killed in a very specific way. You saw what I did to Leo and the others. Were you given instructions to hit her heart, then her head?"

I really don't want to discuss my techniques or my clients with an admitted cop. "I told you, I don't take instructions. Why does it matter?"

I'd never seen this side of Bobby before, the absolute authority. "Because it'll tell me whether it was just a disgruntled human or one of our own that wanted her dead. Did you finish the job? Who was your client?"

I couldn't answer right then. I literally couldn't. I tried but I was suddenly fighting for air. I couldn't breathe. Sue couldn't breathe. Something was very wrong.

I grabbed at my throat. I sucked air through my nose and mouth but it didn't satisfy the need. I couldn't tell Bobby what was wrong but he understood it.

"Now what in the hell is going on?" he asked. He pulled his weapon as I dropped to my side in the dust. He moved with lightning speed toward the hanger. I wished I could have followed, but all I could do was fight for air. Somebody was killing Sue and I couldn't stop it. I couldn't break free. When Bobby left he took the shields with him. Now we were dying together. The noose had finally closed and it was strangling me.

Couldn't breathe. No air. I started seeing spots and white bursts of flowers. I felt Sue's eyes open for a brief instant. Jerry stood above her, his face expressionless. He was blurry through the thick plastic sheet that he held over Sue's face. She couldn't fight. I couldn't fight.

I don't want to lose you, I thought at Sue. It was my last thought. The flowers collided and grew until my vision was white. Then the world slipped away.

Chapter 31

The air smelled like lush exotic flowers. The mid-day sun heated the cloud of mist over the porch where I stood into a golden blanket that was suffocating enough to even silence the insects. Imagine New Orleans in August.

This was worse.

I'm not good at waiting under the best of circumstances. I'm patient as all get-out but patience is a skill. Waiting, though . . . it removes choice. It's out of my control. Makes me tense.

Sue was still unconscious. Over a week had passed. Bobby saved her life and mine, but he could only do so much. They're not completely positive that she's alive. Her body is working but that could just be me. Breathing with her, my heart beating in unison with hers—it's become unconscious. I only know she wasn't in my head.

Carl has spent hours on intercontinental calls with top Sazi doctors, but there aren't enough mated pairs in the world for them to know—and I'm the only one to have ever mated to a full human. Naturally. Just my luck.

Of course we had to tell Carl everything because he went on the plane with us to the island. Bobby lost a lot of energy and had to feed. Carl's dealing with the knowledge. Kind of.

John Corbin arrived on the island yesterday with a psychiatrist from one of the big packs. Elizabeth Perdue, M.D., Ph.D. Dr. Perdue, Betty, is a specialist in "normalizing" the Sazi experience. Not for me; for Carl.

John is completely fascinated with the whole shapeshifter thing. He laughed that he has a couple of patients who *swear* that a dog once talked to them. Until now, he's just been tolerant and treated it as a mild psychosis. Even though he's sworn to secrecy, I'd be interested to watch his next session with *those* people.

He's been as excited as a kid at Christmas, being able to spend hours talking to Dr. Perdue. He told me that he's been on a waiting list for one of her seminars for almost a year. He said she's done some really cutting edge research papers about treating human trauma victims. Laura thinks he's *at* one of her seminars. We used the same story with Carl's people. He had to do some juggling in the office to be here. They'll even have seminar materials to bring home, from a talk that was already in the works a few months from now.

I didn't even know they *did* waiting lists for psychiatric seminars. Live and learn.

Bobby wasn't pleased at having to tell both John-Boy and Carl. He told me that telling them had been "approved" by the Council. If the approval hadn't come through, Bobby would have killed them. I reminded him that they've been Family for years. Nobody will talk.

He just hissed. He was in snake form at the time.

Later on he decided that having another doctor and psychiatrist who can keep their mouths shut could be useful to the Sazi. If Carl can get a grip.

I watched Bobby's multi-colored body slither down a mossy trunk toward an unsuspecting seagull. Loops of him were still draped like garland on the lowest branch. We measured—nose to tail, he's thirty-three feet long when he hasn't eaten. He loses some length with a full stomach. He can take down a full-grown goat as a single meal. I'm still fascinated by watching him hunt and hey, there's nothing better to do.

He's patience personified, but fast as a rattler. If he can get his teeth into prey, it doesn't escape. After he catches something, he wraps his body around it, and then slashes at it with a mouthful of sharp teeth and eats it by swallowing it whole in slow gulps. Like he had Jerry, except for the swallowing part. He has a vindictive streak too. Eye for an eye.

Jerry tried to suffocate Sue. Bobby wanted him to know what it felt like.

Wish I could have watched.

Bobby got a confession out of Jerry before he iced him. It apparently had nothing to do with Leo. I was simply competition. If getting rid of Sue would hurt me, Jerry would do it. He never figured there was anything wrong with doing it. He was more like Scotty than me. He wouldn't have lasted long though—Carmine had said no.

I'd found out a lot of stuff that happened during the airport incident. Like how Carmine and the boys got there: Jocko called them on his cell phone when he came to for back-up. Jocko always liked tag-teams.

Jocko still doesn't know anything about anything. He was hurt so he got a ride from Jake to a hospital. He'll be fine. Jake is unaware too, but Carmine had to be told since he's sleeping with Babs. One wrong scratch without silver and poof, insta-wolf.

Bobby moved a little too slowly this time. The seagull spotted him and jumped into the air just ahead of his mouth. It flew up into the canopy of trees and scolded him with a sharp piercing cry.

"Better luck next time," I called. He turned his head, still suspended in mid-air as though attached to a wire. His head is as big around as my fist and the middle of his long body has a diameter just slightly less than my waist. His red-gold eyes focused on me and he spoke. I still haven't gotten used to seeing that snake mouth move and hearing words come out. I keep expecting someone to step out from behind a tree and yell, "Gotcha!"

"You ssstartled it," he complained. "You owe me dinner." Burning coffee soared over the top of his jungle vine scent—almost indistinguishable from the surroundings.

"Excuses, excuses. You're just getting slow."

He flicked his tongue at me indignantly and lifted his body into the tree to wait for the next victim.

Snakes. They're all alike.

Wow. Suddenly I know how a snake thinks. I reflected

on all I had learned in the past few days. It made what I had endured over the last year seem so unnecessary. I leaned on the railing of the porch and stared into the jungle. The island belongs to Carmine and Linda. It's a good place to lie low, both from the cops and the crooks. Leo had friends, and I worry more about them than Sommers and Vito Prezza combined.

I wish Babs had told me things, given me some clue how to survive in this new world. I should have listened to what she *did* say. But she was running from what she did. She didn't want to admit her transgressions; she tried to pretend that it—that I—never happened.

Babs committed crimes but they weren't what I expected them to be. It was okay for her to use her abilities to defend herself. It was okay to kill me. She screwed up when I lived and became one of them. That violated the Sazi's equivalent of the prime directive. It's a death sentence crime, and Bobby is one of the executioners.

As Bobby tells it, any crime that a Sazi commits which would result in imprisonment in a human jail past any full moon puts you in Wolven's arena. They are judge, jury and executioner. No appeals. No second chances. The rule is simple. Break the law—whether or not you get caught by the humans, and discipline is swift and harsh. Either you are beaten or killed. And the beating isn't like a slap on the wrist. You get thumped on either by your pack leader or by a Wolven agent. The methods used depend on the type of animal doing the discipline. Could be claws, teeth—or, in Bobby's case, being crushed.

There's a bank of lawyers to defend a Sazi in human courts in case the crime is minor. If it's major . . . the Defendant won't be showing up. Ever.

Since Babs attacked me in self-defense it was the equivalent of a misdemeanor. For that Bobby would have just slapped her around a bit. But her dumb move was not to tell them I survived. Plus, she didn't mentor me. If you do accidently bring someone over, you're supposed to make sure that they are trained in the ways of the Sazi. She was supposed to teach me to hunt and instruct me on the use of my magical abilities—I didn't know I had any—to make sure that no humans ever see us. That's their second big rule. Bobby was impressed at how I handled not being seen, using the hotel room for my changes.

Babs's crimes got her a beating. It was bad enough that she's been laid up for almost a week now. Death and pain. Typical Family enforcement, although Bobby didn't like the comparison.

Bobby also did something that he called "claiming damages" on my behalf. Apparently, I was entitled to thump on her myself for making me a wolf. But I didn't know to ask and there was no family or pack to ask for me so he took the role of "concerned protector."

Babs didn't look real pretty for a few days, and still isn't quite herself. Bobby was thorough. But she was surprised not to be killed outright; she had expected to die. That's why she hid the truth. She was afraid.

He was lenient but didn't have to be. Wolven stands behind their people. Whatever decision the field agent makes is what goes. I would think that would lead to some abuses, but when everyone can smell lies I suppose that makes the thought less attractive. Bobby told me that he's in for a beating himself from his supervisor, Fiona Monier, a French cougar with a mean streak.

Wolven agents get full latitude when watching and enforcing, but aren't supposed to get involved. Helping Sue and me with Leo, and killing Jerry when he was suffocating Sue will get Bobby in trouble. He told me as much in the hangar but I didn't understand then. I guess the comment about taking a strip of hide is literal. Ouch.

Bobby's hoping to show mitigating circumstances. If he had done his job quicker, Leo wouldn't have been around to kidnap Sue. Of course, saying that he didn't do his job probably won't win him a friend, either.

I've been getting a crash course in the rules over the past couple of days while we've been waiting. It kills time. That's what I keep telling myself. On the plus side, it *is* fascinating.

I've also been getting biology lessons. I found out from Bobby that since I became Sazi, my body clock has slowed down to a crawl. We live decades longer than humans. Some Sazi have even survived centuries although that's rare.

Also, doctors are no longer necessary. Alphas can heal almost anything. I'm not that powerful, but I can probably drop the health insurance. Never did like the HMO, anyway. For serious wounds to non-alphas, the Sazi have "healers", who use magic to mend wounds—like Bobby had.

When I woke up in the plane hours after Jerry tried to kill us, I was healed but I couldn't feel Sue. I tried. I blew open every door, attached every connection I could, but nothing worked. Her body is living. I know. It's part of me now. I feel each breath, every heartbeat. But the part that's *Sue*, that indefinable spark of consciousness, is missing.

I left Bobby to his hunt and walked in the cabin. I laughed when I first saw the place. Calling this a cabin is like calling the Taj Mahal a bungalow. Forty-five hundred square feet on the first floor. The upstairs is the same.

Betty and John were earnestly talking at the kitchen table. Betty's dark blonde hair was in a bun at the back of her neck. She was wearing a white cotton tank top and shorts that stretched tight over heavy thighs. Betty tells me that she's a grey wolf, same as me, and I know she is because she smells like one. She doesn't strike me as a wolf though. It's hard to explain. She's supposedly the second most powerful female in the Colorado pack but she doesn't *smell* aggressive. She smells steady and warm, a calming presence. Like John-Boy. I'm having a hard time thinking of her running through a forest or ripping out a deer's guts.

I moved past them. Betty watched me out of the corner of one eye. I could feel it. She's been watching me a lot. She's tried to talk to me, tried to initiate some sort of therapy but I've avoided her. What's to discuss? If Sue lives, life is good. If she dies, I go with her. Not much else to say.

Good morning, gorgeous! I whispered into Sue's mind. She lay on a polished brass poster bed in a room with bamboo pattern wallpaper. A sea-soaked breeze ruffled the curtains on the French doors and caught the fan blades spinning overhead. The fan and the rustling lace were the only sounds in the large muggy room. It was only slightly cooler inside than out. I hate the heat but quiet is a nice change.

Betty and John both told me that a person in a coma can hear. They comprehend but can't respond.

I tried to ask Carl what might help bring her out of this—he *is* the medical doctor. He just snorted and said, very annoyed, "Why ask me? I don't understand a damn thing that's going on. Go ask the snake or the wolf in the next room." Then he took another swig straight from a nearly empty bottle of rum.

Okay then.

The teak floors creaked under my weight as I walked toward the bed. I sat down lightly on the edge. Sue still looked pretty rough, what with the surgery and then the near-suffocation. I watched her sleep. I keep telling myself it *is* just sleep. I moved a strand of hair from her pale silent face. The breeze pushed it back. Someone had placed her hands on her stomach, one over the other. Only the slow movement of her chest and the faint color in her cheeks reminded me that she's still alive. I touched her hand, slipped my own through it and squeezed softly. There was no tingle to the touch. Her scent was flat, like sterile soil with no breath of wind. That worried me the most.

"How are you doing today?" It felt strange talking to her like this. I'd rather be doing something—hitting a wall, screaming, fighting. Anything but just waiting. If I threw myself off a cliff at least I'd feel *something*. But I don't dare injure myself. She's too fragile.

My ears picked up sound from the next room and I looked up sharply.

"We interrupt our regularly scheduled programming for a special report," came a loud voice-over. I didn't even know that there was a signal to the island. I decided to listen in.

"This is Erin Stewart coming to you live from the 7 News Center."

Erin Stewart? She's from back home. I took my hand out of Sue's and stood. I walked toward the living room. I stopped in the doorway and leaned on the jamb. Linda was sitting on the couch, facing away from me. The television was on and the pretty black woman with poofy hair was speaking.

I heard Babs's voice from the kitchen. "Put it on pause for a second, Linda." Ah. It was a *tape* of a broadcast. I could watch it later.

I stepped back into the room with Sue, but heard Babs walk across the room and sit down. I glanced out briefly just as Linda hit the play button again, but then my eye caught the photo of a man and woman on the small box behind the anchor. I knew them from somewhere.

"We have just received in our offices a box which contained one of our Channel 7 video cameras. The whereabouts of the news crew who were in possession of this camera are still unknown. The footage that we are about to show you is very graphic in nature. We recommend that small children and those with limited tolerance to violence leave the room." The same wording was repeated at the bottom of the screen in type—I guess for the hearing impaired.

The picture changed to show a petite blonde woman with a microphone in a scene I recognized. I felt my heart in my throat.

The woman on the screen spoke. "This is Cindy Sigala with 7 News. We're here at the old airport where new development will soon transform this desolate scene into one of activity and progress." She motioned with her hand. "Several local construction companies unveiled plans today for a new factory outlet mall that will provide hundreds of new jobs for the area and give a needed economic boost to the region." Suddenly a scream sounded in the background and I felt panic tighten my chest. It was Sue.

"Shit!" I meant to say it soft but it came out loud. The girls started and turned toward me. The picture stopped as Linda hit the pause. The image of Sue, half out of the van with Leo gripping her hair froze on the screen and flickered.

Linda looked embarrassed. "Oh God! Tony. I'm sorry. I didn't know you were there."

"What's this?" I pointed at the screen.

Babs spoke as well as she could. Her mouth was still a mess. "'Armine put it togeth'r from the news coverage." I vaguely remembered the news crew; the sun glinting off the camera lens. It was just fragments of memory.

Betty was instantly beside me. I hadn't heard her move. "It's understandable if you don't want to watch this, Tony. If it's too soon just say so."

I didn't look at Betty. My eyes were glued on the screen. The look on Sue's face was part fear and part pain. It was suddenly hard to breathe. Could I go through this again? I glanced backwards at Sue's still form on the bed. Maybe there was a clue, something I'm forgetting that might help. No. I had to do this.

"Run the tape," I said in a flat voice. Betty watched me. Hell, everyone watched me. Betty glanced at John. He pursed his lips and then nodded. Betty must have agreed because she stepped back and gave me room.

Linda turned back toward the set but glanced over her shoulder at me more than once. She pointed the remote and pressed a button. Sound returned: wind and fast breathing.

The cameraman turned to the scream automatically. The reporter, quick on her feet, continued to report as though it was rehearsed.

"Ladies and gentlemen," she said with a hushed voice. "We are apparently on the scene of an attempted kidnapping. David, are you getting this? A black van has just pulled into the airport and a woman is being forcibly removed from it. She is obviously being moved against her will. Wait! Two men are opening doors on one of the hangers and a Boeing cargo plane is exiting. Can you get a close-up on that, David? Can you see anyone's face?"

The camera's view moved in closer and I watched again Sue's abduction—this time from a third person point of view.

"All of the men appear to have guns," said Cindy's disembodied voice. The scene played out just as it happened.

"The woman looks familiar; she might be a celebrity. One man appears to be the leader. He seems to be letting the woman go free. Okay, she's running now. Wait! Somehow he caught up to her. In fact he passed her by and caught her. He seems to be toying with her. Oh, God! He's slapped her to the ground!"

My eyes narrowed. Leo deserved everything he got.

This was about where I came in. Everybody in the room was glued to the screen, including myself.

"Now he's dragging her toward a small metal building. None of the men are doing anything except loading the plane. David, do you have your cell phone on you? We need to call this in to the police!"

I arrived in the picture in wolf form just then. I nearly knocked the cameraman over. Oops.

I'd only seen myself once before, on the video Babs made. I have mostly grey fur with a white star on my nose and a black and white neck ruff and tail. Pretty traditional markings. I must have run right by the news crew and not even noticed. Of course, I was a little preoccupied.

"What was that?" asked David.

"It looks like a dog. He's running right for the man with the girl!"

"All right! Attadog! Look at him go after the bad guy! Wow, that must have hurt. Think it's a police dog?"

Linda and Babs were echoing the cheers.

"Must be," agreed Cindy who had pretty much given up on reporting. "It's sure big enough. Oooh, look. There's another dog now!"

"*That's* a dog?"

I watched myself fight from a different angle. I felt my body move in reaction to the visual from the video and I split my attention between the images in my mind and the screen.

You fought wonderfully, I thought to myself.

Hold it. When did I start talking to myself in third person? I glanced sharply at Sue who was still inert on the bed.

Sue? I asked in my mind. There was no response.

"C'mon, big guy," muttered David. It brought my attention back to the video. He zoomed in on the dog fight. "Get the bad dog." Somehow they had picked sides and decided that Leo was the bad dog. Pretty astute of them.

"Look at that!" Cindy's voice was thick with horror. "They *shot* the woman! That man with the sandy hair. Oh my God!"

Time stopped. There was a buzzing in my ears. I watched the bullet spin her around for the second time. Watched her fall to the sand once again. A shudder passed through me.

"That was right through the heart," said David, appalled. "She'll never make it."

"Did you get that?" Cindy's blonde hair was in the edge of the picture now. "That black guy shot the second dog! Now they're shooting at him. He shot the sandy-haired man with the gun! Now he's taken a bullet. My God! This is a bloodbath!"

"Look at the dog." David didn't turn the camera to me and Sue. He knew where the bread and butter was. "He's going to the girl. Must have been her pet. They're both hurt pretty bad."

A pause. "—Cin, they'll never be able to use this on the air."

Bobby was the only one still standing when the bullets stopped. Suddenly he turned and looked right at the camera.

"Uh, oh," said David, moving the camera from his eye. The view turned sideways and most of the heads in the room moved with it unconsciously. It's instinct. "We've been spotted! Take off, Cindy. I'll hide the camera. We can come back for—" The picture went dead. There was a pause.

I wonder what Bobby did with the crew. I'd ask but I didn't really care.

The picture returned to the News Center. Erin was speaking again.

"That was the scene earlier today. Police arrived at the scene based on a tip from an unknown source. Perhaps the same source that returned our camera. Police have been unable to locate any bodies at the scene. Both the black van and the cargo plane have disappeared. However, 7 NewsCenter has learned the identities of several of the participants."

The screen behind the desk flashed a publicity still of Sue when she won the lottery. I smiled at the excited look on her face but then glanced again at her still form. Sadness won and the smile faded.

Then the screen split and showed a close-up from the video. "The woman apparently killed in a kidnap attempt was Susan Quentin. We profiled Ms. Quentin after she won the $268 Million Lotto jackpot last year. Her family has been unavailable for comment but we have learned that Ms. Quentin's sister, Bekki Meyers, reported her abduction from the Southside Mall parking lot earlier today."

Another picture flashed. This time of Leo. It was a mug shot. One front, one side, with a number on his chest. "The man first involved that later disappeared is known to Las Vegas authorities as Leopold Scapolo, AKA 'Lucky Leo'".

He was? I never heard that one.

"He has been indicted on multiple counts of money laundering and racketeering. He is also suspected of being involved in the abduction and murder of several Las Vegas showgirls."

Next a fuzzy picture of me flashed. It was an older photo but I didn't know from where. "This man is known to local authorities as Tony Giodone. Sources at the police department have indicated that they believe this name is an alias." Good guess.

"Mr. Giodone recently had a warrant issued for his arrest for first degree murder."

Yeah, well, they would still have to prove it. Frankly it didn't matter anymore. Bobby warned me that if I didn't change careers, he'd be visiting me again, and it wouldn't be a social call. Guess I was going to be the one to bend after all.

Happiness suffused through me. Damned if I knew why.

Erin continued, "We spoke with Detective Robert Sommers of the Fourth Precinct Homicide Division." Bob appeared on the screen, live from the airport. He looks even worse on television.

"Detective, do you believe that we will ever find any of the bodies seen on the video?"

"Well, Erin," he said, "we've had forensic crews out at the airport since we received the tip about the shootings. There is definitely some evidence that matches the video. We have put out an APB for the van and have requested air traffic control to advise us of any radar anomalies during this time. If they're out there we'll find them."

"But will you find any bodies?"

He shook his head and shrugged at the same time. "I doubt that those who survived would carry the bodies with them. We plan to use infrared spotting from our helicopter as soon as the sun goes down. We believe if they're buried nearby we'll find them." If there had been anything to find that might work. I knew what Bobby did with the bodies. They won't be found. Bobby slept in the jungle for the first couple of days on the island because of *that* meal.

The screen went blue just then. "Okay, this is where we spliced it," said Linda. "Hold on."

The picture started and it was Erin again. New outfit, same hair.

"This is Erin Stewart. We're *live* at the Glendale Funeral Home where a memorial service is being held for kidnap victim Susan Quentin. We have been requested to remain outside during the service out of courtesy for the mourners. It appears that the service is just now ending and people are beginning to exit."

"They already had a memorial service?" I asked. "Sort of rushing it, aren't they?" I was abruptly angry at the callousness and the greed.

Blackened coffee filled the room. It emanating from Linda. "You don't know the half of it, sweetie. Watch and learn."

Erin moved forward quickly, forcing the cameraman to double step to keep up. She approached a young woman wearing black. Her eyes were red and swollen. Hey, it's Lee.

Wait. Lee who?

From where I used to work. The friend that I stayed with that night. Nice to know she missed me.

What?! Sue? I asked in my head. Are you there? I ignored the video and turned and walked back into the bedroom. Sue was still out. There was no movement. But when I touched her . . . tiny fingers of electricity. Faint as a dream.

Tony? said a voice in my head but then disappeared. I called again; nothing. Was I imagining it?

Immediately Betty was beside me. Power crackled from her and boiled over the top of me, and I began to understand why she was a big dog.

"Talk to me, Tony. What's happening?" She placed a gentle hand on my shoulder. She smelled concerned and curious.

"She was here. Just now. But she's gone again." I shook my head, fighting to think.

Intelligence burned behind Betty's hazel eyes. "The video," she said slowly. "Keep watching. Maybe it's breaking through."

I understood what she meant.

I strode back into the front room, crossing in front of Linda and Babs. They both suddenly smelled afraid. I ignored the grumble from my stomach at the succulent scent. I haven't been eating well lately.

I took the remote from Linda and hit the rewind button while it was still playing. I backed up the tape to the point where Lee came on screen. I sat down beside Linda on the sofa, my entire focus on the screen.

"Excuse me, Miss?" said Erin. "Were you a friend of Susan Quentin?"

"Suzi," she replied, which made Erin repeat, "Excuse me?"

"Her name was *Suzi*, not Susan. It was her given name. But she liked to be called 'Sue'."

"So you *were* a friend?"

Lee nodded. "I like to think so. We were real close a few years back but we sort of drifted after she won the Lotto."

Warm fuzzies ran through me. They were mingled with sorrow. I called to Sue again. No response. I knew it was her. It had to be.

"Stopped seeing all her old friends, huh?" prodded Erin. "Money went to her head?"

Lee look appalled. "Oh, god, no! Not Sue. Not ever!" She leaned close to Erin, who lowered the mike to chest level. Lee apparently forgot that she was on film, "It was that family of hers! Her mother just took over her life! Once her mom moved in, Sue couldn't even breathe without asking permission . . . and her sister! The money-grubbing witch! God, I could tell you stories!"

Erin's pretty brown eyes lit up and she tipped the microphone toward Lee. "Feel free."

Lee must have noticed the camera. She suddenly got shy. "No, no. This isn't the day for it. I'd better keep my mouth shut." Then she moved hurriedly into the crowd.

Erin picked a new target. Bekki was moving from the main crowd of family and heading toward the waiting black limos. She was wearing a designer black outfit and wore a small pill-box hat with a veil. She didn't look sad at all. Big surprise.

There *was* surprise in my mind at the cynicism.

Another search. Nope. Still nothing.

"Excuse me? Mrs. Meyers? You're Bekki Meyers, right? Sue's sister?" Erin poked the microphone directly in Bekki's path. No problem. I didn't feel any guilt at all for that.

"Can't you people just leave us alone!" Bekki said, slapping the microphone aside. She kept walking toward the limos but Erin walked in step with her. She voiced the question that I just had.

"I was just wondering. Isn't this service sort of soon after the alleged murders? No bodies have been found yet and police are still hopeful that some people survived. Your sister might still be alive."

Bekki stopped then. She turned and faced the camera. She was angry. "I watched the video. It was a direct hit. My sister is dead! Do you understand that?"

She suddenly looked startled. She took a deep breath and added more calmly, "It's time to get on with our lives. We need closure of this awful thing. I have my children to think of. They need to move on. Suzi would have wanted that."

Says who? came an angry voice in my head. I locked onto it, held it.

Don't go! I asked—begged—commanded.

I can't wake up, Tony! Why can't I wake up? Then she was gone.

I looked at Betty. She was watching me, not the screen. My face probably held the panic I felt. So close. Damn it! I hit pause again.

"She was here again." Only Betty understood what I meant.

"Don't fight it, Tony," she said calmly. "Don't fight her. Just watch the tape. Let *Sue* watch the tape."

I took a deep breath and then let it out slowly. I punched the play button once more.

Erin Stewart's face took on a sly look when she asked Bekki, "What about the money? Your sister was a very rich woman. If there's no body, will your sister's estate ever be probated?"

Ah. There's the trick. No body, no money. Bekki's lips grew tight. Erin had struck a nerve. "Our attorneys have informed us that the law requires that we wait for seven years before we can probate."

"How do you feel about that?" She stabbed the mike in Bekki's face. She had scented blood. I wonder how many reporters are Sazi. I'll have to ask Bobby.

"No comment."

Abruptly, the microphone was pulled sideways by a slim well-manicured hand. I knew those fingernails!

"Oh God!" said Linda and dropped her head into her hands. Her scent changed to hot desert winds. "Here comes the embarrassing part! I looked like such a harpie!"

The camera turned to give a full face view of Linda. She was wearing a wide-brimmed hat with a veil. I couldn't see the dress but it was probably black. Although with Linda you never know.

Babs patted Linda's arm soothingly as she watched the screen through spread fingers. "s'okay," Babs said softly. "You 'ad erry 'ight to be angry." Linda turned to her and smiled. I smelled warmth and caring flow from Babs. Bread and sugar and musk.

"Well I have a comment!" Linda said sharply on the screen.

The camera stepped back, so all three women would be in the picture. Erin spoke, "You're Linda Leone, right? Owner of Carlin's Restaurant? Did you know Sue Quentin?" At least she picked up on the "Sue" the first time she was corrected. Some reporters never get the hint.

Bekki wanted to leave but it wouldn't be viewed well. I watched her eyes dart this way and that looking for an escape. Still, she seemed fascinated by Linda.

"Yes, I'm Linda Leone. Yes, I own Carlin's and yes, Sue was a very dear friend of mine." I felt Sue's happiness and gratitude at the admission.

"Sue says thanks," I said quietly to Linda. She gave me a startled look.

Just go with it, I told myself. Just relax. I leaned back into the soft cushions and watched.

"What did you want to comment on?" asked Erin. She seemed to have forgotten the question.

"You asked how the family felt about having to wait seven years to probate Sue's will. *Sister dear* here didn't have a comment. I do." Her voice rose until it drowned out everything surrounding her. Erin handed her the microphone and Linda addressed the assembled crowd. It wasn't big, probably thirty people.

"I've just spent the past two hours with Sue's friends and family. I've listened to the bickering, the sniping and the griping. This was *supposed* to be a memorial service for Sue. I came because I *thought* that I'd hear nice things about my friend. I did. From her other friends. But I guess it's true what they say. You can pick your friends but you can't pick your family." Bekki's eyes shot open and her jaw dropped. Myra looked furious. Her lips thinned just as Bekki's had earlier.

"All I heard from her family were complaints." She turned to Erin so suddenly that the reporter took a step back in reflex. Her brown eyes were startled.

"Know what her family thinks about waiting for the money? They're *pissed!* All of them." She imitated them one by one.

First Myra. She did her perfectly. Cold, with a whiny nasal quality. "'This is all Suzi's fault! What could she have been thinking? How am I going to get by?'" Linda glared into the camera. "Like she had a *choice* or something! She was *kidnapped!*"

Next came Bekki. A younger version of the same whine. "'Oh no! Seven years! Can you believe it? We should sue that attorney! The law should be changed. It's right there in living color. The woman is dead! I'm entitled to my inheritance!'"

Then another voice. "'How will I ever survive on the pittance that the trust gives me? I have a lifestyle to uphold. My children will be homeless in days!'"

It sounded just like Mitzi. I let the knowledge fill me because I knew it was Sue. I'd never met Mitzi. I felt Sue's thoughts swimming just behind my own. I felt angry and sad.

"That's what the family thinks about it! You people *make me SICK!*" She turned her back on the stunned group and tossed the microphone back to the closely following reporter.

Erin caught the mike on the fly. There was a scrambling hiss. She opened her mouth twice before she could speak. "Okay, then." She took another tack, "Um. Mrs. Leone. It's well known that even though you are married you have occasional . . . *relationships* with other women. Was Sue Quentin your lover?"

Anger and embarrassment filled me but I fought it down by being amused. Linda can take care of herself.

On the screen, Linda turned to the reporter with a look that could cut stone. "I *said* that Sue was my *friend.* If you know I'm bisexual, and in an open relationship, then you also know that I'm not shy about it. Nor am I embarrassed. If I had *meant* that Sue was my lover I would have *said* so!" Her voice rose with each word until it was a controlled yell in Erin's face. Small drops of spittle landed on the microphone. "How *dare* you even ask that! Sue's sexual preferences are none of your business! God! You're as bad as her family! Let the woman rest in peace."

Tears were rolling down her cheeks unchecked. Linda glared at the reporter until Erin's eyes dropped. Then she turned on her heel, slipped an arm through Babs's waiting one, slipped her other arm around Carmine and leaned into them, crying. Carmine put a caring arm around his wife while Babs turned and gave the reporter a look that could not only *cut* stone but should be able to turn Erin *into* stone. I found out after Linda arrived that Carmine hadn't said a word to them. They didn't know we were alive that day.

There was a stunned silence on the screen for a moment. Then Erin spoke. "Um, this is Erin Stewart, from Sue Quentin's memorial service. Back to you, Angela." The video clicked off. The entire group of us sat in dazed silence as the screen went dark.

Rage filled me and I let it. Homeless? Homeless! For God's sake! The trust gives her two hundred thousand a year. She's going to starve on that? What the hell is she doing with the money? I felt Sue's anger burn along my body like a flame. Her outrage and pain.

It's okay, I thought at her, You have the right to be angry. Tell me how you feel. Tell me all of it. I stood and walked toward the bedroom. Betty followed me like a ghost. My peripheral vision caught John and the others as they trailed in our wake.

I sat down on the bed, touched Sue's cheek with my hand. The tingles grew while I stroked her face.

"Wake up, Sue. Time to get up, sweetheart," I said to her sleeping form.

I can't! I can't wake up, Tony. Help me! I didn't know how. I looked at Betty. She was waiting patiently for some word. Her scent was masked by the sweet antifreeze curiosity drifting from the others assembled.

"She can't wake up. She's here." I tapped my temple. "But she can't wake up."

I looked to the group for any suggestions. Carl was out cold at a table in the corner. His snoring head was half underneath his left arm. His right fist was tight around the neck of a bottle. Still rum but the bottle was white this time. He smelled thickly of alcohol and sweat. Damn it, Carl. Why now?

Nobody understood what the problem was. How could I explain it?

Betty gripped my arm. She pulled me back. "Let me take a look at her." I moved aside for her. I shifted back a dozen steps. I felt Linda move up behind me. She rested cool hands on my arm and I let her. She laid her head on my shoulder and we watched the doctor work. Sue and I both felt comforted by her touch.

Betty leaned over Sue until I couldn't see her anymore. The room was strangely silent. Tough with so many people present. There was an air of solemnity. I felt Sue in my mind. She was worried. What if this was all? If she never woke up, never lived again.

I wouldn't consider that as a possibility.

A flash of light appeared over Sue's head. Trust a doctor to carry a penlight. The light flicked once, then twice. The white embroidered flowers on the pillow cover gleamed briefly.

Determination's hot metal filled my nose suddenly as Betty stood. Without any warning she slapped Sue hard across the face. What the hell!

Sue's head shifted violently sideways. Honeyed hair spilled over her face and her whole body rocked slightly. A vicious backhand brought her face back to where I could see it. The crack of the slap filled my ears and filled my mind with fury.

I broke away from Linda and was across the room faster than thought. A sound erupted from me—part howl, part roar. All rage. The third blow never reached Sue. I grabbed Betty by both shoulders and fiercely threw her sideways. She sailed across the room. Her back hit an oak and brass entertainment center that filled one corner near where Carl was slumped.

Carl woke in a flash as the cabinet disappeared in a rain of splinters, metal and broken glass. A shard of glass sank deep into her neck. I felt my eyes go. The beast inside was trying to lunge out. Betty's eyes glowed golden as she looked at me. Her lips pulled back and she growled low and deep. I didn't care. I answered with a growl of my own. She smelled confident and anticipatory. Her power raced over me; nearly as strong as Bobby. I think she intended to frighten me off.

Whether I was too angry or too stupid, it didn't work.

She would die for hitting my mate or I would die trying.

Thick orient spice crawled and clawed over the sweet copper blood. It urged me on, making me want the battle. I didn't need to look behind me to feel the fear from the humans. The tang was strong enough to make me salivate. The sound of the turning fan assaulted my ears. I was almost to her. My body tensed to fight. I saw her adjust her footing to spring.

"Tony?" came a tentative voice from the bed. Simultaneously, a burst of intense color exploded in my brain. Sunsets in the middle of the day.

I felt my heart stop. I turned in a flash. I had no words. Sue was sitting up with a slightly distressed look on her face. But her eyes were open. Her pale face was blushing. She smiled at me and I felt my eyes burn.

I ignored Betty. I hoped she wouldn't dive for me. In two steps I was at the bed with Sue in my arms. I hugged her tight. A pained sound reminded me that I could hug a little *too* tight. I eased her back and put pillows behind her so she could sit upright.

Long moments passed. I just stared at her. I couldn't keep a grin off my face. When I finally turned to the group, Linda had happy tears rolling down her face. Betty stood off to the side. Her arm was twisted at an odd angle. The shard of glass in her neck was pushed out by the flesh around it. When it was nearly out she reached up and plucked it away. She didn't admit the pain. She was stronger than I had credited her; I had underestimated her.

"Hey," I said to Betty with embarrassment, "I'm really sorry. I didn't understand . . ."

She waved it off with her good hand. "I forgot about the mating. You aren't an alpha so I didn't think you could hurt me." She looked at her arm with chagrin. "My mistake."

Carl narrowed his bloodshot eyes to stare at Betty. There was an injury and he was still a doctor—mostly. His voice was thick and slurred. "I think that arm's . . . um, unlocated."

She nodded seriously. "I could use some help." Actually, I didn't think she needed any help at all and *certainly* not from him. But maybe it's what Carl needed to hold on. Pretty good shrink. They moved into the other room where he had his black bag.

Sue smiled at me and then laughed. "Won't they be surprised when they find out I gave it to the geese?"

I frowned at her, unable to make the subject leap. It took me a moment to realize that she was commenting on the last thing she remembered: her funeral on the video.

"You gave your fortune to the geese?"

"Well, to the Department of Wildlife. I want them to tear down the house and make a preserve out of the grounds. I went to the attorney just before I had lunch with my sister. I changed my will and cut them all out."

Linda burst out laughing. The tears flowed so hard she couldn't speak.

"What's so funny?" asked Sue.

"Oh, God!" exclaimed Linda, gasping for breath. "They were so angry at the service because the lawyer wouldn't tell them what was in your will. He said until you were officially dead he couldn't reveal the contents. But your sister was so sure that you hadn't changed the will, because you told her that you *intended* to, not that you *had.*"

Sue looked chagrined. "She was so weirded out at even the prospect that I felt guilty. I fudged a little. I actually thought about going back to the lawyer and ripping it up. But I didn't get the chance. Vinny grabbed me right when we were coming out of the restaurant."

"They were making plans at the service about the things

they were going to do. Bekki is going to build a custom house and your Mom is going to travel. They plan to borrow and borrow and borrow some more against their future fortune."

She hooted loudly. "And it goes to the birds! Oh, Sue! That is priceless. Seven years of waiting and the *geese* get a new pond!" Linda laughed until tears rolled down her face.

Sue's mood changed and she smelled sad and angry. Her voice slid across my mind. They really didn't care. Didn't love me. I always knew it but part of me still can't believe it. I hugged her against me.

Then she turned her head to me, still snuggled against my shoulder. "Tony? Now what? I don't want to see them again, not ever. But where will we go?"

"What? You don't like the island? You told me *exotic*."

"But not forever," she said quietly. "Where will we live?"

I looked at her with confidence. "I don't know, sweetheart. But we'll find somewhere."

Bobby pushed himself off from the wall. I hadn't realized he'd come in. Sue looked at him and I smelled fear's tang rise from her. "It's okay. Bobby's a cop."

She nodded nervously and bit at her lip. "That doesn't mean that I'm not afraid of him." Okay, good point.

Bobby looked serious. Sweat beaded on his bare upper body. He was wearing faded jean shorts. That must be for Sue's benefit. Bobby is abnormally accustomed to going naked. Or maybe I'm abnormally accustomed to clothes. He tells me I'll get over it. "Wolven will relocate you, Sue. Tony needs to be with a pack—with other wolves. It'll take some time but we've got packs in Boulder, Minneapolis, and Chicago. There are packs in Anchorage and the Ukraine, too, but they're Arctic climates. You probably wouldn't like it." He sighed and it spoke volumes. "I'll do what I can but you might have to stay here for awhile while we sort it out. It's a slow process."

Longer? In this heat? Inside is fine, but outside is— well, a jungle. God, what I wouldn't give for a sudden snowstorm. Oh well. It was hard to bitch with Sue's hand solidly in mine and tingles racing through my body.

Betty and Carl came back in the room. Carl looked at little better. Maybe Betty could help him after all. Betty was carrying two white boxes. One big, one little. She came over to the bed and gave me the small package. The larger one was placed gently near Sue's feet.

"What's this?" I asked.

She shrugged. Her eyes were bright with curiosity. "I was told to give these to you as soon as Sue woke up."

Bobby frowned and it matched the one on my face. At least I didn't hear anything ticking inside the boxes. No smell either.

I opened my box first. Inside the plain white shirt box was white tissue paper. I opened the tissue paper and found a group of official looking documents. Without removing the documents from the box, I looked at each one.

Wow. Definitely impressive. "We apparently have different definitions of slow," I said to Bobby, amazement tinging my voice. "Okay, I admit it. I'm impressed." I shook my head. "Goddamn show-off."

He frowned and moved a little closer. "I don't understand."

I handed him the documents. There was a driver's license, worn-looking and ready to expire next March. It was from Illinois and showed my given name, J. Anthony Giambrocco, Jr. Giodone is my dad's name. I took it after my mom died. Dad rigged a phony birth certificate and everything. My real name is pretty safe because I've never used it.

There was a matching birth certificate. A certified copy of my real one. Quick work. I gave a little chortle at the matching license and certificate for Sue—oops, sorry, for Jessica Susan Giambrocco. I was betting from the condition of the license that there was a full dossier to match the names. Good identity people take pride in their work. The size and shape of the last paper made me nervous.

Bobby looked at each document in amazement. I smirked at him. "Guess I'm going to Chicago, huh?" Nice of him to decide for me. Probably best. He had told me about the various packs and their leaders.

Lucas Santiago is the alpha of the Boulder pack. He's strong, proud, and incredibly noble. Nope. I wouldn't fit there.

Minneapolis is headed by Josef Isaacson, a hard working Norwegian. Eh. Maybe.

Chicago, though—Chicago is led by Nikoli Molotov. I jokingly asked Bobby if he had an "explosive personality." I thought it was funny. Bobby didn't. "I wouldn't *ever* say that around him if I were you," he said solemnly.

"Jeez, I was just kidding. You know, Molotov cocktails?" I nudged him in the ribs.

"I caught the joke, Tony. I'm not stupid. But you don't understand. He's the *same guy*. He's been around since Czar Nicholas's court. He's Russian Mafia and runs Chicago with an iron fist. He's not a pleasant soul."

Ah. That's the one. My kind of world. I had no objection.

Bobby smelled sort of stunned. He kept shaking his head as he looked at each document. He turned each one, examined them, looked out the window at the muted sunlight through them. He handed them back to me with a seriously pissed off expression.

"Who in the *hell* do you have photos of, doing what?"

Sue and I looked at each other in surprise. "You didn't do this?"

He moved toward the bed and tried to grab at the box. "No! Hell, even I don't know anyone with enough stroke to get them. Was there a card? Anything at all?"

I shrugged. I hadn't looked. I let him take the box. He pulled the tissue paper out of the box and shook it lightly. A small note fell on the bedspread. Sue picked it up. The paper was thick and linen. The handwriting was masculine.

She read it out loud. "I've arranged for you to stay in Chicago. Nikoli will treat you well or answer to me. I've already paid your tribute. Don't let him tell you otherwise." She gave a little laugh. "It's signed Lucas Santiago." She looked at me with a curious expression. "Do you know him?"

I shrugged. I didn't. She looked at Bobby. His mouth had dropped as she spoke. The white box, brilliant against his ebony skin, dropped to the floor from his unexpectedly limp hand. Everyone else in the room was riveted to our conversation. Betty stared at us with a similar expression.

It took Bobby several tries before he could speak. "Know him? Yeah. *Every* Sazi knows him. He's a Council member. But how the hell do *you*?"

I had no answer.

"Why don't you open your box, Sue?" Betty suggested. I looked at her. She seemed as surprised as Bobby at the turn of events. The breeze blew through the open doors again, fluffing Sue's hair across her face. It blew her fragrance right at me. She smelled of summer forest and kitchen spices. I hadn't realized how much I missed the scent of her feelings while she was gone. Her every emotion was like sunlight off crystal; intense and startling.

She tried to pull the large box closer to her. Bending was still difficult. She gave a little grimace so I reached over and placed the box on her lap. It was heavy and about as long as a rose delivery box but wider. She lifted the lid. Taped to the white tissue paper was a note. Again, she read it to the group.

"If Chicago doesn't work out, you're always welcome in Boulder, Suzi. You and Tony both." She said it with surprise and amazement. "It's signed Lucas." She turned her head to me, her feelings mildewed with amazement. "I don't know him, Tony! Why is he doing these wonderful things for us?"

I didn't have an answer. I just shook my head. "What's in the box?"

Everyone moved closer as Sue opened the tissue paper. Under the tissue was a layer of rich green velvet. The thick antifreeze of curiosity overpowered my nose and I sneezed repeatedly. So did Babs and Betty. When we finished, the silence was so thick that I could hear every heart in the room.

I looked in the box. Inside was a plastic figure, a foot or so high, with red matted hair trimmed around a war-torn face. There was a ponytail at the top of the head. Green plastic eyes over a painted smile matched the stained and torn green velvet dress she wore. I smiled. The doll was ravaged as only a four-year-old could manage.

There were confused looks from those assembled. Betty seemed most confused of all. Why would someone go to the trouble to wrap this wreck of a doll like a treasure?

I wasn't going to spoil the surprise. It was Sue's story.

Sue's smile came slowly; recognition turned to joy. "Jessica!" She picked up the doll and hugged it to her tightly. Tangerines and cookie spices rose from her in a burst.

I'd wager two to one that Lucas has white fur.

Sue looked at me with shining eyes. She put the doll carefully back in the box and smoothed the dress reverently. She gently touched the red nylon hair. She was nearing tears. Happy and sad both. But her curiosity finally got the better of her. She reached for the papers I was holding. She looked at the picture on the license and smiled brightly at the listed weight. She cocked her head and looked at me, "I like Jessica and Susan but why Ge-am-brock-o?" She stumbled over the name.

I looked at her intently for a moment. "Because I'll share. If you want to use my name, I'd let you." I could see Linda grinning out of the corner of my eye. I swallowed hard. It had been thrust on me; hardly a choice. But how could I give up rainbows and sunsets?

"Oh, what the hell. I don't do subtle well. I love you, Sue. I *want* to spend the rest of my life with you. Will you come to Chicago with me? Be my mate? Be my wife? Please?" I held her hand and waited for a reply.

I stayed out of her head with effort; I had to let her decide for herself. No prompting. Plus, I was a little scared of what I would find if I looked.

Her face moved from confusion to astonishment and finally to absolute glee. She threw herself into my arms with a joyous cry. Her scent was tangerines and cinnamon and baked apple pie. Sweet musk and baking. Amazing how humans, even without being able to smell the emotions, find comfort in the scents of caring. The scents of love.

It was answer enough. I held her tight against me while

the others looked on smiling. I rolled in her scent. I let the sweet tingles fill my body. The Sazi looked on enviously. The others could only guess.

I was suddenly looking forward to a new life with a new love. Years and years of learning and being together. Sue didn't even look at the last paper. She didn't have to. She saw it in my mind. Sure, we're mated. But we were born human—and American.

It was a marriage license.

A GIFT HORSE

"I want you to pay me for my horse," Slocum said to the maharajah.

The mahout let out a wordless cry of rage and rushed forward, swinging his hooked stick at Slocum. Slocum deflected the stick with his left arm and reached out with his right hand to clutch the mahout's throat. Gasim's eyes bulged as Slocum squeezed. The mahout tried to twist away but was off balance from his headlong rush. Slocum stepped back, turned, and sent Gasim crashing facedown in the dirt.

Slocum picked up the hooked stick and turned toward the maharajah, who had watched with an amused smile dancing on his lips. Behind the prince, Ali scrambled to get a clean shot without hitting his master. But it wasn't necessary. Slocum grabbed the pole with both hands and broke it with a snap that rang out like a gunshot. He threw the pieces onto the mahout's limp body.

"You fight splendidly," the maharajah said. "I will give you a new horse, but you must agree to be my scout."

DON'T MISS THESE
ALL-ACTION WESTERN SERIES
FROM THE BERKLEY PUBLISHING GROUP

THE GUNSMITH by J. R. Roberts
Clint Adams was a legend among lawmen, outlaws, and ladies. They called him . . . the Gunsmith.

LONGARM by Tabor Evans
The popular long-running series about Deputy U.S. Marshal Long—his life, his loves, his fight for justice.

SLOCUM by Jake Logan
Today's longest-running action Western. John Slocum rides a deadly trail of hot blood and cold steel.

BUSHWHACKERS by B. J. Lanagan
An action-packed series by the creators of Longarm! The rousing adventures of the most brutal gang of cutthroats ever assembled—Quantrill's Raiders.

DIAMONDBACK by Guy Brewer
Dex Yancey is Diamondback, a Southern gentleman turned con man when his brother cheats him out of the family fortune. Ladies love him. Gamblers hate him. But nobody pulls one over on Dex . . .

WILDGUN by Jack Hanson
The blazing adventures of mountain man Will Barlow—from the creators of Longarm!

TEXAS TRACKER by Tom Calhoun
Meet J.T. Law: the most relentless—and dangerous—manhunter in all Texas. Where sheriffs and posses fail, he's the best man to bring in the most vicious outlaws—for a price.

JAKE LOGAN

SLOCUM'S
SWEET REVENGE

J

JOVE BOOKS, NEW YORK

THE BERKLEY PUBLISHING GROUP
Published by the Penguin Group
Penguin Group (USA) Inc.
375 Hudson Street, New York, New York 10014, USA
Penguin Group (Canada), 10 Alcorn Avenue, Toronto, Ontario M4V 3B2, Canada
(a division of Pearson Penguin Canada Inc.)
Penguin Books Ltd., 80 Strand, London WC2R 0RL, England
Penguin Group Ireland, 25 St. Stephen's Green, Dublin 2, Ireland (a division of Penguin Books Ltd.)
Penguin Group (Australia), 250 Camberwell Road, Camberwell, Victoria 3124, Australia
(a division of Pearson Australia Group Pty. Ltd.)
Penguin Books India Pvt. Ltd., 11 Community Centre, Panchsheel Park, New Delhi—110 017, India
Penguin Group (NZ), Cnr. Airborne and Rosedale Roads, Albany, Auckland 1310, New Zealand
(a division of Pearson New Zealand Ltd.)
Penguin Books (South Africa) (Pty.) Ltd., 24 Sturdee Avenue, Rosebank, Johannesburg 2196,
South Africa

Penguin Books Ltd., Registered Offices: 80 Strand, London WC2R 0RL, England

This is a work of fiction. Names, characters, places, and incidents either are the product of the author's imagination or are used fictitiously, and any resemblance to actual persons, living or dead, business establishments, events, or locales is entirely coincidental.

SLOCUM'S SWEET REVENGE

A Jove Book / published by arrangement with the author

PRINTING HISTORY
Jove edition / June 2005

Copyright © 2005 by The Berkley Publishing Group.

ISBN: 0-515-13955-6

JOVE®

Jove Books are published by The Berkley Publishing Group,
a division of Penguin Group (USA) Inc.,
375 Hudson Street, New York, New York 10014.
JOVE is a registered trademark of Penguin Group (USA) Inc.
The "J" design is a trademark belonging to Penguin Group (USA) Inc.

PRINTED IN THE UNITED STATES OF AMERICA

10 9 8 7 6 5 4 3 2 1

1

The Grand Tetons rose majestically in front of John Slocum. He wiped sweat from his forehead with his frayed bandanna and took in their soaring purpled beauty after the endless miles of flat Wyoming grasslands he and his traveling companions had crossed in the past week. Spring was turning into summer, and the cool breezes whipping down the tall mountain slopes would be appreciated. If they ever got there.

"You need help?" Slocum called. He craned his neck to see if Hugh Malley could fix whatever trouble he had gotten into this time. Hugh's sweetheart, Darlene, sat in the driver's box of the flatbed wagon and looked peeved at the delay. Slocum shared her irritation, but Darlene had added to the time they had spent on the trail with her insistence on avoiding anything that looked like a ravine, hill or possible rattler den. If things ran smooth as silk and there wasn't anything to complain about, she could make up a new problem at the drop of a hat.

Slocum heaved a sigh. It was Darlene's wagon, not Hugh's. Hugh was a hard-rock miner looking to find a decent job. Slocum had come across them in Central City, Colorado, and had struck up a friendship with Hugh. If he

1

had known Darlene was going to be part of their journey
north out of Colorado and then westward diagonally
through Wyoming, he might have agreed on some other location closer to Central City.

Darlene was a good-looking woman, but she spent most
of her time worrying about things she couldn't change. She
tossed her mane of long brunette hair and let the feeble, hot
prairie breeze pull it into a small banner proclaiming her
gender, as if the well-filled bodice of her gingham dress
and the occasional glimpse of her well-turned ankle and
calf didn't tell the tale properly. Slocum had to admit he
would not have minded a roll in the hay with Darlene, had
she not been so firmly attached to Hugh. But that would
have been it. To have her nagging and worrying on a permanent basis could wear down any man.

That might be why Hugh had chosen to be a hard-rock
miner—he was buried under tons of rock twelve hours a
day and only had to worry about firedamp, cave-ins and a
dozen other ways of dying quickly. The last thing he would
likely hear would be the groaning of timbers or rock crashing downward to crush him, which had to be better than
Darlene's constant carping.

"Can't figure what's wrong, John. Can you take a look
and see what you can do?"

John hid his irritation as he turned his horse about and
walked back to where the right rear wagon wheel had con-
trived to wedge itself in a deep rut blocked by a large rock.

"We can roll the wagon backward and avoid the rock,"
Slocum said, seeing the problem right away. He wondered
why Hugh hadn't seen this himself. Jumping down, he
went to put his shoulder to the wagon to help Hugh.

"Wanted to talk to you, private-like, John," Hugh said in
a low voice. "What can I do to quiet her down? Darlene's a
fine gal; don't get me wrong, but she never stops flapping
her gums."

Slocum knew better than to say a word. Darlene wasn't

his woman, and Hugh had to figure out how to deal with her on his own. Sooner or later it would occur to him that they weren't married, and he would take off to find his own destiny.

"What's holding the two of you together?" asked Slocum.

Hugh braced himself against the wood side and heaved. The wagon came out of the rut and rolled free of the rock blocking the way. The broad-shouldered, heavyset Welsh miner was easily twice as strong as Slocum, but his mind worked slower. Far slower. It took him a few more seconds of laborious thought before he answered.

"She's a bit like my old ma. Think that's it? I want what my pa got?" Then he grinned ear to ear, showing a broken front tooth and another one that had been repaired with bright gold. "And she's mighty good between the sheets. You can't believe the things she can do when she puts her mind to it."

"Don't need to know that," Slocum said. He dusted off his hands and looked at the Grand Tetons glowing a hazy purple in the distance. No matter what, they would go their separate trails in another day or so. He had decided to part company and see what the high country had to offer this summer.

"How far is it to some town?" Darlene called. "We've still got hours and hours of daylight. I don't want to spend any longer on this godforsaken prairie than I have to. I want to sleep in a bed with a fine feather mattress and pillows. How I miss real pillows. Not that your shoulder's not fine, Hugh, dear," she said ingratiatingly.

Slocum mounted and rode west again.

"I'll scout a trail so this doesn't happen again," he said as he passed Darlene, who was hunched over in the driver's box and waiting to get rolling again. "That'll speed up our trip. I think Hoback Junction is only about fifteen miles off."

"Is that Hoback Canyon running to the southeast?" Hugh asked. His eagerness made Slocum wonder what the miner had heard about a gold or silver strike there. But then, Hugh didn't much care what he mined. Coal, lead, silver, it was all the same to him. He actually enjoyed being underground pecking away at the earth's bones to pry loose a few tons of pay dirt, whatever that might be.

Slocum shielded his eyes from the bright Wyoming sun and saw mountains running in that direction. The Grand Tetons loomed ahead, a spine of rock stretching away to the left, towering peaks to the north.

"Could be. It's been more 'n a year since I rode this way, and I don't remember. Anything special there for you?"

"Hoback Junction will be a good place to stay," Darlene said. "It's larger than the rest of those miserable so-called towns we've passed through."

"You been there before?" Slocum asked.

"Why, no, but Hugh has spoken so glowingly of the spot, it has to be far larger than even Central City."

Slocum wasn't so sure but said nothing. It wasn't his place. He spent the rest of the day scouting a trail for them and was about as happy as a man could be when they saw the outskirts of Hoback Junction a little before sundown. Slocum glanced over and saw Hugh and Darlene all lovey-dovey and sitting close to each other in the driver's box. The rest of the world might not even exist.

Slocum looked around for a decent saloon to wet his whistle as they rode down the main street, but he didn't see one. The town probably had a big population of Mormons, who didn't cotton much to others drinking whiskey since it was against their religion. But Slocum had ridden through-out Utah Territory and had always found some establish-ment serving a nip. He might have to look for it, but it was here. This was too close to Fort Bridger to the south and the Oregon Trail to the north for alcohol not to be a prof-itable commodity.

"There!" cried Darlene. "A hotel. A nice-looking one. The first since Central City!"

"Go on, get us a couple rooms," Hugh said. "Me and Slocum will poke around to see what jobs're available."

"You mean you want to imbibe liquor," Darlene said in her snippy tone. "Well, go ahead. Get soused. Just don't expect to sleep in the same bed if you come in reeking of demon rum!"

Hugh bent over and whispered for more than a minute. Darlene finally smiled and then gave him a little peck on the cheek. From what Slocum could tell, Hugh was doing just fine keeping her corralled.

The miner jumped to the ground and let Darlene tend the rig. He looked up at Slocum with big brown eyes and a grin that wouldn't quit. "Where's a good watering hole?" he asked.

"See one anywhere?"

"Nope, but there's got to be a place where a nickel'll buy a beer." Hugh was more cheerful than he had been in the month since leaving Central City. Slocum figured that was because he had finally sent Darlene off and was free to get liquored up.

Slocum and Hugh wandered through the streets, politely nodding to the locals and keeping their ears open. Without having to ask, Slocum soon found a street running toward the south of town where there was a bit more coming-and-going than along the other streets in Hoback Junction.

"You got the knack, John. That's only one of the things I like 'bout you," Hugh said, slapping Slocum on the back. The two went into the saloon and looked around. Slocum was used to boisterous singing, bawdy women running around, exposing their privates in an attempt to lure drunks upstairs so they could rob them, or even women barkeeps leaning over to coax their customers into drinking just one more round. This place didn't even have a sign proclaiming its name.

A man with a bushy mustache walked back and forth behind the bar, looking bored. His apron was almost clean, attesting to the lack of work. Seeing Slocum and Hugh Malley lit his face.

"Come on in, gents. I kin tell you got the look of trail dust 'bout you. How's about a shot of whiskey?"

Slocum considered, then shook his head. He dropped a dime on the bar.

"Two beers."

"Comin' up," the barkeep said, not put out by his inability to foist off some of his trade whiskey on the newcomers. He dropped the warm, frothy beers in front of them.

"What's the prospect of minin' jobs around here?" asked Hugh, taking a sip of his beer. From the face he made, Slocum knew it wasn't the best beer west of the Mississippi. He sipped at his own. Bitter.

"Not a whole lot, truth to tell. Most everyone's gone west to the Comstock Lode to paw through them danged rocks." The barkeep tipped his head to one side and studied Hugh. "You look like a miner, not a prospector."

"That I am. My pa and his, too, was hard-rock men from Wales. No coal mine's too deep or ore too hard for me to pick out."

"Save your spiel," the barkeep said. "There's no minin' in the area. Hoback Junction is just that—a crossroads, north-south and east-west. Was, at least."

"What happened?" Slocum wasn't sure he wanted to know, but from Hugh's hangdog look, he needed someone to keep up his end of the conversation. Listening to tall tales told by a bartender was better than Hugh's depression.

"I ain't one to spread gossip, mind you," the barkeep said, and Slocum knew he was the very person to do so. "I heard it with my own ears."

"It?"

"The most mournful sound you ever did hear. Some folks from up Minnesota way claim it's a wendigo. A critter that used to be human but has become an animal, livin' out in the woods and eatin' moss off the north side of trees.

Blood runs from the eyeball sockets! And the wendigo wants to be human again, but he can't. Regular food makes him puke."

"Good thing," Slocum said, reaching over and taking a pickle from a jar on the bar and biting into it. "Leaves that much more food for my friend and me."

"This ain't no yarn," the barkeep insisted. "Half the town's heard the moanin' and cries! Ain't that so, Jethro? Little Pete?"

From the table at the rear of the saloon came mumbled agreement. Slocum paused, wondering what was going on. If the barkeep had been funning them, the other two would have chimed in with even more outrageous claims. Instead, they looked scared.

"At night?" asked Hugh, obviously taken in by the narrative.

"Night, day, 'bout anytime. Strangest echoes all the way from down in Hoback Canyon. Nobody's been brave enough to go find out what's makin' the sound." The bartender lowered his voice, leaned forward and said confidentially, "You get bit by a wendigo and you become one, too. Nobody's stupid enough to tangle with trouble like that."

"Only in Hoback Canyon?" Slocum asked. "Or does it move around?"

"Moves. Last anyone'd heard, the sounds was comin' from up north, in the country this side of the steam vents in the ground. 'Course that was Whiskey Sam what heard it, so nobody's sure whether to believe him or if he was just havin' more of his hallucinations. They get real bad when he don't have enough money for a pint of his pop-skull."

Slocum had traveled through the Yellowstone area many times and had always marveled at the pools of boiling water standing on the ground and the geysers spewing steam far into the air. But anyone living in this part of Wyoming wouldn't mistake the screech of water blasting upward for a tortured soul pissing and moaning.

"You don't look like you're believin' any of it," spoke up a man at the far end of the bar. He hiccupped, then turned his shot glass over so the barkeep could not refill it. Slocum was impressed. Most men kept drinking until they fell over. This one had a sense of when to call it quits. Or so he thought until the man made his offer.

"I'd pay a hunnerd dollars to find out what's makin' them weird noises."

"Put your money where your mouth is, Mr. Glenn," said the barkeep.

"Here it is." The man pulled a fat wallet from his inner coat pocket and counted out a hundred dollars in scrip. Slocum saw Hugh's eyes go wide at so much money. Even though it was only paper money, it was still more than the miner had seen in the past several months.

"What'll it take to collect that?" Hugh licked his lips, then drained his beer.

"Don't," Slocum cautioned. He had seen about every con game played, and this smelled of one.

"What does a man have to do to collect that bounty?" Hugh pulled away when Slocum tried to calm him, to get him to think more before agreeing to something that wasn't likely to pan out.

"Give you ten dollars if you see whatever it is makin' the noise," Glenn said. "All of it if you bring it back alive."

"What if I shoot it and drag its carcass into town?"

Glenn hiccupped, then slammed his hand down on the money.

"All yours, but I get to stuff it and hang its head on the wall in my office."

"What do you do?" Slocum asked.

"Mr. Glenn there, well, he's the town banker. He's worryin' that the noises'll drive off folks. Hasn't so far, but if they keep up, Hoback Junction might end up a ghost town."

"Who keeps the money?" Slocum had no interest in

such a wild goose chase. A wildcat could make mighty strange sounds. Echoing down a canyon, magnified by distance or altered by peculiarly shaped rock formations, even the most common of animal noises could sound downright unusual. If a new steam vent had worked its way to the surface, it might be blowing through rock like a man whistling for a horse. The steam might be venting through a very long rock chimney to change the sound. Slocum thought of a dozen ways odd sounds might be made, and none of them was worth a hundred dollars to discover.

Hugh Malley thought different.

"I'll find out for you," the miner said.

"Who holds the money?" Slocum refused to let his friend get swindled, though he couldn't see how it would happen. Neither Glenn nor anyone else in Hoback Junction could bilk Hugh out of money he didn't have.

"I'll see to it, 'less you got somebody else in mind," said the barkeep. "Them boys'll vouch for me. Hell, they'll vouch for Mr. Glenn. He's a man of his word." The bartender laughed. "Owns damn near most of the town. No reason for him to cheat you. And he's not the only one who wants to know what's makin' them noises."

"I'd put up five to find out, too," said one of the men at the rear of the saloon.

"You don't have that much. Shut yer tater trap," said his partner.

"I'll do it!"

Slocum motioned for another beer. He paid for Hugh's second one, also, but his mind was racing. This was as good a time as any to part company with Hugh and Darlene. They were good people, but the trip across the flatlands of Wyoming had drained all the milk of human kindness from Slocum.

"We want to see what you drag back, mister," the barkeep said. "Ever'one in town'll want to see. You'll be a hero!"

"And I'll be moving on," Slocum said softly to Hugh.

"You and Darlene can split the money. I think I'll mosey north. Montana is a sight cooler in the summertime than other places. There ought to be enough spreads up there looking for a bronco buster or just a plain old wrangler."

"We can go on this here hunt together, John. The pair of us stand a better chance of runnin' whatever it is to ground and capturin' it. Split the money," Hugh said, but Slocum saw how it was. Hugh Malley thought of this as his new start, his stake, his way of impressing the hell out of Darlene. From the way Hugh and Darlene acted, Slocum could see them getting hitched.

"I'm not thinking of settling down here," Slocum told him. "Let's get a good night's sleep, then go our separate ways in the morning."

"You've been a good partner, John."

Slocum and Hugh shook hands, but Slocum knew Hugh Malley was pleased that he was giving in to wanderlust.

The next morning Hugh headed southeast into Hoback Canyon to hunt for his wendigo, and Slocum cut due north toward Yellowstone.

2

Riding across Wyoming had made Slocum yearn for mountains, really tall mountains like the Grand Tetons. The Front Range of the Rockies was nice, but Slocum preferred the look of these immense, towering peaks. They promised a freedom that no longer existed in Colorado, where settlers and miners were moving in to plow the land and dig endless gopher holes into the once pristine rock.

He sucked in a deep breath and tasted pine and fir and fragrant plants growing in abundance all around him. This was his kind of land, and he had missed it while struggling across the Wyoming prairie with Hugh and Darlene in tow. They were good people, and he had fancied that Darlene had given him the eye more than once, but they weren't the kind of folks who appreciated being on their own. Hugh liked the security of working for some mine owner who sapped all that was valuable from both the ground and the miner, and Darlene sought what she might never find on the frontier: happiness.

Slocum wished he could share his feelings with them. Hugh might decide roaming around above the ground was a better way to live and Darlene could find satisfaction other than in what she bought at some store or what others thought of her.

As he rode, Slocum began to get the uneasy feeling of being watched. The Wind River Reservation wasn't too far off, and he had caught gossip about the Indians not taking kindly to their new land. A few hotheads always snuck away, but seldom did they go on the warpath and do much mischief these days.

But those hotheads might make a bit of a name for themselves if they lifted a solitary traveler's scalp. Slocum felt the back of his neck beginning to itch as he looked around for trouble.

He thought he spotted it, too.

Riding at an angle off the trail did nothing to erase the uneasy sensation that was mounting by the minute. Slocum knew better than to discount these feelings; he had gotten through the war by trusting his instincts, and it was obvious to him now that someone was riding on his back trail. That wasn't too unusual but being unable to spot them certainly was. He was an expert when it came to tracking and hunting—both as hunter and hunted.

He was being hunted now.

Slocum drew rein and sat with his leg curled around the pommel for a spell, waiting for something to happen. The men following him would make a mistake, if they were road agents intent on robbing him. When nobody appeared Slocum knew he had Indians dogging his trail. An outlaw, especially a white man, would be too eager and would never bide his time to strike at the right moment.

Reaching for his rifle, he froze. Movement in the bushes some distance away might have been a breeze he didn't feel where he sat. Slocum left his Winchester in its scabbard and slid his leg back down so he could get his foot into the stirrup. The small movement might have been a fox or even a rabbit, but he didn't think so.

Slocum put his spurs to his horse's flanks and trotted

back toward Hoback Junction, but not far. He cut off the road again, circled and came to a spot where he could get a better view of the bushes that had swayed so suggestively.

A Crow Indian poked his head out and looked around. Not seeing Slocum, he motioned and two more followed. They wore paint, but Slocum wasn't sure what it meant. He wasn't as familiar with the Crows as he was with other tribes. If he had seen a Cheyenne or an Arapaho with paint adorning his face, he would have known if they were celebrating, hunting or on the warpath.

He doubted these three were hunters. Why act so sneaky? They certainly weren't celebrating. That left the least palatable of the choices. Slocum waited for them to move on and try scalping a settler or another pilgrim along the trail.

He cursed under his breath when he saw that they weren't deceived by his circling around to spy on them. Two split from the third and went to the far side of the road, as if to lay an ambush. The third stood his ground, then slowly surveyed the countryside. Slocum stood stock-still, but his horse betrayed him with a nervous whinny.

The brave let out a war whoop and shook his rifle high above his head. He unerringly sighted in on Slocum.

Slocum swung about and galloped off toward the town he had left hours earlier. He knew he could never reach it but wanted to decoy the Indians from his real path. He had no intention of killing his horse with a pointless chase when the trio of Crow must have ponies that were rested and capable of overtaking him before he got halfway to Hoback Junction. He watched carefully, then cut off the road when he came to a rocky patch that afforded him the chance to walk his horse a dozen yards before reaching soft dirt again.

He knew this wouldn't throw the Crow off his trail if they were any kind of trackers, but it gave him another half hour to do what he could to more effectively disappear.

Ducking low he made his way through scrub oak until he reached a stand of pine. The pine needles crushed beneath his feet and released a fragrance that caused him to inhale deeply. He was grateful for the calming effect but more grateful that the needles hid his horse's hoofprints so well. He dodged through the forest until he came to a small creek and followed it higher into the mountains before he reached a point where he was tired and his horse started to stumble from exhaustion.

Slocum figured he had either lost the Crow or left them far enough behind to take a short break. He let his horse gobble knee-high grass at the edge of a small clearing while he ate a cold meal and drank from a stream.

There was no good reason for the Crow to pursue him this long. He had done nothing to them and wasn't likely to ride to the nearest Army fort to tell of off-reservation braves. Slocum lounged back and watched the clouds slip through the intense blue sky. His mind drifted along with the billowing, puffy white clouds until he heard a twig snap.

Like lightning, he swung around. His hand flashed to the ebony handle of the Colt Navy slung in its cross-draw holster. He had the six-shooter aimed, cocked and ready when a Crow brave slowly stood, his rifle pointed at Slocum.

"This looks to be a Mexican standoff," Slocum said. He wasn't sure the brave understood. Then he saw a flash of triumph on the man's face and knew he understood everything perfectly. Slocum was the one who didn't know what was going on.

Without even acknowledging the other two behind him, Slocum lowered the hammer on his six-gun and returned it to its holster. He raised his hands. Let them think he had eyes in the back of his head and saw the two Crow with their rifles trained on him. He saw a flash of what might have been admiration on the face of the Indian before him.

"We're not enemies," Slocum said. "I mean you no harm. I was just passing through."

"Not enemies?" The Crow laughed harshly. "You put us on reservation and starve us!"

"You can share what little I've got in my saddlebags," Slocum said.

"We can take it!" screeched the brave.

Slocum remained calm. If they had intended him harm, the two behind him could have filled him with holes. It had been foolish to rest so long, but he had thought he'd done a better job hiding his trail than he evidently had. Either that or these three were just a tad short of being supernatural in their tracking skills.

"Take that which is offered freely by a friend," Slocum said. "It's yours."

"You can't stop us!"

"I don't want to. I want to share with my new friends."

This confounded the brave. He scowled, then stomped forward. His two companions moved around to flank him. Neither of their rifles left Slocum.

"You are not like the others," said the brave who was doing all the talking. The other two looked at him skeptically. "Why are you here?"

"As I said, just passing through."

"You have heard it?"

This stopped Slocum in his tracks. He didn't know what the Crow meant.

"I have heard many things."

"You will help kill it?"

"What do you mean?" Slocum was at a loss to figure out what the brave meant. "I do not hunt your deer or elk."

The Crow made a dismissive gesture, then pushed down the rifles of the other two braves. They spoke rapidly for almost a minute before turning back to a puzzled John Slocum.

"You listen good, then you help kill."

"All right," Slocum said. "Would you share my food?" He saw the expression on the men's faces. They had spent a good deal of the day on his trail and had not eaten. He went to his saddlebags and took out what food he had stashed for eating on the trail. Slocum decided he could hunt for a rabbit or two in the coming days. The food was better used cementing his friendship with the Indians.

They ate, slowly at first and then voraciously when they saw he wasn't going to stop them. Slocum's entire larder was cleaned out by the time the sky started turning dark.

"It comes now," the one brave said. "It always comes now, when the sun sets."

"What does?" Slocum barely had the words out of his mouth when he heard a mournful sound. At first he thought it was the wind. Then he saw a slight movement in the tall lodge pole pines around him. Whatever it was, this was not a sound born of the wind.

It grew in intensity and was like nothing he had ever heard before. Just when he started to get uneasy, a loud trumpeting sound echoed through the mountains and distance devoured the sound entirely.

All he could do was look at the three frightened Crow warriors and wonder what he had just heard.

3

"Have you seen what makes that sound?" Slocum asked. The three braves shook their heads and looked more scared than ever.

"Let's find out," he said, which caused their eyes to widen. He stared at them for a moment. Here were three young bucks who would go fearlessly into battle and die, if need be, but they wouldn't track down whatever made such an odd sound. In a way he didn't blame them, but his curiosity was running wild.

"Great Spirit not want to be disturbed," said the spokesman for the trio.

"You are good friends," Slocum said, eager to get after whatever had caused such a ruckus. He was beginning to think that the banker in Hoback Junction might not have been amiss to put up a hundred dollar reward for identifying whatever creature made such a noise.

Slocum hoped it was a creature and not a man. There didn't seem to be pain in the trumpeting cry as much as there was challenge.

He rode slowly upslope, leaving the three Crow braves behind him in the gathering dark. As he worked his way through the shadowy forest he heard their horses heading

17

in the opposite direction. Slocum wanted to find a bluff where he could look down and see as much territory as possible.

Within twenty minutes he found a hundred-foot cliff looking over the trail he had ridden before the Crow had begun stalking him. Twilight plunged the trail into inky darkness but Slocum waited, more impatiently than usual, for the moon to poke up above the distant mountains. The lunar light cast a silvery glow over the world, but nowhere did he see anything moving that might have made the peculiar sound he and the Indians had heard.

"Not somebody's drunken nightmare," he allowed. Slocum continued his vigil staring into pitch blackness until his eyelids began to droop and he finally found it impossible to remain alert. He pitched camp, grabbed a quick meal and then spread out his bedroll, thinking that new sounds would probably wake him.

The next thing he knew, dawn was breaking. The night had been as peaceful as any he could remember. But the memory of the booming cry lingered. It was not the product of a drunken imagination, not when he and three Crow braves had heard it, all of them as sober as a preacher on Sunday morning.

He picked his way down the side of the mountain and back onto the main trail, intending to hunt for tracks of something large enough to make such a noise. Slocum had not ridden a mile when his horse stepped on a pile of rocks, stumbled, let out a loud neigh and then tried to rear. He fought to keep his seat. By the time he had settled the horse's jangled nerves, he saw that he wasn't going to do any more riding; the horse was limping badly on a bruised right foreleg.

Disgusted, he dismounted and led the game horse back toward Hoback Junction. It wasn't the end he had envisioned for his hunt. It was close to dusk when he got back into town and stabled his horse, giving the stable boy an extra fifty cents to see that liniment was applied to the sore leg as long as it took for it to get better. Until his horse recovered, Slocum wasn't going anywhere.

"John!" He turned at the call and saw Darlene waving from across the street. "I hoped I'd see you again, John," she said, giving him a quick hug that lasted a fraction of a second longer than was proper for them being in public and all.

"Where's Hugh?" he asked. "Out searching for the noise-maker?"

"He found a hunting party and joined it as a scout. Mr. Glenn said there was no problem if he took another job, if he was the one who solved the mystery. That was certainly a relief since our funds were getting mighty low."

"So he gets paid while he's looking for the critter making the noise?" This had worked out better for Hugh Malley than it had any right to. "I'm glad."

"I don't know how long he'll be gone. Scouting is such arduous work. Look at how much time you spent away from us on the trip from Central City, and that was across mostly flat prairie land."

Slocum didn't bother to tell Darlene he had spent more time on the trail than necessary because he knew they had wanted privacy. He wondered now who it was that the woman was more interested in bedding. She was a handsome woman, not exactly pretty but someone to give a second glance at as a gent walked past. She stood about five-feet-four and had long brunette hair and cat-colored eyes that sparkled like they had gold flecks in them. It was her ready smile and dimples that might have been her best feature, though.

She flashed that smile and showed those dimples now.

"My horse pulled up lame, and I had to return," Slocum explained. "Might be a day or two before the horse can walk again." He knew that the strong liniment might fix the horse up by morning, but somehow that wasn't what Darlene wanted to hear. Slocum found himself more and more interested in finding out what she *did* want.

"We can have some dinner, then," she said almost primly. "I ate at a restaurant down the street this morning, with Hugh, before he rode out to the maharajah's camp."

They went down the street and into the small café to take seats by the window.

"Maharajah?" Slocum asked. He thought he had heard the word before but couldn't rightly place when or where.

"An Indian fellow of some exalted rank. Royalty, I believe."

"Indian? Like a Crow or Cheyenne?"

"No, silly," said Darlene, reaching over and putting her hand familiarly on his. "East India, not like an Indian from these parts. He is a king or something. Royalty."

"Oh," Slocum said. He was more inclined to worry over ordering dinner than he was about some foreigner who had come to Wyoming, probably to bag a buffalo or two to mount on the wall of his far-off palace.

"He is very regal looking. I saw him when Hugh rode out with him this morning. The maharajah gave him a horse, a fine stallion that must be a thoroughbred."

"I prefer quarter horses," Slocum said, working around the chicken and dumplings he had ordered. Trail victuals were all right but nothing matched freshly baked bread and dumplings straight out of the pan.

"Well, it was a fine-looking horse worth a great deal of money, I'm sure."

Slocum and Darlene finished the meal in silence. He started to tell her of his hunt for the creature making the sounds that he and the Crow braves had heard but never quite got around to it. Another sip of coffee or a piece of peach pie, something always got in the way.

Sated, Slocum leaned back and looked at Darlene. She was a good-looking woman, he decided, but he was not the kind to cut in on another man's woman, especially one who was as good a friend as Hugh Malley. Still, from the covetous glances she gave him, he knew what was on her mind. A good meal followed by a tumble in the hay would make the end of the day about perfect.

A sudden tumult outside brought Slocum around to stare through the window.

"That must be your maharajah," he said. A man dressed in what looked like cloth chased with gold thread rode in a magnificent carriage. He was swarthy, with jet-black hair and a long, straight nose. Slocum had never seen that many kings or princes, but this had to be what a prince or maharajah looked like. Fine clothing, the flash of jeweled rings on most of his fingers, a carriage pulled by two prancing white horses, and seated beside him was a woman whose beauty took Slocum's breath away.

"Let's go get a closer look," he said. Slocum fumbled in his shirt pocket and dropped a few greenbacks onto the table and went to the door just as the carriage drew past.

The woman beside the maharajah looked his way. Slocum felt an electric surge pass through him. Then she was gone and Hugh came riding up, waving his hat and howdying with any of the townspeople who would return his greeting.

"John, Darlene!" Hugh bent over and stroked Darlene's cheek before straightening. "Pretty fancy, eh?"

"Malley!" called the maharajah. "Attend, please!"

"Gotta go." Hugh blew Darlene a quick kiss and cantered off to ride alongside the carriage.

"I wish we could have found out more," Darlene said, frowning. "It was rude of the maharajah to order him about like that. He might work for him, but Hugh is certainly not his slave or servant."

"Royalty thinks different," Slocum said, but he had to agree with Darlene. The maharajah wanted to make a big impression more than he wanted to show common courtesy. The Indian potentate descended from his carriage amid retainers bowing and scraping. To Slocum's disgust, Hugh jumped from his horse and similarly bowed as the maharajah passed by.

"Please see to buying the supplies we need," the maharajah ordered Hugh in a haughty voice, then dismissed him with a wave of the hand, which sparkled in the late-evening light from all the gems on his rings.

"Go on, talk to Hugh while he buys the supplies," Slocum said. "I'll see what this gent has to say." Slocum couldn't keep his eyes off the slender woman who descended after the maharajah. Her ebony eyes locked with his again, and Slocum felt the electric tingle once more.

"Wait!" the maharajah called and motioned Hugh to him. They spoke at length, then Hugh reluctantly mounted and rode from town with only a quick, stolen glance over his shoulder at Darlene as he left. The maharajah spoke rapidly in a singsong tongue that sent other servants rushing about to buy the supplies instead of Hugh.

"I wanted to say more than hello to him," Darlene complained.

Slocum and the maharajah stared at each other for a moment, then the man smiled slightly, beckoned to his entourage and walked down the middle of Hoback Junction's main street as if he passed out handfuls of money to the citizens instead of simply smiling at them and saying a few words here and there.

"Please, John. Can you help me see Hugh? This isn't right, the way he chased him off like a naughty boy sent off to bed without his supper."

Slocum said nothing but felt inclined to go along with Darlene. Watching the Indian prince swagger along the main street like he owned it and everyone he saw caused Slocum's hackles to rise. But the sight of the woman accompanying the maharajah caused another portion of Slocum's anatomy to stir.

• • •

"John, are you sure we can get into the camp this way?" asked Darlene. The woman's nervousness increased the closer they got to the maharajah's bivouac outside town. "There must be sentries everywhere."

"I know," Slocum said. He had easily avoided the three men with the thick bushy black beards and the fierce, fanatical eyes. Whatever they looked for, it wasn't a man and woman slipping through the shadows and getting closer to the maharajah's camp. Slocum wouldn't want to tangle with any of the men, but they were ineffective lookouts.

"There's the maharajah's tent," Slocum said. It didn't take much guesswork to figure that out. The tent stood almost fifteen feet high and billowed softly in the late-night wind. The cloth appeared to be something more than the waxed canvas used in most Army tents. The symbols painted on the sides were strange and of unknown significance, but moving inside, silhouetted against the sides, were two people.

Slocum immediately recognized the maharajah. It took a few more seconds to decide that the other dark outline moving slowly back and forth belonged to the woman who had ridden with him. The shadow robbed the woman of her subtle curves and utter, exotic beauty and reduced her to little more than a smudge in the night.

"Where would Hugh be?"

"Servants' quarters," Slocum said. Darlene looked at him sharply, but he was not joking. He pointed to an area near the rope corral. Hugh wouldn't have been hired only to scout, a skill he almost totally lacked. The maharajah would want to get his money's worth and make him tend the horses and any other livestock they had with them.

He guided Darlene through the camp unobserved. She let out a squeal of glee when she saw Hugh sitting on a rock, working away at polishing a harness. Slocum thought it was a strange thing to be doing in the middle of the night but he said nothing.

"Darlin'!" Hugh grabbed his sweetheart and spun her around. "How'd you get here?"

"John brought me," she said. "Why didn't you talk to me back in town?"

"There's a lot I have to say and, well, that maharajah don't like his men lollygaggin' about." Hugh looked over at Slocum and grinned weakly. "He wanted all this here leather shined up before the morning hunt."

"He won't notice, not if he's actually going to hunt," Slocum said. "Buffalo?"

"I think so. I told him there was a herd east of town."

"Is there?" Slocum hadn't seen any trace of buffaloes when they had ridden into Hoback Junction the day before.

"I think so. I was going into Hoback Canyon and felt the ground shaking. That'd be a big herd, wouldn't it?"

Slocum knew herds of buffalo had been counted of upward of several hundred thousand, but not recently, not after the Europeans had taken a fancy to buffalo robes and the hunters had thinned the herds almost to extinction.

"Could be," he allowed. "I'll let the two of you have some time together."

"I can find my way back to town, John," Darlene said, looking at Hugh with admiration in her eyes. Admiration and more than a tad of lust, Slocum saw. He got almost twenty yards off into the woods beyond the maharajah's camp when he heard it again.

It was the same sound he and the Crow braves had heard the night before. Only it was closer. Much closer. Slocum turned slowly and located the noise coming from a draw not a hundred yards away. He touched his six-shooter but decided there was no need for it. Whatever made the sound was too big for a mere six-gun to be of any use.

But Slocum could find out what made the sound.

It came again, grew louder, more insistent. Mingled with it, under its strident call, came a human voice speaking words Slocum could not understand. This time he drew his six-shooter but knew he had a target that would die if he plugged it.

The furor died down and the normal night sounds returned to his sharp ears. He made his way through the darkness with unerring skill and found the ravine where the ruckus emanated. He stared for a moment, then laughed until tears ran down his cheeks. He holstered his Colt Navy and brushed the tears away.

"What is so funny?" came a soft voice from his right. Slocum turned and saw the woman who had ridden with the maharajah standing in shadow and wrapped in a dark brown cloak that completely hid her body. Her eyes sparkled as she stared at him. "Is our elephant so funny that you laugh at him?"

"Folks in these parts think it is a ghost or some Indian spirit."

"Perhaps they are right. We are Hindu and believe in reincarnation. The elephant might be possessed of the spirit of someone from a former life."

"I wouldn't know about that, but elephants are circus creatures," Slocum said. "They shouldn't be the cause of so much commotion. The people in Hoback Junction might take it into their heads to organize a hunt." He knew this was the furthest thing from their minds. The citizens of that fine small town were terrified, but when they found out an elephant made the sounds that frightened them in the middle of the night, they might turn nasty with anger.

"You do not fear the elephant," the woman said. She moved toward Slocum, gliding rather than walking. She stopped a few feet away, and he caught the scent of an exotic perfume. From this distance he got a better look at her face and saw that she wore a bright red dot between her eyes. The thought flashed through his mind that it was like a bull's-eye, but he said nothing.

"You are different from others of this continent we have met."

"My name's John Slocum. You are?" He politely touched the brim of his hat.

"I am called Lakshmi," she said.

"You married to the maharajah fellow?"

She eyed him for a moment, then turned away without answering. Lakshmi stared at the elephant in its pen.

"It is a very powerful beast, but very gentle, unless provoked."

Slocum knew a warning when he heard one. He wondered why she thought it necessary to caution him as she had. Before he could ask, a heavy hand clamped on his shoulder. Slocum turned, his six-shooter half out of its holster as he came around. He recoiled when a knifepoint lightly pricked his belly.

"Ali is my protector," Lakshmi said. She spoke rapidly in Hindi to Ali, who drew back but kept his hand on Slocum's shoulder.

"If he doesn't let go of me, I'll beat him to death with his own arm." Slocum saw Ali react and knew the man spoke English, or at least understood it enough to know he had been threatened. Lakshmi hurriedly spoke. Ali backed off, releasing his grip.

"It is not wise to anger Ali," the woman said. "He is a fierce, formidable enemy."

"Cemeteries are full of the fierce and the formidable," Slocum said.

"You are either very brave or very foolish," Lakshmi said.

"Which do you think?" asked Slocum.

"Foolish," the woman answered without hesitation. She pursed her lips as if pronouncing a death sentence. "Very foolish. Now leave or Ali will feed you to the elephant."

"And here I thought they ate hay and not meat."

Lakshmi turned and stared at him. A tiny smile came to her lips. The smile faded quickly as Ali stepped between them. She drew her heavy cloak around her trim shoulders

and drifted silently into the night, Ali following closely.
Slocum turned from the impenetrable darkness where Lakshmi had vanished back to the elephant in its pen. He
shook his head in disbelief and wondered if the banker
might pay him the hundred dollars for discovering what
made the strange nocturnal noises.

Slocum shrugged it off. Let Hugh Malley collect his
due. He was probably going to earn every penny he made
from the haughty maharajah and deserved a bonus for putting up with such insufferable behavior. Slocum fetched
his horse and rode back to town, vowing to get back on the
trail at first light.

4

Slocum examined his horse's bruised leg and decided it was healed enough to push on. The night before, as he rode back from the maharajah's camp, he had worried that he had thrust the horse back into service too soon, but the valiant roan had not hobbled or even missed a single stride along the trail. Still, Slocum worried. He did not want to be in the middle of nowhere and have the horse break a leg because he had pushed it too far too fast.

"We'll be on the trail soon. No hurry," he said, patting the horse's neck. Slocum tended his gear while the roan fed. He took special care of his two six-shooters, the one he carried slung at his left hip in a cross-draw holster and the other wrapped in oilcloth stashed in his saddlebags. He had learned the value of keeping a second pistol handy back during the war.

Thoughts of blood and death fluttered through his mind. He had ridden with Quantrill and had never been one of the wallflowers when it came to killing. The Raiders would gallop into a Yankee town shooting at anything that moved. Like the others, Slocum had been festooned with six-guns, firing until one emptied and then switching to another and another. He often carried as many as ten six-shooters,

29

which gave him the firepower of an entire squad of soldiers. The rest of Quantrill's Raiders were similarly armed.

Since those days, he had carried only two six-guns and those had served him well, when added to his trusty Winchester.

He was almost finished oiling his rifle and making certain the cartridges fed smoothly into the chamber when he heard a flurry outside the stables. He glanced up to see Darlene looking around wildly. Her hair was in disarray as if she had ridden through a tornado, and her brown eyes were wide and frightened.

"John!" she called. The woman rushed into the stables and grabbed for him. "You've got to help!" She clung to him like she was drowning and he was her only hope for salvation.

"What's wrong?" Darlene wasn't the hysterical sort. She might nag a man to distraction but during the trip from Colorado Slocum had never seen her get anywhere near this upset.

"It's Hugh. He's dead!"

For a moment Slocum stared down at the woman. Her words came as if from a distance and in some foreign tongue he only vaguely understood. Then his mind snapped free and began to work. He had left Darlene in the maharajah's camp with Hugh not twelve hours earlier, and now his friend was dead.

"How'd it happen?" Slocum asked.

"We, you left me, and we went off to—" Darlene turned even paler, and her hands trembled as she lifted a handkerchief to her lips. She sucked in a deep breath, composed herself and started her explanation again. "After we had enjoyed one another's company, I started to leave to return to town when someone called to Hugh."

"Someone? Who was it?"

"I don't know who it was. I never saw him. He was some distance away and barked out the order from behind a tent for Hugh to follow him. Only a couple words. 'Come. Now!' No more'n that. I thought he might have meant someone else since I couldn't see him, but Hugh seemed to know that he was the one being ordered around."

"Was it the maharajah?" Slocum remembered how bossy the Indian prince could be.

"I . . . I honestly cannot say. It rather startled me, and I didn't pay any attention, Hugh and me just having—" Darlene swallowed hard and dabbed at her teary eyes. "I went to ride off when I heard that horrid noise. Hugh had told me it was an elephant. I saw one once back in Illinois at a traveling circus, but never saw the one the maharajah keeps. Until then. After he screamed, I raced to the elephant pen. It was Hugh, but the scream wasn't a word or a call for help. It was just a . . . scream!"

"Did you find him? Hugh?"

"I heard the trumpeting and then one last shriek of pain and rode to the pen where they keep that nasty beast and saw blood and Hugh on the ground and—"

"Calm down," Slocum said. He knew it was difficult for the woman to lose her lover and find his crushed body, but he wanted to get the details. He owed it to Hugh to be certain it was an accident. The way Darlene posed it, Hugh Malley might have been the victim of a murderer in the maharajah's camp. Hugh knew nothing about elephants, and anyone luring him close to the beast could easily have sicced it on him.

"What did you do when you found him?"

"I tried to get someone in their camp to help, but they all ignored me. I rode right back to find you, John. I knew you'd know what to do."

"Come on," Slocum said, taking her by the arm. "We'll tell the marshal and get to the bottom of this."

"I never thought of that," Darlene said in a choked voice. "I'm glad I came to you."

Slocum's mind turned and tumbled as they walked

down the middle of the street hunting for the marshal's office. Hugh might have blundered into the elephant pen and been trampled, but it obviously had happened immediately after someone had called him away from Darlene. That person obviously hadn't stuck around after the elephant did a dance on Hugh's body, which made Slocum mighty suspicious.

"Marshal!" Slocum called out to a weedy-looking man with a dull silver badge pinned on his vest who was sneaking from the office. He looked as if he might have just robbed the place and wanted to escape without being seen. The lawman turned and looked as if he could spit.

"Whadya want?"

"There's been a death out at the Indian maharajah's camp," Slocum said.

"People die all the time," the marshal said. "Ain't no concern o' mine. Undertaker's down the street a ways. Doniphan's his name. Digger Doniphan we call 'im here in town."

"We're not looking to bury him, not right away," Slocum said. "I think he was murdered."

Darlene sobbed a bit harder, and the marshal got the look of a trapped rat. His eyes darted back and forth as if he were hunting for some escape route, only to have Slocum block his retreat.

"What makes ya say a thing like that?"

"Let's go out to the Indian's camp and see firsthand."

"I got work to do here in town," the marshal said.

"Look, Marshal . . ." Slocum waited until the man got the idea and gave him his name. Slocum felt as if he had pried a fleck of gold from drossy rock.

"Rothbottom," the marshal said reluctantly.

"All right, Marshal Rothbottom," Slocum said, his voice taking on an edge. "I'll tend to this matter myself. Might be since you're so busy, you'd want to deputize me so whatever I do is done all legal-like."

"Why'd I go and do a damfool thing like that? I don't know you from Adam."

Slocum moved enough to show the worn butt of his Colt Navy.

"I'm going to find out if Hugh died from an accident or if someone murdered him, like I'm thinking. If I don't ride with a badge on my vest, then I do what I need to do on my own. Hugh Malley was a good friend."

Rothbottom swallowed hard. His Adam's apple bobbed in his scrawny throat like a cork float on a fishing line.

"I'll git my horse." The marshal hurried off without another word.

"What a terrible law officer," Darlene said. She wadded up the handkerchief in her hand, as if she had her fingers wrapped around Rothbottom's throat. Again Slocum found himself sympathizing with the woman, but he knew that force would never get the lawman out to the maharajah's campsite, no matter how satisfying it might be to have his fingers curled around that bony neck.

"Don't expect much from him," Slocum said. He guided Darlene back to the stables. As much as he wanted to protect her from further pain, he had to be sure she pointed out everything in the camp accurately. Slocum figured the marshal would cut and run at the first sign of anything not matching from one telling to the next, and having Darlene there to explain what she had seen stopped the lawman from taking that easy course.

They caught up with Marshal Rothbottom less than a mile down the road. The lawman wasn't making too good a pace, but Slocum found it interesting that Rothbottom knew where the maharajah's camp was and headed straight for it. Nobody else in town seemed to have any idea where the fancy-dressed Indian prince had camped—and they certainly had not known what was causing the odd noises trumpeting through the Grand Tetons and destroying their peaceful slumber.

"How long has the maharajah been in these parts?" Slocum asked.

"Dunno." Rothbottom shrugged narrow shoulders and made a point of staring straight ahead, never meeting Slocum's steely green gaze. As they rode, Slocum sized up the man and found him wanting. The six-shooter riding in the lawman's holster had flecks of rust showing on the metal. The gun would probably blow up from lack of cleaning if he ever tried using it. Worse than this was the marshal's general slovenliness. On the trail a man got mighty dusty and baths might be a week or two apart. That was one reason to go to town—other than saloons and bottles of whiskey and nice cool beers. A bath now and again might even be good for a body. But apparently Rothbottom and soap were distant strangers.

"There's the maharajah," cried Darlene, standing in the stirrups. Her dress fluttered about revealing her ankles and calves, but she was oblivious to such immodesty. She focused completely on the prince and the tight knot of burly men with him. In daylight, Ali appeared even larger than Slocum had thought, towering over his prince by half a head. Ali's shoulders were an ax-handle wide and he stood silently, his dark eyes missing nothing and his powerful arms crossed on his chest.

Slocum saw the twin daggers sheathed at Ali's waist and reckoned the man could use them, in spite of their decorative jeweled hilts.

"Prince," Darlene called, almost falling from horseback in her rush to find out about her sweetheart's death. "The elephant! It stomped on Hugh, Hugh Malley, and—"

"Silence," the maharajah ordered, holding up a mahogany brown hand. No trace of emotion flickered on his face. Slocum decided the prince would be a ferocious card player with such a poker-faced expression.

"What brings you out to my humble encampment, Marshal?" The maharajah bowed slightly in the direction of the skinny lawman.

"This here lady thinks her man got stomped on by yer elephant. That so?"

"Alas, Marshal, it is so. A tragic accident. He was unaccustomed to dealing with such a large creature, and my pet was startled by an unknown man's presence. Perhaps Mr. Malley thought to, what do you call it? Count coup!"

"That's what the Sioux do," Slocum said. The maharajah pretended to confuse Indian war behavior with what a white man might do, thinking it would insult or infuriate him. Slocum had a gut-level feeling that everything said and done was for his benefit, not for the marshal and certainly not for Darlene because of the way the Indian prince had dismissed her earlier questions. "Hugh was called over to the pen by one of your men."

"Which one?" demanded the marshal. "Point the varmint out, and I'll ast him a question 'er two."

Slocum looked at Darlene but knew the answer before he saw her crestfallen expression. She had already told him that she had no idea which of the men in camp had summoned Hugh. It might even have been the maharajah himself.

"She doesn't know," Slocum said, answering for her. Darlene had passed the point where shock possessed her and was now moving on to a building rage that her man had been killed.

"Then there is no point in continuing this inquiry, is there, Marshal?" The maharajah made a shooing motion with his hand and sent his retainers—all but Ali—scuttling away like crabs.

"Don't reckon there is," Rothbottom said. "You want to lug the body on back to Hoback Junction or plant him out here? Like I said, Doniphan's Funeral Parlor's the best we got in town. Only one, truth be told."

Slocum wondered if the marshal got a kickback from each body referred but he said nothing. The marshal grumbled a mite about coming this far for nothing, then touched the brim of his hat politely in the direction of the maharajah and rode off.

"You are free to claim the body," the prince said, "but the condition is rather horrifying to anyone of a gentler persuasion." For the first time, the maharajah made a small bow in Darlene's direction.

"I'll see to it. Where's the elephant that trampled him?"

"Ah, my mahout has taken the animal in question to the lake to bathe."

"Mahout?"

The prince sneered slightly at Slocum's lack of understanding.

"The keeper, trainer, perhaps you might even say rider? No, driver. All of those terms apply."

"Is he the one who called for Hugh to go to the pen?" asked Slocum.

"I know nothing of this. It was a tragic accident and nothing more." The prince cast a sharp look at Slocum, as if accusing him of trying to ensnare with words. That was exactly what Slocum had tried to do, but the maharajah was a slippery character.

Slocum and Darlene rode to where the elephant had been penned. Before they got there Slocum saw the tracks left by the massive beast leading in the direction of the lake, as the prince had said. Slocum wondered if it would be worth the effort to follow the elephant and its mahout, as the maharajah had called him, to the lake. By now any trace of Hugh would be washed away. Slocum wasn't sure what he could have expected to see other than an elephant's bloody foot.

"There's the pen," he said, pointing to a large, muddy section of the meadow where the elephant had been kept. "There's Hugh." Slocum went cold inside when he saw how the elephant had completely crushed his friend. The chest was a gory ruin, but Hugh's face haunted Slocum the most. It was untouched but had the most incredible mask of pain etched on it Slocum had seen this side of an Apache torture session.

"I . . . I'll see to it, John." Darlene looked at him disconsolately. "There's nothing that can be done, is there? The marshal isn't inclined to even ask questions. How do you prove the maharajah knew anything about it?" Tears flowed freely now. "There's nothing to gainsay what the prince said about it being an accident."

Slocum knew Darlene was right. But he refused to let the matter drop.

"Get Hugh back to town. That Doniphan fellow, the undertaker Rothbottom mentioned, ought to do as well as any. I want to turn over a few damp rocks to see what crawls out from under them."

"You will be back, John? For Hugh's service?"

He nodded. What else could he do or say?

Slocum helped the woman wrap Hugh Malley's body in a blanket, then sling it belly-down over the back of a horse from a nearby corral. Slocum didn't bother asking if they could borrow the horse. He suspected the maharajah would consider it worthwhile if all the payment they required to drop inquiries into Hugh's death was the price of a single horse.

"Go on back, Darlene," Slocum said. "I've got a prince to track down."

Darlene slowly walked away, leading the horse with Hugh's body across it. Slocum mounted and picked up the maharajah's trail to see how the prince spent his days. It might mean nothing, but Slocum wasn't so sure.

5

The trail to the lake showed huge hoofprints. The elephant.
Slocum picked up the pace when he found the maharajah's
ornate wagon parked alongside the lake, abandoned. The
prince had ridden from his camp to the lake in his fancy-
ass wagon, which carried more luxuries than most hotels
Slocum had seen west of Denver. A quick glance inside
showed it had been left intentionally. Everything was
placed precisely, as if a servant had made a final effort to
leave it perfectly.

Footprints in the soft earth showed where at least four
people had left the wagon and gone to mount horses.
Slocum frowned, trying to figure out what was going on.
Small footprints might belong to the woman accompanying the maharajah. Lakshmi she had said her name was.
But Slocum could not figure out who rode the horses and if
any of the party rode the elephant. He remembered the
traveling circuses he had seen. The rider had perched on
the head just behind the elephant's ears, using his knees
and feet to kick and steer. One rider Slocum had seen also
carried a pole with a hook on the end of it to poke and prod
the big beast. It had seemed incredible to Slocum that this
was all it took to control the elephant, but the rider—ma-

hout, the prince had named him—didn't even use a bridle
or saddle.

Following the tracks was about the simplest thing
Slocum had done in ages. The elephant's big footprints
were easily the size of a dinner plate. Larger. The immense
weight crushed down grass and dirt. As that thought
crossed Slocum's mind, he turned a bit colder inside. Such
immense weight had also crushed his friend to death. As he
rode, Slocum wondered how Darlene was doing. It would
take her considerable time to get Hugh's body back to
Hoback Junction since she was walking alongside her
horse with its grisly burden. He couldn't see her doing the
logical thing by mounting behind the body and letting the
horse get both of them back to town. She wouldn't want to
even touch the corpse.

The valley opened and turned eastward onto a broad
prairie. Slocum pulled his hat brim down to shield his eyes
and scanned the terrain for some sign of the maharajah's
party. Such a large group accompanied by an immense gray
elephant could not have vanished as surely as they had.

Slocum continued along the trail but had to work harder
now that the knee-high grass began hiding the trail. They
had mashed down the grass as they passed through, but it
was remarkable how quickly they had come this way. It
was as if the maharajah had rushed to this spot for some
reason.

A ravine cut across the prairie in the sudden fashion
found on the plains. The ground ran directly to the edge,
dropped off precipitously, and stretched straight as an ar-
row eastward. The spring runoff coupled with sudden summer rains shot thousands of gallons of water through here
in the blink of an eye.

The gravelly arroyo was dry now. Slocum stood on the
bank trying to figure out what had happened. Two of the
maharajah's party had ridden down into the ravine for
some reason. Their tracks disappeared within a few yards,

but he thought they had continued traveling east. The remainder of the horses and the elephant had followed the bank. Slocum wiped sweat from his face, then continued to follow the tracks.

Death came as fast as a lightning strike.

Slocum had ridden out onto a barren plain when he heard the unmistakable thunder of buffaloes stampeding. He swung about and spotted the dust cloud off to his right but couldn't tell how large the herd was or where he might find sanctuary. He knew better than to get into the ravine. His roan, with its still tender leg, could never cross the rocky-bottomed stream in time. Backtrack? Gallop ahead and test the horse's leg? He had to get a better look at the herd's direction before choosing. Guess wrong and he would die.

Slocum knew he couldn't wait too long. The dust cloud obscured the lead buffalo and the sound frightened his horse. Slocum fought to keep the roan from bucking and running. It was as likely to choose wrong as he was.

"Go!" Slocum cried, raking the horse's flanks with his spurs when he caught sight of the buffalo at the head of the herd. He got the roan running at an angle, surging forward in the direction the maharajah had already taken. With a bit of luck, Slocum would reach the edge of the herd and slip away with little danger—if the herd wasn't too large. The buffalo hunters in earlier years had decimated the herds but the buffalo had come back, although not in as great a number.

Head down, racing the wind, Slocum headed across the prairie. His horse's nostrils flared and whites showed around its eyes. Fear lent speed to the roan, and for a brief instant Slocum thought they were going to make it. Then the horse's leg gave way, sending Slocum somersaulting forward. He hit the ground hard, rolled and staggered to his feet, only to lose his balance and crash down hard.

Scrambling, he came to hands and knees, then heaved up, toes digging into the ground to sprint back to the roan.

His horse had stepped in a prairie-dog hole. White bone showed through the flesh. Slocum drew his six-shooter but didn't put the horse out of its frightened misery. The buffalo herd would do that fast enough.

Slocum raised his six-gun, knowing the .36 caliber bullet had no chance at all of bringing down the buffaloes charging toward him, not when hunters used .50 caliber Sharps and had to be superb marksmen. But he couldn't outrun the edge of the herd on foot and was damned if he would simply stand and be kicked to death without putting up some fight.

He fired at the trio of buffaloes that had broken off from the main herd and were racing toward him. He was lucky in one respect. The mass of heaving, snorting, thundering beasts would pass to his right. But what was the difference being trampled by hundreds or only three? They had seen him and in their own frightened run came straight for him.

Slocum saw a long spark blast off one buffalo's horn where his feeble bullet had hit it. In its fear, the buffalo never noticed and plunged on. Slocum stood his ground, firing methodically.

Then he blinked in surprise. The buffalo tumbled to the ground. The one beside it crashed into its hump and fell amid great bellowing. Slocum looked at his Colt Navy and shook his head. It wasn't possible to bring down a buffalo with a handgun. He looked back and saw the third buffalo drop to its knees, then somersault forward because of its great speed. Its body flopped onto the ground and lay twitching.

Slocum had not fired at this buffalo. He was out of ammo.

He heard a new sound over the dwindling roar of the buffalo herd. An elephant crashed through the grass. Slocum turned and saw the huge gray beast emerge from a cloud of brown dust. Riding atop it was the mahout, balanced on the neck immediately behind the ears as Slocum had seen years before. But a large fringed canopy had been added. In this ornate box sat two men, one with a large rifle resting on the edge. Slocum saw the setting sunlight glint off the barrel as the maharajah raised it and silently, arrogantly, acknowledged Slocum's existence.

As the elephant approached, Slocum took the time to reload his six-shooter. He knew now what had spooked the buffalo and caused the stampede that had almost taken his life. The Indian prince was out hunting. From the direction where the herd had begun its mad charge across the prairie rode the rest of the man's party.

The four riders had acted as beaters to get the herd into motion.

"Mr. Slocum, how odd to find you out on the Wyoming grassland at this time of day," the maharajah called. He said something in Hindi. The mahout brought the elephant to a bouncing halt a few yards away, then forced the elephant to its knees so the maharajah could dismount. As the prince did so, he handed his rifle to Ali, who also had been in the elaborately decorated box strapped onto the elephant's back.

"Your men spooked the herd. I could have been killed."

"Why, yes, that is so," said the maharajah. He looked startled when Slocum reared back, intending to deliver a roundhouse punch that would have decked the man. Slocum checked his swing when he saw Ali aiming the heavy hunting rifle at him.

"You are angry. Why is this so?"

"You said it. Your men could have gotten me killed." Slocum looked to where his horse still struggled. He pointedly turned his back on the maharajah, went to his horse and put it out of its misery. Only then did he return. He considered what it would take to similarly put Ali out of his misery but discarded the idea. The maharajah's servant still had the heavy rifle snugged up into his shoulder, ready to defend his master.

Slocum jammed his six-gun back into his cross-draw holster.

"You are angry," the maharajah said, as if the thought had never occurred to him before that any lesser mortal could share such emotions with someone of his exalted rank.

"Almost getting killed for no reason makes me mad. Having to shoot my horse makes me *real* mad," Slocum said, not trying to hide what he felt.

"You ruined the master's hunt," said the elephant wrangler. The man scowled as he tapped the long rod against the palm of his hand. The wicked hook at the end could do a considerable amount of damage to a man in a fight. Slocum wasn't going to let it go that far. If the elephant driver took so much as one step forward, Slocum would drop him with a bullet in his heart. He had reached the end of his patience.

"Be quiet, Gasim," the maharajah said. "He does so like to please me, but sometimes he oversteps his bounds."

"Were you doing the shooting or was he?" Slocum lifted his chin and pointed, Navajo style, at Ali. Ali might have been turned to stone, rifle to his shoulder with his aim directed at Slocum's head.

"He cleans my guns, nothing more. I do the shooting. Have you ever been on a tiger hunt? No, of course not. There are no tigers in this land of yours. Only the wooly buffaloes and other, lesser animals."

"You've never tangled with a grizzly bear," Slocum said.

"A grizzly bear? Why, no. Is it ferocious?"

"It could rip apart your tiger," Slocum said, knowing what a bear could do against a mountain lion. He reckoned a tiger was only a striped cougar.

The maharajah laughed with gusto. "You have such a sense of humor, Mr. Slocum. The tiger is cunning, dangerous, quick, the most difficult of all wild game to hunt. I have lost no fewer than forty beaters and bearers during my tiger hunts. It is a man-killer and a man-eater."

The four riders came up. Slocum was surprised to see Lakshmi rode one of the horses, then remembered the smaller footprints at the lake where the maharajah had probably mounted the elephant for the hunt. Close beside her rode a small, dark, intense man who glared at Slocum. Slocum was beginning to think no one in the maharajah's party cottoned much to him.

The feeling was mutual.

Except for the way Lakshmi kept looking at him. Her servant eyed him like that man-eating tiger the maharajah talked so much about, but her dark eyes held something more pleasant.

"I want you to pay me for my horse," Slocum said. "If your beaters hadn't stampeded the buffalo herd, it would never have galloped across a field where there were so many prairie-dog holes."

The mahout let out a wordless cry of rage and rushed forward, swinging his hooked stick at Slocum. Slocum reacted instinctively. He deflected the vicious stick with his left arm and reached out with his right hand to clutch the mahout's throat. Gasim's eyes bulged as Slocum squeezed. The mahout tried to twist away but was off balance from his headlong rush. Slocum stepped back, turned and sent Gasim crashing facedown into the dirt.

Gasim lay stunned for a moment, then leaped to his feet. This time Slocum's punch was already on the way and connected with the mahout's belly. The elephant wrangler doubled over, his chin in exactly the right position for Slocum to bring up his knee into it. Gasim's head snapped back, and he fell to the ground, out like a light.

Slocum picked up the hooked stick and turned toward the maharajah, who had watched, an amused smile dancing on his lips. For a split second that enjoyment turned to fear when he saw Slocum's expression.

Behind the prince, Ali scrambled to get a clean shot without hitting his master. But it wasn't necessary. Slocum grabbed the pole in both hands and broke it with a snap that rang out like a gunshot. He threw the pieces onto the mahout's limp body.

"You fight splendidly," the maharajah said. "I will give you a new horse, but you must agree to be my scout."

Slocum turned and walked off without a word. It was a long way back to Hoback Junction, but if he kept a steady pace he might make it before noon the next day.

6

It took Slocum longer to get to Hoback Junction than he had thought. Blisters slowed him and he spent two nights under the stars, sleeping with his head propped against his saddle and his blanket pulled around him. Both nights his dreams were haunted by visions of Hugh Malley being stomped on by the huge gray elephant. The maharajah stood off to one side, laughing uproariously. Floating through the dream, though, was the exotically lovely Lakshmi with her beguiling smile and mysterious dark eyes all for Slocum.

He awoke each morning unrested and grumbled more with every step he took. As he finally reached the outskirts of town, he dropped his saddle and went into the cemetery. The new grave in the otherwise desolate graveyard drew him like a magnet. He laughed ruefully when he read the inscription.

Here lies Hugh Malley
A life in mines
Eternity underground

Darlene had a sense of humor he hadn't expected. Then he sobered. It fit Hugh. The man had been from Wales and his entire life was spent in hard-rock mines. Slocum had seen the man's like before. Hugh Malley could talk rock, drilling, mining, anything having to do with being underground like some men talked about women or the big poker hand where they had won enough money to choke a cow. The difference was obvious, though. Hugh knew mining and Slocum had never caught him in an outright tall tale or lie when it came to his abilities as a miner.

Slocum's resolve hardened. Marshal Rothbottom wasn't likely to do anything to bring the maharajah to justice for Hugh's death. Whether the prince was personally responsible mattered less to Slocum than somebody being punished. His hand drifted to the butt of his six-shooter. He wouldn't mind mixing it up with Ali again. Or the mahout, Gasim.

If Slocum had to pick a place to start asking his hard questions, it would be with Gasim. The elephant driver was unpleasant, but Slocum had seen any number of good-hearted men who acted liked jackasses. He had the gut feeling Gasim had showed his true face when he had attacked with the hooked staff.

Slocum left Hugh's grave with a silent vow to plant the man's killer in the same cemetery, hefted his gear and walked the remaining mile to town. Dusk gave Hoback Junction softer edges, and the gaslights hadn't been turned on yet. Slocum dropped his saddle and sat on it, watching the sun set over the Grand Tetons. Such beauty mixed with ugly death—that summed up the way Slocum looked at the world.

"John?"

He glanced over his shoulder to see Darlene behind him. He had not heard her come up since he had been lost in thought.

"I saw Hugh's grave. You did good putting that marker on it. Hugh'd like it."

"Thank you. It took 'bout all my money, but he deserved

it." Darlene looked around at the bustle of the townspeople and heaved a deep sigh. From that angle, Slocum got a good view of her breasts rising and falling under her somewhat dirtied blouse. She turned and set her skirt whirling around. Slocum stood quickly to keep himself from getting distracted even more by her feminine charms.

"I'm about tapped out, too," Slocum said. He did not bother going into the story of how he had lost his horse. Getting another, even if he could find one with as stout a heart, would cost a fabulous amount of money. Maybe a hundred dollars since this was a frontier town willing to bilk anyone passing through.

Darlene turned and looked at him with a soft, unfocused stare.

"We should team up," she said. It was clear to Slocum what she meant. Darlene was a good-looking woman, but Slocum wasn't sure he wanted to take up with the sweetheart of a dead friend. She was more likely to be seeking out anyone to cling to, to take care of her, to lean on because Hugh was gone. Slocum didn't want that kind of attachment from her because it would be for all the wrong reasons.

"Hugh has to be avenged," both of them said at the same time.

Slocum looked at her and then laughed. Darlene did think a lot like him. That wasn't necessarily a good thing. Or was it?

"I've got a hotel room for one more night," she said. "Gets mighty lonely in that big bed without Hugh."

"Darlene—" he started.

"John, I don't want anything from you. Nothing but a night where I can forget Hugh. For a spell. In the morning we can go our separate ways."

"Or maybe we can figure out how to get some justice for Hugh," he said.

"I want that," she said. "As much as I want you. Now."

Darlene moved closer and looked up at him. For a moment Slocum thought she was going to violate all the laws about public decency and kiss him, but she stopped an inch shy. He felt her hot breath and soaked up some of the heat from her body.

Slocum stepped back. Darlene caught her breath, then let it out in a sigh of relief when he stooped to pick up his gear and came back to her. Side by side they went to the hotel without saying another word and trooped up the rickety stairs. The second floor was full. So was the third. Darlene had a tiny room crammed in under the sloping roof on the fourth floor. The big bed she had mentioned was hardly wide enough for one person, but Slocum doubted they would be doing much sleeping.

"Drop your saddle over there," Darlene said, pointing to a small chest where guests could store their clothing. She moved closer and boldly said, "And drop your pants here."

Slocum heaved his saddle to the top of the chest. By the time it crashed down, Darlene was already working on his jeans. As she opened the buttons on his fly one by one, he carefully unfastened the buckle on his gun belt and laid it aside.

"So big," she cooed, reaching into the fly and teasing out the thick shaft, which had been hidden away for too long. Darlene moved even closer and brushed her lips across the underside of his fleshy rod. Then she made a giant gulping sound and devoured him totally. Slocum's knees went weak as he reached down to run his fingers through her dark hair to balance himself.

"Go on, stroke my hair. I like that," Darlene said, pulling away from him for a moment. She returned immediately, kissing, licking and then gently sucking on the thick tip that bobbed about harder and bigger with every feathery touch of her mouth.

Slocum did as she asked, his fingers moving over the thick strands of her soft, long hair. Every time he stroked back, Darlene moved her head forward and took a little more of him into her mouth. Slocum quickly got the idea and began guiding her in the motion he liked most by the way he ran his fingers over and through her thick locks.

A slurping sound filled the tiny room and worked even more erotic magic on Slocum. He had wondered, now and then while they were all out on the trail, what Darlene might be like, but he had not dwelled too much on such fantasies since she and Hugh had been together, and Hugh Malley had been a friend.

The thought crossed Slocum's mind that this wasn't the right way to honor the man's memory and then vanished for good. Hugh was dead and buried. Whatever fleshy bond Hugh and she had before was now gone. Darlene needed him now as much as he needed her. It was a good trade.

Darlene gobbled and sucked and licked until Slocum's knees began to sag. His legs turned watery as sensations rippled throughout his loins, and he knew he was not going to withstand much more of the woman's oral assault.

Slocum turned slowly, letting Darlene come along with him. Then he sat on the edge of the bed. Darlene looked up. Her eyes turned up to look at him. Slocum saw gold flecks in those eyes. He knew he had hit the mother lode by the way Darlene worked so avidly.

"You're so big," Darlene said again, her fingers curling and uncurling around his steely stalk.

Slocum did not answer with words. Instead, he reached down and took her shoulders, gently drawing her to her feet. Darlene was much shorter but now towered over the seated Slocum. Looking straight ahead, he could see bare flesh poking through the single gap in her blouse just above her navel. He began working on her blouse to get the buttons free to expose more of her luscious skin. He did not work quickly enough for her. Darlene helped with the tiny pearl buttons and quickly revealed the naked swells of her firm breasts. The coral tips were surrounded by brownish, bumpy plains that drew Slocum's mouth as surely as Darlene's had found their target at his crotch.

Slocum licked from the underside all the way to the top of each breast in turn. Darlene purred like a contented cat and arched her back, trying to get more of her succulent flesh into his mouth. Slocum teased her with the promise of more, only to draw back and do something else.

He kissed those rock-hard nubs cresting each mound of snowy flesh, only to kiss his way to the deep valley when she tried to shove her chest forward and let his mouth engulf her tender flesh.

He toyed with her nipples, then suddenly spun the woman about. Darlene let out a cry of surprise and reached out, catching herself on the cedar chest where she had stored her clothing.

Bent over, her behind jutting up into the air, Darlene gasped with joy when Slocum ran his hands up under her skirts. His hands found her sleek legs and worked quickly up to her naked thighs. Slocum's hands parted those thighs and then he hiked her skirts up around her waist to expose her bare hindquarters.

"You don't wear any of those frilly undies most ladies prefer," Slocum said.

"Does that bother you?" She looked back over her shoulder as she braced herself on the chest. Darlene widened her stance enough to emphasize what sort of answer she wanted to hear.

"It excites me."

Slocum showed her how much. He bunched her skirts around her waist and stroked over the smooth curves of her rump. The flesh trembled at his touch. He ran his hand faster and faster over her naked cheeks until he felt friction building.

"I . . . I'm getting so hot, John. And damp inside. I—" Darlene let out a yelp as Slocum lightly spanked her bottom. He continued to spank until her hindquarters were a rosy red and she sagged forward, half lying across the chest.

Then he moved into position. Slocum pushed down his pants around his ankles and kicked free, stood and placed his hands on her flaring hips. Before Darlene could say a word, Slocum's hips spoke for them both. He slid forward, the chunky tip of his manhood bouncing along the woman's nether lips. The pinkly scalloped gates protecting her innermost secrets fluttered gently and then opened to the fleshy invader.

Slocum slid fully into her.

For a moment, the world spun around him. He caught his breath and savored the intense sensations rampaging throughout his loins. The warmth that surrounded him became more intense. Then Darlene gasped. Slocum felt as if a gloved hand tightened around his manhood. She gasped and moaned and then sighed.

"So nice, John. I . . . I didn't know it could be like this."

"It won't be for long," Slocum said. "It'll get better."

Slocum began moving with deliberate speed. Deeper into her gently yielding body, then an agonizingly slow retreat that built both their desires to the breaking point. Slocum hesitated as he stayed between the fleshy curtains of her most intimate recess, then he plunged back with more speed. The friction that he had built using his hands across her rounded bottom now magnified internally as he slid with assurance ever deeper into her body.

Darlene began bucking and thrashing about, impaled on his thickness. Slocum reached down and caught her around the waist to keep her from inadvertently escaping. He pushed forward and braced her upper legs against the chest. Darlene sprawled forward so her breasts were flattened across the wooden lid of the chest, and she grasped the far side to keep from slipping to one side. When

Slocum felt this new buttressing, he began thrusting with more power, trying to bury himself even deeper within her.

Darlene shrieked with uncontrollable pleasure as the tension mounted. Her hips began moving in quick, tight circles and then pushed back to fit perfectly into the circle of his groin as she silently begged for more. Slocum was the man to let her have it. He knew he could go on a bit longer. But not much. The way she sounded, the way she felt, the way she responded so powerfully took its toll on his control. Slocum began to lose control and then all restraint fled. Hips flying like a shuttlecock, he sank faster and faster into Darlene's yearning interior. Her molten center welcomed him eagerly, cradled him tenderly, massaged his entire length as it slipped back and forth and then crushed him as a new wave of desire washed through her body.

Slocum felt the fiery tide rising within and then lost all control. A roaring in his ears blotted out Darlene's new cries of ecstasy.

Slocum held Darlene's hips for a moment longer, then fell back and sat on the edge of the bed. She sank to her knees, then swiveled about to sit cross-legged on the floor to stare at him. She was flushed. Her cheeks were as rosy as the ones he had spanked and her eyes blazed with erotic fire.

"More," she said breathlessly. "I want more. It's never been this good."

Slocum was willing, but it took a spell for him to do much about it. He found it a mite restrictive making love in the bed since the ceiling sloped down so low, but as he had always been told, where there's a will there's a way.

He had the will and he found the way, much to their mutual delight.

7

Slocum's eyelids flickered open, and for a moment he thought he had been tossed into a bramble bush. He pulled back and saw he was staring at the back of Darlene's dark-haired head. The short hairs on her neck looked spiky this close. He edged away, then got out of the bed, careful not to bang his head against the sloping ceiling. He pulled on his pants, then got into the rest of his clothes. He finished buckling on his gun belt before the woman awoke.

"John?" She rolled over in bed and let the sheet fall away from her chest to reveal the twin glories he had so delighted in the night before. "Where are you going?"

Slocum started to answer but realized he didn't have a good answer for her. He sat on the cedar chest and looked at her as a shaft of morning sunlight slanted in through the narrow window mounted at the top of the room. It was as if she were a performer on stage caught in a spotlight.

"I don't know. I have to get some money. There must be a job going wanting around town," he said.

"What about Hugh? You can't let him lie uneasy in his grave. Somebody in the maharajah's camp killed him. I'm sure of it. He was murdered!"

"I know," Slocum said. If a woman had told him the details of Hugh Malley's death without him personally seeing that it was all true, he would have thought she was hysterical. But Slocum knew. Ali might have done the killing or, more likely, the mahout, Gasim. He couldn't even discount that they were all involved.

He believed the maharajah knew of the death and had brushed it off. Whether the Indian prince had ordered Hugh's death was something Slocum intended to find out. It didn't matter that much to Slocum if the maharajah and his servants were all strung up—or ended their miserable lives with bullets in them—if they were guilty of Hugh's death.

"I can get a job, John. I know how to do all kinds of things."

"I know," Slocum said, grinning.

Darlene blushed and chastely drew up the sheet to hide what Slocum had already seen.

"I didn't mean that. I'm not that kind of girl. I've worked in stores. I kept books at a bank. I've even cooked for an entire crew of cowboys on a ranch, though I wasn't anywhere near as good as the regular chuck wagon cook."

"That's fine," Slocum said. He was glad Darlene could get along without Hugh, though he wondered because of the way she had clung so to the miner as if he were her only hope of survival. Slocum had to consider that Darlene and Hugh had been in love. That made her desire to see Hugh's killer brought to justice all the more important.

"You're skeptical. I can earn enough—honestly—to get you a new horse. Then it's up to you."

"A horse is a mighty expensive proposition," Slocum said. "It'd take too long to save that kind of money, what with the need to live off what you make along the way." His mind turned over everything and came up with only one possible way of finding Hugh's killer. It didn't suit him much, but he had done worse in his life. Much worse.

"So what do your propose to do?" Darlene turned indignant now that she thought he was going to steal a horse and simply ride out of Hoback Junction without bringing Hugh's killer to justice.

"Get your job," Slocum said, "and I'll take one that's already been offered to me."

"Much obliged for the ride," Slocum said to the wagon driver. The young man worked at the Hoback Junction general store and brought fresh supplies to the maharajah's camp every other day. In return for helping load and unload, Slocum had avoided walking back to the prince's campsite with his saddle balanced on his shoulder.

"You want a job, Slocum, and I'll see that Mr. Gutherie hires you on. We kin sure use the extra help these days."

"Got a job here," Slocum said, looking at the ornate tents gently flapping in the fitful prairie wind. Nobody stirred in the camp, but it was late afternoon. If the Indian prince and his servants had any sense, they'd follow the Mexican custom of a siesta during the hottest part of the day.

Slocum saw that they didn't have that kind of sense. The maharajah, seated in his fancy carriage, drove toward the camp from an obviously long trip across the Wyoming grasslands. Slocum didn't see any large caliber rifles so he figured the maharajah had been hunting something other than buffalo. Or maybe he had just been sightseeing.

As the carriage drew closer, Slocum saw Lakshmi seated behind the prince and Ali, who drove. Her servant sat stoically in the rear of the carriage, eating dust kicked up by the large wheels and struggling hard not to show any discomfort.

Ali pulled back cruelly hard on the reins and stopped the carriage a few yards from Slocum. The prince jumped lightly to the ground and strutted over, eyeing Slocum from top to bottom. A sly smile turned into a sneer.

"You have returned. As a common laborer?" He motioned to the driver of the supply wagon to leave.

"Go on," Slocum told the young man. "Thank Mr. Gutherie for the offer of a job, but I reckon I've got one here. Isn't that so?"

"Of course it is," the maharajah said, grinning even more broadly. The sneer had turned into an evil leer. "You will scout for me."

"Need a horse," Slocum said.

"Of course you do. Go to the elephant pen and tell Gasim to give you one from my remuda. Choose well. The horse must have stamina enough to keep up if I choose an all-day excursion."

"Like you did today?" Slocum saw the lathered team and welts where Ali had whipped the horses unmercifully.

"You are a man who misses nothing. This is perfect for a scout. You will find me a bear. A grizzly, you called it. I would hunt one to see if it is as ferocious as a tiger." The maharajah made his dismissive hand gesture. "I think not, but it will be an interesting experience, no matter how tame this bear might actually be."

"Whatever you say," Slocum said, swallowing his pride. The prince laughed as he went off to his tent without so much as a backward glance.

By this time Lakshmi's servant had popped out of the rear of the carriage and come around to help her to the ground. Ali drove off, snapping the reins and further abusing the team.

"Enjoy the tour?" Slocum asked Lakshmi.

She appeared surprised that he had spoken to her. She looked at her servant, then in the direction Ali had driven.

"It is not safe to speak to me. He is very possessive."

"The maharajah? What harm is there in exchanging a few civil words? Or is that the problem?"

"What do you mean?" Lakshmi blinked. Her ebony eyes drew Slocum in like a whirlpool sucks in unsuspecting sailors. Her nut-brown skin gleamed with a thin sheen of sweat from the hot afternoon sun, which made her about the loveliest woman he had seen in months. Darlene was far out of this elegant princess's class.

"From the way he treats folks, common civility is a rare commodity in these parts."

"He is a prince, a ruler of many, many people. He does not have to be polite when he has the power of life and death in his hands."

"So in India he can order a man killed and that's it? Somebody does it?"

Again Lakshmi glanced in the direction of her servant. Slocum got the idea that the man was less her servant than the maharajah's spy. He thrust out his hand.

"My name's Slocum. Pleased to meet you."

Lakshmi's servant recoiled, staring suspiciously at Slocum's outstretched hand. Then he looked from the open hand to Slocum's face.

"I am Valande." The man was short, sturdy and carried a pair of ornately gilded daggers at his belt. A pink scar running from a ruined ear to his jaw marred his otherwise handsome face. "Is this proper?" Valande suddenly asked Lakshmi.

"We are not in India. The customs here are strange," Lakshmi said. "Go, prepare my tent."

Valande hesitated. Again Slocum had the feeling the servant wanted more to hear what Lakshmi might say than to obey her. He finally bowed his head and walked away slowly, his good ear tilted slightly backward in their direction.

"He is a loyal servant," Lakshmi said.

Slocum waited to be sure Valande was out of earshot before he said, "Are you sure?"

"He is a spy," Lakshmi said unexpectedly, "but do not let on. The maharajah would kill him."

Her burst of honesty took Slocum aback. He had anticipated protests of innocence and loyalty.

"What about you? Do you tell the prince everything he wants to hear, too?"

"You are not a foolish man, Mr. Slocum. Do not act churlish." With that, Lakshmi hurried to her tent. Slocum saw the flap of the maharajah's tent move slightly although the faint afternoon breeze had died completely. Either the maharajah himself, or possibly Ali, had been watching from across the common area between the tents.

Slocum hefted his saddle and set off for the elephant pen to find Gasim. It took the better part of ten minutes to get there. He was tuckered out by the time he reached the area. The elephant wallowed in a mud puddle at the far end of its pen. Slocum approached and scratched its head. The knee-high stone fence that formed the pen was so flimsy that the elephant need only kick out to topple it. It wasn't even high enough to prevent Slocum from jumping it. If he could do that, so could an elephant standing fifteen feet tall.

"What do you want?" Gasim appeared like a ghost. Slocum swung around, dropping the saddle to protect his body if the mahout tried to stab or shoot him. Gasim stood with his arms hanging at his side. He might not be friendly but he wasn't going to stab Slocum in the back. Not right now.

"Why does the elephant stay in an enclosure like that?" Slocum pointed to the law rock wall. "Seems like it could jump it and be halfway to Cheyenne by morning."

"Elephants do not jump. They cannot."

"It can't step over that wall?"

"No. I wanted to dig a foot-deep trench. That would serve the same purpose but the ground dirt is like rocks."

"Sun-baked," Slocum said.

"Yes, that is so. It is not like India where the ground is soft from many rains." Gasim looked almost human for a moment as he fondly remembered his native land. The expression vanished quickly. "What do you want?"

"I've hired on as the new scout. The maharajah said you'd let me pick a horse from your corral." Slocum looked around and wondered where the horses were kept. He suspected that elephants and horses were a bad mix to corral together and that decent riding animals might be a distance off.

"You work for the prince now?"

"That's what I said."

"Clean the pen," Gasim said. A smile showed broken teeth. "You must muck the pen."

"Got a shovel?"

"Use your hands."

"That what happened to Hugh Malley? You ordered him to do your work for you and when he refused, you had your elephant stomp on him?"

Gasim took a step forward, hands balling into fists. Slocum estimated the distance and knew the mahout would never be able to land a single punch. Slocum had been in too many bar fights to let anyone have the first blow.

"You refuse? You miserable cur?"

Slocum tossed his saddle directly at the mahout. Gasim was a wily fighter and knew better than to try to catch the gear, but he still staggered as he sidestepped the flying saddle. Slocum swarmed in behind and let fly with a straight jab that connected and knocked Gasim to the ground. The mahout sat there, looking more startled than hurt. Slocum figured no one had ever decked him before.

Slocum gestured for the mahout to get up so they could continue the fight.

"Gasim!" The name snapped with all the authority of a whip being cracked.

Slocum glanced over his shoulder and saw the maharajah sauntering up, Ali close behind. The maharajah's servant held his hand near a sheathed dagger at his belt. If he touched the hilt Slocum was going to throw down on him. A bullet always beat a thrown knife.

The maharajah rattled off a sharp string of commands in Hindi that caused Gasim to bow his head. He got his knees under him but remained in a kneeling position so he could touch his forehead to the ground.

Slocum decided Gasim was no further threat, but he watched Ali closely.

"If that's what you expect from all your hired hands, reckon I'll be moving on," Slocum said. He glanced from Gasim to Ali.

"He should not have been so impudent," the maharajah said. "He will be punished. Please stay, Mr. Slocum. I am in need of a good scout."

Slocum saw that Ali left his hand so that his thumb hooked under his belt, near the hilt of his knife. Slocum faced off against the servant, turning his side to the prince.

"You might need me but I can't say I feel the same for the rest of your men."

The maharajah said something in a tone equally as sharp as he had used to address Gasim. Ali crossed his arms over his chest and glowered.

"He is overly protective of me. When he saw how you had manhandled Gasim, Ali thought you were a threat to me."

"No threat, if I get my horse and I don't have to muck the elephant's stall."

The maharajah's eyes widened, then he laughed.

"You do not have to clean up after this noble creature or the other en route from Cheyenne."

"You've got another of those beasts coming?"

The maharajah's eyes locked with Slocum's.

"The young one on its way here is a special elephant. A baby, hardly more than eight feet tall. But a special one. A white elephant."

"Royal elephant," muttered Gasim, never lifting his eyes.

"Yes, a royal elephant."

"A white elephant?" Slocum wondered about that. He had seen snow hares with perfectly white fur. Other creatures that didn't hibernate and had to eke out an existence in the snow also turned white in season, but elephants were creatures from jungles. Hot jungles.

He thought the maharajah was pulling his leg.

"Mr. Slocum, go find yourself a horse in my corral." The maharajah smiled his superior smile. "I am sure you will find one that pleases you." The maharajah made his dismissive gesture to hurry Slocum on his way to the remuda on the far side of camp, then began berating both Ali and Gasim in his native tongue. Slocum quickly left the trio behind to find the corral.

Slocum chose a white stallion.

8

Slocum found life in the camp mostly boring. The maharajah's servants tended the prince constantly, administering to his every whim. What Slocum couldn't figure out was Lakshmi's position in the pecking order. She rode with the maharajah often and he treated her differently, although not too politely. Lakshmi might have been a wife, but Slocum got the feeling she was more of a mistress or concubine. Valande was her servant but the man spent as much time elsewhere as at her beck and call, often leaving her alone in her tent.

Seeing that Lakshmi was by herself so often emboldened Slocum. He thought he might find out the truth of Hugh's death from her more easily than from any of the servants. Getting the maharajah to admit that he was responsible for either killing Hugh or ordering him killed was a pipe dream. Whatever evidence there might be, Slocum had to unearth it by himself—or with Lakshmi's help.

He finished currying his horse and returned it to the corral on the south side of the camp, as far from the elephant pen on the north as possible. Slocum found the servants tight-lipped and almost fearful of him. That might be from whatever Ali or Gasim had said about him, but Slocum got the distinct impression that horses and elephants did not mix well. He considered asking the mahout directly but wanted nothing to do with Gasim, if possible.

Even thinking of the mahout made Slocum's spine tingle. He vowed to never turn his back on Gasim and that wicked dagger he carried at his belt. He added Ali to the list of men to never trust, if there was even a hint that the maharajah's opinion of his scout changed.

Slocum looked around the camp and saw only a few servants scurrying on errands that he knew nothing about. Valande was gone, and Lakshmi was alone. Slocum edged closer to the woman's tent. If she was something less than a wife, she might be willing to help him. Slocum had to admit some mistresses were more loyal to their men than wives, but he had seen the way Lakshmi looked at the maharajah and the high-and-mighty way he treated her.

She would help him find out what had really happened to Hugh Malley.

Slocum veered away from Lakshmi's tent when Ali came out of the maharajah's quarters and stood, arms crossed on his broad chest. He glared at Slocum, who politely touched the brim of his hat and kept walking. Out of the servant's sight, Slocum cursed his bad luck. Another few seconds and he could have slipped in to talk with Lakshmi. But Slocum decided his luck might have changed when he saw Valande hurrying out of camp, looking around furtively.

Slocum made sure that Ali remained at his post outside the prince's tent before following Valande. Lakshmi's servant looked too sneaky not to be up to something he shouldn't be doing. Hanging back, Slocum knew he would have no trouble finding Valande's tracks in the grass and soft dirt. Crushed grass stalks took an hour or more to pop back. Lakshmi's servant was only a minute or two ahead.

Taking his time, Slocum trailed Valande into the foothills

a mile away from the camp. Something warned Slocum to approach cautiously as he neared a particular tumble of rock. This place hadn't been selected solely because it was well away from camp. There had to be something more—and he reckoned it was because anyone hidden in the rocks could watch the approach.

Slocum crouched in tall grass and waited patiently. He had lost sight of Valande long since, but his caution paid off. A flash of sunlight off metal high in the rocks showed him where a sentry watched the trail to the meeting spot. Moving slowly to prevent the grass from betraying him, Slocum edged along until he reached a barren stretch below the rock where he had seen the reflection.

From here it was a matter of speed mixed with a healthy dollop of quiet. Slocum swarmed up the rock, barely disturbing a lizard sunning itself. Otherwise, no guard would have heard his approach.

". . . not so," came the voice floating on the still air. Slocum wiggled forward on his belly to see Valande and Gasim. From the way they stood almost nose to nose, Gasim was Valande's superior and was berating him for some infraction.

The conversation, if it had ever been in English, turned back to Hindi. All Slocum had to go on was the way the two men stood and the tone of their voices. Valande had done something woefully wrong and was getting chewed out for it.

This added to his knowledge of who was in charge in the maharajah's camp. The Indian prince was at the top of the heap, but Gasim was further up the ladder than Lakshmi's servant. From the terse replies Valande made, he had little to report and this did not set well with Gasim.

Slocum slipped back knowing he wasn't going to learn anything eavesdropping. Ali might outrank Gasim, but not by much. Ali's power probably came from being the maharajah's personal servant rather than his elephant driver.

Deciding not to try to beat the two servants back to
camp, Slocum found a comfortable niche in the rock and
waited. Ten minutes later Valande hurried away, shoulders
slumping and his stride that of a defeated man. Less than
five minutes after he had vanished into the tall grass on his
way back to camp, Gasim followed. His head was held
high and, although Slocum could not see his face, he was
confident in his stride.

Long after Gasim disappeared, heading for the elephant
pen, Slocum sat and thought as he sucked on a long blade
of grass. He could not see that the maharajah had much to
do with Hugh's death but Gasim had to know what had
happened. If anyone controlled the huge beast well enough
to get it to trample a man, it was Gasim. And Valande
might be a part of the plot.

For two cents, Slocum would have strung up the entire
lot of them, but he had to be sure he missed nothing. He
wanted to know what had happened and who was responsible for Hugh Malley's crushing murder.

Knowing that he would be missed in camp if he lingered too long, Slocum slid from his cranny in the rocks
and returned to camp by a route that made it appear he had
been off on the prairie rather than up in the rocks. Men
who met secretly like Valande and Gasim had to be up to
something suspicious. It took less than twenty minutes to
reach the spot where he had pitched his camp and sink
down to think a bit more on what he had seen.

"Mr. Slocum, are you ready for a hunt?"

Slocum straightened from pretending to clean his gear
to see the maharajah, resplendent in a black velvet jacket
chased with gold threads in curious patterns. Behind him
stood Ali, a heavy rifle held in the crook of his arm.

"What are we hunting? More buffalo?"

"I have bagged enough of those shaggy beasts. While
there is some thrill, hunting Cape buffalo is more challeng-
ing."

"What's a Cape buffalo?" asked Slocum.

The maharajah laughed his superior laugh and said, "A large black monster that roams southern Africa. It is quite sporting to kill one."

"Only used one shot," Ali chimed in.

The maharajah made his chopping hand motion to silence his servant, but Slocum saw the man was secretly pleased that his marksmanship was noted and appreciated.

"We shall hunt for these wild cats you call pumas or cougars."

"Mountain lion," said Slocum. "They go by a lot of different names."

"We shall see if they are a match for the tiger."

"You going to take along a big company?" asked Slocum. "Cougars turn wary if they hear a lot of men coming."

"No beaters?" Ali seemed disappointed.

"Mr. Slocum is the expert on these wild beasts. Very well," the prince said, slapping his thigh as he came to a decision. "Get Gasim. We shall hunt from the back of the elephant."

Slocum started to point out that a handful of men could spook a mountain lion enough to send it running for the timberline. An elephant would chase any self-respecting mountain lion into the next county. As fierce as the cougars could be, they avoided humans through long and painful experience. In earlier days when only mountain men prowled the slopes of the Grand Tetons the cats might have been more prone to attack, but they had learned when more and more men came to settle the land that avoidance was better than attack. Eat one small child and packs of hunters pursued until the killer cat was run to ground, gunned down and skinned.

"They're scarce critters," Slocum said. "We might not spot one the first day."

"Then we prepare for many days. However long it takes.

Tell Gasim," ordered the maharajah. Ali bowed slightly, took a step backward and then turned to leave.

"You will not shoot, Mr. Slocum. Only I will hunt this mountain lion. It is to be mine and mine alone."

Slocum nodded. He had no quarrel with any mountain lion in these parts. From the abundance of game he had seen, any cat was likely to be fat and sassy but probably not stupid. It might be necessary to track one to its lair.

"Let the hunt begin!" The maharajah whistled as Gasim brought the lumbering elephant to a spot a few yards distant, then forced it to kneel so the prince could mount and settle himself into the small box on the animal's back. Slocum took a few minutes to saddle his powerful white stallion and almost five to catch up with the maharajah.

Slocum saw that the elephant's stride was long, powerful and ate the distance like a simple repast. If he was going to scout, he had to remain in front of the elephant. He trotted alongside and called up to the prince.

"There's a canyon a few miles ahead. I'll scout the left branch since it leads higher into the mountains. You might wait at the junction until I see if I've found anything."

The maharajah called down something Slocum didn't catch over the steady clopping of the elephant's hooves and the rattle of his own horse's shoes against a rocky patch. He figured it didn't matter, waved and galloped ahead.

Less than ten minutes later, he slowed to a walk and enjoyed the country the best he could. It was lovely this time of year, but then Slocum found the mountains to be endlessly fascinating in any season. He rode to the junction of the intersecting canyons and cut left. Ahead stretched a U-shaped valley with plenty of hilly sections on either side to accommodate a small pride of mountain lions. He remembered this country from an earlier trip through the Grand Tetons and focused his attention on one spot in particular near a stream where four game trails ended.

Slocum hobbled his horse a hundred yards away, then

sat in the crook of a tree to watch and wait. Deer came along with a few smaller animals but it wasn't until an hour before sundown that the cougar silently padded up to the stream and sniffed about for dinner. Other animals had left some time earlier. The cat drank its fill, then slipped into afternoon shadows on the far side of the stream.

Slocum had found his quarry.

He jumped from his tree limb and worked the hobbles off his stallion, mounted and headed back to fetch the maharajah. Slocum hadn't gone a half-mile when he spotted the tall, lumbering elephant coming toward him. At first Slocum thought something was wrong. Then he saw the maharajah leaning out, his rifle swinging this way and that as he hunted for his cougar.

Gasim used a hooked pole to prod and his knees to steer the huge elephant up the middle of the valley while Ali rode a prancing horse some distance behind, as if to make sure no one sneaked up on the maharajah.

Slocum watched in disgust as the elephant came up.

"Why didn't you wait where I told you? You could have frightened off the cougar," Slocum said.

"I am a maharajah. I do not wait," said the prince, glaring at Slocum. "Have you found the prey?"

"There's a stream about a mile in that direction," Slocum said, jerking his thumb over his shoulder. "Wait! Don't go charging there. The cougar left, heading deeper into the valley."

The maharajah craned his neck as he studied the lay of the land in that direction. From his vantage, he could probably see a couple miles farther than Slocum.

"There is a trail ahead. A game trail, but it leads into the hills to the left."

Slocum hadn't known that but was unwilling to let the prince know.

"That's why they call them mountain lions," he said. "You might have to go after the cat on foot."

"That's no fit way for a prince to hunt," Ali said. The swarthy man glowered at Slocum.

"This puma is not as ferocious as a tiger," the maharajah said. "I will ride up here. There is more skill required shooting from the *howdah* on the back of an elephant."

Slocum didn't see that as very sporting but kept his peace. He wheeled his horse about and trotted off up the valley, angling toward the left wall to find the trail the maharajah had spotted from elephant-back. Here and there the mountain lion had stepped onto muddy ground and left a big paw print. Slocum had gotten a look at the cat but hadn't realized it was this large. From the size of the paw, it might be eight feet long.

"This way," Slocum called. He knew such loud voices would spook the cougar and send it along its way. Hunting any animal for the thrill of simply killing it wasn't something Slocum cottoned to much. Eat it, fine. Shoot it to keep it from killing livestock, fine. There wasn't any point in stuffing it or putting its head on a wall. If you needed its hide to keep warm, fine. There were any number of reasons to kill an animal, but the maharajah's desire to bag something he hadn't already killed wasn't too high on Slocum's list.

Let the cougar get away. Some rancher might regret this later in the winter when the cat went after a lamb or calf, but that was someone else's trouble.

The elephant lumbered past as the prince spotted his quarry and leaned far to one side of the box to get a good shot. Slocum and Ali jockeyed to get to the side so they could catch sight of the cougar.

"Watch out!" Slocum's warning came too late. The elephant passed by a rock. A tawny flash showed itself suddenly as the cougar pounced. Talons flashed and its powerful jaws opened to clamp fierce teeth on the elephant's side. The teeth failed to penetrate but the mountain lion slid down, leaving behind bloody tracks from its claws.

The elephant trumpeted in pain and shook all over. Slocum saw Gasim fighting to keep his seat, but the way the elephant tossed its head about made it impossible to remain in control. The mahout went flying through the air. But the real problem came as the elephant fought to swing about and defend itself against the cougar. Short tusks of yellowed ivory raked at the cougar and caused the cat to dance away.

All this jerking about loosened the strap holding the maharajah's box. Slocum saw it begin to tilt precariously. Then the prince went flying as the elephant trumpeted its attack and charged forward. The cougar snarled, pawed at the huge, angry, wounded beast and then raced off into the woods where the elephant wasn't likely to follow.

Slocum sat astride his nervous horse, staring at the carnage.

Then things got even more confused. The wounded elephant tossed its massive head, bellowed in triumph at chasing away its enemy and trotted off, back into the valley.

"I'll take care of the maharajah," Slocum shouted to Ali. "Stop that elephant."

To his surprise, the servant obeyed without question. Slocum jumped to the ground and ran to the prince's side. The man lay in a pile of torn jacket and ripped, baggy trousers that soaked up the blood leaking from a nasty gash on his leg.

"I am well," the maharajah said, rolling over. He winced and pressed his hand into his leg. "A wound." As if marveling at such a condition, he lifted his hand and stared at his own blood. "I am wounded in battle with a savage mountain lion!"

Slocum was so angry he could spit.

"Press a cloth against that cut and you'll survive," he

said. Slocum looked around for the mahout but didn't see Gasim. "I'll find your elephant driver."

"Ah, Gasim, yes, go fetch him. He must be punished for causing such a calamity."

Slocum stalked off, then slowed and eyed the ground suspiciously. Cougar tracks. He looked around. The mountain lion that had attacked the elephant had run into the woods a hundred yards away. Then he stared at the ground in front of him. Definite cougar tracks, but these paw prints were smaller.

"Two cats," he cried. Slocum whipped out his six-shooter and ran forward, shouting at the top of his lungs. He saw where Gasim had been thrown down a rocky incline to come to rest at an awkward angle. Gnawing on one arm was a smaller mountain lion—the female he had seen drinking at the stream.

Slocum fired in the air and forced the mountain lion to back away, growling deep in its throat. Gasim's blood dripped from its jowls. The cat let out a feral growl, then bolted into rocks farther down the hill, leaving behind its supper.

"Gasim," came the maharajah's deriding voice. "You made one mistake too many. You fool, you stupid fool."

Slocum's grip on his Colt Navy tightened as he considered shooting the maharajah where he stood. All that stopped him was Ali returning with the elephant.

9

"Your Highness!"

Slocum turned to see Ali returning with the elephant. The maharajah immediately went to stand in front of the wounded animal. Slocum thought that was about the dumbest thing he had ever seen since the powerful elephant could trample the man and never notice.

Like it had Hugh Malley.

"We must go immediately. It's too dangerous for you to remain here," said Ali.

"Nonsense. I have hunted tigers. This mountain lion has its charm."

Slocum looked at the bloody marks on the elephant's side and wondered where the appeal was for the Indian potentate. An animal this large wasn't in danger of dying, but the mountain lion's dirty claws might infect the bleeding wounds—or even cause the elephant to go berserk with pain. That would give the maharajah a real hunt. He could shoot his own elephant.

"Return to camp, sir," Ali said. Slocum saw true concern in the man's dark eyes.

"You do not order me, Ali," the prince said coldly. "I will return to the camp because it is what I must do." The

75

maharajah looked at his dirtied, torn clothing and the gash on his leg that still bled sluggishly. "I need Lakshmi to tend my injuries."

"At once, Highness!"

"I'll ride your horse," the maharajah decided. "Tend the elephant since Mr. Slocum is not likely to be capable of such, uh, wrangling they call it."

Slocum sensed an oblique insult but the prince was right. He could tend a herd of cattle, stop a stampede, do things with horses that the Indian prince could only dream of, but getting a wounded elephant back to its pen was not a chore he wanted.

Slocum and the maharajah mounted as Ali began pushing and shouting at the elephant to get it moving. He had to trot when the beast decided to set the pace just a tad faster than a man could walk, but Ali made no complaint.

"I must bag a mountain lion," the maharajah told Slocum as they rode side by side. "It is a wily adversary, more than I expected from any creature on the North American continent. I am pleased."

"You're pleased?" Slocum shook his head. "You lost your elephant driver and got banged up and you're pleased?"

"Gasim!" cried the maharajah. "I forgot about him when Ali brought the elephant. We must not leave him where he fell." The prince jerked on the reins and turned his horse to return.

"You need to get your leg bandaged," Slocum said. "I'll fetch the body."

"He is my servant. I will do what is necessary to see that his body is not defiled."

Slocum looked at the man and wondered what the hell that meant. He wasn't going to violate the corpse and resented the implication that he would.

"He must be tended properly and the body returned to India," the maharajah said, seeing Slocum's anger. "Religious ritual must be performed to ease his soul on its journey."

"The Celestials render the flesh off the body and send bones back to China," Slocum said. That had never made much sense to him, either, but shipping bones was a better choice than getting an entire body ready for a month-long trip to India. Slocum was more inclined to bury the dead where they fell.

"The Chinese," the maharajah said with distaste. "They covet my land of Rajasthan and will invade someday. How can we stop those faceless, numberless hordes?"

Slocum was more worried about retrieving Gasim's body than some potential invasion of a land he couldn't even locate on a map. Two mountain lions still prowled the area and one had a taste for human flesh. It took close to ten minutes to reach the top of the incline where Gasim had been thrown by the rampaging elephant. Slocum drew rein and frowned as he studied the rocky slope.

"I don't know where the body is," Slocum said. "This is the spot where he took a tumble." Slocum pointed to the cut-up ground, dislodged rocks and even some flecks of blood on rocks a few feet down the slope. Whether the blood came from Gasim or the elephant, Slocum didn't know. But this was the spot where the mahout had fallen.

Now Gasim's body was gone.

"The mountain lion might have dragged off the body," Slocum said.

"Then we track it and save what portion of the body that we can," the maharajah said.

"I'll do it. You don't have a rifle."

"I'll take yours. You have your sidearm."

Slocum bristled at the notion of the prince using his Winchester, but it made sense. Slocum knew the man was an expert marksman after seeing how he bagged one buffalo after another during the stampede. Two guns were certainly better than one when it came to a bringing down man-eating cougars, but it still didn't set well with him. He pulled the rifle from the saddle scabbard and passed it to the maharajah.

"A light rifle, hardly worth carrying," the maharajah said as he examined the Winchester. "Good enough for rabbits, perhaps, but nothing more demanding."

Slocum dismounted and made his way downhill without answering. That rifle had saved his life more than once. It wasn't a Sharps .50 or the heavy caliber rifle the maharajah favored for hunting, but it could bring down a deer—or a man.

Slipping and sliding on the loose gravel, Slocum reached the spot where the cougar had savaged Gasim. Blood had spattered everywhere. But farther downhill Slocum saw something that made him cautious. He drew his six-shooter and looked around, every sense alert for trouble.

"The mountain lion?" called the maharajah. "Do you see it?"

"Quiet," Slocum said. "Gasim wasn't dragged off by the cougar. His body was taken by Indians."

"Of course it was. *We* are Indians," the maharajah said sarcastically.

"Crow," Slocum said. "He was taken by Crow Indians, and I don't think he's dead. There's too much blood. Dead men don't bleed."

"I shall join you." Before Slocum could wave back the prince, he crashed and slid noisily to stand beside Slocum. His dark eyes worked over the land and he slowly nodded. "You are right."

"Thanks for the vote of confidence," Slocum said dryly. He had already spotted the tracks leading away down a draw, which took a sharp bend and hid anything in its gravelly bottom. The Crow might be laying in ambush a dozen yards off.

"Why do you call these natives 'Crow'? When those

who captured Gasim might be other tribes? Is there something in these tracks that identifies them?"

Slocum cursed under his breath since he didn't want to yammer endlessly.

"I ran into Crow hunters earlier. I assume these tracks were made by them or others in their party."

"But you do not know."

"Quiet," Slocum snapped. He cocked his head to one side and listened hard. The wind had picked up a little and whispered through distant leaves, making it hard for him to pick out the sounds mingled with those he needed to decipher most. Turning slowly, Slocum could hear the faint conversation.

"There," Slocum said softly. "The Crow are over there."

"How is it you know they are Crow?" The maharajah refused to let the matter drop. It didn't matter which Indians had taken Gasim. The result would be the same. The maharajah's elephant driver would end up with his scalp lifted if they were hostile. Even if they weren't, the Indians might mistreat the wounded man enough to kill him. Slocum doubted they had seen anyone with that exact skin color, even Mexicans coming this far north to trade. That curiosity might be enough to keep Gasim alive a bit longer.

"Follow close behind," Slocum said. "I doubt they have sentries out, but splitting up will double our chance of being spotted."

"What is happening?" The maharajah tipped his head to one side as he finally heard what Slocum already had. "Are they performing strange heathen rites?"

"They want his scalp for their belts," Slocum said, not wanting any talk at all as he approached the camp. Walking quickly and silently, he went directly along the bank of the arroyo until he got to the wooded area where he heard distinct voices.

Slocum was within a dozen paces of the copse when shadows broke off from two trunks and stepped into the fading afternoon light. He looked down the barrels of two leveled rifles in the capable hands of Crow warriors.

One let out a shrill whistle and brought four other braves running. Slocum put up his hands so they wouldn't shoot.

"I would speak with your chief," Slocum said. His Crow was spotty at best so he stuck with English. The men obviously understood because they whispered among themselves.

"Come." The nearest brave motioned for Slocum to head toward their campsite. Slocum glanced over his shoulder but didn't see the maharajah. He heaved a sigh of relief. There was no telling what kind of trouble the prince might get them into. Slocum's best chance of getting out with his own scalp—and Gasim still alive—lay in palavering with the party's leader. The brave might not be a chief but Slocum knew he had to treat him as such.

He stepped into the clearing where two small fires sputtered. The evening meal was yet to be prepared because the Crows were too interested in their captive. Gasim was tied to a nearby pine tree, his hands behind him. His eyelids fluttered, and he hardly recognized Slocum. But he was alive.

Slocum hoped they'd all be able to brag about that when morning came.

"I greet the great chief of the Crows," Slocum said, holding out his hand. A brave beside him made a grab for his six-shooter, but Slocum moved too fast, sidestepping so the man missed.

"Kill him," spoke a young buck. He looked like a stripling compared to some of the others, but his voice carried the sharp edge of command that set him apart. He might not be a chief—yet—but there was no question that he was in charge of what looked to be a hunting party.

"Does a chief give such careless orders? I thought better of the Crow and their leaders." Slocum took a calculated risk and spat into the fire. His spittle sizzled and a thin column of steam rose.

The Crow shot to his feet, his hand flashing to a knife sheathed at his side. Slocum couldn't help noticing that the jeweled hilt was identical to the one on Gasim's blade. The Indians had already begun divvying up their prisoner's belongings.

"You mock me!"

"Yes," Slocum said. "I thought I spoke to a great chief with wisdom. Am I wrong?"

"No," the brave said, scowling.

"What will you trade for your prisoner?" Slocum indicated Gasim. For the first time since coming into camp, he thought they might get out wearing their hair. Then Gasim's eyes went wide and he struggled, but he wasn't looking at Slocum.

A quick glance over his shoulder confirmed the worst. Slocum saw the maharajah strut into camp as if he owned it. He didn't even have the Winchester leveled at the Crow braves but carried it over his shoulder like a soldier on parade.

Gasim rattled off a long burst of Hindi, but the maharajah ignored his servant as he came to a spot a few paces away from where Slocum stood by the fire.

"Primitives, the lot of them," the maharajah said.

"Primitives who'll scalp you if you get them mad," said Slocum. "And maybe they'll scalp you even if you don't piss them off."

The Crows stared at the prince, one even coming close enough to run his fingers over the maharajah's fancy velvet jacket. The threads caught the firelight and turned to liquid gold. That first touch was tentative, almost fearful, but the next was bolder. Soon, all the Crows were running their hands over the jacket.

"A mighty chief like you should have a coat like that," Slocum said to the young buck leading the hunting party.

"It is yours. A gift from another mighty chief."

The maharajah looked a bit surprised.

"Give him your coat," Slocum said. "Don't argue."

Slocum had to give the prince his due. The man was quick enough to understand the situation so that he shucked out of the jacket and even held it for the Crow brave to slip into. To Slocum's surprise, the jacket might have been tailored for the Crow. It fit perfectly.

"A fine gift to show friendship between our people."

"His skin and his," said the Indian, rudely pointing to Gasim and then to the maharajah, "are the same. Not like the white man's flesh."

"I am from a far-off land," the maharajah said. Slocum shook his head slightly. He didn't want the prince mucking up the exchange. It had gone well so far. The Crow turned around and around, fascinated by the way the light reflected off the golden threads in the jacket.

"He would take his brother back to this far-off land," Slocum said. "We will trade for the one you have tied up."

"Pants," the Crow said suddenly. "I want." He pointed to the maharajah's baggy trousers.

Slocum was afraid this would be a problem, but the maharajah agilely shucked off the pants and handed them to the brave, adding a small bow that was not lost on any of the Crows. They hooted and hollered and looked on top of the world. Slocum hoped they weren't also interested in taking the maharajah's silk underwear.

"You are a mighty chief and mighty chiefs keep their word. Release your prisoner," Slocum said. The brave made a gesture identical to that used so familiarly by the maharajah. Two braves hurried to Gasim's side and cut the ropes holding his hands. Slocum was pleased to see that the mahout had enough strength to get to his feet and unsteadily walk over to them. To support him now would jinx the deal.

"Come to our camp," Slocum said graciously since he

wasn't giving away anything that belonged to him, "and we will give you many more gifts, gifts worthy of a great Crow chief."

Slocum silenced the maharajah with a look, but the man seemed pleased at the notion of the Crows coming to his camp.

The Crow nodded once, then crossed his arms over his chest. Slocum saw how the brave's fingers continued to stroke over the intricate patterns formed by the threads on the jacket. Gasim struggled to walk but the mahout left the Crow camp on his own. When they reached the spot where Slocum and the maharajah had left their horses, Gasim reached the limits of his strength and collapsed.

"Put him on your horse," the maharajah said in his usual imperious tone. "He cannot walk in this condition."

"He's lost a lot of blood," Slocum said. A quick examination showed Gasim's wounds were clotted over but serious enough to require him to stay in bed for a week or more. Even then, his injuries might not heal properly since the mountain lion had ripped away part of the muscles in his upper arm.

The maharajah had already ridden off, head high in spite of his semiclothed state. Slocum settled Gasim and then mounted, steadying the man. The powerful stallion hardly noticed the extra weight as they trotted to catch up. Slocum would have joshed anyone else about returning to camp in only baggy underwear but decided the maharajah was not the joking type.

They reached the camp around midnight. To Slocum's surprise everyone was still awake, probably alert for the return of their master. Lakshmi's eyes went wide when she saw Gasim, then she quickly averted her face when the prince dismounted. They exchanged quick bursts of Hindi, but the woman never looked at the partially clad man, as if it was forbidden. Slocum began to wonder what the relationship was between Lakshmi and the maharajah. If they were married, seeing him in such dishabille wouldn't be that unusual.

Lakshmi bowed deeply and backed away from the maharajah. Ali held open the tent flap for his master, then vanished inside after him.

"I need some help with Gasim," called Slocum. To his surprise, Lakshmi hurried over. She did not seem uncomfortable at the sight of so much dried blood.

"He is nearly dead," she said, as if accusing Slocum of being responsible for Gasim's condition.

"We got him away from a party of Crow hunters. They took a fancy to him because of the color of his skin. They might be Indians, but they don't see folks from India in these parts."

"This wound is from an animal bite." Lakshmi's fingers expertly probed Gasim's shoulder and biceps.

"A mountain lion mauled him. Are you a nurse?"

"I am trained in many disciplines," Lakshmi said. She looked at him and those impenetrable ebony eyes took on a spark of fire, just for a moment. Or was Slocum reading something that wasn't there? She hurriedly summoned servants and ordered them to take Gasim to a tent.

Lakshmi turned to Slocum and started to speak when the maharajah returned, fully dressed once more.

"You have performed a great service, Mr. Slocum. While you lost us the mountain lion, you saved our favorite mahout. Take this as a token of our thanks." The prince held out a small box.

Slocum took it and opened the lid. For a moment he was not sure what he was looking at. Lakshmi gasped and muttered under her breath, "Such a fine diamond!"

"Thanks," Slocum said. "I'm glad that Gasim is getting the medical help he needs."

He stared at the large rock inside the box as the maharajah left, trailing Ali and Lakshmi. He had seen diamonds before but never one the size of a large pebble. It had to be

worth a fortune. Slocum looked around but he stood alone
in the middle of the maharajah's camp, as if everyone else
had simply evaporated. He tucked the box into his pocket
and tugged on his stallion's reins, getting it moving toward
where he had pitched his camp. He might not be any closer
to figuring out who killed Hugh Malley but he was a sight
richer, thanks to the maharajah's reward for saving Gasim.

10

With the huge diamond rubbing against his chest as it bounced around in his shirt pocket as he rode, Slocum headed into Hoback Junction to see Darlene. The constant reminder of the diamond told him he was rich when he sold it—and that he wasn't likely to figure out what killed Hugh Malley if he got the money and rode on. Had the fancy diamond been a bribe so Slocum would do just that? The miner was dead and was hardly more than a faint memory in the maharajah's camp. If the prince had ordered Hugh's murder, it was unlikely Slocum could get any of the servants to fess up. It was even less likely he could get Gasim or Ali to speak of his friend's death.

Slocum laughed ruefully. The one most likely to confess was the elephant, and Slocum didn't speak the animal's language. Not like he did horses, He patted the neck of the powerful white stallion the maharajah had given him and sobered a mite. Was he willing to forget Hugh and how he had died because the prince had bought him off? Slocum touched the diamond and wondered if that hunk of gemstone meant as much to him as getting this fine horse.

The maharajah was a clever man and obviously knew everyone's price. Slocum hardened at the thought of being bribed and not even knowing it. Resolve grew until he came to a decision. He wasn't going to give up on finding who had killed Hugh and why. It might have been that Hugh had seen something people in the camp wanted to keep secret. That would be a good road for Slocum to begin traveling once he returned from town.

The day was hot and only a feeble breeze blew across the Wyoming prairie, but the Grand Tetons rising to his back reassured him. He was in the middle of hills and only saw the grasslands because of the direction he rode. Given a few more days, he would solve the mystery of who killed Hugh and why, then be on his way to the upper slopes of the mountains where it was cool and peaceful and there wasn't nary an elephant to be heard trumpeting.

Hoback Junction seemed particularly empty for midday, but Slocum paid scant attention as he looked around for a jeweler's store. The closest he came was next door to the land and assay office. A big sign outside listed all the items of precious metal that would be purchased "for a fair price" inside. Diamonds weren't listed, but Slocum had confidence that he could get enough money for the rock to keep him from sleeping in the stables.

He went into the shop and looked around. His nose wrinkled at the pungent stench of spilled chemicals. The chemist, decked out in a heavy canvas apron and thick gutta-percha gloves, looked up.

"What kin I do fer ya?" He didn't sound too eager to leave his experiment. A bluish liquid in a clear Mason jar awaited a twisted hunk of metal the man held in clamps just above the surface.

"Go on, finish whatever you're doing. I'm in no particular hurry," Slocum said. The chemist grumbled, then dropped the bit of metal into the blue acid.

"Aqua regia," the chemist said. "Dissolves damn near anything. Got me a good silver ore sample here. But you don't wanna hear that, do ya?"

"What can you give me for this?" Slocum drew out the diamond in its box and lifted the lid to expose it to the faint light slanting through the solitary window in the shop.

"I declare," the chemist said, picking up the diamond and peering at it closely. "This real?"

"Reckon so," Slocum said.

"You got it from that India fella, din't ya?" The chemist took the stone to the dirty window and dragged it across the surface with a screech that put Slocum's teeth on edge. A shiny cut in the glass testified to the diamond's authenticity, not that Slocum had doubted for a moment that the maharajah would give him a worthless hunk of glass.

"What'll you give me for it?"

"Ten," the chemist said, dropping it on the counter.

"Ten thousand?" Slocum's eyes widened.

"Ten dollars. I ain't got no market fer that thing. Nuthin' I kin do to break it up into smaller hunks, though I heard tell of diamond cutters doin' that."

"Ten dollars?" Slocum was getting angry. "It's worth more than that!"

"Not to me, not to nobody in Hoback Junction. You want top dollar fer it, you take it to New Orleans or maybe St. Louis. Don't think you could get more 'n five hundred for it in Frisco, 'less it caught the eye of one of them high-priced whores." The chemist chuckled at a private joke. Slocum asked what was so funny. "Well," said the chemist, "I was thinkin' you could give that to the best lookin' whore in all of Frisco and get yerself laid for the next twenny years. I'll give you fifty for it!"

Slocum tucked the diamond back into its box and left without another word. He hadn't expected this. If the man had offered a few hundred, Slocum would have been inclined to accept, but fifty dollars was a tiny fraction of what it was worth. As he walked, his ire settled. The chemist was right. Who in Hoback Junction, Wyoming, wanted such a fabulous precious stone? Most of the women, the ones who had any jewelry at all, wore rhine-stones and were happy for that speck of flash.

The diamond might be worth more than the land under the entire town but did him no good if he couldn't find anyone interested in buying it.

Slocum went to the hotel and asked after Darlene, only to find that she had taken a clerking job at the general store. He went to the store and looked around. It was empty.

"Hello? Anybody around?" he called. From the back of the store he heard movement and went to see. A young boy, hardly thirteen, played like a cat with a mouse he had trapped in a cracker box.

"Where is everyone?" asked Slocum. The boy jumped like he had been stuck with a pin.

"Sorry, mister. Didn't hear you come in. My pa left me in charge since he and the rest have ridden out to take care of things."

"What are you talking about?" Slocum had the feeling he wouldn't like what he heard. Hoback Junction seemed unnaturally empty right now.

"They got themselves a posse together and went out to string up all them Indians. Well, they ain't Indians like we know. Those brown-skinned fellows what killed Hugh Malley."

"Darlene," Slocum muttered.

"Yep, she convinced my pa and a dozen others around town. She rode with 'em. She's not all that good-lookin', but she rides like a man. And I heard her cussin'. She can cuss a blue streak, too."

"I bet she can," Slocum said. "When did they leave?" He hadn't passed them on the road as he came into town.

"Oh, they left 'fore dawn. They was gonna split up and go at the Indian camp from a couple different ways so none of them varmints could get away. They was a little a'feared of that elephant. Don't much blame 'em, but I'd sure like to see it 'fore they kill it."

Slocum doubted the maharajah would care much if the posse shot all his servants, but if they touched one bristly hair on the elephant's back, he would use that rifle of his to take out the men one by one. With such a large caliber rifle, he could shoot them from horseback at a half mile and never even need to squint.

"There's supposed to be another of them elephants comin' to town."

"What's that? Another elephant?" Slocum remembered something the maharajah had said about this.

"Bein' brung in from Cheyenne, or so I heard," the boy said. "Cain't say why since they don't look to be good for much, other 'n scarin' the little kids." He obviously did not place himself in this group.

Slocum left the general store without another word. Darlene had whipped the townspeople into a blood frenzy that would end up in too many more deaths. She wasn't content letting him poke about and wanted revenge for Hugh herself.

As Slocum galloped from town he saw Marshal Rothbottom leaning against the jamb of the door leading into his jailhouse. The peace officer glared at Slocum but said nothing. Slocum wondered if Rothbottom knew half his town was out ready to string up anyone with strange clothes and smelling of elephants or if he was completely oblivious to what went on around him. It didn't matter since the outcome was the same either way.

Someone was going to die, and it wasn't necessarily the one responsible for Hugh Malley's death.

As he rode at such a quick pace, even the powerful horse began to tire. Slocum changed gait, then had to stop for a spell to let the horse cool off and regain its breath. Slocum was in a hurry to get to the camp to warn the maharajah, but only because *he* wanted to be the one who found who had killed Hugh Malley. Slocum knew a lynch mob such as the one Darlene had gathered would care nothing for truth or justice. They'd be whipped into a murderous frenzy and whomever they came across would be the victim—guilty or not.

As he brought the horse into a walk, Slocum saw dust from off to his left. The spectacle of the Grand Tetons was dwarfed, however, when he saw that the approaching rider was the lovely Lakshmi. Her long black hair flowed behind her, caught on the wind like some delicate banner. Expensive clothing glinted in the sunlight and the occasional jewel on her person added to the belief that a drop of sun had come to earth to shed its brilliance. To his surprise, Lakshmi was an expert horsewoman and flowed well with the animal straining so under her.

"Mr. Slocum!" she called. "Please. Help. We need your help."

"Whoa, slow down," he said as she jerked back on the reins. Her horse dug its heels into the ground and sent up a dusty curtain all around. By the time she had settled down, they were almost leg-to-leg but facing in opposite directions. This gave Slocum a perfect look at her finely chiseled features, the darkly beguiling eyes and the strange red dot painted on her forehead.

"Ali, they have Ali. They caught him some distance from camp. They were sneaking about. I happened to see them and told the maharajah. He told me to ride to town and get the marshal."

Slocum snorted in contempt at the idea Marshal Rothbottom would do anything to help. In a way, Slocum was surprised that the peace officer wasn't with the crowd, helping them knot the hangman's noose.

"Where is he? Not in camp?"

"I avoided the road to ride here, but no, you are right. Ali is several miles toward the foothills. The maharajah must have sent him on a hunt for berries or—oh, I do not know! I saw them shoving him back and forth. His hands were tied. A woman wanted the men to 'string him up,' she said."

"Darlene," Slocum muttered. Louder he asked, "How long ago was that?"

"Not more than ten minutes. Even with my detour off the road, not more than that."

"Dismount. Give me your horse," Slocum said, thinking fast. "I can't gallop mine long enough to get there since I've already tuckered him out, but your horse is still fresh."

"Very well," Lakshmi said, unsure of what was happening. She dismounted. Slocum jumped from saddle to saddle. The spirited mare Lakshmi had ridden tried to show him who was boss, but he quickly settled the mare's nerves.

"Go back to camp, but if it looks like the posse's coming, hide out until they're gone."

"All right," Lakshmi said, but it was to Slocum's back. He bent low over the mare's neck and used spurs and reins to urge the horse to full gallop. The mare wasn't as strong as the stallion but had not been ridden into the ground already.

The distance flew past and then seemed to drag when Slocum picked up tiny sounds ahead. The noises became more distinct, and then he heard men crying out angrily for blood. It hadn't taken long for the posse to become a lynch mob, and they were going to string up Ali for the hell of it.

The mare faltered and almost fell but recovered and kept on galloping gamely until Slocum reached a tall oak with a thick limb. The first thing he saw was the hangman's noose dangling over the branch, swinging slowly in the sluggish Wyoming wind.

A dozen yards away the posse had gathered in a circle and shoved a bound Ali back and forth to get him dizzy and disoriented. Darlene sat astride her horse, watching with a fixed expression that sent shivers up Slocum's spine. He had seen men with tombstones in their eyes before but never a woman so intent on a man's death.

"Who was it?" she demanded. "Who murdered Hugh? Tell us and we'll let you go."

"You will kill us all," Ali cried. For his impudence, a man swung his rifle and caught the Indian on the back of the head. Ali stumbled forward and fell to his knees. The men began kicking him until he stood again. His back was straight and his chin held high in defiance. They could kill him, but they'd never get him to implicate anyone in Hugh's death.

"He's not going to say a word. String him up," Darlene said, as cold as Judge Parker sending another man to the gallows.

"Wait a minute," Slocum shouted. "Are you sure he's the one who murdered Hugh Malley?"

"What's the difference?" Darlene asked. Slocum ignored her. She incited the crowd to violence, but he had to throw water on their fiery tempers if he wanted to save Ali. Worst of all, he didn't actually *want* to save the Indian servant. Letting him swing at the end of a rope was probably too good for him, but his death wouldn't answer the real question of how Hugh had died.

Or why he had died.

"You want the real killer. String this one up and you might get him, but you might let the actual killer go scotfree," said Slocum.

"Then we gotta introduce 'em all to a good ole-fashioned Western necktie party!" shouted someone in the crowd.

"Hang the innocent with the guilty? How'd you like it if Marshal Rothbottom worked like that back in Hoback Junction? He might take it into his head to arrest the lot of you for stringing up the wrong Indian."

"They look alike," another in the crowd said. "You sure," he called to Darlene, "that this varmint's the right one?"

"She doesn't know who killed Hugh any more than you

do—than I do," Slocum said. He saw some weaker sisters in the crowd wavering. He kept talking and finally drove a wedge through their resolve. Slocum caught his breath and held it when he saw the maharajah riding up. The prince carried one of his powerful hunting rifles. There was no telling where he had been. He probably had waited some distance off, ready to shoot anyone trying to actually hang Ali. Seeing Slocum easing the lynch mob away from their murderous ways, he chose to show himself.

Slocum wasn't sure that was a good thing, especially if the maharajah acted uppity like he had a yen to do.

"Good afternoon," the maharajah greeted, as if he had simply come upon fellow travelers along a road. "Out for a constitutional?"

"What's that mean?" asked a ruddy-faced man.

"For your health, sir. Are you British, by any chance?" The maharajah's question confused the man. Slocum had to admit he wasn't alone. What was the prince up to?

"Me a Brit? Hell, no. I hail from down around New Braunfels, just outside of San Antonio in Texas."

"German?"

"Reckon so. Leastways, my pappy was so that makes me half German. My ma was a mestizo from down in Mexico, but we're all Texans through and through."

Slocum didn't interrupt. The peculiar questioning went on as the maharajah went from man to man asking if they were of British descent. By the time he had finished, the posse had lost all sense of purpose. Nothing Darlene could do stirred them to the same need for blood that had brought them from town.

"Take your manservant, Maharajah," Slocum said. "See that he's tended."

"Quite," the prince said, eyeing Slocum. The maharajah grabbed Ali by the collar and pulled him over the hindquarters of his horse, hands still tied behind him. When he rode back toward his camp, the spirit left the lynch mob entirely. They drifted away by ones and twos until only a fuming Darlene was left.

"We could have got the truth from him. He would have told who was responsible for Hugh bein' tramped on like he was."

"This isn't the way to find whoever's guilty," Slocum said. "I told you I'd find out, and I meant it. Get on back to town. Let me keep poking around. They don't trust me enough to talk, but I'm finding out plenty."

"Such as?" Darlene glowered.

"I'll let you know when I can tell you for sure who murdered Hugh," he said.

"You better or I swear, John, I swear you'll be swingin' from one of them oak tree limbs!"

Darlene rode off, madder than a wet hen. But Ali hadn't gotten his neck stretched.

Slocum mopped sweat from his forehead, then turned the mare back toward the road and Lakshmi. This was his first and best chance to talk to the woman and find out what she knew of Hugh's death—and the strange questions the maharajah had asked of the crowd.

11

Slocum found Lakshmi standing beside his horse along the road. He wondered if Darlene and the rest of her lynch mob had ridden past, but he doubted it from the anxious expression on the Indian woman's face. She knew nothing of the outcome and would have known immediately if Darlene had come this way.

"Is everything all right?" Lakshmi asked anxiously.

Slocum dismounted and handed her the reins to her horse. He had used the mare as lavishly as he had his own stallion. Both horses were lathered from heavy, hard riding and deserved to be cleaned, curried and fed in addition to getting a good, long rest. Slocum found himself smiling a little at the idea that he deserved the same.

"Ali almost got his neck stretched," Slocum said. From her puzzled look, Lakshmi had no idea what that meant. Slocum explained.

"The barbarians!" exclaimed Lakshmi. "They would murder an innocent man!"

Slocum didn't share the exotic woman's appraisal of Ali—or anyone else in the maharajah's camp. Hugh Malley had been murdered, and it was passed off as an accident with no investigation of the circumstances at all.

"We should rest the horses," Slocum said, looking around. "Over yonder." Slocum pointed to a meandering stream some distance from the road. The grassy area on either bank would give the horses something to nibble, and a few low-growing stunted trees afforded a bit of shade.

"I must return to the camp."

"Ali's fine," Slocum said. "The maharajah showed up after the crowd had decided to go home. He took Ali back."

"They are not hurt?"

"Nope," Slocum said. He was already walking his stallion to the stream. Lakshmi could do as she saw fit, but his expert eye caught signs that her horse would not go far before collapsing. Lakshmi had ridden it hard from the maharajah's camp, and Slocum had given it an even more strenuous run.

"You are right," Lakshmi said, a smile dancing on her lips. She brushed back her midnight-dark hair and lifted her chin slightly to let the gentle breeze caress her face. She closed her eyes and let out a small, contented noise like a kitten purring. Slocum studied every plane of her beautiful face, her lush body, the tempting way the wind pressed her elaborate dress against her body and then released it, taunting him.

Lakshmi opened her eyes and stared straight at Slocum. He caught his breath. He worried that she might not like the intent way he studied her, her body, everything about her. If anything, she welcomed it.

"Come," she said, reaching out and taking his hand. Together they walked to the stream. "We should rest along with our horses."

"Reckon so," Slocum said. The way she looked at him told him they wouldn't be doing much resting. He quickly unsaddled the horses, hobbled them so they could crop at the knee-high grass and drink from the stream and not wander away. As he turned back, he stopped.

Slocum stared.

"Sorry," he said, not sorry at all. Lakshmi sat under a gnarled oak tree entirely naked. She had shucked off her dress and anything she had worn under it. Her mahogany skin shone in the light filtering through the gently dancing leaves, casting tempting shadows here and there as the wind picked up a little.

Lakshmi had breasts the size of large apples and twice as tempting. Her waist was narrow and her hips wide. She sat with legs drawn up slightly to occasionally reveal the dimly seen, furred patch between her thighs. She reached out. Long fingers rippled as if she had no bones in them as she beckoned him toward her.

"Are you sure about this?" he asked.

"You Americans are so formal at the wrong times," Lakshmi said. "What is it about me that you do not want? Do I not have fine breasts?" She cupped her teats and lifted, then pinched the already hard nubs capping each. She sucked in her breath as she gave herself a jolt of pleasure. "Or can it be my belly is too fat?"

Lakshmi lounged back slightly as she ran her long fingers across her firm, flat stomach. Those fingers pointed lower. She saw Slocum's attention—and how he responded.

"Perhaps you do not think this region is desirable? Too tangled? Not lush enough?" Her fingers stroked over her privates even as she moved her legs to alternately give Slocum a bold view and then a more chaste position with her legs drawn up tightly.

"Or do you think I am inexperienced? I know the *Kama Sutra* well. From personal exploration, not merely academic study."

"What's that?" Slocum dropped his gun belt and was kicking off his boots when Lakshmi laughed.

"I should show you. The *Kama Sutra* is not to be talked of. It is to be exalted by action. Intimate action."

"I've got to agree. I'm in favor of doing rather than talking, too," Slocum said. He dropped his shirt and began working off his jeans. He was aware of how Lakshmi stared at him with rising desire. Her fingers no longer strayed to other parts of her body but remained hidden between her legs. Her hand moved up and down, and Slocum knew what she was doing—what he wanted to be doing.

He watched her closely as her hand stroked up and down and her arousal mounted second by second. Slocum responded to the sight by getting harder. He stepped closer and looked down at her. He felt a tremor pass from head to toe at the beautiful sight before him. The sleek nut-colored skin, the hair and breasts and legs—it was all enough to get any red-blooded man excited.

Slocum knelt and gently parted her legs to expose her nether regions. One of her fingers curled around and disappeared inside that moist, tight recess.

"Let me put something else there. Something we'll both enjoy a whale of a lot more."

"No!"

Her sharp refusal startled him. He could not have read her wrong. She was the one who had stripped off her clothing to entice him. And her arousal was obvious. The brown nub on each teat was hard and pulsing with need, begging for his lips and tongue and attention. Her chest heaved up and down as her heart raced. Why did she tell him "no"?

"We must proceed slowly if I am to show you one page of the *Kama Sutra*."

"What's that mean?"

"It is the Hindu book of love," she said. Her tongue slipped out and made a quick circuit of her lips. She fixed her dark ebony eyes on his green ones. Then she reached out, and he knew she wasn't turning him down. She wanted to show him how Indians made love. He was so throbbingly hard that he would have hung upside down from a tree limb if that opened her book of love to the right page.

He jerked when her fingers lightly brushed along the

sensitive underside of his erect organ. She tapped and stroked, then pinched. The difference in sensations took him by surprise. Slocum fought to keep control.

"You see, there are many ways of stimulation," she said softly. Lakshmi moved closer so her hot breath gusted into his ear. A wet, darting tongue touched his lobe and tried to stuff itself into his ear before moving on. Lakshmi kissed and touched with her tongue to leave a wet spot before blowing on it. Cool, hot, neutral, aroused, she guided him through all possible sensations.

He tried to kiss her but Lakshmi drew back.

"Let me do for you," she said softly as she rubbed her breasts against his naked chest. He felt the hammering of her heart. She seemed cool as a cucumber, but he felt the heat from her radiating into his body. Slowness in her movement masked her desires.

"Build slowly," Lakshmi said. Her mouth moved fleetingly across his. Her tongue stroked his and then found a new target.

"This is fine, but I'm getting mighty excited," Slocum said. "Have been getting more excited from the first day I set eyes on you. You're about the prettiest woman I've seen in a month of Sundays."

"The prettiest," Lakshmi said, her breath coming faster now. "And the most skilled. I have watched your soiled doves as they made love. They know nothing."

"You've what?" Slocum thought he was past being flabbergasted by anything anyone could say or do. He was wrong. "How do you know what goes on between a whore and her customer?"

"The maharajah has sampled their wares," Lakshmi said, continuing her oral assault. She added the lightly dancing fingertips to her stimulation of every inch of Slocum's body.

"And you watched? Did he know?"

"Of course. He ordered it. I was not distressed at the request. I desired it. In India, lovemaking is an art. Here, it is more like a rodeo."

"Yeehaw!" cried Slocum. This brought a laugh to the woman's lips.

"You are so different," she said. "I must show you much so you will be pleased with me."

Slocum tried to answer and found the words all jumbled in his throat. Her hands had both dropped down to his manhood. Lakshmi moved her hands up and down, in concert and in different directions. Whatever she did excited him that much more. Slocum was harder and hotter than he remembered ever being.

"I should do something for you," he said.

"You are. Can you not tell?" Lakshmi shoved her chest forward again and he felt her heart hammering away.

"I want to do more."

"You will. Oh, you will!"

With her gentle urging Slocum sat cross-legged on the ground so she could straddle his waist. Slocum gulped as he felt the sensitive underside of his manhood rub against the crinkly nest between Lakshmi's legs. She circled his waist with her legs and tensed, pulling her body in closer so she sat on top of his thighs, their privates working slowly as her body undulated. She was dancing to a tune Slocum didn't share. He was eager to enter, but she restrained him.

Just as he was sure he could not hold back another instant, she pressed and pushed and moved in such a way that it was possible. Every time, he found himself brought to a higher level of excitement, barely restraining himself—but succeeding.

He lifted a bit off the ground, but she silently pushed him back down using only the pressure of her hips. She wrapped her arms around his neck and began kissing.

Slocum thought he knew everything there was about kissing, but he quickly learned there was more. And Lakshmi showed him. Not only did she kiss but also her roving fingers sometimes intruded.

Slocum found himself sucking on her fingertips and then her tongue, only to have delicious sweet-wine lips against his. She engaged him perfectly as she ran those knowing fingers down his spine, outlining every bone and sometimes pressing in forcefully.

Every time she did something new, he jerked and thought he would lose control. But he didn't and found himself aching for her more than he ever had for another woman. Still she wouldn't give him the release he sought.

Lakshmi began moving her hips in slow, subtle circles. First she rotated clockwise and then reversed her course. Her body rubbed into the underside of his manhood and promised paradise—but never quite delivered. This teasing caused him to reach a new plateau of arousal.

"I want—" That was as far as he got. Lakshmi's hips rose and she moved still closer. This time, however, as she descended she enveloped him entirely.

"Now," she whispered hotly in his ear. "Do for me what I have done for you. Make me yearn for what only you can give me."

As much as Slocum wanted to lift her up, flop her onto her back and sate himself, he realized she was offering him far more than a sudden physical release. She was offering him the sexual experience of a lifetime.

He could not duplicate the delicate motions of her fingers. Besides, he did not know the right spots to press and stroke that would send the electric volts of delight into her body. His callused fingers did their best to stroke and stimulate. He ran his hands down her sides, traced out ribs, then slipped across her lower back, cupped her firm buttocks with his strong fingers and began to knead as if he had found two mounds of tasty brown dough. Buried within her, he found a different way of exciting both himself and her as he twisted about in a corkscrewing motion.

Slocum knew she was responding to his ministrations by the way she uttered tiny animal noises. More than this he felt her tensing around his hidden buried length. He gulped and kept going in spite of the tensions reaching the breaking point inside. She massaged him with hidden muscles and then threw her head back, letting her hair fly about wildly. Slocum realized he could not keep going much longer.

He lifted her a little off his lap and then let her settle down slowly. This up and down movement brought even more violent reactions in the supple woman. She jerked about like a whip being snapped and then let out a louder, longer cry of releasing desire. This almost ended Slocum's valiant efforts to keep his control.

She crushed him as desire blasted through her. Slocum kept up the slow movement until Lakshmi reached down and found the hairy bag dangling under his long shaft. As he moved her body up and down, she began massaging it with her fingertips. The feathery touches coupled with the inner heat and moisture leaking out around his thick, fleshy plug set him off. He made no effort to hold back. The sensation ripping through him was too intense for that.

He heard Lakshmi crying out in ecstasy again, as if she were in the distance. The marvel of their lovemaking shook him and unleashed something more than simple physical pleasure. Slocum held Lakshmi close and then slowly disentangled their arms and legs to lie in the grass under the tree. He looked into her lovely face. The woman's eyes were closed and her expression was one of contentment. Eventually, she opened her eyes halfway.

"You have read the *Kama Sutra*, also."

"Never heard of it before today."

"You are a natural talent."

"I had some powerful inspiration," Slocum said. For a spell they said nothing more, content to let the warm Wyoming breeze caress their bodies as they lay still.

It was some time before Slocum asked, "What are you to the maharajah? You're not his wife, are you?" Slocum was startled at the reaction this caused. Lakshmi sat bolt upright, her eyes wide.

"His wife? You joke! We could never marry. That would be a travesty."

"Any man'd be a fool not to have you under him. Or over him or any of those positions you were talking about."

Lakshmi almost smiled, then turned somber.

"I am more than a servant but less than a concubine."

"A mistress?"

"Not that. The prince and I have never . . ." Lakshmi made a vague gesture with her long-fingered hands, indicating what she and Slocum had just done. "It is more complicated than that."

"What do you do for him?"

"I am a secretary and translator, since I speak languages he does not. And anything else he might want done."

Slocum didn't quite understand but let it drop. He had other questions to ask of Lakshmi and felt the moment would slip away like tickling a slippery rainbow trout if he failed to ask now.

"What's the dot? The red spot on your forehead?"

Lakshmi blinked and frowned.

"You jump from one thing to another. But this? This is *bindi*," she said. "It is made of turmeric mixed with other spices. It shows many things. In some regions of Rajasthan only married women wear it. In others, a white spot means unmarried but not available. In my case, it means unmarried but . . . skilled."

Slocum didn't bother asking what skill that might be. He had found out firsthand. As fascinating as it was to hear her murmuring, soft voice and look into her dark eyes, Slocum had other fish to fry.

"What's the maharajah want? He's not just hunting wild creatures to put in his trophy room." Slocum remembered how peculiar the prince had acted afterward when it was obvious that Darlene's lynch mob wasn't going to string up Ali.

"I am not sure. He has not confided this in me, nor has he asked for me to gather information. I do know this: He is most interested in anyone of British citizenship."

"What?"

"He hired your friend because he was British."

"Hugh was Welsh. A coal miner. What earthly use would Indian royalty have of someone who grubbed out a living a mile underground?"

Lakshmi shrugged her bare shoulders, causing a delightful jiggling reaction down lower. Slocum forced himself to ask a couple more questions.

"What do you reckon he wants with a Brit? It's not just any Brit, is it?"

"I think he looks for someone in particular, but as I said, he does not trust me with such information." Lakshmi turned slightly toward him so he got a better view of her lovely breasts. He saw that the nips were hardening again—just as he was down low.

"How many pages are there in your book?" Slocum asked. He reached out and lightly touched her cheek. She turned her head a mite and kissed his palm.

"Many," she said in a low, husky voice. "Many, many pages. We should not dawdle if we are to get through one or two more."

"Only one or two?"

"I do not want you to learn too much," Lakshmi said, kissing his chest and looking up with her limitless dark eyes. "You would have no further need of me."

"Don't be so sure," Slocum said. "And don't think

everything's in that book of yours. I might be able to show you a trick or two."

"Do it!" Lakshmi said eagerly.

Slocum did.

12

Slocum worried about Darlene back in Hoback Junction and the trouble she might be getting into. He didn't want to ride along, always watching his back trail and worrying that a lynch mob was going to swoop down on the maharajah or Ali or any of the others in the Indian camp. Slocum wanted to find out the details of Hugh's death and work from that base. Somebody had done his friend in, and Slocum was going to find out who.

Then the guilty party would pay. With his life.

Slocum and Lakshmi had returned to camp after twilight bathed the camp in long shadows and turned the tents into some exotic far-off location. The elephant bellowing in the distance added to the feeling of being transported into another world. Or was he only thinking of his unique lovemaking with Lakshmi? He had never experienced such sensations before and wanted more, like some opium addict.

But Lakshmi had been summoned immediately by the maharajah and had vanished into the prince's tent for more than an hour. Slocum had hung around, studying the camp routine and wondering how the labor was divided among the servants. Most of them were lower caste. Slocum was getting a feel for the differences in class status. Not all of them were treated as slaves. One group could dictate to another, but then bowed deeply when a higher caste came along. The maharajah was at the top of the pecking order, but Slocum couldn't figure where Lakshmi fit in. She was a woman and lower status, or should have been. Yet her caste, whatever it was, allowed her to dictate with almost the same authority as the maharajah.

Almost.

Slocum saw how her servant, Valande, spied on her. Valande and Gasim were in cahoots, with the mahout higher in caste. But why did Lakshmi permit such spying? Slocum scratched his head. She was no fool and had to know she had a traitor in her own employ. The only thing Slocum could decide was that Lakshmi knew and fed bogus information to Valande for her own purposes.

Or was the situation in the maharajah's party entirely beyond his comprehension?

Slocum had watched Valande, Gasim and Ali moving about, watching Lakshmi and the maharajah and one another but never coming together to compare notes. He had finally given up around midnight and unrolled his blanket for a decent night's sleep. The commotion in the camp just before dawn brought him awake. He heard footsteps coming in his direction and reached for his six-shooter, keeping it out of sight under the edge of his blanket.

"The maharajah wants you. We hunt today," said Ali, looking as impassive as if his face had been carved from a block of walnut wood.

"What are we going after?"

Slocum spoke to empty air. Ali was already halfway back to the main area of the camp. Slocum stretched and tucked his six-gun away. His belly grumbled, but he decided it was better to present himself for the day's hunt rather than grabbing a fast breakfast.

He hurriedly pulled on his boots and saddled his stallion before leading it to the maharajah's tent.

Slocum was not surprised to see the man facing east, eyes closed as he waited for the sunrise. As the first rays touched the prince's face, his eyelids opened slowly to take in the full beauty of dawn in Wyoming.

"You are ready, Mr. Slocum?" he asked without turning. Slocum thought the prince was worshiping the sun, but that didn't jibe with what little he knew of the Hindu religion.

"What are we hunting today?"

"Bear. Your stories of these ferocious animals have piqued my curiosity. I have decided that the mountain lions were not such ferocious beasts, after all."

"Clawed up your elephant, and Gasim isn't likely to get full use of his arm back," Slocum pointed out. "That's mighty ferocious in my book. Especially since we never even got a good shot at the puma."

"That the elephant is injured is a shame. I fear we cannot use it until it heals since the wounds have become inflamed."

"Did I hear you say that you're shipping another one from Cheyenne?"

"A special elephant, one more fitting for a maharajah. The large gray elephants are useful but not suitable for truly regal travel. I intend to move on in a few days, when the white elephant arrives."

"Never seen a white elephant," Slocum allowed. "Saw an all-white man once. An albino, they called him. White hair, skin whiter than bleached muslin, though his eyes were pink like a rabbit's."

"You would be disappointed then. The Indian white elephant is not white but dust-colored. Most unusual."

"And fit for royalty to ride," Slocum finished. From the hot flash of anger this inspired, Slocum thought it was better for him to keep quiet.

"Ali will range ahead and beat the bushes today," the

maharajah said, his ire subsiding as Gasim brought a horse for the man to mount. Gasim dropped to hands and knees and let the maharajah use his back as a stool to mount.

Slocum swung into the saddle. He caught sight of Lakshmi peering out of her tent. She smiled and waved almost shyly to him, then ducked back inside. Slocum had to use his spurs to catch up with the maharajah and Ali, both of whom had rocketed from camp and were heading toward the mountains.

"Does Ali know what spoor to look for? You might want me to scout and let him hang back," Slocum suggested.

"Ali is a clever man. He will know," the maharajah said. "I want to have a word with you."

Slocum tensed. In spite of what Lakshmi had said, she might belong to the maharajah in ways other than sexual. The maharajah certainly wouldn't take kindly to Slocum and Lakshmi being together the way they had. Slocum shifted a little in the saddle so he could get to his six-shooter if the need arose. He didn't want to gun down the man, but he had seen how good a marksman the prince was. If he drew the rifle riding at his knee, the maharajah would be a formidable foe.

Slocum didn't want it to come to a shootout between a pistol and a high-powered rifle.

"Do you know any Britishers?"

The question took Slocum by surprise. Of all the things he had expected, this was not it.

"I have since learned that your friend Malley was not British, not technically, but a Welshman. That is most unfortunate."

"His death or that he was Welsh?"

"Why, both, naturally," the maharajah said, his eyebrows rising in twin arches. "You do not think Mr. Malley's death was accidental, do you?"

Since Slocum thought the maharajah might be implicated, he held his tongue.

"I am more interested in finding a British citizen. To your knowledge, are there any in the area?"

"I was just passing through," Slocum said. "There might be some. Usually are, though I know more Irish and Scotch than British."

"No, not Irish. Not Welsh or Scotsman. The man I seek must be from London."

"What's your interest in this gent?"

"Ah, look, Ali is signaling to us. Perhaps he has found bear scat or other sign."

Slocum looked around and nodded. This was the type of country bears preferred. Mountainous, a stream running not far off probably loaded with trout, plenty of fodder growing here and up the side of the mountains where a bear could make a den. Bear country.

Slocum touched the rifle riding in his saddle sheath but knew better than to use it. The prince wanted to make the kill. Besides, Ali might not have found a bear at all. Slocum didn't trust the man's tracking ability all that much. In the jungles of India he might be good, but this was the West.

The maharajah broke open the breech of his rifle and shoved in the heavy cartridge.

"Yes, I do so love the British. I should find one of their number among the throngs out on the Wyoming grasslands."

Slocum looked sharply at the maharajah, wondering if he was being sarcastic. He could not tell from the man's tone, but the words indicated he wanted something more than a pleasant conversation or afternoon tea with any British citizen he found.

"There!"

Slocum sat bolt upright in the saddle. Ali had flushed a bear, and it was a big one.

"Brown bear," Slocum said in a low voice, not wanting to draw any more attention to himself than necessary. "Not a grizzly."

"So it is not worth shooting?" The maharajah lowered his rifle and hesitated as if thinking it over. His horse began backing and threatened to bolt and run as it caught the bear's scent. The prince controlled it with his knees while he brought the rifle to his shoulder again.

"It's coming this way!" Slocum grabbed for his rifle, but the approaching bear caused his stallion to rear and paw at the air. Slocum was off-balance and fell heavily to the ground. He struggled to get to his feet but couldn't get traction on the grassy stretch where he lay sprawled. He rolled, grabbing his rifle as he got out of the bear's path.

The maharajah's horse let out a frightened neigh and finally forced him to grab for the reins. The horse ran away with him, leaving Slocum to face the bear on his own. He kept rolling as he pulled the rifle in close to his body, then he slammed against a rock and came to a sitting position. From this awkward posture he brought the rifle up and squeezed the trigger.

The hammer fell with a dull thud.

Slocum hastily levered another round into the chamber and immediately felt the new cartridge jam in the action. He struggled to clear the breech, but the bear roared and charged straight for him. Ali had been too effective in flushing their quarry.

Slocum dropped the rifle and sprang to his feet. His hand flashed for his six-shooter and whipped it out to fire point-blank at the bear's head. He saw the bear recoil as the .36 caliber bullet smashed into the heavy-boned skull directly between the eyes, but the slug wasn't heavy enough to do any damage to such a powerful beast. Slocum had struck it at the thickest portion of its skull and had only enraged it further.

He tried to scramble up the rocks behind him, but the bear was on him in an instant. Powerful, hairy arms circled him and tried to crush the life from him. Slocum winced as claws cut painfully into his back, holding him in place against the bear's broad, smelly chest.

Slocum had heard stories of how mountain men had escaped such a deadly embrace. No man was strong enough to fight a bear, even a brown bear, but many were brave enough and clever enough to know the habits of such an animal.

Slocum went limp in the bear's grip. He closed his eyes and held his breath, hoping against hope he did not appear alive any longer. Bears ate live food. He had to convince the bear that he was dead. No matter how powerful the shaking, Slocum remained as limp as a dishrag. With a furious roar, the bear threw him a dozen feet. Slocum hit the rock, felt skin being ripped off and let himself slip down. He hoped his acting was good enough to convince the bear he was dead.

The brown bear roared in rage. A loud report sounded and rock chips showered down on Slocum's face. He winced. Opening one eye a fraction he saw that the bear had lost interest in him because the maharajah was firing methodically at it with his powerful rifle.

Roaring as it reared on hind legs, the bear issued its challenge to the maharajah. Then the bear reconsidered its defiance and dropped to all fours. With impressive speed, the bear headed for the thicket a dozen yards away and vanished from sight. Slocum continued to lie doggo, not wanting to risk having the bear come roaring back.

"I say, Mr. Slocum, are you dead?"

Slocum opened his eyes. The maharajah stood over him, the rifle pointing directly at his chest. For a moment, Slocum wondered if the real threat came from this man rather than the bear, but he figured the maharajah could have plugged him at any time.

"I'm scratched up but still in one piece—I think." Slocum winced as he tried to move his left arm. His shirt was soaked with the sluggishly flowing blood from the claw tracks on his back.

"I fear I missed the monster. He was a powerful beast. But you say he was not a grizzly?"

"A brown bear," Slocum said, standing. Every bone in his body ached as he moved, but he was alive. He had always wondered if the tall tales spun by the mountain men were true on how to keep from getting killed by a bear. He wished he could stand all of those rugged men a drink for actually telling the truth.

It had saved his life.

"I must find Ali. Where did he go?" The maharajah rode away, clutching his rifle and looking about for his servant.

Slocum picked up his rifle and examined the action. He went cold inside when he saw how the jammed cartridge had been bent. He pried it loose and saw several scratch marks on the side of the brass. Slocum looked around and found the first round that had misfired. The primer was missing. He had tried to fire a defective shell, then had pumped in a bent cartridge.

Someone had sabotaged his rifle and hoped it would kill him.

It almost had. Now he was fuming mad.

13

The ride back to camp was slow and, for Slocum, both thoughtful and painful. Every move, every bounce, every time he twisted just a little caused pain to lance into his back where the bear had clawed him. But the pain vanished into a dull ache when he considered how someone had tried to kill him. A jammed rifle while bear hunting was not quite a death sentence, but it was damned close. There was no question that someone had tampered with the first round so it would not fire. They knew anyone having a hang fire on one round would hastily lever in a second.

This had been bent in such a way that it jammed the action. By the time Slocum could have cleared it, the bear would have had him for lunch.

"It is a pity we could not track the bear. For such a large creature, it proved very elusive," the maharajah said. "We might have found it had you been in better condition, Mr. Slocum."

"Sorry," Slocum said sarcastically. "I didn't mean to spoil your hunt by getting mauled."

"Oh, do not worry over it. There will be other days, other bears. If this was not the ferocious grizzly of which you spoke, perhaps we can flush one of them. That would provide a fine hunt."

Before Slocum could tell the maharajah what he thought of the idea, he caught sight of a dozen horses tethered outside the camp. He hardly thought it possible that Darlene had assembled another lynch mob, and if she had, would they be so bold as to ride into the main camp? Mobs tended to be cowardly and preyed on solitary men. To tangle with all of the maharajah's servants would be nothing short of a major war.

"What's going on?" demanded the prince from horseback. He looked down his long nose at the men gathered around the largest of the fire pits in the camp.

"That's Marshal Rothbottom," Slocum said in a low voice. "He's the local law."

"I know who it is," the maharajah said testily. Slocum quieted down. He remembered how the lawman had been loath to come out before and reckoned the maharajah had paid him off. By showing up like this, all bets were off because the marshal had enough firepower riding with him to enforce any law.

"Glad to see you, Your Highness," Rothbottom said. The marshal hitched up his gun belt and looked as if he had eaten something that didn't set well with him. He chewed on his lower lip a moment, then squared his shoulders. "We got business here. Law business. A complaint's been lodged 'gainst one of your folks."

"Gasim?" Slocum looked around but did not see the mahout.

"Who? Nope, Slocum, ain't the elephant driver fella," said Rothbottom. "It's that woman yonder."

Both Slocum and the maharajah were speechless when two deputies dragged Lakshmi from her tent.

"Yep, that's the lady what had charges filed 'gainst her."

"What's she charged with?" asked Slocum.

"Attempted murder. Reckon there'll be other charges

since she didn't actually succeed. Disturbin' the peace, most likely, and dischargin' a firearm inside the town limits of Hoback Junction. That'll keep her locked up 'til we kin get this all squared away."

"Who'd she try to kill?" Slocum saw the confusion and outright terror on Lakshmi's face. He guessed that police taking away a suspect in India was the same as a death warrant. She reached out for Slocum—or was it the prince?—and got manacles clamped around her slender wrists. In a flash she was chained and hauled away.

"We can settle this matter. You said the matter was an attempt at murder." The maharajah rode closer to the marshal, but Slocum saw this wasn't going to work. Rothbottom had men coming up behind him with rifles and shotguns to prevent him from being intimidated or bribed. They weren't going to be robbed of a prisoner this time.

The maharajah was oblivious to the signs as he swung down to the ground and smoothed wrinkles from his dusty clothing. With an easy move, he rested the heavy rifle in the crook of his left arm.

"Who was shot at?" Slocum rode closer and dismounted to put himself on the same level as the marshal. He still towered over the man but didn't make the lawman feel as much like a rat trapped in a corner by standing on the ground.

"That friend of yers," Rothbottom said.

"Darlene?" Slocum wasn't too surprised. If she couldn't get a lynch mob to string up one of the maharajah's men for killing Hugh, she would come at the Indians from another direction.

"We gotta git on back to town with our prisoner." Rothbottom pushed Slocum out of the way. Slocum resisted for a second, then stepped away. This wasn't the place to make a fight of it.

"You'll let her have visitors?" asked Slocum.

Rothbottom chewed a bit more on his lip, then nodded briskly.

"Them's the rules. Only one at a time, then only if'n she wants to see ya."

"Wait, you cannot do this. She is under my protection."

"Wrong, Maharajah," said the marshal. "She's under mine now."

Slocum grabbed the maharajah's wrist to keep him from bringing up his hunting rifle and doing something he would regret. He wasn't supreme ruler here and would end up in a cell next to Lakshmi—or worse. The posse was hungering for a fight. If the maharajah started it, they'd feel all the more righteous about the outcome.

Ali growled like a dog. Slocum favored him with a glare, then tightened his grip on the maharajah's wrist.

"Let it be," he said softly. "We'll work this out, but not here, not right now."

"Do not *ever* touch me," the maharajah said angrily. He jerked free, and stalked off to his tent, Ali trailing behind. Several in the posse snickered and made vulgar comments about a man who wore baggy trousers like that, but the marshal had enough common sense to shut them up before trouble started. They might prevail in a fight but not before several of them ended up candidates for the potter's field outside of town.

Slocum watched the maharajah disappear into his tent and the marshal's posse ride off with Lakshmi, heading back to town. Slocum cursed a blue streak at how dumb Darlene could be, then headed for his campsite to tend to his rifle and check the rest of his ammo for tampering. It took him close to an hour to get himself patched up and his horse and rifle tended before he headed into town. He expected to see the maharajah also preparing to see Lakshmi but the prince had gone to his tent in high dudgeon and had not shown his face. That suited Slocum just fine. It was better if he dealt with the marshal to get Lakshmi free since he wasn't as likely to ruffle the lawman's feathers.

Then he'd have to talk to Darlene and settle matters

once and for all. If she kept butting in, he wasn't likely to ever find out what had happened to Hugh Malley.

As Slocum rode into Hoback Junction he saw a definite change in the sleepy town. Men strutted up and down the street, carrying rifles or wearing iron strapped to their hips like gunfighters. None of them looked as if they had any idea how to use those six-shooters but that made them even more dangerous—they thought they did.

"Figured you'd be along sometime soon, Slocum," greeted the marshal as Slocum dismounted beside the jailhouse. He couldn't keep from wincing as pain drilled into his back and arms. "What's wrong with you? You look all chewed up and spit out."

"Tangled with a bear," Slocum said. His other shirt had been ruined, clawed into bloody tatters. The one he wore was his spare, and it had seen better days.

"Yeah, sure," the marshal said, not believing a word of it. "You want to come on in and palaver a spell? She's been askin' for him, but I reckon she'd be happy to see you."

The inside of the jailhouse was hot and dusty, causing Slocum to choke.

"Be glad you don't have to sit round here waitin' fer some lawbreakin' jist so's you kin go breathe some fresh air," Rothbottom said, trying to make a joke.

"What'll it take to bail her out?"

"Can't do that. I'd have a riot on my hands. The citizens of this here town have taken it into their heads to run off that Indian prince fellow. When they found out the boogeyman scarin' 'em all was an elephant, well, mad don't hardly describe it."

Slocum understood that. The townspeople had been worked up over spirits of the dead and strange monsters lurking in the Grand Tetons, maybe spawned in the Yellowstone geysers, and had discovered an odd, if commonplace reason for the sounds that had scared the bejesus out of them. They were as mad at themselves for being frightened as they were at the maharajah for bringing the elephant into their mountains.

That made them all the more dangerous. Slocum remembered the sight of the men prancing up and down the street with six-guns strapped on their hips when not one in a dozen had worn such deadly hardware a few days earlier.

"It's not right holding Lakshmi without bail. She didn't kill anyone, after all."

"She'd hightail it at the first chance. She don't live here, after all."

Slocum didn't bother pointing out that if Lakshmi turned tail and ran it might be the best for everyone concerned. He looked past the half-open door into the cell area. The calaboose had all of four cells, made from inch-wide strips of iron riveted together into a cage.

"You wanna go on back and talk, Slocum, you kin do it. But don't take too long. Folks might get kinda uneasy if you're too chummy."

Slocum let the marshal take his Colt Navy and pushed past the door. It had hinges that didn't work, even a little. Once in the cellblock he saw they were rusted completely through.

"John!" Lakshmi rushed to the wide strips of iron and tried to reach through but couldn't do it satisfactorily. That didn't stop her from skinning her knuckles touching his hand.

"What did you say to Darlene? Anything?"

"I do not know this woman! She is the one who came to town with you and Hugh Malley, but I do not know her. Why should I threaten to kill her as they say?"

Slocum made small talk, mostly letting Lakshmi vent her frustration as he studied the jail. The cage only went around on four sides. The door was a separate piece, and the back wall with the heavily barred window in it was not protected by the strips. Slocum wondered if a stick of dynamite would blow out the wall and not kill anyone in the small cell. He doubted it.

"I'll talk some sense into her," Slocum said. "If she drops the charges, the marshal has to let you go."

"The people of this town," Lakshmi said, shuddering. "They will not let me go. What have I done to them to deserve this?"

"Who's the Britisher the maharajah is hunting for?" Slocum asked.

"I do not know!" Lakshmi began crying. She buried her face in her palms and shook silently. "Why do you ask that?"

"Might be it has something to do with the way the folks are treating you," Slocum said. "Or not. This might all be Darlene's doing."

Lakshmi looked up and forced herself to be calm.

"I know nothing about Hugh Malley's death. Gasim said it was an accident. I believe him."

"If the maharajah told Gasim to kill Hugh and then lie, saying it was an accident, would Gasim do that?"

"Yes," Lakshmi said in a small voice. "But why would he?" •

"Might have something to do with why he's hunting for a Brit," Slocum said. He didn't think the maharajah would have been so disappointed that Hugh was Welsh that he had him killed, but Hugh might have said or done something to spark such an end.

"Slocum, git your ass outta there. Vistin' hours're over," Marshal Rothbottom shouted from the office.

"I'll get you out of here," Slocum said.

Lakshmi said nothing. The expression on her face told him she doubted that he could do anything for her. That made Slocum all the more intent on freeing her from the jail. He slid between door and jamb back into the outer office and retrieved his six-shooter.

"Don't go stirrin' up trouble now, Slocum. You hear?"

"I understand, Marshal," Slocum said, but that was exactly what he intended doing.

He stepped out of the tiny, close jailhouse into the fresh air and felt a wave of relief wash over him. He didn't cotton much to jails at the best of times, and this was hardly a good time. The only bright spot Slocum could see was that it was Lakshmi locked up inside and not him. With any luck, Darlene would talk to him and they could settle this matter in a few minutes.

Slocum went to the hotel and asked after Darlene, but the clerk said she had checked out. He looked into the general store where Darlene had a job clerking and was told she was in a small building out back. Slocum stopped and gathered his wits. The outbuilding was hardly the size of a coffin, but Darlene was getting free rent here while she worked at the store. From the way the storeowner had talked, though, she wouldn't be here much longer unless she got to work fast. There wasn't room for slackers in Hoback Junction.

Knocking on the door, Slocum waited. He heard scraping noises from inside. Right hand on his six-gun, he pushed the door open with his left. Darlene sat on a three-legged stool beside a cot. She dragged her fingernails endlessly over the top of a small table. Darlene looked up with listless eyes.

"Hello, John."

"Are you all right?" he asked. Whatever had happened to her seemed to have unhinged her mind.

"As good as anybody can be who's almost been killed." Darlene's voice rose in pitch until it was downright shrill. "She tried to kill me. The bitch tried to shoot me!"

"You saw her?"

"I, yes, I saw her." Darlene looked away, studying the scratch marks in the table as if she might discern who had killed Hugh there. Slocum heard something more in her words and hesitation.

"You don't rightly know who shot at you, do you?"

"Her. The Indian bitch! She did it. It had to be her."

"Why?"

Before Darlene could answer, an unearthly screech filled the air. Slocum sprang to his feet and dashed outside, looking around. Screams of panic came from the streets. A new sound replaced the screech. Slocum recognized instantly the exultant trumpeting of the maharajah's huge elephant.

Leaving Darlene behind, he dashed into the street and looked toward the jailhouse in time to see Ali pulling Lakshmi into the small box fitted on the elephant's back. The wall of the hoosegow had been pulled out. Slocum guessed the elephant was more versatile than he had imagined. He slipped his six-shooter back into his holster as Ali urged the elephant to a fast trot out of town.

Slocum looked around. No one was to be seen. All the citizens of Hoback Junction had taken cover at the first sign of the elephant. In a way he couldn't blame them.

But he knew the fear would wear off and be replaced by anger soon. Then they would get their ropes and guns and go hunting for elephant—and Lakshmi.

14

Slocum stood in the middle of the street and wondered how long people had to be gone before a town became a ghost town. Hoback Junction was well on the way if it meant no-body was wandering the streets, no curtains pulled back for fearful looks from the safety of houses, and the law had abandoned the town. Ali, astride the elephant, had spooked the citizens something fierce. Slocum heard movement and turned to see Darlene stumbling out into the street from the mercantile, looking confused. Slocum went to her.

"Are you all right?" Darlene spoke as if someone else put the words in her mouth. "I don't want you hurt, John. You're all I have left. Hugh's dead. And everyone else?" Darlene looked around, as Slocum had been doing. Her tear-filled eyes did no better finding the people of Hoback Junction than his sharper ones had.

"They'll come out of their holes eventually," Slocum said. He put his arm around Darlene's shoulders and steered her to a rickety wood chair on the boardwalk in front of the general store. He gently pushed her down into the chair and knelt in front of her.

"What am I supposed to do, John?" she asked.

"Tell me what happened last night. When someone shot at you."

"I was going to my room behind the store." Darlene pointed vaguely in the direction of the rear of the store. "It was quite dark. I heard a strange sound, very soft, rustling. Like silk rubbing against more silk. Then I saw light reflecting off a gun. I screamed and she fired. That horrid woman. The one you call Lakshmi."

"So you saw her face?"

"Well, no," Darlene admitted. "It had to be her, though. Who else wears silk around here?"

"The men in the maharajah's camp do," Slocum said, remembering the maharajah's own silk trousers. The servants even had jackets made of silk. It was a tough material, light and cool for traveling in tropical climes. For an American, silk was a luxury item. For the Indians it was a useful material, and one the maharajah certainly could afford for himself and those in his employ.

"They do?"

"Could it have been a man who shot at you?"

"The wrist," Darlene said, thinking harder now. "It was a bit thick for a woman's wrist. But I don't know. It might have been, but I think it was Lakshmi."

"Do you want it to be the woman?" Slocum saw the way Darlene's cheeks flushed as she looked away guiltily. She had some idea what might have gone on between Slocum and the seductive, exotic woman. Darlene had lost one sweetheart and obviously had her sights set on Slocum. He wasn't the kind who could be corralled and branded by any woman, and jealousy was only going to get people killed.

Slocum didn't want one of them to be Lakshmi.

"I want them to all leave," Darlene blurted. "Please, John, find who killed Hugh and why. I need to know why they'd do such a horrible thing."

Slocum worried that it might have been an accident, but his gut told him there was more boiling under the surface

calm at the maharajah's camp than met the eye. But whatever was there, he doubted Lakshmi would try to kill Darlene. There was no reason he could think of for the Indian
woman to do such a thing.

"I'll find out what happened to him," Slocum said. "You
keep to yourself and don't go raising any posses." He tried
to make it sound light and upbeat but wasn't sure how well
he succeeded.

Slocum left Darlene and found his horse. By now a few
of the townspeople poked out of their hidey-holes but
nowhere did he see Marshal Rothbottom. The lawman
might be hiding in the back cell of his jail, if it hadn't been
completely destroyed when Ali got the elephant to free
Lakshmi. More likely, the marshal was halfway to the next
county.

Swinging into the saddle, Slocum trotted from Hoback
Junction and headed directly for the maharajah's camp. He
needed more information than he had to find out what was
going on. He shook his head remembering how innocently
this had started. The people in town had heard strange
noises, and Hugh had gone after the reward. He had been
trampled to death soon after.

Slocum had almost reached the Indian prince's camp
when he heard Lakshmi calling his name. He drew rein and
looked around but did not see the woman.

"Here, John, over here." Lakshmi stepped out from beside a tree alongside the road. Her expression was tense.
Slocum knew she had reason to be worried, not knowing
when the marshal would get his posse together to come after her for breaking out of jail.

"You've certainly stirred the pot a mite since the last
time I saw you," he said. "Why'd you break out of jail? I
told you I'd talk to Darlene. She admitted to me that it
might have been a man who shot at her. All she saw was a
hand holding a gun. She thought it must be you because
she heard the sound of silk sliding against silk."

"But all the men wear silk clothing," Lakshmi said, dismayed.

"She would have dropped charges," Slocum said. "Now you've got to dodge the marshal for jailbreak."

"I did not want to leave. I was going to do what you said, but Ali came with the elephant." Lakshmi looked even more distressed.

"We can smooth it out, but you're going to have to pay for the damage to the jailhouse," Slocum said.

"Please, that can wait. I have found something, John. I was going through my brother's papers and—"

"Your brother?" Slocum was confused. Lakshmi looked at him. Her thin eyebrows rose and the red *bindi* dot between her eyes seemed to crinkle with the beginnings of real humor. For the first time Lakshmi smiled broadly, even if she did not laugh outright.

"My brother," she said. "I thought you knew. The maharajah is my brother."

"I didn't even guess," Slocum said.

"He is not a maharajah, either. He is only a raja. Still important but lesser in rank. Our father might one day be maharajah, but I do not believe it will happen."

"That's all?" Slocum asked. "Your brother's not really the high muckety-muck he's been pretending to be?"

"No, no, John. He is quite an important man, but he puts on airs when he is abroad. Please," she said in exasperation. "I found why he came to your West. He is looking for a British citizen, a remittance man."

Slocum frowned. Many British lords had second and third sons who would never inherit either title or family estates because of the law of primogeniture. Rather than keep a useless drone about, these sons were often shipped off to America where they received a small allowance every month to stay away from the serious business of running the family estates. Most of these remittance men were drunkards and ne'er-do-wells Slocum viewed with the same contempt he did any wastrel unwilling to work for a living.

"Why does he want to find this Brit?"

"I do not know. All I saw was the paper with the man's name. Will Harrison. From maps he lives somewhere on the eastern slope of the Grand Tetons."

"That sure cuts down on where to look for him," Slocum said sarcastically. There must be a hundred thousand square miles of rock on the eastern slope of the mountains.

"I have a specific location." Lakshmi held out a map. Slocum took it and spent a few seconds getting oriented. He turned slowly, matched the map with topographical features of the Grand Tetons and then quickly figured distances.

"Might be a day's ride off. Two at the most. What is this place where Will Harrison is?"

Lakshmi shrugged her lovely shoulders.

"If we find Harrison, what's in it for us?" asked Slocum. "Will your brother fess up to what happened to Hugh Malley?"

"I do not know," Lakshmi said, "but I do know that he will leave Wyoming and America when he finds Will Harrison. I want to leave, John. Please do not take this wrongly. I hate this place. I hate all that has happened, and I miss my own country. In this country no one can tell another's social caste and everything is so wild and confused. I wish my brother had never brought me along."

"You didn't have a choice?"

"He is my brother," she said, casting her eyes downward. "In my country women do not have the freedom they do in yours."

Slocum snorted. Wyoming was different from most other places in the country. From what he had heard, they agitated to give women the vote and even had mentioned the possibility of a woman being governor. But folks in Wyoming were considered strange everywhere else he traveled throughout the West, even—especially—in adjoining Utah Territory.

"I'm not traipsing off to find this Harrison fellow unless I get answers to how Hugh died."

"Please, John, for me. I must leave this place."

"Take that up with your raja brother."

"I . . . I cannot. The reason I rifled through his papers was because of Ali."

"What's he got to do with this?"

"He is not the loyal servant my brother thinks. Ali tried to imprison me."

"But he rescued you from jail!"

"He tried to bind me and hide me in the mountains. He intended to barter me for Will Harrison."

"What's Ali's interest in this remittance man?" Slocum read the answer on her face before she could answer. Lakshmi didn't know. All she knew was the name and location of the man her brother sought.

Apparently Harrison was important enough for Ali to risk royal displeasure by kidnapping a princess and ransoming her for the man. Or maybe what Harrison knew. This was mining country. Maybe Will Harrison had found a rich mine and the maharajah was somehow involved in ownership.

Slocum shook his head. It felt as if it might break apart it ached so. None of that made sense. The only way to find the truth was to find Will Harrison.

"Let's go," Slocum said.

"What are you saying, John?" Lakshmi's eyebrows arched again.

"I can't leave you behind. Ali would catch you. And if he couldn't, he might decide to kill your brother if he thought you had told him anything. Does the maharajah even know you've been busted out of jail?"

Lakshmi shook her head and looked miserable.

"Then we're going to find Harrison and get to the bottom of this. Do you have a horse?"

"No, I escaped on foot. What am I to do?" Lakshmi sounded almost panicked.

"I'll steal a horse. Then we'll go see Harrison ourselves. You stay out of sight."

Slocum was taken aback when Lakshmi threw her arms around his neck and kissed him hard on the lips. He felt her body melting to match the contours of his. Worse, he began to respond to her passionate kiss. Slocum pushed her away.

"I'll be back as fast as I can."

Lakshmi caught her breath, then let it out in a sudden gust. She dropped her eyes and nodded.

Slocum slipped into the maharajah's camp and got a horse with gear without anyone seeing him. He returned to Lakshmi and they were on the trail heading deeper into the Grand Tetons within a half hour.

15

"Were there other papers in your brother's files?" asked Slocum. It was hard for him to get around the words and the notion that Lakshmi was the maharajah's sister. "Something else he could use to find Will Harrison?" Slocum worried that the maharajah's henchmen would take out after Lakshmi and figure reaching Will Harrison first was the best way to capture her again. From everything he had seen at the camp, the servants always jumped when the maharajah gave an order, but such instant obedience could cause hatred of their master. Slocum didn't know what would have turned Ali against the maharajah but it had to be something potent that had built over the years.

Slocum sucked on his gums a moment, reflecting. Lakshmi might have gotten confused. It was possible that the maharajah had ordered Ali to break his sister out of the Hoback Junction calaboose and then keep her safely out of sight until they finished their hunt for Will Harrison. She might have interpreted that as being kidnapped by Ali working on his own. There was too much he didn't know and even more that he simply guessed at.

Lakshmi did not answer right away. Slocum looked at

her as she took a sharp bend in the trail. She might not have heard him since she looked to be as deep in thought as he was. He had a powerful lot of facts to sort through, not the least being her relationship to the maharajah. A female maharajah—whatever that'd be called—obviously had less power than royalty in other countries. Slocum had heard that Great Britain, at one time a couple hundred years back, had a queen on the throne. That might have been unusual, but Lakshmi showed no hint that she held any power other than the servants scuttling around her brother's camp. Her own servant spied on her and looked to be in cahoots with Gasim.

All the servants were in league against her, Slocum decided, since Ali had broken her out of jail only to try to get the information out of the maharajah where Will Harrison was. The pot was definitely coming to a boil.

He caught up with Lakshmi. She looked at him and smiled weakly.

"You are a savior, John. I do not think I could have found Harrison without you."

"We haven't got him yet," Slocum pointed out. "Why didn't your brother plow right on up into the mountains and find him on his own? The map isn't that hard to figure out."

"I do not know," she said. "He was spending a great deal of time hunting. He is a great hunter and has bagged many tigers in India, but his heart was not in it. He was waiting, but I do not know why."

"Did he suspect his own servants might have wanted Will Harrison for their own purposes?"

"I don't know. I know so little. I just want to go home."

Lakshmi's shoulders sagged as she rode. Slocum wondered what was going on between her and her brother. Why had he brought her to America at all? There was too much he didn't know, but at least he had the map Lakshmi had stolen from the maharajah's tent. Slocum held it up and matched it to the mountains ahead. The beauty of the

Grand Tetons vanished as he studied the canyons and peaks, the location of lakes and rivers.

The distance to the mountains was deceptive because of the clear air. On the plains he often felt as if he rode in a fog, unable to see more than a mile or two at a time. But here in the mountains, he could look down and out and see for miles and miles. It made Slocum a little heartsick thinking that Hugh Malley would never see this. Then he smiled ruefully. Hugh Malley would not have appreciated these vistas. He had been a hard-rock miner whose idea of a good view was a new vein of ore a mile underground.

"Let's break for something to eat," Slocum said. They had been on the trail for better than four hours, putting a considerable number of miles behind them. It was time to let the horses rest.

"There's a good spot," Slocum said.

"I want to keep going, John," Lakshmi said. "The sooner we find this Harrison the sooner I can go home."

"And leave me behind?" Slocum's tone was light, but Lakshmi acted as if he had stabbed her.

"I am so sorry, John. I did not mean it like that."

Slocum waved off the apology. He jumped to the ground and hobbled his horse so it could eat without wandering off. At last he got a chance to look around without having to struggle with the map while on horseback. Something about the lay of the land bothered him, and he couldn't put his finger on what it might be. They were at the juncture of three valleys, one going deeper into the Grand Tetons, the one they had just traveled and another coming in at an angle.

"What's wrong?" Lakshmi asked.

"The other canyon. That one," Slocum said. "I wish I had a map showing where it led."

"Back toward Hoback Junction, I should say."

"You're probably right. That might be the canyon where Hugh Malley was supposed to go scouting for the weird noises in the night." As Slocum spoke, he thought of Hugh and how long ago it seemed that they had driven into Hoback Junction. He could have been in Nevada by now if he had kept on the trail. Slocum glanced at the powerful white stallion cropping grass. And he would never have been given such a fine horse—or lost the roan he had ridden from Colorado.

Lakshmi and elephants and nearly being killed had filled less than a week to overflowing.

"Why do you worry so about it?" asked Lakshmi.

"Don't rightly know," Slocum said, but the canyon might provide a shortcut into the Grand Tetons where they headed.

"How much farther do we have to go?"

Slocum mopped the sweat on his forehead as he studied the valley stretching ahead of them. As he put his hat back on his head a bullet jerked it from his hand and sent it flying through the air. Slocum dived for cover, shouting at Lakshmi.

The woman stood and stared at him as if he had gone crazy.

"Someone's shooting at us. Get down!"

Another shot kicked up dirt at Lakshmi's feet. This got her moving. She ran toward him, but a barrage of shots cut her off. Slocum drew his six-shooter and knew there was no point in using it. The sniper taking potshots at them used a rifle and was some distance away. The report from the rifle was muffled, and Slocum wasn't sure he even knew where the bullets were coming from.

"Stay down. I'm going after him." Slocum shoved his Colt Navy back into its holster, cast a quick, covetous glance toward his horse and the Winchester rifle resting in the saddle scabbard, then knew he could never get that far. He had to take the fight to the ambusher right away.

Keeping low, Slocum dodged back and forth amid new fire from the hidden rifleman. He reached a rockfall and caught his breath. Slocum looked back to be sure Lakshmi was staying out of the line of fire but didn't see her. He took that as good news. She was hiding and not likely to get ventilated.

Or was she?

Slocum pressed his back against the large rock and looked straight up along the curve of the boulder. He heard nothing; he saw nothing. He was sure this was the direction the shots had come from, but that didn't mean the sniper had to stay put. Slocum looked back toward where his and Lakshmi's horses nervously milled, rattling their hobbles but not panicking yet. Both had been around gunfire enough not to rear unless the slugs came mighty close.

Slocum wanted to call to Lakshmi but decided not to. He glanced upward into the rocks again and made his decision. Rather than making his way through the jagged rocks to reach the spot where the sniper had shot at them, he edged along the base of the rockfall, then cut back toward the spot where he had left Lakshmi.

On the way Slocum spotted a fresh footprint in soft dirt and knew he had been right. The sniper had taken several quick shots at them to lure Slocum away from Lakshmi, then had headed for the woman like a bee flying back to its honey hive.

Slocum slipped his six-shooter from its holster and got ready to kill. He hurried along, not worrying as much about falling into another trap as saving Lakshmi. Slocum wasn't surprised when he saw Ali holding a rifle on the woman.

Slocum gestured that Lakshmi wasn't to give any sign that he was behind the Indian servant, but she was a lousy actress. Her eyes widened, she turned toward him and said something in Hindi and gave Slocum away. Ali whirled about, his rifle blazing as he came. Bullets ricocheted off rocks and drove Slocum to cover.

"Run!" he shouted to Lakshmi. But the woman stood

frozen to the spot, whether in fear or simple indecision he could not say. All Slocum could do to help her was fire a couple rounds in Ali's direction.

"I will kill her!" shrieked Ali. "Go away. Leave us alone. You do not know what you are meddling in."

"Why don't you tell me?" Slocum began circling, angling to get a better shot at Ali. The man was clever enough to change position so any shot Slocum might take that missed its target would endanger Lakshmi.

"You cannot know. It is forbidden. I have taken an oath. Go! Leave us!"

"You'd kill the maharajah's sister?" Slocum played for time. He wanted Ali's attention split in as many ways as possible, but it didn't work. The servant ignored the wild shots Slocum sent his way and concentrated on capturing Lakshmi. He knew this was his trump card and nothing was going to sway him from taking her prisoner.

Slocum threw caution to the winds and launched a full-scale frontal assault. He pounded hard and fast to the spot where Lakshmi had stood, but the woman was nowhere to be seen. Neither was Ali. Slocum knew better than to stand in the middle of a clearing, gawking at their sudden disappearance. He flopped to the ground and wriggled like a snake until he found their footprints crushed into the tall grass. He followed fast and found them twenty yards away, at the edge of a stand of trees.

Like a prairie dog, he popped up and looked around, then went back to ground. Lakshmi made no effort to struggle or hold Ali back. Slocum cursed such bad luck on his part that she was such a willing victim. If she had kicked him or fought the least bit he could have gotten a good shot at Ali.

Slocum heard Lakshmi's voice and followed it. A loud slap silenced her, but he had the right direction now. He angled from the footprints toward the new position and knew instantly that Ali had laid a trap for him. He backpedaled and listened hard. Lakshmi made no further outbursts. That meant Ali had allowed her to call out that single time to lure Slocum.

He circled wider and came at the spot from a different direction. A man hunched over, pistol clutched in his hand. But it wasn't Ali.

"Don't move and you might live to see the sunset," Slocum said to Valande. Lakshmi's servant jumped as if ants had invaded his baggy trousers. "Drop the six-shooter," Slocum ordered sharply. He sighted in on the Indian servant and waited to squeeze off the round that would take the man's life.

Valande understood his problem and dropped the six-gun.

"You do not understand," Valande said. "I try to catch Ali. He has kidnapped my mistress."

Slocum hesitated. Valande had made a career out of spying on everyone in the maharajah's camp, especially Lakshmi.

"What are you doing out here?"

"Ali took her from the jail. I followed. I must save her from him."

Slocum lowered his six-shooter just a mite, then realized he had been tricked.

"I will shoot you, Slocum," came Ali's cold boast. "I will enjoy it. You have meddled where you were not welcome."

From the corner of his eye Slocum saw Ali had his knife to Lakshmi's slender throat. A single quick movement would behead her in a bloody fountain. Slocum turned back to Valande and saw the servant scooping up his dropped six-shooter, but it wasn't to fire at Ali. Valande pointed his pistol at Slocum.

"It is as you said, Ali," Valande said. "He is a fool. He tried to rescue her."

"Be quiet," Ali said. Lakshmi struggled a little, but Ali

drove his knife into her soft throat, bringing a tiny bead of blood to mar the flawless mahogany flesh. To Slocum, Ali said, "The map. Give me the map she stole from the rajah."

"No, John. Don't. I don't know what they want with Will Harrison but—" Lakshmi's words died in a gurgle as Ali circled her throat with his powerful arm and squeezed. Lakshmi went limp.

As Slocum started for Ali, Valande fired his pistol. The man's aim was poor and the slug ripped in front of Slocum, tearing up a patch of grass. But it was enough to stop Slocum in his tracks. That bullet could as easily have blasted out Lakshmi's heart.

"You have done well," Ali said to Valande.

Slocum watched and cried out to Valande, but he was too late. Ali drew a small pistol from the broad silk waistband of his trousers, aimed and fired in a smooth, deliberate motion. Valande's arms rose as if on strings, then he sank straight down. Ali's bullet had caught him in the middle of the forehead and killed him instantly.

"The map," Ali said. He pointed the small pistol at Slocum. Seeing this had little effect, he pointed the gun at Lakshmi's head. The woman was still unconscious at his feet and was not going to dodge. Slocum didn't see how Ali could miss at point-blank range. Frustration rose to the point of cold hatred for the Indian servant. Slocum certainly could not cover the ground between him and the armed man before the bullet robbed Lakshmi of her life.

"What's so important about Will Harrison?" Slocum reached into his pocket and pulled out the many-times-folded map. He held it far from his body, hoping Ali's attention would focus on it rather than the more obvious target Slocum presented.

Ali sneered at such a transparent ploy and shifted the gun straight to a point in the center of Slocum's chest. Slocum twitched in anticipation of the bullet driving a hot leaden path through him.

16

Slocum figured he was a goner. He couldn't outrun a bullet, and at this distance Ali wasn't going to miss.

The sudden trumpeting of an elephant startled both men. Ali jerked about at the sound. Slocum felt the heavy footfalls of the monstrous beast through the ground under his boot soles. The instant Ali whirled and his pistol turned away from its target, he found himself contending with more than the sound of a charging elephant.

Slocum dived. He took two quick steps, launched himself and stretched out his arms to circle Ali's waist. He caught the gun hand in the cordon of his arms as he clamped down hard. Ali fought but was off-balance and staggered back. Slocum winced as a hot streak passed along his leg. Ali had fired in spite of his hand being tangled up in Slocum's embrace.

They crashed to the ground, rolling over and over. Ali's pistol discharged again, but it missed Slocum this time. He concentrated on getting his hands around the Indian's muscular throat. Try as Slocum might, he found the man too sinuous and strong. Slocum flopped away, gasping for air after Ali kicked him in the belly.

"G-get him!" Slocum pointed in the direction Ali had lit

143

out but the maharajah, from his vantage high on the back of the elephant in his decorated carriage box, either did not hear or chose to ignore the warning.

Slocum sat up, bent double for a moment and sucked the wind back into his lungs. He got to his feet and hurried to Lakshmi. The woman's eyelids flickered, but she didn't awaken. Slocum left her on the ground, grabbed his fallen six-shooter, then picked up the one Valande had dropped when Ali had killed him.

He looked up and swallowed hard. The maharajah had almost run him over with the charging elephant, but the gargantuan beast had stopped a few yards away. Gasim sweated heavily as he struggled with the rampaging, nervous creature. For a moment Slocum thought the elephant would toss the mahout from his perch behind the huge head, but Gasim clung tenaciously and his experience using his feet behind the ears controlled the beast's worst impulses.

"Is she hurt? I will kill him with my bare hands if that pig has harmed her!" The maharajah scrambled from the small *howdah* carrier on the elephant's back. He did not wait for Gasim to get the elephant to its knees but slid over the bulging gray side, gripped the straps and used them to lower himself.

"She's all right," Slocum said. "Did you see where Ali went?"

The maharajah knelt at Lakshmi's side and cradled her head. He looked up at Slocum.

"You saved her. Thank you for this inestimable service."

"Ali wants to kill us all," Slocum said. "Where'd the son of a bitch go? Did you see him before you came down from the elephant?"

The maharajah shrugged. "I think he went up the slope, where the elephant cannot go."

"I didn't expect to see the elephant this far up in the mountains," Slocum admitted.

"You forget your history. Hannibal crossed the Alps with an army led by war elephants."

Slocum stared blankly at the prince. He had no idea who Hannibal was, but he had heard of Hannibal, Missouri. He refrained from asking if this wasn't another of Mark Twain's wild tales.

Slocum eyed Gasim as the mahout dismounted and began tending to the elephant. The gashes on its broad gray side where the cougar had clawed it were covered with a thick yellowish paste that seemed to take any soreness or pain from the animal.

"What about him?" Slocum pointed at Gasim. "Can you trust him?"

"I have no choice," the maharajah said. "Who else can control the elephant? My other one is due to arrive soon, but until then, I am forced to use the battle-weary veteran."

"What?" Lakshmi stirred. Her brother immediately caressed her cheek. Lakshmi's eyelids fluttered.

"John?" She recoiled slightly seeing it was the maharajah who held her rather than Slocum. "I am sorry. I did not know."

"You are well, my sister. That is all that matters."

"Hate to burst your balloon," Slocum said, "but that's not all that matters. Ali is on the loose. I've got a score to settle with him."

"Is he the one?" asked Lakshmi. Seeing the maharajah's perplexed look, she added, "The one who killed his friend, Hugh Malley."

"That was an accident," the prince said. "It is of no concern."

"I—" Lakshmi started to speak but fell silent when she caught Gasim's eye. Slocum touched the six-shooter at his side and wondered how loyal the mahout was. The maharajah obviously found it difficult to believe any of his servants could turn on him. Slocum didn't bother pointing out how both Ali and Valande had tried to kill his sister.

"I'll go after him," Slocum said.

"It is not a good idea to split one's forces," the maharajah said. "We will rest before continuing on—together."

Slocum felt as if he were being pulled into the mountains after Ali. The Grand Tetons were lovely, but he wanted to add a stream of blood down their slopes. Ali couldn't escape punishment for kidnapping Lakshmi and trying to kill her. In his gut Slocum thought Ali was responsible for Hugh's death, too. The servant was the kingpin in the revolt against the prince's authority.

"Who is Will Harrison and why are you hunting for him?" Slocum addressed the question to the maharajah but looked squarely at Gasim. The mahout's impassive face might have been carved from a block of mahogany, but Slocum thought he saw a slight twitch around the eyes. Gasim knew more about this hunt than he was letting on— and certainly had a greater interest in finding Harrison than was likely for an injured elephant driver.

"This is of no concern to you," the maharajah said. "It is a matter of honor and duty."

Slocum fell silent. It sounded as if the maharajah wanted to kill Harrison. That made sense in a way, but it struck Slocum as a long way to go to carry on a blood feud. India was half the world away. Maybe on the other side of the Alps the maharajah's Hannibal had crossed.

"We rest, then we go after Will Harrison," the maharajah said firmly.

For the first time since Ali had put his pistol to Lakshmi's head, Slocum hunted for the scrap of paper Lakshmi had found in her brother's files. He hunted for it but it was gone. He didn't remember dropping it but things had been mighty hot for a spell and a tattered piece of paper had not been his primary concern.

"I will talk to Gasim about the elephant," the maharajah said. He glanced from Slocum to his sister. A look of disapproval was evident. "I shall return quickly."

"He saved my life," Lakshmi said, a little too stridently for Slocum's taste. Pleading with the maharajah wasn't the way to gain anything.

"I won't let any harm come to her," Slocum said. "On my word."

"Yes, on your word," the prince said glumly. He took Gasim by the shoulder and aimed the mahout toward the elephant, now noisily enjoying a meal of knee-high grass. When they were out of earshot, Slocum spoke to Lakshmi.

"Ali has the map. I must have dropped it when he was threatening you."

"It does not matter. I remember it well." She smiled weakly. "From my brother's viewpoint, it is all I do well."

"I wouldn't say that," Slocum said, grinning. "I hope you and him haven't been going through the *Kama Sutra* page by page together." He laughed when she blushed furiously and averted her eyes. It broke the tension and Lakshmi finally had to laugh, if a bit uncomfortably.

"You are a strange man, John Slocum. I like that."

"I'll tell you what I don't like. I don't like Ali being on the loose," Slocum said in a low voice. He saw the maharajah and Gasim completing their discussion about the elephant. Whatever was said did not set well with the prince. His expression matched the summer storms that regularly boiled over the jagged mountain peaks and came crashing down into the unsuspecting valleys.

"We can sneak away, for a while. There are so many things I must show you," Lakshmi said. "So many ways that I might repay you for saving my life."

Her brother stalked back and stood, hands balled on his hips as he glared at them.

"We must wait. The elephant is unable to continue for a few hours. By then it will be too dark to find Will Harrison."

"What of Ali?" asked Slocum.

"Pah. He is a nothing. An outcast. A *mieccha*!"

"What's that?" asked Slocum. "Sounds as bad as calling a gent a lily-livered, no account snake in the grass."

"Worse," Lakshmi said. "It is the castless of our society. The untouchable. No one has anything to do with them. They are beneath contempt and notice."

"We will find Will Harrison in the morning," the maharajah said decisively, as if this made it so. He struck a fine pose, but to Slocum that was all it was. Bluster and show for Lakshmi's sake and nothing more.

"You have a map for finding him?" Slocum saw a slight smile twitch the man's lips as he looked at his sister. He knew she had stolen the map from his files.

"I have the real one," he said softly. Reaching into his jacket, he pulled out a sheet of paper identical to the other, but from the quick look Slocum got, he saw significant differences. Slocum let out a little sigh of relief. The map Ali had was a fake, a decoy the prince had planted in his belongings against such a theft.

"I am not so stupid after all, eh, Mr. Slocum?"

"Never said you were," Slocum replied but that had been exactly what had crossed his mind. He looked over his shoulder in Gasim's direction and said in a whisper, "What of him? Can he be trusted?"

"Gasim? No more than the others," the maharajah said. "And no less. He is a loyal retainer. He is from Afghanistan, a *wilavatis*. What the British call a mercenary."

"So he's likely to sell out to the highest bidder? What can Ali offer him that you can't?"

"You go on so about Ali. Forget him. He is untouchable. His name will never again pass your lips."

Slocum wasn't going to argue the point. Knowing that Gasim had fought for money made it all the more likely he could be bought. As rich as the maharajah looked, he didn't seem the kind to spread the wealth around among his hired hands.

"I'll pitch my bedroll over yonder," Slocum said, pointing to a clump of trees some distance away.

"What am I to do for my tent?" asked the maharajah. Seeing Slocum's expression, he suddenly grinned and said, "Ah, the American reluctance to serve one's better. That is all right. Lakshmi can pitch it."

"What about Gasim? If you offer him enough, he'll likely do it." The sarcasm was lost on the prince.

"He must tend the elephant. The beast's wounds are substantial and must be tended and permitted to heal properly. I do wish the other elephant had arrived before we left Hoback Junction."

"How many of those elephants do you have?" Slocum asked.

"Many. I am a mighty king of the Rajput."

"He is only a rajah," Lakshmi said, "but already he thinks of the day when our father is gone and he is a real maharajah."

"Be quiet, woman," the prince said.

"Where's your gear?" Slocum asked, cutting off a tirade. "I'll pitch your tent for you."

With ill grace the maharajah showed Slocum how the gear had been stowed in the elephant carriage. The tent was light and easily handled until a breeze kicked up, blowing down forcefully from the upper slopes. Slocum's sharp sense of smell caught a hint of rain on the wind, but he could not decide if they were in for a sudden shower or if he was only catching the edge of a storm on the far side of the mountains.

"The silk is quite waterproof," Lakshmi said, helping him with the ropes holding the tent upright. "It is a fine material."

"Makes better shirts than tents," Slocum said. "I won a silk shirt off a gambler in San Francisco once. I had to get a tailor to let out the shoulders but it wore real good."

"Do you still have it?"

Slocum shook his head. He had gotten a lot of blood on it—none of it his—and had found it impossible to remove. He had buried it with the owlhoot who had tried to kill him with a hunting knife.

"I will see that you get another. One with the royal insignia of Rajasthan on it."

She laid a hand on his arm and looked up at him from beneath her long dark lashes. Slocum started to tell her to wait until her brother had bedded down for the night and then he would bed her, but tiny sights and sounds came to him that brought him around.

"What is it, John?"

"I don't know." He slid his six-shooter from its holster and took a couple steps in the direction of the temporary elephant corral. "Stop!" he shouted. Slocum brought the six-gun up and fired in a smooth motion, but the range was too great for him to hope to hit Ali.

"John, no!" Lakshmi tried to hold him back. He jerked free.

"They've got your brother. Ali and Gasim, the son of a bitch. In cahoots!"

He had been right about the mahout, and it galled him he had not been able to convince the maharajah to watch his back better. At a dead run, Slocum got to the spot where Gasim had penned the elephant by simply digging a shallow trench around it. Slocum remembered that elephants could not jump, but this looked too easy. Why didn't the elephant simply step across it?

All such thoughts vanished when he saw Ali dragging the maharajah off. The prince was not putting up much of a fight.

"Let him go!"

Ali took a quick shot with his small-bore pistol. Slocum didn't even flinch at the soft *pop!* when it discharged. He tried to get a good shot at Ali, but the man used the maharajah as a shield, forcing Slocum to get closer or risk killing the man he tried to rescue.

"There, there they are!" shouted Gasim.

Slocum spun, leveled his pistol and fired at the mahout. Gasim threw up his uninjured hand in surprise, then dodged into the woods and fled. Slocum hesitated. He could go after the mahout, but Ali had the prince.

By the time he returned to the trail, Ali and his kidnap victim had disappeared.

Slocum backed toward camp, then reluctantly went to fetch his horse only to find a desolate Lakshmi standing and staring at him.

"The horses," she said in a choked voice. "They are gone. Stolen!"

"Ali's smarter and sneakier than I gave him credit for," Slocum said in disgust. "And he's got your brother."

"With the real map," Lakshmi said.

Slocum had no answer for that. He had made one bad decision after another today, and now a man's life hung in the balance. He turned slowly and stared at the elephant in its crude pen.

"What the hell?" Slocum said. "What's one more blunder?" He grabbed Lakshmi's hand and pulled her along. "Show me how to steer that damned thing," he said.

"What thing is that?" She dug her heels in and stared at him in disbelief as it dawned on her what he intended doing.

"The elephant," he said, confirming her worst fears. "How do we saddle up and ride that elephant?"

17

"He would die before he gave any information to Ali," Lakshmi said. She saw Slocum's expression and got mad. "My brother is destined to be a king one day, possibly someday soon. He is of noble caste and places honor above all else."

"Maybe so," Slocum allowed, "but I suspect Ali can get mighty persuasive. There are things Indians do with knives that no man—" Slocum broke off his angry tirade when he saw her face. "I meant Plains Indians. Sioux. Crow. Arapaho and Cheyenne."

"We have evil men who also know how to torture, but Ali is not of their caste. He is evil but does not possess such knowledge."

"It doesn't take much to figure out how to make a man scream if you don't care if he lives after you're finished," Slocum said. He stopped at the edge of the shallow trench Gasim had dug and stared at the elephant. The gray mountain of flesh bellowed loudly, raising its trunk high and looking the world like it meant to stomp on him. Slocum uneasily looked down at the shallow trench and wondered if such a small pit would contain its fury. He would have preferred to be standing on the north rim of the Grand Canyon looking at the elephant on the south rim.

"If only the horses had not been taken," Lakshmi said. "We could go after them right away."

"I suspect Gasim had a hand in that," Slocum said.

"But he never left the elephant's side," Lakshmi said. "Every time I looked, he was here."

"You weren't always looking at Gasim," Slocum said.

"I did look at you. A little." Again the shyly averted eyes contrasted so with her bold sexuality. "But I am sure Gasim did not leave the elephant." Now Lakshmi's voice rang with conviction.

Slocum wasn't inclined to argue. How Gasim had crept about and made off with the horses so Ali could nab the maharajah was something of a mystery that could wait to be solved later. Right now he was faced with four tons of angry elephant.

"Might be I could follow Ali on foot," Slocum said uneasily.

"Are you not the mighty bronco buster? That is the term, is it not?"

Slocum was stung by Lakshmi's sarcasm. He settled his Colt Navy, made sure the leather keeper was securely snugged down over the hammer to keep it from bouncing out of the holster, then stepped across the shallow ditch and was on the same side as the elephant. They were on an island of dirt in the middle of the vast Grand Tetons, and Slocum had never felt more alone. He stared up at the massive beast and was encouraged when it did not charge him. It had two short, yellowed ivory tusks capped with gold balls to prevent the elephant from inflicting serious injury on its handler.

Slocum shivered as he stepped closer. A toss of that great head and the lightest brush of a tusk would send him flying through the air, body broken and on his way to being entirely dead. He wished he could sell those tusks to some piano company for keys, *then* approach the towering gray brute.

He took another careful step forward, remembering this was the beast that had stomped on Hugh Malley and crushed the life from his body as easily as a man might snuff out a match.

"The elephant is a gentle soul," Lakshmi said from behind him. "Take the long pole, the one with the hook, and approach him. Tap him on the side of the head to turn him, then apply the shaft forcefully behind his knees to get him to kneel so you can mount."

"Sounds easy enough," Slocum said. He was sweating but he was not as frightened as he had thought he might be this close to the elephant. What Lakshmi said seemed true. The elephant showed little fear of him. This was no supernatural wendigo. It was flesh and blood, and Gasim had controlled it as easily as Slocum rode a horse. If the mercenary could do it, so could Slocum. He had worked with all kinds of animals in his day, although never one this large.

Doing as Lakshmi suggested, he found it easy enough to get the elephant to turn the way he wanted, but when he swung the pole and whacked it loudly behind the front knees, it bellowed and tried to rear. Its trunk lashed out like a thick whip and the deadly tusks forced Slocum to retreat.

"The hook! Use the hook!" Lakshmi cried. "Do not let it behave this way toward you!"

Slocum reacted instinctively and caught the elephant's large flapping ear with the hook. Using both hands on the pole, he pulled hard. Both his feet left the ground as the elephant tossed its head, but Slocum hung on and hit the ground again. He kept pulling on the hook until the elephant settled down.

"That's working," he said in surprise. He tried to swing the pole to tap the elephant's knees again but didn't have to. The elephant was already dropping down clumsily.

"Now we can go," Lakshmi said brightly. She jumped

the ditch and came over, scrambling up the side of the elephant into the ornate carriage. The *howdah* leaned precariously as she entered and finally settled down.

"Don't get too comfortable," Slocum said. "You have to leave me some room."

"But, John, you are the mahout. You ride on the neck."

Slocum stared at the still-obedient elephant and knew he had to move fast or he'd lose his nerve. He took a running jump and shinnied agilely so he could straddle the elephant's neck, feet dangling on either side. His boots pressed into the backsides of the elephant's floppy ears, and he wondered about using his spurs.

Then it was all he could do to hang on. A rope around the elephant's neck provided a halter for him to grip, and this kept him from being tossed off as the beast regained its feet.

"How do we get it out of its pen?"

"I put down rocks and brushed dirt over them. There is a bridge," Lakshmi called from the carriage. "The elephant will walk across it with no problem. Now quit talking. Find my brother!" The imperial command in her voice would have offended Slocum had he not been working so hard to steer the elephant where he wanted it to go. The beast saw the dirt bridge and crossed it quickly, letting out a triumphant bellow before breaking into a trot.

"How do I slow it down?" Slocum asked. He had no bit and bridle to control the elephant. Worse than not having any way of keeping the elephant's speed down, the sun was now setting behind the towering mountains and turning the landscape into an eerie twilight when viewed from this elevation.

"I do not know. You are the mahout. Do whatever a mahout does," Lakshmi said unhelpfully. "I will keep the lookout for my brother. That is the expression, isn't it?"

Slocum didn't answer. He used the hooked pole to tap

on one side of the elephant's head and then the other as he felt his way to a better control. He figured he knew how to get more speed from the elephant, but that wasn't what he wanted in the gathering gloom of dusk.

"To the right," called Lakshmi. "They are riding down an arroyo. A rocky ravine. I see them. My brother looks to be hurt!"

Slocum was getting the hang of controlling the elephant and steered it down into the draw. The elephant liked the sandy, small-pebbled ravine floor better than the more heavily rock-strewn path above. Legs reaching out, the elephant more than matched the speed of Ali's horse. When the maharajah began stirring, Slocum thought they had a chance of overtaking the kidnapper.

What would happen then he didn't know. Ali could kill the maharajah with a single slash of a knife or bullet to the brain. Slocum had his Colt, which was unsuitable for long-distance shooting, but he might spook Ali's horses and throw them off stride. He was willing to do anything because he had no idea how much longer his luck would hold and he would remain in control of the elephant.

"Does the elephant respond to voice commands?" Slocum called back to Lakshmi.

"I do not know. The mahout always speaks in low tones so the passengers are not disturbed."

Slocum grumbled under his breath. Gasim probably had taught the elephant a long list of words to control it, but Slocum knew none of them and doubted his cuss words would affect the huge beast one way or the other. He looked up to see Ali's horse beginning to turn skittish at the rapid approach of the elephant.

Slocum drew his six-gun and fired a single round for effect. He wanted to know if the elephant would react as much as he wanted Ali to get down and make a stand. The maharajah was tossed belly down over Slocum's white stallion and stirred weakly. From what Slocum could tell, the prince's hands were bound and he was lashed into place. The maharajah would be no help in getting himself free.

The weight of the rescue fell entirely on Slocum's shoulders.

Slocum did what he could to direct the elephant to Ali, but there was no way he could stop the rampaging beast. The elephant shot past Ali, but Slocum did succeed in getting between the kidnapper and his victim.

"Can you get down and go to your brother?" Slocum called but knew that wasn't possible. The elephant continued down the ravine at top speed. Lakshmi would be dead in a thrice if she tried to dismount now.

"John, there, look!"

Slocum craned his head around and saw Gasim running for the maharajah. His face glowed with rivers of sweat in the early night starlight, showing the intense effort he had made getting here from the spot where the prince had been kidnapped. Slocum couldn't imagine how hard and fast Gasim had run to match both horse and elephant.

"What's he yelling?"

"I cannot make it out," Lakshmi said.

Slocum did what he could to get the elephant turned around. It took close to a quarter mile to swing the ponderous beast about by using his feet on the ears and whacking with the hooked pole, but once he aimed back up the ravine, the elephant began its wild charge again. It had only two speeds. Dead stop and all-out.

As the elephant trampled its way back along the draw, Slocum leaned over and fired several times at Gasim, who was trying to do something to the maharajah. The mahout looked up in surprise and shouted something in Hindi. Then the elephant was past.

"John, he is trying to help. He is not with Ali!"

"What?" Slocum struggled to control the elephant's

charge again. The beast trumpeted noisily, sending echoes up and down the mountains.

"Gasim is helping my brother! He said to tell the elephant *chota*."

"What's that mean?"

"Little. I think it tells the elephant to slow, to not go so fast!"

Slocum began shouting the command as he leaned back, as if he were in the saddle of a quarter horse working to rope a calf. To his surprise, the elephant slowed it headlong pace and then came to a halt.

"Not going to try steering any more," Slocum said. He slid to one side, grabbed a floppy ear and then let himself down to the ground. The elephant glared at him for the ear pull but remained standing and stationary.

Slocum ran back to where Gasim worked to get the maharajah free of the ropes binding him to the stallion. The mahout was having little luck because Ali fired sporadically, forcing Gasim to return fire. The nearness of flying lead spooked the stallion, causing Gasim to divide his attention three different ways. When Slocum arrived, the odds changed.

Reaching down, Slocum pulled out the thick-bladed knife he carried in his right boot top. A quick slash severed the ropes holding the maharajah and sent the prince crashing to the ground. He groaned and his dark eyes fixed on Slocum, but the glare was more damning for the fall than thankful for releasing him from bondage.

"Get him to the elephant and clear out. Take Lakshmi with you."

"You can do nothing against Ali. He is a maniac," Gasim said, panting harshly.

Slocum worked to reload his Colt Navy. He led his rearing stallion away to where it would be out of the line of fire while Gasim helped the prince. The maharajah's feet were still tied, forcing him to hop clumsily. Gasim muttered constantly. Maybe it was encouragement or maybe it was something more vitriolic. Whatever the mahout said, it kept the prince moving and out of Ali's sights.

"Get to the elephant," Slocum said. "I'll hold him down." With a steady fire into the clump of bushes where he thought Ali was hiding, Slocum made sure the renegade servant could not get a decent shot at his prince.

Slocum saw Gasim order the elephant to drop to its knees and boost the maharajah into the carriage with Lakshmi. The mahout jumped to the elephant's neck and positioned himself, making *hut-hut-hut* noises to urge the elephant to greater speed.

The elephant awkwardly rose, then started back up the draw at a speed that amazed Slocum. What the elephant did, it did well.

He turned his attention back to the bushes but saw no movement. He might have gotten in a lucky shot and killed Ali, but his gut didn't tell him that. As Slocum began a slow sneak toward the spot where he thought Ali had taken refuge, he heard a single shot ring out.

The *pop!* matched that of the small pistol Ali had—but it didn't come from ahead. Slocum swung about and saw Gasim throw up his hands and begin to wobble. Ali's shot had hit the mahout.

And the elephant was charging along at full speed again with Lakshmi and her brother helpless in the carriage.

Slocum rammed his six-gun back into the holster and sprinted for his horse. He had to stop the rampaging elephant somehow. He hoped something occurred to him before he got up to it because he was as dry of ideas as the Mojave was of water in the middle of summer.

With a loud Rebel yell, he put his spurs to his stallion's flanks and raced off, hoping he could rescue Lakshmi and her brother.

Somehow.

18

Slocum kept the horse plunging up the arroyo at a breakneck speed even the elephant could not match. Slocum
pulled even and looked up. Gasim hung precariously, flop-
ping about as the elephant loped along out of control.

"Are you all right?" He tried to see if Lakshmi and the
maharajah were still in the carriage but couldn't spot them.
He hadn't passed them in the ravine so they must still be
crouching inside the *howdah*, trying to stay out of sight and
Ali's line of fire.

Slocum pushed his stallion closer to the elephant with
its rapidly driving long legs. The horse tried to balk, but
Slocum kept after it until he came to a rope halter dangling
from around the elephant's neck. He took a deep breath
then cast caution to the winds. Kicking free of his stirrups,
he launched himself across the divide between horse and
elephant. His grasping fingers caught the hemp rope. For a
brief instant he felt it slipping through his grip, then he
clamped down hard enough to swing about. He crashed
into the side of the elephant, disturbing its rhythm. The elephant bellowed in surprise and anger and began to slow as
it tried to pull him free using its powerful trunk.

Slocum clambered up the side of the great beast, hurting it as he dug spurs into the tough gray hide. Slocum hated to injure the elephant further, but it was either that or be flung off. Slocum didn't want to die, and he didn't want to sacrifice the maharajah and Lakshmi, either. Grimly climbing, he came to the spot where Gasim was tangled up in rope. The man was dead. His sightless eyes gave no hint what he saw on the other side. Slocum vowed not to join him to find out anytime soon.

Pushing Gasim back, he sat in front of the mahout and began shouting the single word he knew.

"*Chota, chota!*" The elephant had endured enough punishment for the day and obeyed. Slowly, ever so slowly, it obeyed until Slocum sat astride the massive head on a completely stationary creature.

"John? John!"

Slocum glanced over his shoulder and saw Lakshmi hanging over the edge of the carriage.

"Get your brother out. Can he move?"

"We need to dismount when the elephant is kneeling. It is only fitting for a rajah and—" Lakshmi quieted when she saw the fire in his eyes. Slocum cared nothing for the perquisites due royalty. He wanted off and away from this mountain of a creature before it took it into its head to trumpet its pain and rage and race off again.

"I'll see what I can do," Lakshmi said.

"Hurry it up." Slocum swiveled about and tried to untangle Gasim from the rope around the elephant's neck. Failing, he used his knife to sever the rope. The dead mahout crashed to the ground. This sight as much as Slocum's goading got Lakshmi to help the maharajah out of the carriage.

"No!" she shrieked as the prince slipped from her grip. He slid over the bulging gray side and flopped hard onto the ground. Lakshmi quickly followed, landing heavily and sitting beside her brother, rubbing her ankle. She glared up at Slocum.

He slid his leg over the top of the elephant's head and dropped the fifteen feet to the ground. The impact shook him, but he was ready for it and hit with bent knees. He stumbled a few steps and then came up, looking around for any sign of Ali.

"You can't let the elephant go," the maharajah said. "Not until I get my other one in from Cheyenne."

It was too late. The elephant took it into its head to go exploring, and Slocum let it go without trying to stop it. He was fed up with dealing with the monster.

"You did well for someone with no training," the maharajah said. "You should train to, uh, wrangle elephants. I will hire you and take you back to India!"

"Like hell," Slocum said. He dusted himself off, then saw that Lakshmi was all right. Her ankle was a little swollen, but she was able to walk on it if she did not try to go too fast. Slocum fixed her a rude crutch out of a fallen piñon branch before turning to the maharajah.

"You owe me an explanation," Slocum said. "What's Will Harrison to you and why is Ali so eager to kill you to keep you from getting to him?"

"I do not know Ali's motives," the maharajah said, "but I have sworn an oath that binds me by honor."

"What's your beef with Harrison?"

The maharajah pulled himself upright against a tree, took a deep breath and then launched into his story.

"His father, the Lord of Swansea, was a noted soldier in India. Unlike many of the British officers, he worked with my people and did not impose his will unreasonably. While it is going too far to say he was beloved, he was certainly respected."

"By you?" asked Slocum.

"I loved the man like a father," the maharajah said. "He saved my life and he worked for seventeen years to keep my father in power as maharajah. If possible, Lord Swansea is family to all of us."

Slocum glanced at Lakshmi and saw her nodding in agreement. A small smile curled her lips that said more than words might. She shared her brother's assessment of the British soldier.

"What has Lord Swansea asked of you?" Lakshmi watched with wide eyes. Slocum was a little surprised that the woman really did not know why her brother had made the trip to America.

"He is dying of wounds. His oldest son, Robert, was killed in the same ambush." The maharajah looked as if he would spit when he added, "They killed all the thugs who ambushed them. Their fate was too swift."

"So you're here to tell Will Harrison his father's dying?" Slocum scratched his head at this. A telegram would have served the same purpose, or a courier since Harrison seemed to be sequestered in the middle of the Grand Tetons doing whatever he did.

"Will is a remittance man and receives his stipend every month. If that were all, it would be easy to send along a letter to him. No, this is far more serious."

Slocum held his tongue so the maharajah could get to the answer in his own fashion. From the dreamy look on the prince's face, it might take a spell.

"I have sworn *rakhri* in this matter. This means I am obligated to perform a service in return for the years of loyalty."

"But, my brother," protested Lakshmi, "*rakhri* is an obligation of the entire family. You never told me!"

"I am sorry for that," the maharajah said. "I thought to make this a swift journey and an enjoyable one. I selfishly wanted to hunt the buffalo and bear and the mountain lion to return to India so I could brag about it. But more than this, I wanted to return to tell Lord Swansea that his second son had been informed that he was soon to inherit the family estates."

Slocum suddenly understood. The maharajah had said

the lord's oldest son had been killed. By the British laws of primogeniture only the oldest son inherited the family title and estates. With Robert Harrison dead, that meant Will was now fabulously wealthy and no longer had to be sent his monthly pittance to keep him from becoming an annoyance. He had gone from remittance man to wealthy lord in one ambush somewhere in India.

"I can see why this should be news delivered in person," Slocum said. "Harrison wouldn't likely believe it otherwise."

"We have also met, so we will be able to recognize each other. I intended to make a present to him of the white elephant. Such a gesture would affirm my message. For a short while, Will Harrison was a soldier in the British Army, although he quickly proved himself less than adequate for the position. Lord Swansea placed young Will under my tutelage, but while we became friends, he never learned the basics of soldiering."

Slocum wondered if the maharajah was half as good a soldier as he made himself out to be. He might be, but the way his own servants had turned on him belied that. Still, he had kept the mercenary Gasim loyal to him even as Valande and Ali betrayed him.

The maharajah pushed back his sleeve and showed a braided ropy bracelet knotted around his left wrist.

"This is the *rakhri* band symbolizing my duty. Any of my family who see it must help." The maharajah laughed short and hard, almost a barking sound. "Of course I come to a country where there are none of my extensive family to help me, other than my own dear sister." He bowed slightly in Lakshmi's direction.

"And you said nothing of this," Lakshmi said. Her hot eyes bored into her brother's. She was not happy with him, but Slocum guessed even a sister did not show too much anger toward a man who would one day be the king of his country.

"I thought it was a simple chore, one quickly finished. That is why I took so much time crossing Wyoming."

"You're supposed to take Will Harrison back with you?"

"If he will come. His father's injuries are serious. Even if he survives, he will linger for years. He will need his heir at his side to take over the reins of power, to run the considerable estates in both India and England and to perform the social functions of a Lord of Swansea."

"What if he likes it here and doesn't want to go with you?"

The prince looked surprised. "I never considered that. Why, of course he will accept the title. It is his role in life, his duty, his karma." He looked at Slocum as if Slocum's suggestion was the stupidest thing he had ever heard in his life.

Slocum wondered. The few remittance men he had known personally were ne'er-do-wells who lacked any ambition, but one of the reasons for that was their easy life out West. They got enough money to live on, which allowed them to gamble, whore, drink and indulge themselves in any outrageous behavior that occurred to them or their disreputable friends. One or two had made fortunes on their own. Slocum thought of a remittance man in Montana who had used his trickle of funds from his father to buy and build a cattle ranch that stretched a quarter million acres. He might be richer than his father by now. But he was decidedly a different sort of man and not like most of the remittance men Slocum had known.

Why would Will Harrison return to England or even India if his life here was easy and pleasant?

"What's Harrison doing in the mountains? Mining?"

"I believe that is so," the maharajah said. "I don't see your point."

"What if he's hit it big? Gold or silver can make a man a millionaire overnight. Letting packs of dogs rip apart a fox or taking afternoon tea might not be Harrison's idea of a good time anymore."

"He *must* return," the prince said. "It is his duty."

Slocum saw that honor and duty were everything for the maharajah. He understood the powerful tug. While his own family had been alive, he would have done anything for them. Anything. During the war, he had ridden with some of the most vicious murderers on either side of the Mason-Dixon Line and felt closer to them than he did to most folks. They had been a kind of family—or something more, something different but no less powerfully binding.

"You don't have any idea why Ali and Valande were trying to stop you?" Slocum thought on that a moment, then added, "Ali wanted to reach Harrison before you. Why'd he want to do a thing like that?" He knew the answer if not Ali's motive. The Indian servant wanted to kill Will Harrison.

"They were evil men," Lakshmi said. That satisfied her and her brother, but Slocum wanted more. Ali and Valande had trusted positions as servants to a powerful Indian prince. Why sacrifice their lives unless the reward was far greater than any power they might gain working for the future king?

"Ali is still on the loose," Slocum said, "but there's no way to run him down now. He's had considerable time to make himself scarce." He thought for a moment, then asked, "I don't know what became of the map Lakshmi took. You said it was a fake."

"I suspected someone in my camp of wanting to find the map," the maharajah explained, "but I had never thought my own sister would take the map. It was, as you said, bogus. I have the real map here." He patted a pocket, got a strange expression and began fumbling about. "That's odd. It is missing. The map's gone!" He looked at Slocum and held out his hands, palms up, in a gesture of helplessness.

"Any idea what happened to it? Did Ali get it?"

"I don't think so. When would he have taken it? I must have dropped it during the scuffle."

"You don't seem too worried," Slocum said. "Can you find Harrison without the map?"

The maharajah tapped his forehead and smiled.

"I have the information etched here. It is something Will's father taught me. A mere glance at a map will give me full knowledge of it for all time."

Slocum looked at the dark sky and knew that trying to find Will Harrison now was out of the question.

"We'll be off first thing in the morning," he said. "We're going to need some transportation. I've got my horse but—"

"But nothing," Lakshmi said. "Look, the elephant has returned, so we have it also. My brother can ride the horse and you can be my mahout." She grinned broadly at his discomfort at the notion.

"You want me to steer the elephant again? No," Slocum said. "I'm not getting on that monster again. There's no way you can make me. It's too big and too ornery. I can't make it do what I want, either, since it doesn't understand English."

They hit the trail the next morning, the maharajah riding the majestic white stallion and Slocum once more atop the huge elephant.

19

Slocum would never enjoy riding an elephant. The motion was all wrong and nothing compared with a decent horse for going up narrow mountain roads. He kept glancing at the maharajah, riding high, wide and fancy free on the white stallion, and almost envied the man. Almost. The prince had a whale of a lot to do, telling Will Harrison of his brother's death and his father's approaching death. Slocum didn't know how much the news would be leavened by Harrison learning he was going to be the next Lord Swansea. Receiving a white elephant as a gift hardly made the news any more palatable.

This set Slocum to thinking in other directions. Ali's attacks had a focus to them that centered on Will Harrison. Slocum couldn't figure what the maharajah's former servant gained by killing the remittance man.

"There," called the maharajah. "This is the trail leading to Harrison's mine."

"I'm not so sure I can get the elephant up there," Slocum said. He looked down uneasily at the trunk snaking back toward him. He and the elephant were getting along better now, but he lacked the experience to keep it under control if it took off at full speed. Maneuvering up the narrow trail into what might be a box canyon amounted to suicide from where Slocum sat atop the elephant.

"I can go talk to him," the maharajah said. "The mine is only a few miles farther."

"What of me?" called Lakshmi.

"Stay with Mr. Slocum," her brother shouted. He waved, put his heels to the stallion's flanks and rocketed up the trail. "I shan't be long before returning with Will Harrison."

Slocum looked at Lakshmi and smiled.

"How long do you reckon your brother'll be?" Slocum asked.

"One page, at least. Perhaps two." Lakshmi's hot dark eyes fixed on him. He knew instantly what she meant, and it didn't matter which pages from the *Kama Sutra* they chose.

Slocum kicked and prodded and called to the elephant and, to his surprise, got the elephant to kneel so Lakshmi could dismount.

"Wish I knew how I did that," Slocum said, sliding down to the ground. Lakshmi looked at him, licked her lips and stepped closer. Her silken clothing flowed with the gentle wind blowing through the Grand Tetons, pressing the soft cloth sensuously against her body.

"It does not matter as long as you know how to do other things," she said.

"Never had a problem getting mounted," he said. She came into the circle of his arms, pressing her lithe body warmly against his. Their lips met, and Slocum was taken away from the world of the smelly, trumpeting elephant and deadly servants and lost remittance men sought by Indian maharajahs. All that mattered was held in his arms. Lakshmi's breasts crushed hard against his chest in their embrace. Through the soft silken blouse she wore, he felt her nipples beginning to harden into tight points. This pushed his own passions up even more.

"I don't have a blanket to spread for us," he said as he broke off their deep kiss.

"One is not needed."

"Another page out of your love manual?"

"Why, yes," Lakshmi said impishly. "Or are you asking for manual love?" She reached down and unfastened his gun belt and then deftly worked on the buttons fastening his jeans. She caught the fleshy stalk sprouting up from his groin and began running her fingers up and down its hardening length. Every touch was electric and sent tingles of pure joy into Slocum's body. He gasped when her magic touch slipped lower and cupped him. She squeezed and pinched and soothed and stimulated fantastically all at the same time. Slocum snapped to rigid attention like a new recruit on parade for the first time.

"So nice," cooed Lakshmi, "but it does neither of us any good here."

"How—?"

Slocum was quickly suffocated with her kisses again. Lakshmi pushed him backward until his back was up against a post oak tree. Trapped between her passion and the hard wood trunk, Slocum found himself unsure what to do. Lakshmi seemed to know exactly what she wanted, however, and did it.

Her kisses turned softer, subtler as they moved from his lips down to the throbbing rigidity of his manhood. Here she lavished great care on him, her tongue and teeth alternating with her lips to soothe and stimulate. She nipped and kissed, licked and breathed her heavenly hot breath across his aroused flesh until Slocum felt like a skyrocket ready to detonate in the Fourth of July sky.

He let her have her way, running his hands through her silken raven-dark hair. It flowed like water under his hands. He pushed it away so he could see her face as she worked so eagerly at his groin. The sight of the woman's obvious enjoyment from what she did coupled with the feelings lancing into him almost set him off.

Lakshmi sensed this and did *things* to give him a chance to catch his breath and regain control.

"You're too good," he said. Sweat beaded his face now. He wasn't sure how much longer he wanted the Indian princess doing this to him, for him. He wanted to return the pleasures she gave him—and greedily he wanted more for himself, as well.

She looked up. The stark erotic desire graven on her lovely face told Slocum she was enjoying this, too, but he wanted to move on. Maybe he was a pushy American, but he was getting enough of the subtle Indian ways of lovemaking.

"Come on, Lakshmi. Now," he insisted.

"I agree," she said. She stood and began rustling her clothing as she shifted the flowing silks and curtains of gold and pearls that decorated her. Slocum saw her legs flash like teak in the Wyoming sun and then she swarmed up on him so quickly it took his breath away again. Lakshmi's arms circled his neck and her legs wrapped about his waist. He was pushed backward hard against the tree, but more important, he felt the fleecy triangle nestled between her legs opening for his manly probe.

Lakshmi wiggled her hips until he felt her nether lips parting in a lewd kiss on the very tip of his manstalk. Satisfied with this for a moment, Lakshmi kissed him with increasing fervor. When he was ready to demand more, she gave it. Her hips lowered, pressing him completely against the tree trunk. She continued her gentle positioning as he slid easily into her well-moistened slit.

Slocum felt as if he balanced on the edge of the world. He supported her entire body but there was little strain. Braced as he was against the tree, he could take her weight with no problem. Her sleek, strong legs tensed and pulled her hips down. As she relaxed, she slipped away. The movement was small, deliberate, unlike the powerful thrusting that appealed so to Slocum. But the agitation built tensions within him that were akin to those he got being completely in control.

Lakshmi moved about in a corkscrewing motion, back and forth just a little, always spinning about as she moved with increasing zeal. The silks wrapping her body fluttered like bright banners in the afternoon sun but neither of them saw. Both worked furiously with their eyes clamped tightly shut.

Slocum fought to keep control to eke out just a little more pleasure before he exploded like a stick of dynamite. And Lakshmi performed minor miracles with her tiny motions that stirred both body and soul. She paused a moment as only her fluttering pinkly scalloped nether gates touched the end of his shaft. Then she thrust down with speed and determination that matched any Slocum could have mustered.

He felt suddenly surrounded by her warm clinging flesh. The moistness oozed around his thick fleshly plug and dribbled downward, tickling as it went. But the sensations mounted rapidly and such small details were easily overlooked. He concentrated on the waves of heat blasting downward into his loins, ricocheting and returning up the entire length of his manhood.

With hips wiggling, twisting and striving, Lakshmi let out a low groan of sheer pleasure. Seconds later Slocum joined her in carnal release. He clung tightly to her until all his muscles turned to jelly. He sank down the tree trunk, the woman ending up resting in his lap with her legs on either side and a huge flow of silks all about.

"What page was that?" Slocum asked. "I surely did like it."

"There are footnotes," Lakshmi said, grinning. "I can—"

She jerked about when a gunshot echoed from far up in the canyon. Three more rapidly followed. Slocum lifted her bodily, stood and put her onto her feet. He was buttoning himself up as he went to fetch his six-gun where Lakshmi had left it in the grass a few delightful minutes earlier.

"What is happening?" Lakshmi put her hand to her lips when three more shots sounded. One was a throatier roar, like a shotgun, but it was quickly followed by the smaller *pops!*

"Sounds like a gunfight," Slocum said. "Mostly, it sounds like Ali's doing all the firing."

"What are we going to do?"

Slocum saw the elephant contentedly grabbing tall grass with its trunk, pulling the plant from the ground and then stuffing it into its mouth. Nothing was going to budge that creature, and even if Slocum could get it headed in the right direction there was scant room for it along the narrow trail leading back into the canyon to Will Harrison's claim.

"On foot. It's the only way. Stay here," he said as he started up the trail.

"That's my brother! I want to go!"

"You don't have a gun," Slocum said, wondering what argument would work with a princess. "Besides, you have to watch the elephant. It'll likely be our only transportation back to Hoback Junction."

He saw Lakshmi was torn between duty to the elephant and seeing what happened to her brother. Slocum gave her no time to think. He kissed her hard, gently pushed her in the direction of the grazing elephant and said, "I'll be back quicker 'n a flash."

He left that fast, legs pumping hard to get up the slope so he would be out of Lakshmi's sight in minutes. The longer she watched him the more likely she was to try and tag along and make what was a bad situation a whole lot worse. Slocum kept hoping to hear the shotgun's report as he trudged up the increasingly steep trail into the mountains, but it did not come. If it had, that meant Will Harrison was putting up a fight. The single blast from the scattergun might carry some hope if there had not been any pistol shots afterward. There had been, so Harrison had not killed Ali.

Puffing like a steam engine, Slocum had to take a rest. He looked at the winding trail behind, almost expecting to see Lakshmi. She had said India had mountainous regions and she was comfortable in them, but she remained with the elephant.

At least Slocum hoped that she did.

He settled his hat on his head, checked his Colt Navy, then continued on the road winding around the mountainside until he came to a sign nailed on a pine tree proclaiming this to be "Harrison's Hole."

Slocum's heart leapt with joy when he heard the bass roar of the shotgun again. He sprinted up the trail, rounding a bend and finally seeing the shaft sunk into the side of the mountain. Tailings had been puked out like some vile gray stream halfway down the mountainside into a deep arroyo. To one side stood a line shack, now ventilated with new holes in the sides. Slocum looked around and saw a tall, husky man clutching the shotgun as he peered around the edge of the shack. He looked in the direction of the mineshaft, but Slocum saw the danger coming from a different direction.

"Will! Behind you!" he shouted. It was too far for Slocum to get a good shot, even if he could have sent the lead accurately whining past Will Harrison's ear. Ali rushed up from behind the miner and smashed him in the head with a rock.

As Harrison fell, Slocum began firing. His slugs tore more splinters from the side of the shack, but they also forced Ali to duck low to avoid having his head blown off.

"Give up, Ali. You can't get away."

"I killed Hugh Malley, I'll kill Harrison and the maharajah *and* you, Slocum!" Ali knelt as he broke open his small pistol and fumbled for rounds in his pockets.

Slocum gave him no time to reload. He rushed ahead, firing as he went. Ali realized he was a sitting duck and jammed the unloaded pistol into his pocket, then did a strange thing. He grabbed Will Harrison, hoisted the man to his shoulders and ran off with him as if he carried a bag of flour.

Slocum's hammer fell on an empty chamber. He cursed. There wasn't time to reload, even if he had a clean shot. With Harrison draped over the Indian's shoulders, any shot would be risky. Slocum skidded to a halt and looked into the cabin. His heart leaped into his throat.

Lying in the middle of the floor was the maharajah, bleeding profusely. The prince propped himself up on one elbow when he saw Slocum.

"Stop Ali. Kill him!"

"He's got Harrison," Slocum said, going into the cabin. He had to stop the bleeding from the three wounds in the maharajah's chest or the man would be dead soon. He used his knife to cut away the man's expensive silk shirt and sliced strips to bind the wounds. As he worked, the maharajah gasped out the story.

"I got here, talked to Will Harrison. He is going to return to India to see his father." The maharajah winced as Slocum tightened the bandage as tight as he could. "Ali, Ali the traitor! He and Valande were hired by Lawrence Harrison to kill Will."

"Who's Lawrence Harrison?"

"Robert and William's youngest brother."

Slocum understood then. The estate passed from the oldest to the next and on down. If the third brother were ever to inherit, both his older brothers had to be dead. Fighting in India had taken care of Robert, and Lawrence had somehow hired Ali and Valande to see to it that the maharajah never found William, and if they did, that he never lived long enough to enjoy his newfound position and wealth.

"Can you press in hard? There? Good. Let up and you might bleed to death. I've got to get you to a doctor."

"Save Will Harrison. You are not of my royal family, Mr. Slocum, but you should be bound by *rakhri* because of your dalliance with my sister." He held up the wrist with the braided bracelet. "Keep Ali from killing him. I will be all right."

Slocum saw that might be so. The wounds were gory, but now that the bleeding had been stanched, the maharajah might be all right if he didn't open the bullet holes again.

"Don't go digging in the mine for gold," Slocum said.

"I won't." The maharajah smiled weakly. "Will told me there is little gold to be found. This is a dry hole."

Slocum hastily reloaded and started for the door when the maharajah's command stopped him in his tracks.

"Be careful, Mr. Slocum. Return down the road. Ali had his horse in the ravine below the mine. If he follows that, it will take him longer to get to the valley where we left the elephant."

"I hope he won't kill Harrison out of hand," Slocum said.

"He needs proof that he has killed Will Harrison. I do not think he will assassinate him until he gets it."

"What proof?" Slocum saw the maharajah's strength fading as the man shrugged. Such details hardly mattered when overtaking the fleeing kidnapper and his victim counted more.

Slocum put his head down and began running at the fastest clip he thought he could maintain all the way downhill. He was tired from the climb to the mine, but the steep elevation worked in his favor now while Ali had to wind about some distance away. Slocum guessed the arroyo below Harrison's mine joined the larger arroyo where they had battled earlier.

Slocum stumbled several times but kept up his breakneck pace and reached the main road in less than half the time it had taken him to go up to the mine. He saw a startled Lakshmi look up from under a tree where she toyed with a mountain wildflower.

"What is it, John?"

"Your brother's shot up but is going to make it," he gasped out. "Ali's got Will Harrison. Ought to be along on horses anytime. Hear them?" Slocum tried to listen but the thunder of his own pulse drowned out softer sounds.

"Why, yes, horses whinnying." Lakshmi turned and pointed back down into the draw where Slocum suspected the arroyos merged. He was already running for the elephant, now standing and swaying slightly in the cool afternoon breeze. The animal's eyes popped open as Slocum approached. He swarmed up the rope circling the huge neck and settled himself so his feet rested behind the floppy ears.

"Giddy up, you gray behemoth," Slocum growled. He doubted the elephant understood but it began to walk—to run.

He was unable to control its speed as he turned it down the arroyo in the direction of the horses emerging from behind a curtain of tangled green vegetation that had overgrown the mouth of the gulch leading up to Harrison's mine.

Ali rode the white stallion and had Will Harrison draped over the saddle of another horse, the one Ali had ridden earlier. Slocum wasn't sure who was more surprised as the elephant charged headlong toward the men on the horses. He hardly knew that he reacted as he slid one leg over the elephant's head and then shoved off powerfully. Slocum sailed through the air and crashed hard into Ali, knocking the Indian servant to the ground.

Slocum rolled to his feet, drew his six-shooter and aimed it at Ali, but the man wasn't moving. He was knocked out cold.

"Whass that? El'phant?" came the wondering words from a battered Will Harrison. He flopped onto the ground and sat staring at the retreating hindquarters of the elephant as it continued its mad run down the arroyo and out of sight.

Slocum fingered his six-shooter as he stared down at Ali. The man had admitted to killing Hugh Malley, and that was as good a reason for shooting him as any. But Slocum jammed his six-gun back into its holster. Justice would be done, but there was someone else who ought to be there when Ali paid for his crime.

20

John Slocum was footsore by the time the small party made it back to Hoback Junction. The maharajah's injuries were such that he had to ride Slocum's horse. Slocum did not begrudge the prince the use of the white stallion—it had been his before he had given it to Slocum to replace a good horse that had been killed. Nor did he mind that Lakshmi rode with her brother. Will Harrison had ridden Ali's horse due to a broken leg he had sustained after Ali had dragged him from the shack down the rocky slope to the ravine where he had tethered the horses. Slocum didn't mind that all of them got to ride while he and Ali walked.

He liked the idea that Ali stumbled along, each step closer to town harder for the Indian to make because he knew what awaited him.

"There is the town," Lakshmi called from her high vantage point, but Slocum had already spotted the curls of smoke rising from half a hundred chimneys long since. "I'm sorry you have had to walk so many miles, John."

"There was no way I could catch the elephant," Slocum said, not sure if he was sorry about it at all. He had felt out of control every time he had climbed onto the elephant's neck to act as mahout. Still, the elephant was rampaging

181

through the Grand Tetons with no one likely to capture it after the maharajah and his party left.

A slow smile came to Slocum's lips. The Crow Indians would have a fine meal if they could bring down the huge beast. It had enough meat on its bones to feed an entire Crow village throughout the winter. That would be the best outcome of letting the elephant charge up and down the valleys.

"That is all right, Mr. Slocum," said the maharajah. "The other one, a special elephant, ought to arrive soon. When it does, I can present it to Mr. Harrison and we can leave."

"I'm itchin' to get on back to India. Haven't been there in years," Will Harrison said. He had lost a great deal of his British accent during his time in the West, but enough remained that Slocum knew Harrison would regain it quickly. "Hate to think of my dear old dad dyin' like that."

"He is determined and will hang on to life until you arrive, William," the maharajah said.

"Might be so, but I have another problem. What do I do 'bout my little brother, Lawrence?"

Slocum knew what he would do to anyone hiring Ali and Valande to kill him, but he said nothing. This was something Will Harrison had to work out for himself, possibly with his father's consent. He doubted it was a unique situation since there were so many younger siblings of British lords. Not all of them lacked the ambition to take what their older brothers had, by hook or by crook.

"You get a statement from Ali before you leave," Slocum told the former remittance man. "I reckon he'll be willing to spill his guts in exchange for a lighter sentence."

"You will hang me," Ali said. "I am a dead man."

As he spoke, Slocum moved fast, coming up behind the Indian. Ali tried to bolt, hoping Slocum or the maharajah would gun him down. Slocum thrust out his foot and hooked it around Ali's, sending the man crashing facedown to the ground.

By now they were far enough inside Hoback Junction to draw a small crowd, including Marshal Rothbottom. Slocum had nothing but contempt for the lawman, but even Rothbottom had to agree to lock up Ali with so many witnesses against him. The confession made in front of Will, the maharajah and Slocum had to have some validity since it had been freely given, albeit in the heat of battle.

"We got ourselves a murderer, Marshal," Slocum said, pointing at the prone Ali. "He got that elephant of the maharajah's to stomp on Hugh Malley and kill him. There's a damn sight more but if you keep him locked up on that charge, we'll get around soon and give you a bigger list."

"Well, I dunno," said the marshal, chewing on his lower lip. "It's just you folks' say-so."

"It is on *my* say-so, Marshal," spoke up the maharajah. "My injuries are a result of being shot many times by Ali, my former servant and now my sworn enemy!" The prince ripped open his shirt and showed the bloody bandages Slocum had tied around his chest to bind up the bullet wounds. As the citizens saw the extent of the maharajah's injuries, a gasp went up. Slocum knew the bullet wounds looked worse than they were, but the dramatic moment and the response it got convinced the marshal to do something about Ali.

"Come on. I got a special cell waitin' fer ya," Rothbottom said, grabbing Ali by the collar and half dragging him along. "Reckon I kin keep ya locked up for destroyin' half my hoosegow."

"You need to get to the doctor," someone called from the boardwalk in front of the hotel. "Want me to go fetch him?"

"Do it," Slocum said, taking charge. He saw how pale the maharajah looked after his brief speech. "Look after him, Lakshmi. And Mr. Harrison, you ought to tag along and let the doc take a look at your gimpy leg."

"Thank you, Slocum," Will Harrison said. "We needed someone to break the ice and get things movin' around here. Thank you."

"Send me a bale of English pounds when you inherit the Swansea estate," Slocum said. He knew how callous that sounded and it didn't matter. He was tired of foot and soul. But a curious lightness kept him moving along the main street until he saw Darlene.

She stood outside the general store, a broom in her hand. She tossed it aside and ran to him.

"John! You came back!"

"I brought Hugh's murderer in for trial," he told her. She threw her arms around him and buried her face in his shoulder. Darlene began sobbing. Her hot tears soaked into his shirt.

"I didn't think you would, John. I doubted you. I'm sorry. I'm so sorry."

Slocum had nothing to say to that. He held her awkwardly, not sure what to do until he looked down the street and saw Lakshmi watching. Slocum tried to push Darlene away, but she clung to him like a leech. Then he gave up when it was apparent that Lakshmi saw nothing wrong in comforting the woman.

Slocum had to admit to himself, also, that the time with Lakshmi had been good—special. The princess was more skilled between the sheets than most other women he had come across in the West—not that he and Lakshmi had ever found any sheets for their dalliances. Lakshmi gave a special meaning to mysteries of the Orient, and Slocum wished he had more time to explore them. But she was returning to India with her brother and Will Harrison. No matter what had happened between them out on the trail, it was over now. She was royalty, and he was nothing but a saddle tramp.

•

That was fine with Slocum.

"Can we sit for a minute?" He pointed to chairs in front of the store. "Don't want to make your boss think you're falling down on the job."

"Mr. Benton's a nice old fellow," Darlene said, smiling a little now. "So what if he fires me? I've done what I had to do here. You're sure that Ali is the one who killed Hugh?"

"He admitted it in front of me, Will Harrison and the maharajah. I'll make sure the marshal doesn't forget to get statements from them before they leave." Slocum went on to explain how Harrison had come into a vast estate, or would when his father finally died.

"That's a shame," Darlene said. "That his brother died, I mean. Not that Mr. Harrison becoming rich is wrong. From all the gossip I've heard, that mine of his wasn't worth spit." She paused a moment, folded her hands in her lap and then said, "Why'd Ali kill Hugh? I don't understand."

"The maharajah was looking for a young man with a British accent. He had met Will Harrison more than ten years ago and, in spite of what he said, I don't think he believed he would actually recognize him when he found him. Being royalty and all, he didn't dare admit, even to himself, he might single out the wrong man."

"But Hugh was Welsh."

"I'll give the maharajah this much. I don't think he ever considered Hugh to be Will Harrison, but he might have thought Hugh could lead him to Harrison. Ali wanted to stop that at all costs. It didn't matter if Hugh actually was the heir to the Swansea title or might get the maharajah to the real heir."

"He was being paid by the third son to make sure no one found Will."

"And," Slocum went on, "if the maharajah did find him, to be sure that Will never claimed his title."

"Hugh died for nothing," Darlene said in a choked voice. She fought to hold back tears.

"Reckon so," Slocum said. There was no easy way to say it. Hugh Malley had been at the wrong place at the wrong time, and it had cost him his life.

Slocum turned when he heard a great commotion from down the street. He heaved a sigh of resignation when he saw an elephant swinging along, but this one was smaller than the one still roaming the Grand Tetons—and it was a peculiar dusty brown rather than gray.

"It's come!" shouted the maharajah.

Slocum and Darlene went into the street and joined the slow-moving prince and Lakshmi. Both Indians beamed with joy at seeing the elephant.

"This is the most special of elephants in existence," the maharajah said. "It is the rare white elephant."

"Don't look white to me," Darlene said.

"It's more of a title than description," Lakshmi explained. "But it is most rare and valuable."

"What are you going to do? Ride it back to India?" asked Slocum.

"It is yours, John Slocum, for all the valuable service you have given me. Of all Americans I have met, you are the best suited to riding like a maharajah!"

"I can't accept it," Slocum said, involuntarily taking a half step backward. "You said you were giving it to Harrison, as a gift."

"You cannot refuse," the maharajah said sternly. "It is a royal wish. That is the same as a command."

"Lakshmi said you weren't really a maharajah."

"I am yet a rajah, true. I can make such commands. Take possession of the white elephant, John Slocum. It is yours." The prince brooked no argument with his largesse.

"Oh, do, John," urged Darlene. "I have an idea."

"Thank you," Slocum said with ill grace. He touched the pocket where the huge diamond the maharajah had given him earlier still rested. At least he had gotten something of value. "You're letting me keep he stallion, aren't you?"

"That, also. You will be a well-traveled man, Mr. Slocum, on the finest of animals. Now we must go."

"Go?"

"Westward, over the Grand Tetons. Lakshmi has arranged for sea transport from San Francisco. I have horses to purchase and a party to form."

Slocum started to swap his services as a scout in exchange for taking back the white elephant, but Darlene elbowed him in the ribs.

"Let 'em go," she whispered.

Slocum knew she was right. It was hard enough to part with Lakshmi now. Spending another month on the trail with the woman would only make her departure in San Francisco all the more difficult.

"Have a safe trip. The mountains can be treacherous—and there's a rogue elephant on the loose out there."

The maharajah laughed and slapped Slocum on the back. Then he and Lakshmi left.

Slocum stared the white elephant in the eye but got no pleasure from the feeling that the elephant blinked first.

"I have a wonderful idea, John. There's a traveling circus in Cheyenne. If we get the elephant to them, I'm sure they'd buy it for a huge price."

"Think so?" Slocum stroked his chin. He could get the elephant across Wyoming in a week or two, find the circus, sell the elephant and split the money with Darlene. From Cheyenne it wasn't that far to Denver and diamond merchants who might give him a good price for the rock in his pocket.

And spending a couple more weeks with Darlene might not be so bad, either. He could teach her what he had learned from the *Kama Sutra*—and Lakshmi.

Watch for

SLOCUM AND THE SIERRA MADRAS GOLD

317th novel in the exciting SLOCUM series
from Jove

Coming in July!